JOYCE ANNOTATED

SECOND EDITION, *Revised and Enlarged*

Joyce Annotated

NOTES FOR *Dubliners*

AND *A Portrait of the Artist as a Young Man*

Don Gifford

University of California Press / Berkeley / Los Angeles / London

University of California Press
Berkeley and Los Angeles, California

University of California Press, Ltd.
London, England

© 1982 by
The Regents of the University of California

Library of Congress Cataloging in Publication Data

Gifford, Don Creighton.
  Joyce annotated.

  Edition for 1967 published under title: Notes for
Joyce: Dubliners and A portrait of the artist as a
young man.
  Includes index.
  1. Joyce, James, 1882–1941—Handbooks, manuals, etc.
2. Joyce, James, 1882–1941. Dubliners. 3. Joyce,
James, 1882–1941. Portrait of the artist as a young
man. I. Joyce, James, 1882–1941. Dubliners.
II. Joyce, James, 1882–1941. Portrait of the artist
as a young man. III. Title.
PR6019.09Z5335 1981   823'.912   80-29448
ISBN 0-520-04189-5 (cloth)
ISBN 0-520-04610-2 (ppbk)
Printed in the United States of America

  3 4 5 6 7 8 9

This second edition is revised and enlarged from *Notes for
Joyce: "Dubliners" and "A Portrait of the Artist as a Young
Man"* by Don Gifford with the assistance of Robert J.
Seidman (New York: Dutton, 1967).

The translation of Pope Leo XIII's poem "The Art of
Photography" quoted in this book is from *Surface and
Symbol: The Consistency of James Joyce's Ulysses* by Robert
Martin Adams. Copyright © 1962 by Robert Martin
Adams. Reprinted by permission of Oxford University
Press, Inc.

The maps were drawn by Peggy Diggs.

Contents

Preface to the Second Edition

Since publication of the first edition of this annotation in 1967, responses from colleagues, students, and correspondents have made it clear that I had assembled something less than a thorough working annotation of *Dubliners* and *A Portrait of the Artist as a Young Man*. The subsequent experience of preparing *Notes for Joyce: Ulysses* (New York: E. P. Dutton, 1974) made the shortcomings of the first annotations even more disturbingly clear. Obviously, the shortcomings resulted from lack of information, from insufficient saturation in Dublin detail, and from failure to perceive many occasions when Joyce's text might have been made more accessible by annotation. Gradually, I came to realize that I was missing "occasions" not only because I lacked information or awareness, but also because in the earlier fictions Joyce was being too offhand and too subtle. He was not consistently attentive to how much a reader might miss, to how much the suggestive potential of cryptic allusion and "mere detail" depended on the writer's ability to alert the reader, to provide frames of reference, markers, and clues which indicate how the text is to be read, how the trivial and the cryptic could be made to resonate.

Joyce was aware of the literary use he wanted to make of what he called "trivial things" (see p. 3 below), and the technique is there at striking moments in *Dubliners*: in the coin in Corley's hand, the clay in Maria's saucer, but it is the technique of the apprentice, not yet the technique of the master. The two published versions of "The Sisters"[1] provide a case in point. *The Irish Homestead* version (13 August 1904; see Appendix) grew up to become the lead story of *Dubliners* by a process characteristic of Joyce, who, as he rewrote, packed a relatively spare narrative with sugges-

---

1. There is an intermediate manuscript draft of "The Sisters" in the Joyce Collection at the Yale University Library, number E2a in the Slocum-Cahoon *Bibliography*.

tive detail. Several added details suggest that the paralysis from which Father Flynn suffers is not the *result* of the three strokes he has suffered but the *cause* because it is "general paralysis of the insane," or paresis, syphilis of the central nervous system. Old Cotter's innuendoes and the circumlocutions of the other adults in the story are not enough, however, to alert us to the significance of the priest's symptoms; those symptoms might still be read as evidence that the priest is senile, and the suspicions which the adults in the story have of the priest can be put down wholly to what in part they are, Irish anti-intellectualism. To realize the symptoms as those of a specific disease, we need the contrast between the two versions of the story and some prodding by informed critics.[2] But even when the "trivial things" click together as paresis, the story is not *solved* or foreclosed, because paresis does not reduce the old priest to a physical disease but establishes a physical disease which in turn is to resonate as a disease of the spirit and contribute to a heightening of what to the Irish imagination is "the fearfully potent image of the excommunicated or silenced priest."[3] Still, when paresis springs out of the symptoms interpolated into the final version of the story, there is the danger that the revelation will refuse to take its place within the web of significances in the story as a whole—including, for example, the suggestive linkage between "paralysis" and "simony" in the boy's "ears" or the fact that Father Flynn as a young man from a background of poverty showed enough promise to merit training at the prestigious Irish College in Rome.

What I am trying to suggest is that, while "the significance of trivial things" is at the core of the literary technique of *Dubliners* and *A Portrait*, things-significant are not as clearly framed or marked as they are in *Ulysses*, and, as a consequence, it is more difficult to strike a balance between overinterpretation and underinterpretation. The temptation to invent significances for one's own self-aggrandizement is very strong, as is the countertemptation to return the stories to a minimally literal base. For example, echoes of the romance of Tristan and Iseult are present in "A Painful Case." Mr. Duffy lives in Chapelizod (Iseult's Chapel), where at least one Irish version of the legend says Tristan and Iseult consummated their love, and Phoenix Park (the site of the legendary Forest of Tristan, into which Tristan retreated in despair) is also the site of the final confrontation between and separation of Mrs. Sinico and Mr. Duffy and the site of Duffy's devastating self-realization at the story's end. It is therefore tempting to hear echoes of Tristan and Iseult in all the story's details, but the pres-

2. Burton A. Waisbren and Florence L. Walzl, "Paresis and the Priest: James Joyce's Symbolic Use of Syphilis in 'The Sisters,'" *Annals of Internal Medicine* 80 (June 1974): 758–62.

3. Tom MacIntyre, Irish man of letters, in conversation, September 1977.

ence of that bit of Arthurian legend is not to "A Painful Case" as *The Odyssey* is to *Ulysses*. The aura of the Tristan legend is evoked as grace note rather than exploited throughout as, by contrast, the towering presence of Parnell is exploited in "Ivy Day in the Committee Room," conjured up to preside over the hopelessly cramped confines of the Committee Room in Wicklow Street. Another example of an allusion in passing: Stanislaus Joyce remarks that "Grace" has "an obvious touch of parody of The Divine Comedy."[4] The "touch" may be there in Mr. Kernan's fall down the lavatory stairs in the first part of the story (*Inferno*), in Kernan's convalescence in the second part (*Purgatorio*), and in his achievement of the beatific vision in the third part, "the distant speck of red light which was suspended before the high altar" (*Paradiso*). But the parody, while demonstrable, seems to stop there and to remain an in-joke between brothers rather than a pervasively informative presence in the story.

In the prefaces to the first edition of this annotation and to the annotation of *Ulysses* I tried to list at least some of those to whom I have been indebted for information, advice, and reproof. But the list has expanded in so many directions that it threatens to outrun memory, and I hesitate to compile it for fear the list, like the annotations themselves, can never be complete, let alone give each his due.

D. G.
June 1980

4. *Recollections of James Joyce by His Brother* (New York, 1950), p. 20.

Introduction

THE NOTES AND THEIR USE

The primary intention of this volume is to provide a semi-encyclopedia that will inform a reading of *Dubliners* and of *A Portrait of the Artist as a Young Man*. As they stood in 1967 and as they stand now, the notes are not complete, and undoubtedly some of the completed notes will prove inadequate or inaccurate. But the vernacular world of the Dublin on which Joyce so heavily depended for his vocabularies is rapidly receding out of living memory, and the effort to catch the nuances of those vocabularies before they are permanently lost is timely in its importance.

The annotated passages are presented in the sequence of the fictions themselves—not unlike the footnotes at the bottom of the pages of an edition of Shakespeare or Milton; thus this book is designed to be laid open beside the Joyce texts and to be read in conjunction with those texts. That method of reading has its disadvantages. It threatens a reader not only with interruption but also with distortion, since details which are mere grace notes of suggestion in the fictions may be overemphasized by the annotation. Several compromises suggest themselves here: one is to follow an interrupted reading with an uninterrupted reading; another is to read through a sequence of the notes before reading the annotated sequence in the fictions.

I have tried to balance on the knife edge of factual annotation and to avoid interpretive comment. This is something of a legal fiction since it can hardly be said that the notes do not imply interpretations or that they have not derived from interpretations in the first place;[1] but the intention

---

1. See the headnote to *A Portrait*, pp. 129–31 below, for a notable instance of the shadow zone between annotation and interpretation.

has been to keep the notes "neutral" so that they will inform rather than direct a reading. For example: the speaker in "Araby" remarks that he liked *The Memoirs of Vidocq* more than he liked *The Abbot* or *The Devout Communicant* because the pages of *The Memoirs* were "yellow," i.e., because the book appealed to a romantic fascination with antiquities. The notes to this passage in *Dubliners* indicate *The Memoirs* to be the least aged of the three books; the notes also state that *The Memoirs* are "inauthentic and/or unreliable," compiled in the interest of exciting and titillating an audience rather than in the interest of autobiographical accuracy. The neutrality of the "annotation" dictates that the reader be left to draw his own conclusions about the suggestiveness of these details, even though the details themselves can be read as implying that the boy has a preference for romantic fakes with little perception of the objects he observes (as subsequently in the story he romantically distorts "Mangan's sister" and "Araby," with little perception of their realities). The preference for *The Memoirs* thus can be regarded as a detail which is a clue to the way the boy participates in the processes of his own paralysis, but the notes, if they are to be informative rather than interpretative, should leave this development of the detail to the reader, since the detail does not have "meaning" in itself apart from its interrelations with the total context of the story (and with the whole of *Dubliners* as, in turn, the story's context).

The suggestive potential of minor details was, of course, enormously fascinating to Joyce, and the precision of his use of detail is a most important aspect of his literary method (see p. vii above). Early in his career Joyce frequently used religious metaphors for the artist and his processes, and in *Stephen Hero* he couched this fascination with detail in the religious term "epiphanies"—minor details that achieve for a moment a suggestive potential all out of proportion to their actual scale. "By an epiphany he [Stephen Daedalus] meant a sudden spiritual manifestation" when the "soul" or "whatness" of an object "leaps to us from the vestment of its appearance."[2] This passage suggests Joyce's fascination with the ways in which what he called "trivial things" could be invested with significance. But the term "epiphany" has been overquoted to the point where it has become remarkably fuzzy; it is not clear whether the "soul" which is made manifest is inherent in the object itself, or in the artist's response to the object's potential as metaphor, or in the response of a character within a fiction, or in the response of the reader to a revelatory moment in the fic-

2. *Stephen Hero* (New York, 1963), p. 211. In 1904 Joyce used the pseudonym Stephen Daedalus when the first versions of "The Sisters," "Eveline," and "After the Race" were published in *The Irish Homestead*. He used the same spelling for the protagonist of *Stephen Hero* (1904–5), but when he came to recast *Stephen Hero* as *A Portrait*, Joyce changed the spelling to "Dedalus" and separated his hero by one letter from the "cunning artificer" of Greek mythology.

tion. For example, the end of "Araby" raises the possibility of several questions; is the "epiphany," or "sudden spiritual manifestation,." the "soul" of the tawdry, exhausted commercialism inherent in the bazaar? or is it Joyce's perception of the bazaar as the "soul" of romance Dublin-style? or is it the boy-narrator's romantic disillusionment when he reaches the bazaar? or is it our perception as readers of the disparities between the boy's expectations and responses on the one hand and Mangan's sister and the bazaar (and perhaps even the boy's own disillusionment) as objects on the other hand? The term "epiphany" tends to blur rather than direct answers to these questions because its scale as metaphor distracts us from what Joyce is really after—the "significance of trivial things" and the literary techniques involved in developing that significance.

It is notable that Joyce dropped the term "epiphany" from Stephen's discussion of his aesthetic theory in A Portrait and that Stephen mocks the adolescent pretentiousness of his book of epiphanies in Ulysses (p. 40.)[3] Joyce did begin to compile a "book of epiphanies" (1900–1903) in which he attempted to record minor moments in such a way as to develop (without explicitly or discursively so stating) their metaphoric potential. He did not abandon his collection of epiphanies (the dream moments at the end of A Portrait are culled from those notebook fragments), but his interest in the ideal of artistic detachment displaced the overstatement of "a sudden spiritual manifestation" in favor of a precise attention to the handling of detail together with the author's refusal to point, evaluate, or interpret in any direct way the meaning of a detail.

When he was working on the stories that were to comprise Dubliners, Joyce said to his brother Stanislaus:

> Do you see that man who has just skipped out of the way of the tram? Consider, if he had been run over, how significant every act of his would at once become. I don't mean for the police inspector. I mean for anybody who knew him. And his thoughts, for anybody that could know them. It is my idea of the significance of trivial things that I want to give the two or three unfortunate wretches who may eventually read me.[4]

The technical difficulty was how to let the man in the fiction skip "out of the way of the tram" and yet give the reader the sense of "the significance of trivial things" consequent on the man's having been "run over." If we are to count ourselves among the "unfortunate wretches," we have to strike

3. Page references to Ulysses are to the Modern Library edition (New York, 1961) and to the subsequent Vintage edition. To locate all the appearances in Ulysses of characters mentioned in Dubliners and A Portrait consult Shari Benstock and Bernard Benstock, Who's He When He's at Home: A James Joyce Directory (Urbana, Ill., 1980).

4. Quoted from Stanislaus Joyce's Diary in Richard Ellmann, James Joyce (New York, 1959), p. 169.

a dynamic and ever-shifting balance between the sense that trivial details are (and should remain) trivial and the sense that they are capable of revelatory metaphoric significance. What makes the balance difficult is that the excitement attendant on the recognition of a significance can so easily make us forget that the man has only figuratively, not literally, been run over by the tram.

BIOGRAPHY

Joyce depended heavily on the people, events, and environments in his own life for models of the characters and events of his fictions. This is a commonplace of scholarship on Joyce, and indeed much of that scholarship has been devoted to researching Joyce's personal environments and to identifying the autobiographical elements in his work. The notes in this volume intentionally neglect this phase of scholarship on Joyce. Presumably every novelist relies to some extent on the range and vocabulary of his personal experience. In this respect Joyce is not different in kind from other novelists, although he may well be so different in degree as to appear different in kind. But once the event or the person (or even the stick of "Dublin street furniture") is transferred from "fact" to the page (and inevitably transformed in the process), the "true" nature of the event or person loses much of its relevance for the reader who is attempting to grasp the forms and meanings inherent in the fiction itself. This is particularly true if one grants Joyce the achievement of his ideal of artistic detachment.

The "facts" do remain relevant to a study of the writer's biography and of his habits and processes as a writer, and that study can contribute to an understanding of the writer's works, but the contribution is primarily indirect. To know that Cranly is a partial portrait of John Francis Byrne or that Lynch is a partial portrait of Vincent Cosgrave does not particularly illuminate a reading of Chapter V of A Portrait since the "truth to life" (or at least the plural truth—other perspectives, other views) of the two sitters would require a thoroughness and immediacy of observation of them that is probably beyond the capacity of scholarship and certainly beyond the capacity of the well-informed reader. Furthermore, this whole tangled question of Joyce's personal life and its relation to his work has been re-tangled by the comments and objections of several of the people whose partial portraits Joyce rendered in ways that were not always exactly flattering.[5]

5. See the writings of Stanislaus Joyce; John Francis Byrne, The Silent Years (New York, 1953); Eugene Sheehy, May It Please the Court (Dublin, 1951); Oliver St. John Gogarty, As I Was Going down Sackville Street (New York, 1937) and Mourning Became Mrs. Spendlove (New York, 1948). See also Ellmann's sources in James Joyce, passim.

MacCann and Davin provide splendid examples of the ways in which the retrospect of history could distort a reading of Chapter V of *A Portrait*. MacCann is a partial portrait of Francis Sheehy-Skeffington (1878–1916); Davin, of George Clancy (d. March 1921). Sheehy-Skeffington was shot without trial (murdered by a deranged British officer) during the Easter 1916 Rebellion in Dublin because Sheehy-Skeffington's pacifism compelled him to urge British soldiers to stop looting. Clancy, as Nationalist mayor of Limerick, was "foully murdered, by the Black and Tans at night in his home before the eyes of his family" (Byrne, p. 55). The "facts" of the two deaths could easily be read back into *A Portrait*, deepening the shadows in the prior fictional careers of MacCann and Davin. But those careers do not point "ineluctably" toward the untimely and pointless violence of the deaths of the two men. The modern reader should be distant enough from the Dublin of 1900 and its rich play of personality to be able to face Joyce's work squarely as the "fiction" which it is, and to refuse to let the retrospect of fact cloud the prospect of fiction.

The imposition of autobiographical time on fictional time can also distort the way *A Portrait* is read. The fragment of *Stephen Hero* that remains to us is cast in a picaresque narrative time which is a familiar way of imitating the chronological succession of day-to-day, season-to-season in autobiographical time. The narrative time of *A Portrait* does not attempt to imitate chronological continuity; it is discontinuous, episodic, a sequence of portraits rather than a flow of happenings. (To reflect the episodic nature of the novel, the notes to *A Portrait* in this volume are organized not only into five chapters but also into subchapters: I:A, I:B, I:C, etc.)

In autobiographical time Joyce spent three years at Clongowes Wood College (September 1888–June 1891). In *A Portrait* those three years are focused (and summed up) as an afternoon-night-morning in October (chapter I:B) and a Wednesday morning-early-afternoon during Lent—of the following year?—(chapter I:D). Obviously the novel does not ask us to follow a succession of events in autobiographical time but a sequence of tableaux in which the climate of that-time-of-life and the textures of that-phase-of-the-mind are imaged. Nor does it matter that the death of Parnell (October 1891) is an anachronism in I:B (because in autobiographical time Joyce left Clongowes four months before Parnell's death). That death is appropriate in fictional time because it provides an image of the shadowy presence that the world of Irish politics had for the child, Stephen— appropriate to the child-as-child and structurally appropriate as prelude to the political and religious donnybrook of the Christmas dinner in I:C.

The autobiographical years at Belvedere College (1893–98) are focused as one night in May (autobiographically, 1898) in II:C. The five days of Chapter III are also autobiographically Belvedere time (the retreat itself,

30 November–3 December 1896). And here Joyce has juggled time (or paid little attention to it) in the fiction. St. Francis Xavier's feast day, 3 December, fell on Thursday in 1896. In the novel it falls on Saturday; that would mean it is 1898, but it could not have been in Joyce-time because Joyce was already a student at University College, Dublin. As an expanded episode the retreat fits the episodic pattern of the novel, but the narrative presentation of the retreat also imitates chronological succession. The function of this sustained narrative at the structural center of the novel would seem to be that chapters III and IV:A (its afterglow) are to stand not only as tableaux of that phase-in-life but also as sustained and concentrated images of the all-pervasive and fearful presence of religion for Stephen during his coming-of-age in the novel.

In *A Portrait* succession in chronological-autobiographical time is not as important as the succession and juxtaposition of tableaux, of portraits. Subchapters IV:B and IV:C provide paired portraits of Stephen at the end of his time at Belvedere. Chapter V presents four portraits located in University College time (1898–1902), but the "Thursday" of V:A and the evening in Lent of V:C are not precisely located, though clearly we are meant to sense them as toward the end of that phase-of-life. Here again the attempt at a direct correlation of fictional time and autobiographical time could mislead. Stephen's diary in V:D begins on 20 March, which (whether Joyce was aware or not) was a Thursday in 1902 (the autobiographical year of departure). One way to underscore the fictional nature of time in *A Portrait* (and to suggest that it does not matter which calendar year) is to point to the fact that Good Friday and Easter must inevitably fall within the time covered by Stephen's diary, and Stephen takes no notice of those notable days in the liturgical calendar (other than to notice the season as the time when he should do his Easter Duty but refuses).[6]

Far more important to a reading of *A Portrait* than a knowledge of autobiographical time is a sense of the political and cultural climate in Ireland at the turn of the century. The collapse of Parnell's leadership in the Great Split of December 1890, the factional bitterness engendered by the Split and exacerbated by what the faithful regarded as Parnell's martyrdom in October 1891 plunged Ireland into at least a decade of political disorientation. The cultural climate was politicized by the rise of the Gaelic League (1893ff.) and by deliberate intensification of Irish cultural self-consciousness. The artistic climate was characterized by conflicting claims: of the nationalists who demanded an art in the service of a national self-image, of

6. If it were 1902, the entry for 30 March would be the entry for Easter Sunday, and the final entry would be (27 April) a Sunday.

the Catholic and Protestant moralists who demanded an art that would in-
culcate Victorian morality, of the symbolists who urged an art-for-art's-
sake aestheticism—as against the naturalism of Ibsen and Zola and its rejection of what Ibsen called "the aesthetic" in favor of "the ethical, the
prophetic."[7] In this connection it is notable that Stephen's preoccupation
with Ibsen is as absent from *A Portrait* as it is present in *Stephen Hero* (and
in Joyce's own personal interests).

There are, of course, exceptions to this no-biography rule in these
notes, particularly when the persons or events Joyce used as raw materials
have a public or historical existence that provides meaningful perspectives
or points of reference. In general, however, it seems more intelligent to
examine Joyce's complex relations to his raw materials in separate study—
tributary to but apart from a direct reading of the works themselves, and
for that study there is no better place to begin than with Richard Ellmann's splendid biography, *James Joyce* (New York, 1959).

References to *Stephen Hero* have also been omitted from these notes on
the basis that a comparative study of that fragment and *A Portrait* is more
appropriate to a study of Joyce's development as an artist than it is illuminating to a reading of *A Portrait* itself. Indeed, it has proven all too easy to
distort readings of *A Portrait* by importing particulars if not "facts" from
Stephen Hero; see the discussion of "epiphany" above, pp. 2–4, for one
example of this distortion. Another example: in *A Portrait* Stephen's
"beloved" is called "Emma" three times in two pages in III : B; otherwise,
she is "she," never "Emma Clery" as she is in *Stephen Hero*, though once
she is "E—— C——" when Stephen addresses a poem to her in II : B. In
A Portrait she is on stage only twice: at the end of V : A and the beginning
of V : C (and then only fleetingly). Heron and Wallis see her in II : C. For
the rest she is present only in Stephen's recall and in his imagination. But
the tradition of referring to her as Emma Clery persists in Joyce criticism
and brings with it the temptation to import particulars from *Stephen Hero*
in order to lend flesh and blood to the appropriately ghostly presence of
E—— C——. Many critics assume, for example, that the reason she
snubs Stephen in favor of Cranly in *A Portrait* V : C is because Stephen has
offended her by proposing one night of passion as he does in *Stephen Hero*,
pp. 197–99. This gives her a dramatic will of her own which in *A Portrait*
she does not enjoy unless one counts her "reply to Cranly's greeting" in
V : C as response to the fact that Stephen, preoccupied with his "confessor," Cranly, has not raised his hat to greet her. As her "image" floats
through *A Portrait*, she is a technical triumph, a *tour de force* reflection of

7. Ibsen in a letter to Bjørnstjerne Bjørnson, 12 September 1865, q. in *Brand*, translated
by G. M. Gathorne-Hardy (Seattle, 1966), p. 14.

the narcissism of the adolescent poetic imagination, 1890s style. To import her name and an independent flesh-and-blood voice from *Stephen Hero* is to deny Joyce an artistic triumph and to distort a reading of *A Portrait*.

IRELAND AND EXILE

The contemporary American reader may very well be baffled by Stephen Dedalus's dramatic insistence (and Joyce's personal insistence) on exile from Ireland as precondition for artistic enterprise. Why, we might ask, couldn't the artist both remain in Ireland and maintain his artistic integrity? Wasn't there some underground that could be discovered or created? Or is this insistence on exile a latter-day Byronism? One answer to those questions is reflected in the figure of Gabriel Conroy in "The Dead." Like Stephen (and Joyce) he is put off by the Gaelic League and its self-conscious attempts to revive the Irish language and to revive a truly "Irish" culture. Unlike Joyce, Gabriel has remained in Ireland, where he is teased by the militant Gaels (Molly Ivors) as a "West Briton" (a proponent of English culture *and* English rule). Gabriel has not evolved into a writer but into a literary journalist. At best his literary independence is clouded by an inevitable association with the politics of *The Daily Express*, the conservative, pro-British newspaper for which he writes reviews in fiction (and for which Joyce wrote reviews in fact). At worst Gabriel is shown as an insecure panderer to the tastes and demands of the middle-class world around him—as he worries about quoting "that difficult poet," Browning, and tailors his after-dinner speech at his aunts' annual dance so that it won't be "above the heads of his hearers."

Cultural-political confusion would seem to be part of the answer to the question: why exile for the Irish artist? since the Irish revival movement was as covertly political as it was overtly cultural. Any display of cultural (artistic) independence would have immediate political overtones whether they were intended or not. And there was also a corollary problem: English was, in a root way, the language and culture of Joyce and his literate Irish contemporaries, just as it is for the contemporary American. The self-conscious attempt to deny those English roots and to replace them with Irish "roots" was the attempt to substitute an artificial medium for the natural medium (even though the connotations of the English medium were sometimes difficult to accept). One wonders what would have happened in the United States had post-Revolutionary hotheads been successful in their advocacy of French (or German) as the official language of the newly born republic?

The religious environment of turn-of-the-century Ireland adds an interesting dimension to the problem that would have faced the artist-in-residence. In 1890 Ireland was approximately 90 percent Roman Catholic. It is axiomatic that a comfortable majority in a community can usually afford to tolerate considerable deviation from the stated norms within its ranks. But the Irish Catholic community acted instead like a beleaguered minority—tender to the point of paranoia and inclined to "excommunicate" anyone who refused to conform. This minority psychosis can of course be explained as a function of Britain's political and economic dominion over Ireland and as a function of the living memory of British oppression. The Catholic community enjoyed a numerical majority (with all its power to ostracize and discomfit), but at the same time the community was economically and politically in the minority and was inclined to militancy in its reaction. The Protestant minority on the other hand was also beleaguered and intolerant in spite of the political and economic power it derived from English support. The Protestant community regarded Catholics as chronically undependable, subversive, and incendiary; the Catholic community regarded Protestants as continually threatening to erode the Catholic position by coercion, intimidation, and bribery, and by proselytizing.

Both communities were conservative in religion, and both were conservative in politics—the Protestants conservative pro-English, the Catholics conservative pro-Home Rule for Ireland. A significant minority in the Catholic community was inclined toward radical nationalism, but conservative Catholics were suspicious of the "Fenians" (see p. 20 below) and vice versa—as Joyce so clearly dramatizes for the child Stephen in the confrontation at Christmas dinner in *A Portrait*. In a world so bitterly divided against itself there was virtually no middle or anonymous ground for personal independence, and any assertion of independence was liable to be greeted not with unilateral but with multilateral retaliation—a plague-on-both-your-houses in reverse. Joyce's struggle with the Dublin publishers who agreed and then refused to publish *Dubliners* offers a case in point, as do Yeats's and J. M. Synge's, and Sean O'Casey's repeated encounters with Irish intolerance (not to mention dozens of other writers and artists who have had their difficulties); see *Por* C226: 12–13n.

The Irish Free State (1922ff.), which has evolved into the Republic of Ireland, exercised until recently a fairly repressive and Church-dominated censorship.[8] Official censorship has been relaxed somewhat in contempo-

8. See Michael Adams, *Censorship: The Irish Experience* (University, Ala., 1968). This book is useful for the information it presents, but it is hampered by a stiff attempt at an impartiality unaffected by any prejudice against censorship in general and, in particular, against Irish censorship, which was itself intensely prejudicial. Adams does not take into account the ways in which the actions of the censors in effect licensed community harrassment of the writers of banned books, intimidating them and their fellow writers and driving many into exile.

rary Dublin, but there is still a strong odor of unofficial censorship, strong enough to give one a clear impression of how unfriendly the city could have been in the opening decades of this century. For example: the first Dublin performance (October 1977) of Sean O'Casey's burlesque *Cock-a-doodle Dandy* (1949) was introduced with an apology in the Abbey Theatre program lest the play take the audience unawares and anger "religious, national, and social sensibilities . . . especially for [its] undeniably crude caricatures of [Irish] patriots, politicians, and priests."

STEPHEN DEDALUS'S EDUCATION

Stephen's education in *A Portrait* stands in troublesome contrast to contemporary educational practices. His knowledge of Aristotle and St. Thomas Aquinas, for example, is not based on a reading of those authors in context or *in extenso* as it would be in a contemporary university; Stephen's knowledge is based on a study of selected passages, key points or moments, presented in textbooks which advertised themselves as *Synopsis of the Philosophy of* . . . . As Stephen puts it to himself, he has "only a garner of slender sentences." The educational practice of focusing study on memorable key quotations provided the student with a package of quotable phrases and tended to suggest that thought was aphorism. It also made it possible for an individual to appear remarkably learned when he had, in fact, not read very widely.

Stephen remarks in V:A that his aesthetic is "applied Aquinas"; dramatically this assertion is "correct" since Stephen does use a series of semi-quotations from Aquinas as the basis of his explication. Intellectually, Stephen's assertion is somewhat confusing since the semi-quotations from Aquinas are used without much regard for the larger context of Aquinas's work and thought. This confusion has led several critics to challenge Joyce's grasp of Aquinas, and while that is an interesting issue, the pursuit of it takes the reader away from the dramatic fabric of Stephen's discussion in V:A to focus instead on Joyce's mental processes and on Joyce's relation to the history of ideas. The point is that Stephen is presenting his argument in the conventional form dictated by his training; he quotes his authority only ostensibly to develop the aesthetic latent in Aquinas's observations; actually Stephen uses the phrases from Aquinas as a point of departure for his own aesthetic speculation because that is the "language" in which he has been trained to present (and to cloak) his own thought. It is widely assumed that Stephen's aesthetic theory is Joyce's and that Joyce is using Stephen as a mouthpiece, but it can also be argued that Joyce is using Lynch as a mouthpiece when that character remarks that Stephen's discussion has "the true scholastic stink." Stephen's aesthetic may be Joyce's only in part, presented in a language appropriate not to the writer who is about to turn his attention to *Ulysses* but to the coinage of the "young man's" education and to the young artist's romantic inclination, since the aesthetic is not any more "applied Aquinas" than it is applied Shelley.

J. S. Atherton has demonstrated that all of Stephen's quotations from Newman derive not from Newman's works but from a one-volume anthology, *Characteristics from the Writings of John Henry Newman* (London, 1875).[9] Atherton argues that Joyce is trying to give the impression that Stephen is widely read. But Stephen treats his bits of Newman (in the dramatic context of the novel) as parts of a collection of phrases notable for their sounds and rhythms, not notable for their reflection of the context in which they occur or for their reflection of the attitudes of the writer from whom they were taken. This would again suggest the tendency to regard learning not as a grasp of contexts but as an acquisition of quotable moments. The dramatic impression left by Stephen's mental behavior in the novel is not so much that of a mind that has read widely as it is of a mind that has poked around and collected phrases in a variety of places: some of them collected in conformity with the emphasis of his education, as from Newman, Aquinas, Aristotle; some of them collected in out-of-the-way places, as from minor Elizabethans, from Hugh Miller's *Testimony of the Rocks*, from Luigi Galvani, etc. But all of the phrases have been converted from their literary and intellectual contexts to the context of Stephen's personal use. Above and behind Stephen, Joyce on occasion manipulates the bits and pieces as indicators of ironies and evaluations—for example, in V : A when Stephen, the nonconformist, quotes Christian Aquinas to the Dean of Studies, the conformist, who in turn quotes pagan Epictetus, or when Stephen follows a poetic quotation from Shelley with a superficially apt phrase from Luigi Galvani ("enchantment of the heart")—except that Galvani was describing what happens to a frog's heart when a needle is inserted in its spine.

Religious instruction was a regular and required feature of the education Joyce received in fact and which Stephen receives in fiction. Two catechisms were assigned as the basic texts in the courses of religious instruction at Clongowes Wood College in the 1880s and 90s:

> *The Catechism Ordered by the National Synod of Maynooth* (Dublin, 1883), called *Maynooth Catechism* in the notes.
>
> Joseph De Harbe, S. J., *A Full Catechism of the Catholic Religion*, translated

9. James Joyce, *A Portrait of the Artist as a Young Man* (London, 1964), p. 249 n.

from the German by the Rev. John Flander (New York, 1877), cited as De Harbe *Catechism* in these notes.

The catechism or catechisms assigned at Belvedere College when Joyce (and Stephen) were students there in the 1890s are not known. The Rector of Belvedere writes (August 1976) that unfortunately the College's records are "incomplete" on this point. For the purposes of this annotation I have assumed that the Maynooth and De Harbe catechisms were used at both Jesuit colleges and that together they provided the basis for Joyce's (and Stephen's) catechetical saturation.

I have also consulted two other Irish catechisms:

> Rev. Andrew Donlevy, *The Catechism, or, Christian Doctrine . . . Published for the Royal Catholic College of St. Patrick, Maynooth* (Dublin, 1848), cited as Donlevy *Catechism* below.

> *A Catechism of Catholic Doctrine; Approved by the Archbishops and Bishops of Ireland* (Dublin, 1951), cited as *Catechism*, 1951 below.

WOMEN AND THEIR EXPECTATIONS

A middle-class woman's horizons in Dublin at the beginning of this century were severely limited. Apart from marriage or a convent, there were precious few careers open to her, and some of those such as clerking in a shop or going into service implied a loss of social status. If she were skilled, dressmaking and millinery were open to her. With some vocational schooling (a relatively new idea), she might become a typist, a stenographer, and even (though rarely) a secretary. If educated, she could seek employment as a governess or companion or teacher. Otherwise, her only hope was dependency, or . . . see *Dub* C99:2n.

Marriage itself was by no means something that could be expected in due course. After the Great Famine of the 1840s the population of Ireland declined and continued to decline. The marriage rate declined; the average age at which people married rose toward the mid-30s, and the birth rate declined. In Ireland in 1901 52.7 percent of the women of marriageable age in the population (16 years of age and older) were unmarried; 37.7 percent were married; 9.6 percent widowed. The proportion of unmarried increased from 47.7 percent in 1881 to 50.8 percent in 1891 to 52.7 percent in 1901. These are very high rates: what they mean is that Frank's offer to Eveline, in the story "Eveline," is the exception rather than the rule, and it is quite probable that when Eveline turns away from Frank she turns toward a celibate future, a fate like that of Maria in "Clay."

MONETARY VALUES

Joyce uses monetary values (among other incidental "hard facts") as indicators of and clues to his characters' attitudes and status. Since Joyce's technique is to withhold evaluatory comment, these clues can easily be overlooked or misinterpreted. The value of money in Ireland circa 1900 (or in any country foreign in space and time) presents difficult problems for the reader. What does it imply that Eveline Hill in the story "Eveline" receives a weekly wage of seven shillings? What order of poverty and/or exploitation does her wage suggest? A direct and rough translation would start by assuming that the dollar in 1900 was worth five times what it is today; thus the British pound, worth $5.00 in 1900, would be worth $25.00 in 1980. So Eveline's wage would be the equivalent of $8.75 a week in 1980! This would suggest abysmal poverty and cruel exploitation. On the other hand, a somewhat different line of reasoning would lead to quite different answers. *Thom's Official Directory of the United Kingdom of Great Britain and Ireland* (Dublin, 1904), p. 1345, lists the Dublin market prices of four Irish staples: bacon, bread, potatoes, and oatmeal.[10] A comparison of the prices of those staples (plus beer) in 1904 and 1980 suggests that the British penny (1904) had the buying power of 44.25¢ (U.S. 1980); so Eveline's weekly wage would be the equivalent of $37.17 (1980). This would still mean poverty, but of quite a different order. In the late nineteenth century women were still regarded as "temporary employees" in stores and offices, so they were not paid wages on the assumption that they were self-supporting but on the assumption that they lived at home and that the minimal wages they earned would augment an established family income as Eveline's wage does.

The unpleasant tone of the Hill family's relation to money is not economic but interpersonal. Joyce does not imply that Eveline has to give her whole wage to her father because her family is suffering under grinding poverty, but because her father likes to drink and is brutally ungenerous.

10. Bacon, 7d. (seven pence, old style) a pound in 1904; a comparable lean (Canadian) bacon in the U.S.A. (1980) would be at least $3.00 a pound; the British penny (d.) = 43¢. Bread, 5½d. for a four pound loaf in 1904; U.S.A. 1980, $2.36; d. = 43¢. Potatoes, .36d. in 1904; U.S.A. 1980, 25¢; d. = 69¢. Oatmeal, 1.8d. per pound in 1904; U.S.A. 1980, 39¢; d. = 22¢. Average: d. (1904) = 44.25¢ (1980); or one shilling (1904) = $5.31 (1980); or one pound (1904) = $106.20 (1980). These figures may sound way out of line, and yet when we adjust our glasses by recognizing that food was subsidized in the United Kingdom of Great Britain and Ireland in 1904, we still have to take into account a profound transformation of money values in the last seventy-five years. Another Dublin staple (not averaged above), the twenty ounce pint of beer, was a subsidized 2d. in Dublin, 1904, or in 1904 dollars, a nickel. Today (1980) a pint in Dublin costs 55 to 60 new pence or $1.30 to $1.42; the 1904 d. = 68¢ (1980); s. = $8.16; £ = $163.32!

If Eveline had been allowed to keep as little as half her weekly wage for pocket money ($18.50, 1980), she would have been "well off" in relation to her lower-middle-class contemporaries, even though her "living standard" (the possessions and services she could afford) would have been below that of a 1980 Dublin shop girl. But this, too, is a misleading comparison, since the range of consumer choice which the Dublin world would have offered to Eveline would have been much narrower than that available to her modern counterpart, and conversely Eveline would have felt less deprived than her modern counterpart is liable to feel, since the modern shop girl is comparatively less able to take advantage of the opportunities presented (or at least advertised) as within her field of choice as a consumer. If Eveline were to try to live on her own, Dublin, 1904, she could have found a tenement room, furnished for four shillings per week, unfurnished for one shilling sixpence. If she had a few sticks of furniture, she could have found accommodation for just a little more than one-fifth of her paltry seven shilling salary.

The notes on money clues provided in this volume have been worked out with a three-dimensional relativism of the sort applied here to Eveline's salary. These notes are an exception to the intention to keep the notes "factual" rather than interpretive—largely because exact monetary equivalents are not available and would not always be revealing if they were, since it is not only the value of money that has changed but also the relation of money to all aspects of life. Dubliners in the 1890s experienced both depression and prosperity, but they were habituated to fixed currency values and not to the chronic inflation with which we live. Further, the domestic economy of Dublin in 1900 was not a consumer economy as ours is. Staples play a relatively small part in our household budgets; they were central in the lower-middle-class family budget, 1900. A relatively secure salary or wage earner (1900) would not have expected his income to provide anything like the range of goods and services his 1980 counterpart would expect, and most of what a 1980 consumer regards as everyday necessities would have been once-in-a-while luxuries in 1900.

Stephen's scholarship prize of £33 in *A Portrait* II : E provides another sort of example. It was a sizeable sum; the average book in 1900 cost from five to seven shillings; Stephen could have purchased approximately 110 books with his prize. In terms of today's average book prices Stephen's prize would have been worth more than $1000. But that is only part of the story; a £33 prize would have put Stephen in a far more unusual relation to his normal environment (and that of his school contemporaries) than a $1000 prize would put a modern student. A modern student can easily earn that amount of money in a few summer weeks. Stephen and his classmates, if they had been able to work at comparable jobs (and as members of their "student class" that would have been unlikely), would have been lucky to earn £6 in a summer. When, after several years at the University, Stephen does get a job as a schoolteacher (in *Ulysses*), his monthly wage is £3/12/0, about three times Eveline's wage, but it would still have taken Stephen more than nine months to equal his prize money. Finally, impressive as the amount of money must have been in the 1890s, the importance of the prize was primarily the academic distinction that it conferred. (Academic prizes have not kept pace with inflation; a comparable modern student prize in Ireland would still be on the order of £20 to £30—$40 to $60, 1980—even more emphasis on academic distinction.)

Poverty: this discussion of monetary values applies primarily to the middle- and lower-middle-class world in Dublin, the world on which Joyce focuses. The world of the lower depths is glimpsed only at moments, as the "throng of foes" through which the boy passes on Saturday evenings in "Araby" and the "vermin-like life" through which Little Chandler picks his way in "A Little Cloud." "Informed contemporary estimates" put early twentieth century unemployment in Dublin "at anything up to twenty per cent though in the skilled trades the figure would have been appreciably less, perhaps as low as ten per cent."[11] The result (together with the depressed wage scale in Ireland as against wage scales in England) was an appalling poverty:

> About thirty per cent (87,000) of the people of Dublin lived in the slums which were for the most part wornout shells of Georgian mansions. Over 2000 *families* lived in single room tenements which were without heat or light or water (save for a tap in a passage or backyard) or adequate sanitation. Inevitably, the death-rate was the highest in the country, while infant mortality was the worst, not just in Ireland, but in the British Isles. Disease of every kind, especially tuberculosis, was rife and malnutrition was endemic; it is hardly surprising that the poor, when they had a few pence, often spent them seeking oblivion through drink.[12]

AN OUTLINE OF IRISH HISTORY

The world of Dublin in Joyce's time enjoyed a complex preoccupation with history-as-legend and legend-as-history and possessed a rich vocabulary of historical anecdote. Joyce exploits this preoccupation and vocabulary to the full, and it is obvious that a general grasp of Irish history (as the Irish saw it) is indispensable to an informed reading of Joyce's works. The

11. F. S. L. Lyons, *Ireland Since the Famine* (London, 1973), p. 278.
12. *Ibid.*, pp. 277–78.

notes in this volume identify historical incidents and figures; this outline is intended to provide a general framework for the individual notes.

Prehistory The legendary prehistory of Ireland was chronicled as a series of five successive invasions and colonizations—first, the Parthalonians; second, the Nemedians, who were harassed by the Formorians, gloomy giants of the sea; third, the Firbolg (fourth century B.C.?) who were characterized as undersized, crude, and earthy; fourth, the Tuatha Da Danann, the race of heroes; and lastly, the Milesians, the sons of Mileadh of Spain, ideal free spirits and artists, who were regarded as the "ancestors" of the royal clans of Ireland. The historical basis for these legends was apparently a series of migration-invasions. Neolithic flint users were displaced by a small, dark people from the Mediterranean (Firbolg?); they were invaded by the Picts; the final invaders in the fourth century B.C. were Celts from central Europe, followed by Gaelic Celts from southern France and northern Spain. Accounts of these prehistoric invasions and characterizations of the invaders were very much alive in the oral traditions of early Irish history, though the oral traditions only indirectly reflect the complex waves of migration which peopled prehistoric Ireland. Indeed, the "Irish Race" is still frequently represented as enjoying a mythical purity which the rich mix of prehistoric peoples and Celtic invaders belies—not to mention the continuing admixtures that resulted from social and cultural interchange with Anglo-Saxons, Picts, and Scots (sixth century ff.), with the Viking invaders (ninth century ff.), with the Anglo-Norman invaders (1169ff.), and with waves of English colonists under the Tudors and since. To this day the sharp distinctions some Irish make between a Celtic *us* and an Anglo-Irish *them* (and vice versa) can strike a visitor as something of an abstraction.

Third century A.D. The High Kingship of Tara reached its apogee under Cormac Mac Art. Tara thus became the quasi-legendary and symbolic capital of "golden age" Ireland, as King Arthur's even more legendary Camelot was dream-capital of Logres, the ideal kingdom of the Britons.

432 The traditional (but by no means certain) date of the beginning of St. Patrick's mission to Ireland.

634 The great age of Irish missionary enterprise in England and on the Continent began.

795 Viking raids began.

832–70 Sporadic Viking raids gave way to large scale Viking invasions;

Viking strongholds were established in Dublin and Waterford. Irish missionary enterprise declined. Beginning of an extended period of civil strife: Irish against Vikings; Irish against Irish; Irish and Vikings against Irish, etc.

1014 Battle of Clontarf—combined Irish forces accomplished the defeat of Viking power in Dublin and environs (and promptly started fighting among themselves).

(1066 The Norman invasion of England.)

1155 Pope Adrian IV (Nicholas Breakspear), the only Englishman to be pope (1154–59), was said to have granted the overlordship of Ireland to Henry II of England (king, 1154–89), but the Papal Bull, *Laudabiliter*, which is supposed to have made the grant does not exist in the Vatican Archives.

1169 Some of Henry II's lords tried their luck at piecemeal (feudal) conquest of Ireland.

1171 The successes of the Anglo-Norman adventurers in Ireland prompted Henry II to assert his sovereignty and take charge of the invasion. Since that time Irish history has been one long series of Anglo-Irish donnybrooks.

1455–85 The Wars of the Roses in England—the Irish regained a measure of independence while the English were preoccupied at home, but the Irish also supported the White Rose of the House of York (the losers) and eventually suffered the consequences.

1485ff. Henry VII established Tudor policy in Ireland—conquest and colonization. Henry VII imposed English land use laws on Ireland, much to the detriment of Irish agriculture.

1509–47 During the reign of Henry VIII, England sought further consolidation of its power in Ireland and also sought to establish Henry's new Church, much to the displeasure of many Irish dissidents who looked to the Pope and sought support from Roman Catholic France and Spain.

1558–1620 During the reigns of Elizabeth I and James I, a series of Irish revolts gave the English the opportunity to begin the destruction of the old Celtic clan system (onto which the Anglo-Normans had grafted their own feudal system) and to replace it with a "plantation" system under which land was held by Protestant English landlords and worked by the Irish Catholic peasantry. The consequent displacement of the Irish Catholic aristocracy, many of whom fled to the Continent (1607ff.), was called the Flight of the Earls.

1642   While the English were preoccupied with their own Civil War, the Irish proclaimed the Catholic Confederacy and declared their independence.

1649   After he had consolidated his power in England, Cromwell invaded Ireland. The reconquest began with the massacre of the population of Drogheda (to show the Irish what resistance would mean) and was sufficiently punitive throughout to earn Cromwell a well-merited reputation as the "Great Oppressor." The reconquest was also more methodical and more thorough than any previous conquest. Cromwell extended the land "reform" and intensified the strictures against Roman Catholics, who were forbidden to own land, to carry weapons, to hold military commissions or public office, and to worship without restrictions.

1688–1714   James II of England (a crypto-Catholic) was deposed in the Bloodless Revolution of 1688 and fled to France. He was succeeded by the Protestant William of Orange, who became William III of England. The Irish remained loyal to the losing Stuart cause, and in 1689 James II came to Ireland and led the Irish to defeat at the hands of William III in the Battle of the Boyne (1690). The Irish were not only reconquered but also systematically betrayed by English violations (1700ff.) of the Treaty of Limerick (1691). The result was further repressive "reform" which effectively reduced Ireland to the status of a penal colony in the opening decades of the eighteenth century.

Late eighteenth century   Under the leadership of Henry Flood (1732–91) and Henry Grattan (1736–1820) an Irish Protestant political party in the Irish Parliament (Catholics were, of course, excluded from office) undertook reforms, especially for the relief of the oppressed Roman Catholic community.

1782   The Irish Parliament, which had its beginnings in the late thirteenth century, passed Grattan's "Constitution" and established a limited (and historically often overrated) independence under the authority of the British Crown.

1791   The Society of United Irishmen was founded under the leadership of Wolfe Tone (1763–98), Hamilton Rowan (1751–1834), and James Napper Tandy (1740–1803) in an attempt to unite Protestant and Catholic Ireland for the achievement of independence as a constitutional republic.

1795   The United Irishmen shifted from a constitutional to a revolutionary strategy and sought military aid from the French Republic. The French made a series of abortive attempts at invasion—in December of

1796, in June of 1797, and twice in 1798. Wolfe Tone was captured at sea during one of the attempts in 1798.

1795–98 The English took repressive measures, and the oppressive situation was made worse by the formation in Ulster of the Protestant Orange Lodges, which indulged in local and "independent" acts of reprisal against Irish Catholics.

1798 The Rebellion of this year was a tangle of conflicting and poorly coordinated revolutionary attempts. The United Irishmen, with their aspirations for a secular Republic of Ireland, were thoroughly infiltrated by British informers and were crushed. At the same time in the south and west the Catholic peasantry rose in what amounted to a religious civil war; they were also crushed.

1800 The Act of Union dissolved the Irish Parliament (by its own vote) and merged it with the British Parliament in London. The Act was engineered by a good deal of bribery and skulduggery and against the bitter opposition of much of Catholic Ireland and of many Protestant leaders. Several Catholic Bishops supported the Act of Union in the hope, which proved ill-founded, of achieving Catholic Emancipation as the price of their support. The result of the Union was disaster in Ireland: it displaced Irish political power to London, and scores of Irish landlords moved to England to be near the new seat of political power. Meanwhile, the land and the peasants were pillaged by land agents left in charge by the absentees. In effect, a none-too-sound Irish economy was virtually dismantled just as it had begun to recover from the depression of the "penal colony" period.

1807ff. Daniel O'Connell ("The Liberator," 1775–1847) emerged as the political leader of Catholic Ireland (though Catholics enjoyed few direct political rights other than the right to vote). O'Connell used both constitutional procedures and civil disobedience (quasi-illegal "monster meetings" organized to demonstrate Irish unanimity) to agitate for Catholic Emancipation (religious freedom, the right to hold public office, etc.) and for repeal of the Act of Union.

1829 The political pressure O'Connell and others managed to generate resulted in Parliament's acceptance of Catholic Emancipation. O'Connell's further efforts to achieve repeal of the Act of Union were frustrated by increasing dissension within the ranks of his own party and by English conservative resistance to further reform.

1845–48 The Great Famine—the disintegration of the Irish economy had condemned at least half of Ireland's population of just over

8,000,000 (census of 1841) to abysmal poverty and to dependence on the potato as staple food. (At least three-quarters of the land under cultivation in Ireland was devoted to crops, primarily wheat for export, which the poor simply could not afford; the rest of the arable land was used for grazing.) The potato blight appeared in 1845, destroying the potato crop and reducing the poor to famine. The famine (with its attendant epidemics of cholera, etc.) ruined the Irish peasantry and completed the ruin of the tottering Irish economy. British policy had dictated the suppression of industry in Ireland (Ireland was to supply food to industrial England), and the agrarian collapse was a death blow, not only to the peasantry but also to many landlords because many tried to tide their peasants over and were ruined in the process. The population of Ireland fell by 1,500,000 in three years (through death and emigration to America), and the population continued to fall through the rest of the nineteenth century until in 1901 it was just under 4,500,000. The famine has been repeatedly described as "the worst event of its kind recorded in European history at a time of peace."

1848ff. After the famine there was a "devotional revolution," a marked and widespread increase in religious commitment and activity; there was also a marked increase in violent (if minority) demand for political independence. These two impulses and the crosscurrents they generated reflect two interrelated and continuing conflicts in Irish politics: (1) the conflict between (a) those dedicated to the achievement of Irish independence through violence and armed rebellion—Wolfe Tone and the United Irishmen (1798), the Irish Republican Brotherhood or the Fenians (1858ff.), and their heirs including the Irish Republican Army of the post-World War I years and the Provisional I. R. A. of the 1970s; and (b) those dedicated to the achievement of Irish independence through negotiation and through constitutional and parliamentary processes—Daniel O'Connell and apparently Charles Stewart Parnell, though Parnell frequently used rhetoric which suggests that he was straddling on the issue. (2) The conflict between (a) those dedicated to the achievement of a Catholic Ireland (usually styled as moderates, though they had their "bludgeon men") and (b) those dedicated to an Ireland with civil and religious liberties for all (usually styled as Ribbonmen, Fenians, and radicals). Wolfe Tone (and his heirs) were clearly in favor of religious and civil liberties for all; Parnell balanced between the two sides as a matter of political expediency, but after the split in December 1890, he appeared to the remnant of the faithful as more and more the civil and religious libertarian. The Irish Free State when it emerged in the 1920s was Catholic and moderate-conservative in tone and orientation.

The trouble for one who would like to understand political attitudes in Ireland since the famine is that "left" and "right" are all but meaningless terms and that the two conflicts outlined above did not divide people into two camps but into four and multiples of four.

1867 The Fenian Rising—reenforced by returnees from the American Civil War, the Fenians launched an ill-timed and ill-coordinated rebellion that was thoroughly anticipated by the British and summarily crushed. The traditional British reprisals were surprisingly mild.

1869 The Church of Ireland (counterpart of the Church of England) was disestablished in Ireland by act of the British Parliament. Among other things this meant that Irish Catholics no longer had to pay tithes to the Church of Ireland (which owns all the good medieval real estate anyway).

1877 Charles Stewart Parnell (1846–91), an Anglo-Irish Protestant landlord, emerged as the leading figure in the Irish Parliamentary Party. Parnell not only united most of the Irish nationalist groups under his leadership, he also maneuvered his party into a balance-of-power position between the Liberals and the Conservatives (or Tories) in the British Parliament. The strength of his position made it possible for Parnell to force Parliament at least to consider Home Rule for Ireland.

1879 Renewed fear of famine gave added impetus to agitation for land reform; Michael Davitt (1846–1906) organized the Land League. When Parnell subsequently became president of the League, he was able, with Davitt's help, to fuse the two dominant political issues in the Ireland of his time: land reform and Home Rule. Land reform was gradually undertaken in a series of reform bills, 1882–1903.

1882 Two British officials, Lord Frederick Cavendish, chief secretary for Ireland, and Mr. Burke, undersecretary, were murdered in Phoenix Park, Dublin, by the "Invincibles" (a Fenian splinter-group?). The Chief-Secretary was, in effect, responsible to the British cabinet (and to Parliament) for the government of Ireland. The outbreak of violence imperiled Parnell's political campaign for constitutional reform.

1886 Gladstone's first Home Rule Bill was defeated in Parliament to the tune of riots in Protestant Belfast (which violently opposed Home Rule as "Rome Rule"), and Gladstone's Liberal Party began to come apart at the seams, on its way to what George Dangerfield was to call *The Strange Death of Liberal England* (London, 1936).

1887   Letters forged by an Irish journalist named Richard Pigott and published with its blessing by *The London Times* accused Parnell of advocating the murder of landlords and appeared to implicate him in the planning of the Phoenix Park murders. Parnell demanded (and got) an investigation by a Special Parliamentary Commission. Pigott broke and admitted the forgery, while *The London Times* tried to put the whole Irish nationalist movement on trial. Parnell emerged victorious, at the peak of his popularity in Ireland and of his political power in Parliament.

1889–90   Captain O'Shea, one of Parnell's political associates, filed for divorce on grounds of adultery, naming Parnell as correspondent. The divorce was not contested; Parnell's relation with Mrs. O'Shea had been all-but-marriage (and a well-kept open secret). After the divorce was final, the two were married. Parnell was discredited and abandoned by Davitt and by most of the Irish nationalist groups except the Fenians. As a result of the scandal and British pressure, Gladstone threatened to resign as Prime Minister if Parnell were not removed from leadership of the Irish Parliamentary Party. A majority of the Party, led by Timothy Michael Healy, tried to depose Parnell as leader, but, because Parnell was in the chair, managed only to split the party by a vote of 45 to 26 in Committee Room 15 of the House of Parliament in London. The withdrawal of the 45 left Parnell the leader of a truncated party.

After the Split, the Irish Roman Catholic hierarchy, which had held its tongue in calculated inactivity in order not to appear to have intervened, joined in denouncing and openly opposing Parnell's leadership (and the Parnellite candidates he tried to advance in by-elections). The political consensus of the 1880s was shattered, and the bitterness and divisiveness engendered by the Split was intensified by Parnell's increasingly strident attempts to recoup.

1891   Parnell died in England shortly before midnight on Tuesday, 6 October 1891. His body was brought to Dublin on Sunday, 11 October, to lie in state at the City Hall before burial in Prospect Cemetery, Glasnevin. Parnell's life was (and to a great extent remains) a political and personal enigma. Perhaps it is this enigmatic quality which accounts for the violence of the loyalties and antipathies Parnell aroused. Some of this enigmatic quality is reflected in Michael Davitt's assessment of him, "an Englishman of the strongest type molded for an Irish purpose." See F. S. L. Lyons, *Charles Stewart Parnell* (London, 1977).

1892   Gladstone's second Home Rule Bill was defeated.

1893   The Gaelic League was founded—overtly cultural, covertly political, its avowed purpose was the revival of Irish language and tradition.

1905   Arthur Griffith (1872–1922) formed the Sinn Fein (We Ourselves, or Ourselves Alone) movement, conceived at first in terms of civil disobedience and passive resistance to British rule.

Subsequent events   Home Rule for Ireland was almost accomplished on the eve of World War I, but implementation was delayed by Ulster intransigence and then suspended for the duration of the war in a way that exacerbated an already healthy Irish suspicion of British intentions. There were recurrent outbreaks of violence; the most famous was the Easter Rebellion of 1916, which resulted in defeat but at the same time accomplished a profound revival of Irish patriotic spirit and a renewed sense of political unity. At the close of World War I, Sinn Fein and its military organization, the Irish Republic Army, rose against British rule. The I.R.A. managed to frustrate the best efforts of the British Army and the Royal Irish Constabulary (reinforced by recently demobilized British soldiers and called the Black and Tans). The Anglo-Irish War finally wound down in a negotiated settlement that proposed a sort of Irish independence, compromised, however, by the fact that the British allowed the six northern counties of Ulster to vote themselves out of the Irish Free State. This partition of Ireland, together with the civil war (1921–22), which was triggered by dissatisfaction with that and other provisions of the treaty, has marred the tranquility of the "solution" and given rise to sporadic but continuing acts of agitation and violence—as the recent history of Northern Ireland has made all too clear.

GEOGRAPHY

Joyce uses the geography of Dublin extensively and with precise attention to detail in the whole canon of his work. This is at times baffling to the non-Dubliner, since it is not always clear whether the details are merely incidental bits of "Dublin's street furniture" (*Stephen Hero*, p. 211) or whether they are suggestive of larger meanings. The notes in this volume include specific identification of geographical references and, where appropriate, outline the basis for the "larger meanings" involved. A glance at a map of Dublin, 1900, shows an oval city, encircled north and south by canals and bisected on its east-west, longer axis by the River Liffey; the city's shape and pattern make location by "quadrants" generally feasible, and that practice has been followed in the notes.

In some of the stories in *Dubliners* geographical location and direction of movement come sharply into focus as reflections of states of being: of paralysis (as in the circle of Lenehan's wanderings in "Two Gallants"), of

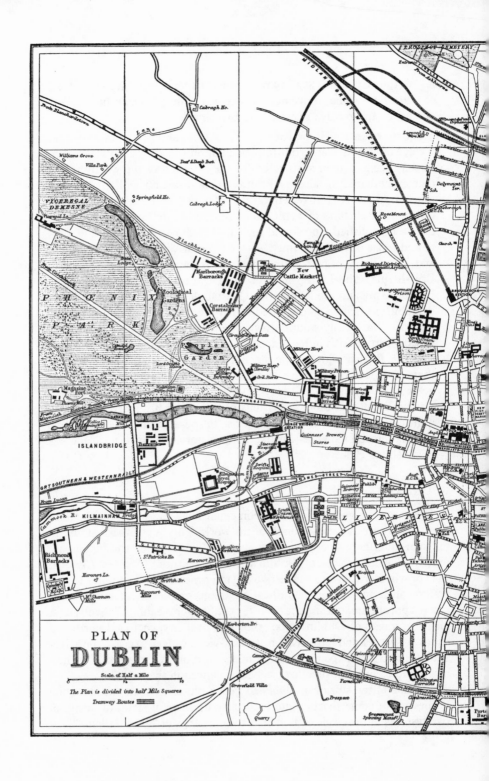

PLAN OF
DUBLIN

Scale of Half a Mile

The Plan is divided into half Mile Squares
Tramway Routes

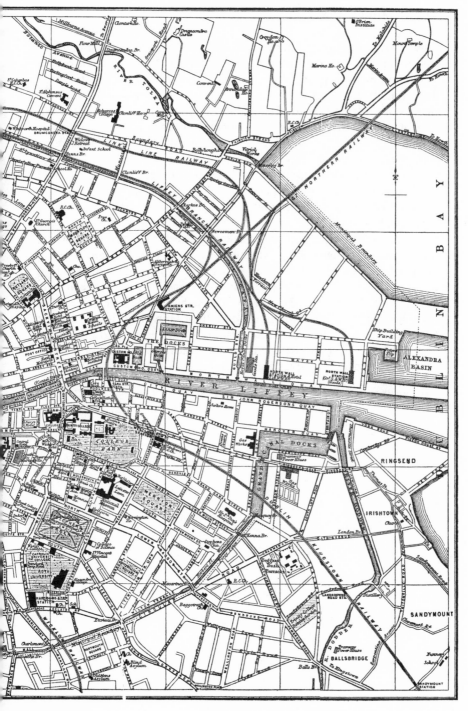

From David A. Chart, *The Story of Dublin* (London, 1907)

illusory, escapist quest (as in the journey toward the Pigeon House in "An Encounter"). Somewhat less sharply, location and direction can be read as suggesting more inclusive patterns in *Dubliners*. The opening stories all involve motion toward the east, toward "exile," toward some principle that promises at least escape from paralysis if not revitalization. In the balance of the volume eastward motion gives way to an increasing concentration in the center of Dublin, the center of paralysis; in the final story, "The Dead," there are glances westward, toward death.[13]

Geography also reflects states of being in *A Portrait*: the displacement of Stephen's family from the affluent resort village of Bray to the suburban village of Blackrock to increasingly poor Dublin neighborhoods spells out the gradual decline of the family's fortunes. Escape toward the east is also a motif in *A Portrait*, notably when Stephen asserts that "the shortest way to Tara is via Holyhead"—i.e., the quickest way to achieve a golden age of literature for Ireland is to create in exile on the Continent. Stephen's final determination on flight and exile holds out some hope of escape and regeneration at the end of *A Portrait*, even though we find out in *Ulysses* that his first attempt at flight from the labyrinth of Dublin has been, like that of Icarus, frustrated. Geographical patterns in *Dubliners* and *A Portrait* are suggestive, but they are emergent and occasional and should not be overstated as dominant principles of order in either of the fictions.

13. See Brewster Ghiselin, "The Unity of Joyce's *Dubliners*," *Accent* 16:75–88, 196–213.

NOTES FOR

Dubliners

(1914)

My intention was to write a chapter of the moral history of my country and I chose Dublin for the scene because that city seemed to me the centre of paralysis. I have tried to present it to the indifferent public under four of its aspects: childhood, adolescence, maturity, and public life. The stories are arranged in this order.

JAMES JOYCE,
quoted in Herbert Gorman,
James Joyce (New York, 1939), p. 150

NOTE ON ABBREVIATIONS

The letters and numerals at the head of each annotated word or phrase indicate edition, page, and line.

C9:1   Viking Compass Edition, edited by Robert Scholes in consultation with Richard Ellmann (New York, 1967), page 9, line 1. (The titles of the stories have been counted as lines.)

pe9:1   Penguin Books (New York, 1976), page 9, line 1.

P19:1   *The Portable James Joyce* (New York, 1968), page 19, line 1.

References to other notes in this volume are labeled *Dub* for *Dubliners* and *Por* for *A Portrait of the Artist as a Young Man* and are designated by Compass Edition page and line number followed by n—as, for example, *Dub* C9:1n.

"The Sisters" was the first of the fifteen stories to be written and the first to be published, in *The Irish Homestead*, 13 August 1904. Joyce thoroughly rewrote "The Sisters" in May–June 1906. The first version of the story is included in the Appendix below.

C9: 1, pe9: 1, P19: 1 (title)   **The Sisters**   Nurses and nuns are called sisters in Ireland.

C9: 7, pe9: 8, P19: 8   **two candles**   Candles are variously interpreted as symbols in the Church. The wax of the candle is symbolic of the Body of Christ; the wick, His Soul; the flame, His Divinity. If two candles: one can be regarded as a symbol of the Old Testament, one of the New.

C9: 11, pe9: 12, P19: 12–13   *paralysis*   Usually assumed to be the result of the three strokes the priest has suffered, but it may well be the other way around, that the strokes have been caused by *paralysis*, since in 1904 the term *paralysis* was frequently used in medical parlance (and by Joyce) to mean "general paralysis of the insane," i.e., paresis, syphilis of the central nervous system. It is possible to demonstrate that in rewriting the story (see Appendix) Joyce not only added the word "paralysis" but also worked the symptoms of paresis into the boy-narrator's recall of the priest's appearance and manner. See Burton A. Waisbren and Florence L. Walzl, "Paresis and the Priest: James Joyce's Symbolic Use of Syphilis in 'The Sisters,'" *Annals of Internal Medicine* 80 (June 1974): 758–62.

C9: 12–13, pe9: 13–14, P19: 14   *gnomon* **in the Euclid**   The Alexandrian Greek geometrician, Euclid, flourished circa 300 B.C. In his *Elements*, book II, definition 2, Euclid defines a gnomon as what is left of a parallelogram when a similar parallelogram containing one of its corners is removed. Gnomon is also the name for the pointer on a sundial (and for the angle at which the pointer is set).

C9: 13, pe9: 14, P19: 14–15   *simony* **in the Catechism**   None of the Irish Catechisms I have consulted for these notes mentions or defines *simony*; all treat the sacrament of Holy Orders and the duties of the priesthood rather briefly. But "Catechism" can also be the boy's word for the courses of religious instruction regularly required in Irish Catholic schools (since one or more catechisms would have been used as the basic text in those courses). *Simony* is named after Simon Magus (Simon the Sorcerer), Acts 8: 18–24, who ignorantly offered the Apostle Peter money for "the gift of God," (i.e., for the power to transmit the

Holy Ghost through the laying on of hands). Hence simony is the deliberate buying or selling of ecclesiastical offices, pardons, or emoluments. In the medieval Church this literal definition was transformed figuratively so that simony meant the prostitution of any spiritual value, any of the seven gifts of the Holy Ghost (wisdom, understanding, counsel, fortitude, knowledge, piety, fear of the Lord) for material comfort or gain. See *Por* C159:16–17n.

C9:18–19, pe9:21, P19:21   **stirabout**   A porridge, usually made of oatmeal simmered in water or milk.

C10:5, pe10:5–6, P20:1   **faints and worms**   "Faints" are the impure spirits that come through the still first and last in the process of distillation; "worms" are long spiral or coiled tubes connected with the head of a still; the vapor is condensed in the worms.

C10:8–9, pe10:9, P20:4   **one of those . . . peculiar cases**   While Father Flynn has not been excommunicated, his relation to the priesthood is somewhat ambiguous, the end of his career shadowed by what to the Irish Catholic imagination is "the fearfully potent image of the excommunicated or silenced priest." See p. viii above and *Por* C160:3n.

C10:20–23, pe10:24, P20:20   **a great wish for him**   In this expression the word "wish" is a translation of the Irish *meas*, which means "respect, esteem" (P. W. Joyce, *English as We Speak It in Ireland* [Dublin, 1910], p. 351). Hereafter this work will be cited as P. W. Joyce.

C11:1–2, pe10:36–37, P20:33–34   **Let him learn to box his corner**   "Corner" is slang for "share" or "proceeds"; thus, "Let him go out and learn to make a living and get ahead in the world."

C11:2–3, pe11:1, P20:35   **Rosicrucian**   A member of an international fraternity of religious mystics, the Ancient Order Rosae Crucis. The order was supposedly revived in the fifteenth century by a German monk, Friar Christian Rosenkreutz (probably legendary) who was mystically in touch with the Great White Brotherhood of Egypt (15th century B.C.). Several small sects which derived their lore from the medieval cabala and from alchemy flourished in the seventeenth and eighteenth centuries. The order was revived in England in 1866 as part of the general upwelling of fascination with the occult in the late nineteenth century. The Order defined its purpose as to expound "a system of metaphysical and physical philosophy intended to awaken the dormant, latent faculties of the individual whereby he may utilize to a better advantage his natural talents and lead a happier and more useful life." The Order was popularly associated with a dreamy, aesthetic withdrawal from worldly concerns.

C11:30, pe11:30, P21:31   **absolve the simoniac of his sin**   See *Dub* C9:13n. The punishment for simony is excommunication, "simply reserved to the Apostolic See"; thus absolution for the sin would have to come from higher clerical authority, i.e., from an authority at least as high as the bishop of the simoniac's diocese, and if the simoniac were a priest, the authority might very well have to be the pope himself.

C11:32, pe11:32, P21:33   **Great Britain Street**   (now Parnell Street) Is in north-central Dublin. In 1895 it was part of a main east-west thoroughfare and was lined with small shops, houses, and tenements. It bisected an area where some of the poorest of Dublin's poor lived.

C11:33, pe11:33, P21:34-35   *Drapery*   *Thom's Official Directory of the United Kingdom of Great Britain and Ireland* (Dublin, 1904; hereafter *Thom's* 1904) lists four draper's shops in Great Britain Street.

C12:8-9, pe12:7, P22:8-9   **S. Catherine's Church, Meath Street** St. Catherine's Roman Catholic Church, a parish church between 83 and 84 Meath Street in central Dublin, south of the Liffey. When attached to St. Catherine's, Father Flynn would have lived at the Presbytery House adjoining.

C12:10, pe12:9, P22:10   **R.I.P.**   *Requiescat in Pace*, Latin: "Rest in peace," a short prayer for the dead.

C12:16, pe12:15, P22:16   **High Toast**   A brand of snuff.

C13:2, pe13:2, P23:4   **the Irish college in Rome**   The plan for an Irish seminary in Rome was first conceived by Gregory XIII (b. 1502, pope 1572-85), but the money allocated for the college went instead to supply Irish Catholics for a revolt against the English. In 1625 the Irish bishops revived the project; they appealed to Cardinal Ludovisi, cardinal protector of Ireland, and he not only approved but also offered to finance the college. It opened 1 January 1628. Before Napoleon closed it in 1798 there had been only eight students a year, but the college had great prestige and produced several famous leaders of the Irish Church. When it was revived in 1826, the student body was expanded to forty students a year. The fact that Father Flynn was educated at the Irish College implies that he was regarded as an outstanding candidate for the priesthood, the more remarkable since he was born in the lower-class neighborhood of Irishtown (see *Dub* C17:5n).

C13:3, pe13:3, P23:5   **to pronounce Latin properly**   I.e., according to the so-called "Roman Method," an elaborate late nineteenth century reconstruction of the way Latin was pronounced in the time of Cicero (106-43 B.C.). The "Roman Method" was the subject of considerable controversy because it challenged both the "Continental Method" (which many regarded as the sacred heritage of the Middle Ages) and the "English Method" (pronouncing Latin words precisely as though they were English, the method still current in English education in 1900).

C13:4, peI3:4, P23:6-7   **about Napoleon Bonaparte**   See *Por* C47: 9-10n.

C13:5-6, peI3:5-6, P23:7-8   **the meaning of the different ceremonies of the mass**   *The Layman's Missal* (Baltimore, Md., 1962) remarks,

> At the heart of every Mass there occurs the account of the Last Supper, because every Mass renews the sacramental mystery then given to the human race as a legacy until the end of time: "Do this in memory of me." [Luke 22:19]. The liturgical rites which constitute the celebration of Mass—taking bread (offertory), giving thanks (preface and canon), breaking the bread and distributing it in communion—reproduce the very actions of Jesus. The Mass is an act in which the mystery of Christ is not just commemorated, but made present, living over again. God makes use of it afresh to give himself to man; and man can use it to give glory to God through the one single sacrifice of Christ. In the missal there are certain central pages used over and over again in practically the same way at every Mass, and therefore they are called the "ordinary" of the Mass. [P. 761]

Around the core of the ordinary, the ceremonies of the Mass vary in accordance with the different seasons of the Liturgical Year; i.e., there are sequences of masses for the yearly anniversaries of "Christ in His Mysteries" and "Christ in His Saints." There are also "votive masses," masses for the sick and for the dead, various local masses for the feast days of special saints, etc.

C13:6, peI3:6, P23:8-9   **the different vestments worn by the priest**   The outer vestments of the priest have distinctive colors symbolically related to the feast being celebrated. *White*, for Easter and Christmas seasons, for feasts of the Trinity, for Christ, the Virgin Mary, and for angels and saints who are not martyrs; *red*, for Pentecost, for feasts of the Cross and of martyrs; *purple*, for Advent, for Lent, and for other penitential occasions; *rose* is occasionally substituted for purple; *green* is used at times when there is no particular season of feasts; *gold* can substitute for white, red, or green; and *black* is the color for Good Friday and for the Liturgy of the Dead.

C13:13-14, peI3:13-14, P23:16-17   **the Eucharist and . . . the secrecy of the confessional**   The *Maynooth Catechism* asserts, "The chief powers given to a priest are: to offer the holy sacrifice of the Mass, and to forgive sins in the sacrament of Penance." It defines the Eucharist as "the Sacrament of the body and blood, soul and divinity of Jesus Christ, under the appearance of bread and wine," and remarks, "Eucharist means a special grace or gift of God—and it also means a solemn act of thanksgiving to God for all His mercies" (p. 53). The Catholic Church regards penance as a sacrament instituted by Christ, in which forgiveness of sins is granted through the priest's absolution of those who, with true contrition, confess their sins. In the process of confession, the penitent is at once accuser, the accused, and the witness, while the priest pronounces judgment and sentence. The grace conferred on the absolved penitent is deliverance from guilt of sin. Confession can only be made to an ordained priest with the requisite jurisdiction. The priest is bound to secrecy and cannot be excused either to save his own life or that of another, or even to avert a public calamity. No law can compel him to divulge the sins confessed to him. Violation of the seal of confession would be the worst sort of sacrilege and would merit excommunication.

C13:17–18, pe13:18, P23:21   the *Post Office Directory*   Between 1500 and 2000 pages in length, including an exhaustive street by street listing of Dublin's buildings and their inhabitants. It was published annually by Alexander Thom & Co., Ltd. but is not to be confused with another annual publication quoted throughout these notes, *Thom's 1904*, 2106 pp., which did include a "Postal Directory" and "Post Office Dublin City and County Directory." See *Dub* C11:33n.

C13:22, pe13:24, P23:27   **responses of the Mass**   Words or phrases spoken by the server in answer to the celebrant, the priest who officiates in the celebration of the Mass. At times the responses can be spoken by a minister (a priest who assists the celebrant) or by a choir or by the congregation. See *Dub* C13:5–6n.

C14:1, pe13:37, P24:5   **in Persia**   The Middle East was widely regarded in the late nineteenth century as a land of romance (with morally permissive and sensual overtones), an ideal escape from the repressive world of Victorian morality and from what William Morris called "six counties overhung with smoke."

C14:28, pe14:29, P25:1   **a chalice**   The ceremonial cup that holds the consecrated wine in the sacrament of the Eucharist (see *Dub* C13:13–14n).

C15:19, pe15:19, P25:28   **And everything . . . ?**   The unstated question is: did Father Flynn receive extreme unction, the final sacrament which cleanses the dying man and prepares him for death, taking away "the effects of sin" and giving "the sufferer the interior strength needed to bear his illness and perhaps to meet death"?

C16:12, pe16:12, P26:21   the *Freeman's General*   For the *Freeman's Journal and National Press*, a daily morning newspaper in Dublin. The paper was editorially pro-Home Rule for Ireland but so moderate-conservative in its point of view that it was nicknamed "the old woman of Prince's Street" (where its editorial offices were located).

C16:33, pe16:34, P27:10   **breviary**   A book containing the daily public or canonical prayers for the canonical hours. The daily recital of the breviary is obligatory on members of the priesthood, on all those in major orders, and on all choir members.

C17:5, pe17:4, P27:17   **Irishtown**   In 1900 a poor, working-class slum just south of the mouth of the Liffey and therefore east and south of Great Britain Street. Traditionally the men of Irishtown were employed in intermittent, pick-up jobs on the docks at the mouth of the Liffey and at the terminuses of the two canals that encircle Dublin. Dubliners still regard Irishtowners as a clannish and turbulent lot.

C17:8, pe17:7, P27:20   **Rheumatic wheels**   For wheels fitted with pneumatic tires.

C17:9, pe17:8, P27:21   **Johnny Rush's**   Francis (Johnny) Rush, cab and car proprietor, 10 Findlater's Place, a narrow street parallel to and one block south of the eastern end of Great Britain Street.

C17:26, pe17:26, P28:6   **chalice**   See *Dub* C14:28n.

C17:27–28, pe17:27–28, P28:7–8   **it contained nothing**   An adaptation of a typically childish question about Church ritual: "What would happen if the priest dropped the chalice after the wine had been transsubstantiated into the body and blood of Christ?" To the lay imagination the question seems an awe-inspiring one, but the answer is quite simple: only the "appearance" of wine would be spilt, not the body and blood of Christ (see *Por* C106:18–19n and C106:33–36n).

C17:28, pe17:29, P28:9   **the boy's fault**   The boy is an acolyte or server who assists the celebrant at the altar.

"An Encounter"

"An Encounter," the ninth of the fifteen stories in order of composition, was completed by 18 September 1905.

C19:3–4, pe19:4–5, P29:4   *The Union Jack, Pluck* **and** *The Halfpenny Marvel*   Popular magazines for boys, published in England by the Irish-born editor-publisher, Alfred C. Harmsworth (1865–1922). *The Halfpenny Marvel* began publication in 1893; the other two appeared in 1894. They were advertised as reform magazines that would replace sensational trash with good, clean, instructive stories of adven-

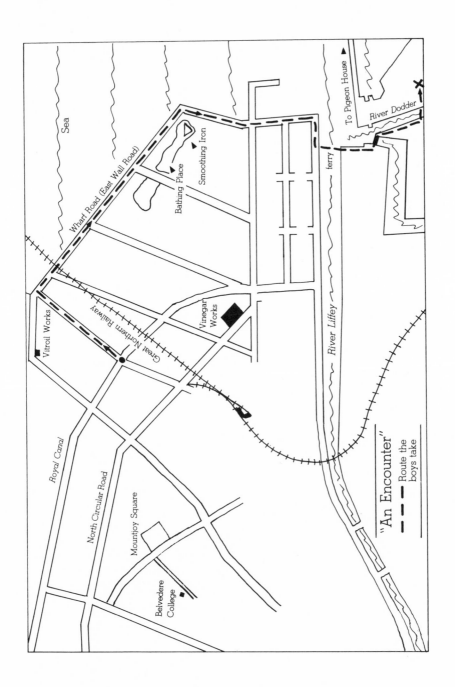

"An Encounter"

▬ ▬ ▬ Route the boys take

Sea

Wharf Road (East Wall Road)

Bathing Place

Smoothing Iron

To Pigeon House

River Dodder

ferry

River Liffey

Great Northern Railway

Vinegar Works

Vitriol Works

Royal Canal

North Circular Road

Mountjoy Square

Belvedere College

ture for boys, what *The Union Jack* called "pure, healthy tales." They
featured stories of American Indians, explorers, prospectors, sailors,
and travelers.

C19:10–11, pe19:12, P29:12   **eight o'clock mass every morning**
I.e., they were extraordinarily devout Catholics, although their devotional exercises would not have made them the outstanding exceptions
in the Dublin of the 1890s that they would be in the U.S.A. of the
1980s. See *Dub* C66:12n.

C19:11, pe19:12, P29:12   **in Gardiner Street**   At the Jesuit church of
St. Francis Xavier in the northeast quadrant of Dublin.

C19:17, pe19:18, P29:19   **Ya! yaka, yaka, yaka!**   A solemn cry of ap-
probation, an American Indian ritual at formal or religious councils (according to the eighteenth-century American interpreter and frontier
scout, Conrad Weiser, 1696–1760).

C19:19, pe19:20, P29:21   **a vocation**   In the religious sense of a spiritual calling and in the secular sense of a job. A modern Dubliner would
assume that in all probability Joe Dillon had discovered his "vocation"
as a result of parental pressure, the parents' pursuit of the status
"devout."

C20:17–18, pe20:16–17, P30:12–13   **Hardly had the day dawned**
In Caesar's *Commentarii de Bello Gallico* (Commentaries on the Gallic
Wars) several of the accounts of a day's campaigning begin with phrases
that could be translated this way. The allusion is apparently not to the
story that follows the stock phrase but to the stock phrase itself, which
is enough to stump Leo Dillon.

C20:25, pe20:25, P30:21   **college**   Belvedere College, a Jesuit day
school for boys, located in Great Denmark Street in the northeast
quadrant of Dublin. Belvedere House itself was a handsome eighteenth-century country house which the expansion of metropolitan
Dublin converted into a town house. The Jesuits acquired it in 1841
and added to its facilities until it was by 1895 a somewhat cramped
quadrangle. The education was thorough and Jesuit in its quality although the school was not as fashionable as Clongowes Wood College
(q.v. *Por* C9:21n and *A Portrait*, Chapter I:B and I:D).

C20:29, pe20:28, P30:24–25   **National School**   The Irish counterpart
of the American public school, although bearing somewhat more re-
semblance to a trade or vocational school with its emphasis on useful
skills. The system of Primary Education was established in Ireland in
1831–34, Intermediate Education (for children thirteen to sixteen
years of age) in the years following 1859. The schools were dominated
by an English, Protestant point of view and were suspected by the Irish

of being part of a British plot to control Ireland religiously and socially as well as politically and economically.

C21:8, pe21:7, P31:4   **The summer holidays were near at hand**   Cf. Luke 21:29–31, "And he spake unto them a parable; Behold the fig tree, and all the trees; When they now shoot forth, ye see and know of your own selves that summer is now nigh at hand. So likewise ye, when ye see these things come to pass, know ye that the kingdom of God is nigh at hand."

C21:11, pe21:10, P31:7   **miching**   Playing truant.

C21:11, pe21:11, P31:8   **sixpence**   Worth between $1.00 and $2.00 in modern currency, depending of course on what it was to be used for, but it would probably have represented at least one and possibly two weeks' allowance for each of the boys.

C21:12, pe21:12, P31:9   **Canal Bridge**   Newcomen Bridge, which carries North Strand Road over the Royal Canal in the northeast quadrant of Dublin.

C21:14–15, pe21:14, P31:11–12   **Wharf Road**   A popular name for East Wall (now East Wall Road). East Wall is a sea wall that runs southeast and then south, confining the River Tolka's delta and preventing the river (and Dublin Bay) from making inroads on eastern Dublin north of the Liffey. The wall had a road along its top.

C21:15, pe21:15, P31:13   **the ferryboat**   Still crosses the Liffey just short of its mouth and about a mile downstream from the eastern-most of the Liffey bridges.

C21:16, pe21:16, P31:13   **Pigeon House**   Originally named after the Pidgeon family, subsequently a fort ("an apology for a battery"), and then the Dublin electricity and power station, located on a breakwater that projects out into Dublin Bay as a continuation of the south bank of the Liffey. The dove (a relative of the pigeon) is also a traditional symbol for the Holy Ghost (Matthew 3:16, John 1:32; see *Por* C149:1–2n). There were far more direct routes southeast to the Pigeon House from Newcomen Bridge than the one the boys outline and eventually take. Their plan is "to stay out of sight," so they circle north before turning southeast and then south toward the mouth of the Liffey.

C21:32, pe21:32, P31:30   **pipeclayed**   Pipeclay, a highly plastic and fairly pure clay of a greyish-white color used in making pipes. In this case it is used to clean and whiten canvas.

C21:34, pe21:35, P31:33   **the mall**   Charleville Mall, on the south bank of the Royal Canal just west of Newcomen Bridge, where the boys are to meet.

C22:8, pe22:7, P32:6   **catapult**   A slingshot.

C22:11, pe22:10, P32:10 **to have some gas with** To joke with, to make mischief with.

C22:15, pe22:15, P32:15 **funk** To fail as a result of timidity or depression. As used below, *Dub* C22:32, pe22:33, P32:33, a jerk.

C22:18, pe22:18, P32:19 **a bob and a tanner** A shilling and sixpence.

C22:19, pe22:19, P32:19 **North Strand Road** A part of the main road from Dublin to the northeast, it begins just southwest of Newcomen Bridge and runs northeast over the bridge to end at the River Tolka, which flows southeast along the northern face of East Wall.

C22:20, pe22:20, P32:20 **the Vitriol Works** The Dublin Vitriol Works Company, 17 Ballybough Road, on the northeastern outskirts of metropolitan Dublin. The Works was a landmark 250 yards west of where the boys turn "right" to walk southeast along East Wall (Wharf Road).

C22:20, pe22:21, P32:21 **the Wharf Road** See *Dub* C21:14–15n.

C22:22, 23, 26, pe22:22–23, 24, 26–27, P32:23, 24, 27 **ragged girls . . . ragged boys . . . the ragged troop** There were both Protestant and Roman Catholic "ragged schools" in Dublin. They were charitable institutions which provided free education and some food and clothing for the children of the very poor.

C22:27, pe22:27, P32:27–28 *Swaddlers!* A contemptuous Roman Catholic term, at first applied primarily to Wesleyan Methodists in Ireland and subsequently hurled at all Protestants. Various derivations have been suggested, but the term remains stubbornly meaningless in spite of its possible suggestion that Protestants are "swaddled" by rigid controls and restrictions.

C22:30, pe22:30, P32:31 **the Smoothing Iron** A bathing place on Dublin Bay off East Wall (Wharf Road). It was named after the shape of an outcrop of rock which resembled a pressing iron and served as the pool's diving platform. Pool and rock have since disappeared in favor of a school and other improvements.

C22:32–33, pe22:33–34, P32:34–35 **how many he would get at three o'clock** Corporal punishment at Belvedere College (and Clongowes Wood College) consisted of being struck on the hand with a pandybat (a leather strap reenforced with whalebone). Boys were never whipped and were flogged only for an extreme offence and then in a very formal way. Punishment was not usually administered informally in the classroom. The offended teacher would instead write the number of blows to be received on a slip of paper and then twist it so that the offender could not read his sentence en route to the place where punishment was administered daily at the end of school hours. It should also be noted that corporal punishment in Jesuit schools in Ireland at the turn of the century was far less threatening and cruel than it was in contemporary English private (in the American sense) schools.

C22 : 33, pe22 : 34, P32 : 35   **Mr. Ryan**   Kevin Sullivan says that "Father Francis Ryan, S.J. . . . was officially assigned to teach Italian and French at Belvedere from 1894 to 1898" (*Joyce Among the Jesuits* [New York, 1958], p. 92).

C23 : 9, pe23 : 9, P33 : 11–12   **Ringsend**   An area on the south bank of the Liffey at its mouth.

C23 : 11, pe23 : 11, P33 : 13–14   **it would be right skit**   It would be very exciting or adventurous.

C23 : 21–22, pe23 : 23, P33 : 25   **threemaster**   A three-masted sailing ship. Much of the world's commerce was still carried by sailing ships in the early years of this century.

C23 : 26, pe23 : 27, P33 : 30   **green eyes**   In medieval tradition Odysseus was said to have had green eyes—the eyes of a vigorous, youthful man, the ultimate adventurer. Green eyes are also the sign of innocence or inexperience and, conversely, of a shifty and undependable person. See *Dub* C62 : 32–33n.

C24 : 8, pe24 : 9, P34 : 13   **the Dodder**   A river which enters the Liffey from the south just short of the mouth of the Liffey and just west of Ringsend.

C24 : 19–20, pe24 : 20–21, P34 : 25–26   **green stems on which girls tell fortunes**   The way in which the fibrous strands of certain plant stems curl when peeled back was regarded as an omen just as daisy petals are in the "he-loves-me-he-loves-me-not" game.

C24 : 23–24, pe24 : 25, P34 : 30–31   **a jerry hat**   A round, stiff felt hat.

C25 : 8, pe25 : 7–8, P35 : 17   **Thomas Moore**   Irish romantic poet (1779–1852), best known for rather mild love songs and laments (from a safe distance) for the depressed state of Ireland. No properly sentimental Irish home was complete without its copy of Moore's *Irish Melodies* (in installments, 1807–34).

C25 : 8, pe25 : 8, P35 : 18   **Sir Walter Scott**   Scottish poet and novelist (1771–1832), best known for his romanticization of the Middle Ages, but more notable for his development of the "romance," which he defined as "a fictitious narrative in prose or verse, the interest of which turns upon marvelous and uncommon incidents."

C25 : 8–9, pe25 : 8, P35 : 18   **Lord Lytton**   Edward Bulwer-Lytton, Baron Lytton (1803–73), English politician and novelist, who wrote not only historical novels (*The Last Days of Pompeii*, 1834) but also romances of terror and the supernatural and of crime and social injustice; these latter are "some of Lord Lytton's works which boys couldn't

read." Public suspicion of the morality of some of Bulwer-Lytton's
novels was reenforced by rumors of scandal in his private life.

C25:23, pe25:24, P35:33   **totties**   Not only sweethearts as the context
suggests but also, by innuendo, high-class prostitutes.

C26:2, pe25:37–26:1, P36:14   **his accent was good**   I.e., in spite of
his physical appearance he was recognizable as an educated person, a
member of the middle class.

C26:27, pe26:28, P37:8   **josser**   In English slang, a simpleton; also
pidgin English for the worshiper of a joss (a god) and suggestive of the
burning of joss sticks (sticks of incense).

C27:7, pe27:7, P37:24   **National School boys**   See *Dub* C20:29n and
C22:32–33n.

C27:17, pe27:18, P38:2   **bottle-green eyes**   See *Dub* C23:26n.

C28:11–12, pe28:12–13, P38:34–35   **in my heart I had always despised him a little**   In II Samuel 6 Saul's daughter Michal sees King
David *playing* "before the Lord" (6:21) "and she despised him in her
heart" (6:16). Her punishment because she is unrepentent: she "had
no child unto the day of her death" (6:23).

"Araby"

"Araby" was finished and added to the sequence of stories in October 1905. It
was eleventh in order of composition.

C29:1, pe29:1, P39:1 (title)   **Araby**   A bazaar, advertised as a "Grand
Oriental Fête" and given in aid of the Jervis Street Hospital (under the
care of the Roman Catholic Sisters of Mercy), Monday through Saturday, 14–19 May 1894. Araby was a poetic name for Arabia and was
suggestive of the heady and sensuous romanticism of popular tales and
poems about the Middle East. The bazaar's theme song:

> I'll sing thee songs of Araby,
> And tales of fair Cashmere,
> Wild tales to cheat thee of a sigh,
> Or charm thee to a tear.
> And dreams of delight shall on thee break,
> And rainbow visions rise,

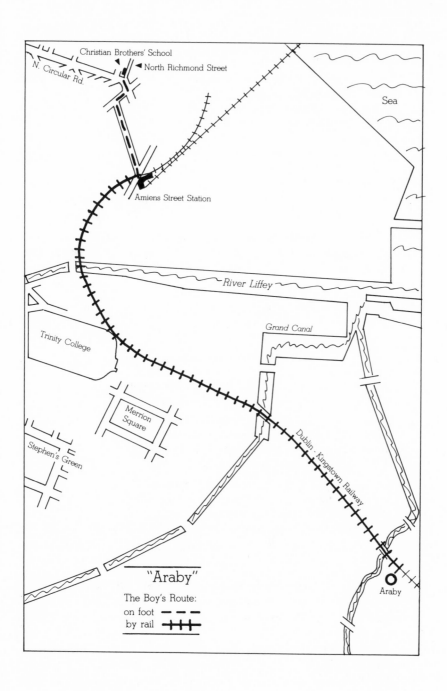

Christian Brothers' School

North Richmond Street

N. Circular Rd.

Sea

Amiens Street Station

River Liffey

Grand Canal

Trinity College

Merrion Square

Dublin - Kingstown Railway

Stephen's Green

"Araby"

The Boy's Route:
on foot – – –
by rail ╅╈╅╈╅

Araby

And all my soul shall strive to wake
Sweet wonder in thine eyes . . .

Through those twin lakes, when wonder wages,
My raptured song shall sink,
And as the diver dives for pearls,
Bring tears, bright tears to their brink,
And rainbow visions rise,
And all my soul shall strive to wake,
Sweet wonder in thine eyes . . . To cheat thee of a sigh,
Or charm thee to a tear!

> Words by W. G. Wills,
> music by Frederick Clay

The first four stanzas of "Araby's Daughter," a ballad by Thomas Moore, suggest the tone of this nineteenth-century fascination with Araby:

Farewell—farewell to thee, Araby's daughter!
(Thus warbled a peri [nymph in Persian myth] beneath the dark sea,)
No pearl ever lay, under Oman's green water
More pure in its shell than thy spirit in thee.

Oh! fair as the sea-flower close to thee growing,
How light was thy heart till Love's witchery came,
Like the wind of the South o'er a summer lute blowing,
And hush'd all its music, and wither'd its frame!

But long, upon Araby's green sunny highlands,
Shall maids and their lovers remember the doom
Of her, who lies sleeping among the Pearl Islands,
With nought but the sea-star to light up her tomb.

And still, when the merry date-season is burning,
And calls to the palm-groves the young and the old,
The happiest here from their pastime returning
At sunset will weep when thy story is told.

> From *Ballads of Ireland*, ed. Edward Hayes
> (Edinburgh, n.d.), 2 : 301

C29:2, pe29:2, P39:2 **North Richmond Street** Off North Circular Road in the northeast quadrant of Dublin. The Joyces lived at number 17 from 1894–96. The street was lined with modest but not poor dwellings in the 1890s.

C29:2, pe29:2, P39:2 **blind** I.e., a dead-end street, which North Richmond Street is.

C29:3, pe29:4, P39:4 **Christian Brothers' School** A Roman Catholic

Male School of the Christian Brothers stood on the northwest corner of
North Richmond Street and North Circular Road. It was a day school
maintained by a teaching brotherhood of Catholic laymen, bound
under temporary vows. The original Christian Brothers' School was
founded at Waterford in southeastern Ireland by Edmund Ignatius Rice
(1762–1844) in 1802, when it was illegal for children in Ireland to be
given a Catholic education. The Christian Brothers were supported by
public contributions; they charged very low fees for their services and
were more interested in practical than in academic education.

C29:7, pe29:8, P39:8   **brown**   The implication of this color is spelled
out in *Stephen Hero*: "one of those brown brick houses which seem the
very incarnation of Irish paralysis" (p. 211).

C29:13, pe29:15–16, P39:15–16   *The Abbot,* **by Walter Scott**   A
novel (1820) which combines history and romance in a rather inventive
version of the story of Mary Queen of Scots (1542–87). Mary is not the
ambiguous devout Catholic and/or "harlot queen" of history but an unambiguously pure and romantic ideal. The novel's young hero is transformed overnight from a youth of no importance into the imprisoned
Mary's page and the all-important guardian of her state secrets.

C29:13–14, pe29:16, P39:16   *The Devout Communicant*   Or *Pious
Meditations and Aspirations for the Three Days Before and the Three Days
After Receiving the Holy Eucharist* (1813) by the English Franciscan
Friar, Pacificus Baker (1695–1774). One nineteenth-century critic remarked about Baker's books that they are "without much originality
. . . remarkable for unction, solidity, and moderation; but we wish the
style was less diffuse and redundant of words."

C29:14, pe29:16–17, P39:16–17   *The Memoirs of Vidocq*   The inauthentic and/or unreliable memoirs (1829) of François-Jules Vidocq
(1775–1857). Vidocq began a promising career as a criminal, became
an informer, and, in 1812, a detective. His career as detective was
somewhat marred by the suspicion that he was as brilliant at playing
the agent provocateur and creating crimes to detect as he was at detect-
ing them. His memoirs present him as a master of disguises and du-
plicities, one who has (with *sang froid*) experienced every possible esca-
pade on both sides of the law. Vidocq, since he (or his ghost writer) was
writing fiction, could manage something for everyone; as the preface to
an American translation (Philadelphia, 1859) points out: something for
the "amateur of fun" interested in humor, for the "reflective reader"
interested in psychology and motive, for the moralist who desires to see
vice and to see it punished, and for the prurient who are interested in
the sexual mores of criminal types, the latter element "pruned down"

by the Philadelphia translators in deference to "American taste when considered (as we consider it) synonymous with decency and decorum" (p. 20).

C29:18, pe29:21, P39:21   **charitable**   In the secular sense of philanthropic generosity and in the religious sense of love for God and for all mankind. See *Por* C148:18n.

C30:9, pe30:9, P40:4   **the cottages**   I.e., Richmond Cottages, a lane off North Richmond Street which was lined with small dwellings for the poor.

C30:15–16, pe30:16–17, P40:12   **Mangan's sister**   No Mangan family lived in North Richmond Street in the 1890s. James Clarence Mangan (1803–49), who lends his name but not his relationship, was a minor but famous Irish romantic poet. He was fascinated by the romantic aura that had been cast over things Middle Eastern by Byron, Moore, and others, and Mangan, though he knew no Arabic at all, liked to pretend that many of his poems were translations from that language. The boy's preoccupation with Mangan's sister can be contrasted with the self-dedication of the speaker in one of Mangan's most popular poems, "Dark Rosaleen" (Dark Rosaleen is a personification of Ireland). The first and last two of the poem's seven stanzas:

> O, My Dark Rosaleen,
> Do not sigh, Do not weep!
> The priests are on the ocean green,
> They march along the deep.
> There's wine from the royal Pope,
> Upon the ocean green;
> And the Spanish ale shall give you hope,
> My Dark Rosaleen!
> My own Rosaleen!
> Shall glad your heart, shall give you hope,
> My Dark Rosaleen!
>
> I could scale the blue air,
> I could plough the high hills,
> Oh, I could kneel all night in prayer,
> To heal your many ills!
> And one beamy smile from you
> Would float like light between
> My toils and me, my own, my true,
> My Dark Rosaleen!
> My fond Rosaleen!
> Would give me life and soul anew,
> A second life, a soul anew,
> My Dark Rosaleen!

O! the Erne shall run red
With redundance of blood,
The earth shall rock beneath our tread,
And flames wrap hill and wood,
And gun-peal, and slogan cry
Wake many a glen serene,
Ere you shall fade, ere you shall die,
My Dark Rosaleen!
My own Rosaleen!
The Judgment House must be full nigh,
Ere you fade, ere you can die,
My Dark Rosaleen.

C31:7–8, pe31:8, P41:5–6   a *come-all-you* about O'Donovan Rossa
A *come-all-you* is a topical song sung on the streets and in public
houses, announced by the conventional introductory line, "Come all
you gallant Irishmen and listen to my song." Jeremiah O'Donovan
(1831–1915) was a Fenian leader whose advocacy of violent measures
in Ireland's struggle for independence, together with his birthplace,
Ross Carberry in County Cork, earned him the nickname Dynamite
Rossa. He was a leader of the revolutionary Phoenix Society (a literary
and political group in County Cork). A priest and an informer turned
O'Donovan and his Society over to the British, but the "Phoenix Conspiracy" trial in 1859 did little except provide the revolutionaries with
free publicity, and O'Donovan was released. After a sojourn in the
United States, he returned to Ireland in 1863 to become business manager of the radical paper, *Irish People*. In 1865 the paper was seized and
O'Donovan was convicted of treason-felony and sentenced to life in
prison. He was treated somewhat inhumanely in prison, and his suffer-
ings made him so famous that County Tipperary elected him to Parliament in 1869 while he was still in prison. In 1870 his life sentence was
commuted to banishment, and he returned to the United States where
he edited *The United Irishman*. He was again in Ireland from 1891 until
1900, although at that time he was a symbol rather than an actor in the
Irish political scene. One street ballad about O'Donovan, "Rossa's
Farewell to Erin":

Farewell to friends of Dublin Town,
I bid ye all adieu.
I cannot yet appoint the day
That I'll return to you.
I write these lines on board a ship,
Where the stormy billows roar.
May heaven bless our Fenian men,
Till I return once more.

I joined the Fenian Brotherhood
In the year of Sixty-Four,
Resolved to save my native land
Or perish on the shore;
My friends and me we did agree
Our native land to save,
And to raise the flag of freedom
O'er the head of Emmet's grave.

My curse attend those traitors
Who did our cause betray;
I'd throw a rope around their necks,
And drown them in the Bay.
There was Nagle, Massey, Corydon,
And Talbot—he makes four;
Like demons for their thirst of gold,
They're punished evermore.

Let no man blame the turnkey
Nor any of the men;
There's no one knows but two of us
The man who served my friend.
I robbed no man, I spilt no blood,
Tho' they sent me to jail;
Because I was O'Donovan Rossa,
And a son of Granuaile.

> From Colm O Lochlainn, *Irish Street Ballads*
> (Dublin and London, 1939), p. 68

Granuaile is the Irish name of Grace O'Malley (c. 1520–c. 1600) a leader of the rebellious in western Ireland and, like the Poor Old Woman (the Shan Van Vocht) and Dark Rosaleen, symbolic of Ireland.

C31:10–11, pe31:10–11, P41:8–9 **I bore my chalice safely through a throng of foes** Chalice implies "that which I idealize or worship," and the whole context echoes nineteenth-century versions of legendary quests for the Holy Grail. Cf. *Dub* C14:28n.

C32:3–4, pe32:4, P42:3 **a retreat that week in her convent** The convent school which she attends is to devote several days to a withdrawal from worldly concerns during which students and teachers will spend their time in meditation, prayer, and attendance at special sermons. There is a notable retreat in *A Portrait*, Chapter III.

C32:11, pe32:13, P42:12 **It's well for you** Obviously, "you're lucky," but the Irish-English idiom frequently carries an overtone of envy or bitterness.

C32:21, pe32:24, P42:24 **some Freemason affair** The Masons were regarded as vigilant, powerful, and subversive enemies of Roman Catholicism. Traditionally, Irish Catholics suspect the Masons of being atheists, though the Masonic Oath requires belief in a Supreme Being (or Architect), and Irish Freemasonry has been essentially Protestant-establishment in its orientation. The aunt is apparently not aware that the bazaar is for the benefit of a Roman Catholic hospital (see *Dub* C29:1n), though she may have simply confused this bazaar with one of two years before, the Masonic Centenary Exhibition and Bazaar in Aid of the Masonic Female Orphan's School, 17 May 1892.

C33:18, pe33:20–21, P43:21–22 **collected used stamps for some pious purpose** She would give them to the local foreign missions officer of the Catholic Church, who would sell the stamps through a stamp-collecting outlet and send the money to Catholic missions overseas (to baptize the heathen).

C33:26–27, pe33:28–29, P43:30–31 **this night of Our Lord** I.e., Saturday night (possibly, the last night of the bazaar which, in historical time, did close on Saturday, 19 May 1894).

C34:9–10, pe34:8, P44:12 *The Arab's Farewell to his Steed* A poem by Caroline Norton (1808–77). The first two and last stanzas (of eleven):

My beautiful! my beautiful! that standeth meekly by,
With thy proudly-arched and glossy neck, and dark and fiery eye!
Fret not to roam the desert now with all thy wingéd speed;
I may not mount on thee again! thou'rt sold, my Arab steed!

Fret not with that impatient hoof—snuff not the breezy wind;
The farther that thou fliest now, so far am I behind;
The stranger hath thy bridle-rein, thy master hath his gold;—
Fleet-limbed and beautiful, farewell!—thou'rt sold, my steed, thou'rt
    sold!

Who said that I had given thee up? Who said that thou wert sold?
'T is false! 't is false! my Arab steed! I fling them back their gold!
Thus—thus, I leap upon thy back, and scour the distant plains!
Away! who overtakes us now shall claim thee for his pains.

C34:12, pe34:11, P44:15 **a florin** A two shilling coin, the equivalent of from $5.00 to $8.00 in modern currency, a sizeable and generous sum for a boy who would be used to handouts of threepence or sixpence.

C34:12–13, pe34:12, P44:16 **Buckingham Street** Lies on the direct route from North Richmond Street south-southeast to the Amiens Street Railway Station (now Sean Connolly Station), just north of the Liffey in the northeast quadrant of Dublin.

C34:18, pe34:18, P44:22 **Westland Row Station** Now Pearse Station, south of the Liffey in eastern Dublin, was linked by the Loop

Line to the Amiens Street Station north of the river. Trains from Westland Row served southeastern Ireland as trains from Amiens Street
served the north and west.

C34:28, pe34:28, P44:33 **a shilling** In context, a rash and expensive
gesture on the boy's part, particularly if he is to have anything left over
for the gift he intends to buy.

C34:34, pe34:35, P45:5–6 **Café Chantant** French: coffeehouse with
entertainment. Baedeker's *Paris and Its Environs* (1907) remarks that
these places of entertainment were a cut below the music halls: "The
music and singing at these establishments are never of a high class, while
the audience is of a very mixed character. The entertainments, however,
are often amusing, and sometimes consist of vaudevilles, operettas, and
farces" (p. 41). Baedeker's word "mixed" carries the veiled warning that
"ladies" might be embarrassed.

C35:1–2, pe34:36, P45:6–7 **two men were counting money on a sal-
ver** Cf. Matthew 21:12–13, "And Jesus went into the temple of God,
and cast out all them that sold and bought in the temple, and overthrew
the tables of the moneychangers, and the seats of them that sold doves,
And said unto them, It is written, My house shall be called the house of
prayer; but ye have made it a den of thieves."

C35:27, pe35:27–28, P45:35–46:1 **two pennies . . . sixpence** puzzling, because it is not clear whether the eight pence the boy has left
(worth roughly $3.00 to $3.50, 1980) would be enough for the gift he
has intended to purchase. Possibly he would have enough if he saved
the four penny return train fare by walking the two-plus miles back to
North Richmond Street, but the money clues are far from as clearly
focused here as they are in "Two Gallants," for example.

"Eveline"

Second in order of composition, "Eveline" was first published in *The Irish
Homestead*, 10 September 1904.

C36:1, pe36:1, P46:7 (title). *Eveline* Compare Thomas Moore, "Eveleen's Bower":

Oh, weep for the hour
When to Eveleen's bow'r
The Lord of the valley with false vows came;
The moon hid her light
From the heavens that night
And wept behind the clouds o'er the maiden's shame.

C36:2-3, pe36:3, P46:9   **the avenue**   The location of the avenue where Eveline lives is not specified, though the implication is that an adjoining and once open area in metropolitan Dublin has been shut in by a development since Eveline's childhood.

C36:10, pe36:11-12, P46:17-18   **a man from Belfast**   In the Dublin scheme of things, suspect as not really Irish but a West Briton, one whose sympathies are with the Protestant English establishment.

C36:10, pe36:13, P46:19   **their little brown houses**   See *Dub* C29:7n.

C36:15, pe36:19, P46:25   **his blackthorn stick**   In Irish folklore the blackthorn was regarded as an unlucky tree whose wood provided the "bludgeon men" with the clubs they used to enforce their political and religious opinions. In Celtic mythology the blackthorn is the "tree of black magic and blasting," associated with a witch's staff of office and in legend supposed to have provided the crown of thorns with which the Roman soldiers tormented Jesus on the eve of the crucifixion (Robert Graves, *The White Goddess* [New York, 1948], pp. 166, 205).

C36:18, pe36:19, P46:26   **to keep** *nix*   To stand guard; nix is slang for no, nothing, and watch out or stop.

C37:13-14, pe37:14-15, P47:14-15   **the promises made to Blessed Margaret Mary Alacoque**   St. Margaret Mary Alacoque (1647-90) was a member of the Visitation Order in France. Her career was marked by a baroque counterpoint of physical and spiritual suffering. In the years of 1673-77 she experienced a sustained sequence of visions which led her to crusade for "public devotion to the Sacred Heart of Jesus." She was beatified in 1864 and hence is called "Blessed" in this story; she was canonized in 1920. The "coloured print" would illustrate the Sacred Heart and would list the promises made through St. Margaret-Mary to those faithful who display in their homes a representation of the Sacred Heart and who receive the Eucharist on the first Friday of each month:

(1) I will give them all the graces necessary in their state in life.
(2) I will establish peace in their homes.
(3) I will comfort them in all their afflictions.
(4) I will be their secure refuge during life, and above all in death.
(5) I will bestow abundant blessings on all their undertakings.

(6) Sinners shall find in My Heart the source and the infinite ocean of mercy.
(7) Tepid souls shall become fervent.
(8) Fervent souls shall quickly mount to high perfection.
(9) I will bless every place in which an image of My Heart shall be exposed and honored.
(10) I will give to priests the gift of touching the most hardened hearts.
(11) Those who promote this devotion shall have their names written in My Heart never to be effaced.
(12) I promise thee in the excessive mercy of My Heart that My all powerful love will grant to all those who communicate on the First Friday in nine consecutive months the grace of final perseverance; they shall not die in My disgrace nor without receiving their Sacraments. My Divine Heart shall be their safe refuge in this last moment.

C37:23, pe37:24, P47:26   **the Stores**   See *Dub* C51:11n.

C38:11, pe38:12, P48:15   **seven shillings**   See "Monetary Values" in the Introduction above.

C38:29, pe38:32, P48:35   **the night-boat**   A steam packet for Liverpool left the North Wall, a quayside dock near the mouth of the Liffey in Dublin, every evening at 8 P.M. Apparently Frank and Eveline plan to transship for Buenos Aires in Liverpool (see *Dub* C39:11n) unless, as Hugh Kenner argues, Frank is a plausible fraud who intends to seduce and abandon Eveline in England; see "Molly's Masterstroke," in *Ulysses: Fifty Years*, ed. Thomas F. Staley (Bloomington, Ind., 1974), pp. 20–21.

C39:3, pe39:4, P49:9–10   *The Bohemian Girl*   A light opera (1843), libretto by Alfred Bunn (1796–1860), music by Michael William Balfe (1808–1870). Balfe was a Dublin musician who conducted, sang, composed opera, and played a virtuoso violin. The opera, in three acts, is set in the romantic vicinity of Presburg in the eighteenth century. The Bohemian Girl, Arlene, born to the nobility, is kidnapped by gypsies in the course of act I. In act II, twelve years later, Arlene has matured into a beautiful woman in the midst of pastoral gypsy simplicity, and only vague dreams of the "marble halls" of her former existence remain to haunt her. She is betrothed to an exiled Polish nobleman turned gypsy. She is then betrayed by the queen of the gypsies and coincidentally recognized by the Count, her long lost father. Back in the luxury of her father's castle in act III, she longs for the freedom of the gypsy life and for her betrothed. All is resolved so that Arlene is to live happily ever after with the best of both worlds. See *Dub* C106:2n.

C39:6–7, pe39:7–8, P49:13–14   **the lass that loves a sailor**   Title of a song by Charles Dibdin (1745–1815), English popular dramatist and songwriter.

> The Moon on the ocean was dimn'd by a ripple,
> Affording a chequer'd delight,
> The gay jolly tars pass'd the wórd for a tipple,
> And the toast, for 'twas Saturday night.
> Some sweetheart or wife he lov'd as his life,
> Each drank and wish'd he could hail her;
> But the standing toast that pleas'd the most,
> Was 'The wind that blows,
> The ship that goes,
> And the lass that loves a sailor.'

C39:8, pe39:9, P49:15 **Poppens** A term of endearment, variant of poppet, obsolete or dialect English for a small person.

C39:11, pe39:12, P48:18 **a pound a month** Not as small a wage as it sounds, since it would have been all pocket money unless he had to supply his own clothes. The experienced seaman's average wage in 1900: £2/10 to £3 per month.

C39:11, pe39:13, P49:19 **Allan Line** Advertised in the *Freeman's Journal*, 16 June 1904, as a steamship line based in Liverpool, England, operating steamships "regularly every Thursday" to the Pacific coast of Canada and the United States. The ships called at South American ports (Rio de Janeiro, Buenos Aires, etc.) and rounded Cape Horn en route to the Pacific.

C39:14–15, pe39:16, P49:22–23 **the terrible Patagonians** At the turn of the century the general term for the several different Patagonian tribes which occupied the southern tip of Argentina was *Tehuelche*. In late Victorian times little was known of them except that they were said to be the tallest of human races, and their nomadic culture was summed up as "low." Legend took over from there and created a race of near monsters.

C39:30, pe39:32, P50:4 **Hill of Howth** Nine miles northeast of the center of Dublin, the hill is the northeast headland of Dublin Bay.

C40:8, pe40:8, P50:17 **sixpence** The more usual tip would have been a penny or two.

C40:10, pe40:10, P50:19 **Damned Italians! coming over here!** There is no evidence of a significant Italian immigration to Ireland during this period; the majority of the Italian immigrants in Ireland were itinerant artisans (stonemasons, plaster workers), performers, or artists—or immigrants on their way home from the United States.

C40:16, pe40:16, P50:25 **Derevaun Seraun! Derevaun Seraun!** "Patrick Henchy of the National Library of Kildare Street [Dublin] thinks this mad and puzzling ejaculation corrupt Gaelic for 'the end of pleasure is pain'" (William Y. Tindall, *A Reader's Guide to James Joyce* [New York, 1959]). Another possibility: Edward Brandabur, in *A Scrupulous Meanness* (Urbana and Chicago, 1971), p. 62, quotes Professor Roland Smith, who regards "Derevaun Seraun" as corrupt for the Irish "Deireadh Amrain Siabran, -ain,"—"the end of song is raving madness."

C40:23, pe40:24, P50:33   **the North Wall**   The quayside dock on the north bank of the Liffey toward its mouth; see *Dub* C38:29n.

"After the Race"

"After the Race" was first published in *The Irish Homestead*, 17 December 1904. Joyce repeatedly said that he wanted to revise the story, but never did.

C42:1, pe42:1, P52:1 (title)   **After the Race**   The race was the fourth annual Gordon-Bennett automobile race, which was held in Ireland on 2 July 1903. It was run against time over a 370 mile course of roads in counties Carlow, Kildare, and Queens, west and southwest of Dublin. The basic purpose of the race was to test, to prove, and to advertise (and thus to encourage improvements in) automobile design and equipment. Twelve cars started the race; three each from France (blue), Germany (white), Great Britain (green), and the United States (red). Only four cars finished. The winner, Camille Jenatzy, a Belgian who drove a German Mercedes entry, accomplished the course in 6 hours, 36 minutes, 9 seconds of driving time. Two of the French entries (both Panhard cars) placed second and third, and one of the British entries (a Napier) survived to finish fourth.

C42:3, pe42:4, P52:3–4   **the Naas Road**   Approaches Dublin from the southwest. See map for *A Portrait*, chapter I, on p. 132 below.

C42:4, pe42:4, P52:4   **Inchicore**   A township on the western outskirts of Dublin and just south of the Liffey—not exactly a township (or slum suburb) for the poor, but dominated by modest lower-middle-class cottages in 1903.

C42:10, pe42:11, P52:11 **The French . . . were virtual victors** See *Dub* C42:1n.

C42:12–13, pe42:13–14, P52:13–14 **the driver of the winning German car . . . a Belgian** See *Dub* C42:1n.

C43:15, pe43:15, P53:9 **advanced Nationalist** A Parnellite, a radical member of the Irish Parliamentary (or Home Rule) Party. The Party flourished in the 1880s, but after the great split over Parnell's leadership in 1890 and his death in 1891, the party was divided against itself under the titular leadership of John Redmond (1856–1918). Redmond's aides, Timothy Healy (1855–1931), William O'Brien (1852–1928), and John Dillon (1851–1927), were rivals as much as they were aides. It was not until 1900 that Redmond was able to restore an appearance of unity to the party, and even then he was not able to restore its vitality and political effectiveness either in Ireland or in London.

C43:17, pe43:17, P53:10 **Kingstown** A town with a large artificial harbor on the southeast headland of Dublin Bay, six miles east-south-east of the center of Dublin (now Dun Laoghaire, pronounced Dun Leary). Kingstown was the terminus for the mailboats that were Ireland's "bridge" to Holyhead in Wales and (via railroad) to London.

C43:19, pe43:20, P53:13 **police contracts** Contracts with the government to supply food to police barracks and jails.

C43:22, pe43:23, P53:16–17 **a big Catholic college** In the 1890s the largest and most prestigious Roman Catholic college (preparatory school) in England was Stoneyhurst College in Lancashire. It was founded in France (1592) by refugee English Jesuits and displaced several times before it came to rest in Lancashire in 1808.

C43:23, pe43:23–24, P53:17 **Dublin University** I.e., Trinity College, because Trinity was the original and has remained the only college in the University. Queen Elizabeth I founded the University in 1591 to further the cause of the Reformation in Ireland. It was traditionally staffed by an excellent faculty, but throughout the nineteenth and in the opening decades of the twentieth century, its small size and its Anglo-Protestant orientation kept it out of the mainstream of Irish (Catholic) intellectual life. F. S. L. Lyons, the present Provost of Trinity, remarks that this separation was doubly reinforced because "from about 1875 onwards the Irish Catholic bishops [had forbidden] members of their Church to attend such an infidel College without a special dispensation" (*Culture and Anarchy in Ireland* 1890–1939 [Oxford, 1979] p. 20).

C43:27, pe43:28, P53:22 **a term to Cambridge** It was not at all unusual before World War I for "young gentlemen" to matriculate at Cambridge or Oxford with no intention of reading for a degree or standing for the examinations but simply for the social status and the possibility of making influential friends which derived from being in residence.

C45:13, pe45:14, P55:12   **Dame Street**   An east-west thoroughfare in central Dublin just south of the Liffey.

C45:15, pe45:16, P55:14   **the Bank**   The Bank of Ireland, in the heart of Dublin south of the Liffey at the intersection of Dame and Grafton Streets and facing the College Green of Trinity College. Until the Act of Union in 1800, the Bank building housed the Irish Parliament.

C45:20–21, pe45:22, P55:21   **Grafton Street**   A street of then fashionable shops that runs south to St. Stephen's Green from the Bank of Ireland and Trinity College (at the eastern end of Dame Street).

C46:8, pe46:9, P56:9   **electric candle lamps**   The height of hotel affluence in 1903.

C46:16–17, pe46:18–19, P56:19–20   **the beauties of the English madrigal . . . old instruments**   Avant-garde intellectual and artistic circles were just beginning to rediscover Elizabethan music and to reproduce Elizabethan and Renaissance instruments at the beginning of the twentieth century.

C46:29, pe46:32, P56:33   **the mask of a capital**   London, not Dublin, was the political and economic "capital" of Ireland after the Irish Parliament was dissolved and united with the Parliament in London by the Act of Union in 1800.

C46:30, pe46:33, P56:34   **Stephen's Green**   A sizeable public park in a fashionable section of east-central Dublin south of the Liffey.

C46:34, pe46:36, P57:2–3   **Grafton Street**   Intersects Stephen's Green at the northwest corner of the square; see *Dub* C45:20–21n.

C47:10, pe47:12, P57:14   **Westland Row**   See *Dub* C34:18n.

C47:12, pe47:13, P57:16   **Kingstown Station**   See *Dub* C43:17n.

C47:17, pe47:18, P57:21   *Cadet Roussel*   A French regimental marching song which originated anonymously in the 1790s. The song is cast in a repetitive, jingling, marching rhythm that invites endless improvisation of new verses. In content, the song mocks the cadet for his oddities. Tradition in France associates more serious connotations with the song than its content would suggest. Seriously, the cadet is regarded as the youth who, unfairly derided (as the new French Republic had been derided), is able with heroic and stoic acceptance to bear his undeserved position.

C47:19, pe47:20, P57:23   *Ho! Ho! Hohé, vraiment!*   A version of the first line of the two line refrain of "Cadet Roussel." *"Vraiment"* means truly, certainly. The second line is, *"Cadet Roussel est bon enfant"* (Cadet Roussel is a good guy).

C47:31, pe47:32, P58:1   **Bohemian**   Unconventional, free-and-easy, or gypsy manners, usually in a context where one would expect middle-class decorum and restraint.

C48:15, pe48:16, P58:21   ***The Belle of Newport***   An allusion to Newport, Rhode Island, as a center of yachting activity and also to Newport's reputation as the vacation capital of the American wealthy, the robber barons' summer showcase.

"Two Gallants"

"Two Gallants" was finished and added to the sequence of stories in February 1906. It was the thirteenth of the fifteen stories in order of composition.

While he awaits Corley's return, Lenehan traces a large circle north, then west, then south, and finally east around the center of Dublin. The implication is that Lenehan's solitary wanderings retrace much of the wandering route he has taken with Corley earlier in the day.

C49:10, pe49:11, P59:10–11   **Rutland Square**   Now Parnell Square, in east-central Dublin, 500 yards north of the Liffey. Lenehan and Corley are en route from the pub in Dorset Street where they have spent the last part of the afternoon south toward the point of Corley's rendezvous.

C50:13–14, pe50:14, P60:14   *recherché*   French: in demand, rare.

C50:17, pe50:17, P60:17   **Dorset Street**   A main thoroughfare from central Dublin toward the north-northeast. Corley and Lenehan would have had their choice of at least fourteen or fifteen pubs on the street in 1903.

C50:17–18, pe50:18, P60:18   **Lenehan**   Appears as a character in the Aeolus, Wandering Rocks, Sirens, Oxen of the Sun, and Circe episodes in *Ulysses*; he is first mentioned on p. 125 of the New York 1961 edition.

C50:26, pe50:27, P60:28   **racing tissues**   Information sheets about horse races.

C50:27, pe50:28, P60:29   **Corley**   Appears as a character in the Eumaeus episode in *Ulysses*, pp. 616–19.

C50:29, pe50:30–31, P60:31–32   **Dame Street**   See *Dub* C45:13n.

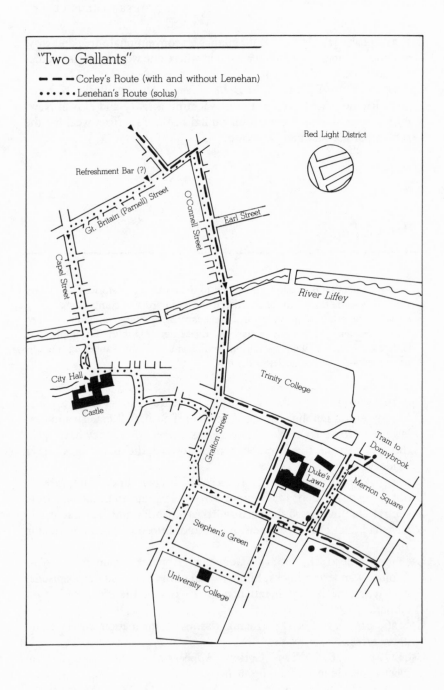

"Two Gallants"

– – – Corley's Route (with and without Lenehan)
• • • • • Lenehan's Route (solus)

Red Light District

Refreshment Bar (?)

Gt. Britain (Parnell) Street

O'Connell Street

Earl Street

Capel Street

River Liffey

City Hall

Castle

Trinity College

Grafton Street

Duke's Lawn

Tram to Donnybrook

Merrion Square

Stephen's Green

University College

C50:30, pe50:31, P60:32 **Waterhouse's clock** Outside Waterhouse and Company, goldsmiths and silversmiths, jewelers, and watchmakers, 25 & 26 Dame Street.

C50:32, pe50:33, P60:34 **the canal** I.e., they walked south to the Grand Canal, which circled the then southern limits of metropolitan Dublin.

C50:32, pe50:33, P60:34 **slavey** A maid-of-all-work (as against higher ranking domestics with defined job status such as downstairs maid, upstairs maid, etc.); her annual salary would be, if she lived in, as Corley's friend does, £6 or £7.

C50:32–33, pe50:34, P60:35 **Baggot Street** A street of fashionable houses and shops in southeastern Dublin.

C51:2, pe50:36, P61:2 **Donnybrook** A suburban village two miles south-southeast of the center of Dublin. It was once the site of an annual fair that became notorious for its brawls, faction fights, and debaucheries—so much so that the name Donnybrook became slang for any scene of public disorder and the fair had to be discontinued in 1855.

C51:8, pe51:7, P61:9 **up to the dodge** Knows how to avoid the consequences of a crime.

C51:11, pe51:10, P61:12 **Pim's** Pim Brothers Limited had a small wholesale-retail empire in south-central Dublin: upholsterers, cabinetmakers and general furniture and carpet warehousemen, Irish poplin manufacturers; their "Stores" were in Great George's Street South, wholesale and retail linen and woolen drapers, silk mercers, hosiers, haberdashers, and leather merchants. The Pims were Quakers and were widely regarded in Dublin as models of sober commercial reliability.

C51:11, pe51:10, P61:13 **hairy** Shrewd, cautious.

C51:27, pe51:28, P61:31 **about town** I.e., out of a job, but with the implication that he is making a living at things barely within the limits of the law.

C51:29–30, pe51:30–31, P61:32–34 **He was often to be seen walking with policemen in plain clothes, talking earnestly** The implication is that Corley is a "stag," a police informer.

C52:2–3, pe52:1–2, P62:5–6 **he aspirated the first letter of his name after the manner of the Florentines** The Florentines aspirate *c* as *h*, thus *casa* (house) becomes *hasa* and Corley, Horley or Whorely.

C52:17, pe52:16, P62:21 **Lothario** In *The Fair Penitent* (1703), a play by the English dramatist, Nicholas Rowe (1674–1718), Lothario is a young nobleman of Genoa, the typified libertine, who seduces Calista, the wife of Altamont, and is killed in a duel by the latter. In Cervantes's

Don Quixote, part I, chapters 33 and 34, "The Tale of Foolish Curiosity," another Lothario is persuaded against his will by his friend Anselmo to test the virtue of Anselmo's wife by attempting to seduce her. Lothario resists the enterprise but finally succumbs, as does the wife. The story climaxes in a web of comic deceptions.

C52:26, pe52:26, P62:31   **girls off the South Circular**   The South Circular Road (which circumscribed the then southern limits of metropolitan Dublin) was a popular promenade for groups of unattached lower-middle-class young women.

C52:33, pe52:33, P63:4   **a mug's game**   A mug is a dupe, one easily imposed upon.

C53:8, pe53:7, P63:14   **on the turf**   In business as a prostitute.

C53:8, pe53:7-8, P63:14-15   **down Earl Street**   Earl Street is one section of a main east-west thoroughfare in central Dublin north of the Liffey, a little more than a block west of what was then the red-light district which Joyce used as the setting for the Circe episode of *Ulysses*. "Down Earl Street" would mean that the car was proceeding east, toward the district.

C53:19, pe53:19, P63:26   **the railings of Trinity College**   They are walking south around the west front of the College, the main facade of which is set back behind a row of iron railings. See *Dub* C43:23n.

C53:21, pe53:22, P63:29   **Twenty after**   I.e., it is 7:20 P.M., Dunsink (Dublin) time. Since it is late August, the sun would have set at about 7 P.M.

C54:6, pe54:6, P64:14   **Nassau Street**   They have turned east and walked along the south side of Trinity College.

C54:6-7, pe54:7, P64:15   **Kildare Street**   Runs south from Nassau Street to the north side of Stephen's Green.

C54:7, pe54:7, P64:15   **the club**   On the corner of Nassau Street and Kildare Street, the Kildare Street Club, a fashionable and exclusive men's club, overwhelmingly Protestant and Anglo-Irish. In 1900 it was, as one member put it, "the only place in Ireland where one could enjoy decent caviar." The building now houses the *Alliance Française*.

C54:11, pe54:11, P64:20   **harp**   A traditional symbol of Ireland's legendary golden age (see Thomas Moore's song, "The Harp That Once through Tara's Halls / The soul of music shed. . ."). The pillar of this harp is in the figure of a semi-draped woman; i.e., the harp bears another traditional symbol of Ireland, the Poor Old Woman who metamorphoses into a beautiful young woman ("Dark Rosaleen") in the presence of her true lovers, the true patriots (see *Dub* C30:15-16n). The figure also echoes the lament of "Lir's lonely daughter" in the Moore song the harpist performs. Lir was the ancient Irish god of the

sea, whose daughter was maliciously transformed into a swan and condemned to lonely wandering until the sound of the bell at the elevation
of the Host in the first Mass to be celebrated in Ireland; then the spell
would be broken.

C54:13, pe54:13, P64:22 **strangers** Traditional in Ireland for the English invaders, the overlords.

C54:14, pe54:14–15, P64:23 *Silent, O Moyle* "Song of Fionnuala,"
by Thomas Moore:

> Silent, O Moyle, be the roar of thy waters,
> Break not, ye breezes, your chain of repose,
> While, murmuring mournfully, Lir's lonely daughter
> Tells to the night-star her tale of woes.
> When shall the swan, her death-note singing,
> Sleep, with wings in darkness furled?
> When will heaven, its sweet bells ringing,
> Call my spirit from this stormy world?
>
> Sadly, O Moyle, to thy winter-wave weeping,
> Fate bids me languish long ages away;
> Yet still in her darkness doth Erin lie sleeping,
> Still doth the pure light its dawning delay.
> When will that day-star, mildly springing,
> Warm our isle with peace and love?
> When will heaven, its sweet bells ringing,
> Call my spirit to the fields above?

(For "Lir's lonely daughter," see *Dub* C54:11n above.)

C54:18–19, pe54:20, P64:28 **Stephen's Green** See *Dub* C46:30n.

C54:19, pe54:20, P64:28 **the road** They cross Stephen's Green
North (a street) to enter the Green itself.

C54:22, pe54:24, P64:32 **Hume Street** Off Stephen's Green East,
about fifty yards away across the northeast corner of the park.

C54:23, pe54:25, P64:33 **a blue dress and a white sailor hat** Blue
and white are color attributes of the Virgin Mary.

C54:29, pe54:31, P65:4 **trying to get inside me** An expression from
the game of bowls, in which a player scores by placing a ball closer to
the target ball or "jack" than his opponent does. If a player bowls fairly
close to the jack, his opponent will try "to get inside" him, to bowl
(often with a spin) so that his ball intervenes between the potential
score and the jack.

C55:4, pe55:2, P65:12 **the chains** Posts with low loops of chain once
separated the park from the street.

C55:9, pe55:8, P65:18 **Corner of Merrion Street** I.e., where Merrion Row (the eastward continuation of Stephen's Green North) gives into Baggot Street to the east and intersects with Merrion Street Upper, which enters from the north.

C55:11, pe55:10, P65:20   **the road**   Stephen's Green East.

C55:30–31, pe55:30, P66:7   **stems upwards**   I.e., in a manner that shows want of sophistication; "properly," the stems should be down.

C56:7, pe56:3, P66:17   **Shelbourne Hotel**   Then (and still today) a fashionable hotel at the junction of Kildare Street and Stephen's Green North.

C56:9, pe56:5–6, P66:19–20   **turned to the right**   I.e., east, into Merrion Row, from which they apparently turn north along Merrion Street Upper and into Merrion Square West.

C56:11, pe56:7, P66:21   **Merrion Square**   One of Dublin's still handsome eighteenth-century squares. In 1900 it was bordered by fashionable residences of professional people, primarily physicians and surgeons.

C56:15, pe56:12, P60:26   **the Donnybrook tram**   Corley and friend would have caught the southbound tram in Merrion Square North. See *Dub* C51:2n.

C56:19, pe56:16, P66:30   **Duke's Lawn**   On the west side of Merrion Square West. It is the lawn of Leinster House, which lies between Merrion Square and Kildare Street to the west in the midst of a complex of buildings that includes the National Gallery and the National Library. In 1900 Leinster House housed the Royal Dublin Society; at present the Irish Parliament sits there.

C56:24, pe56:21, P66:35   **round Stephen's Green**   I.e., down the east side, across the south and up the west side, which gives into Grafton Street.

C56:25, pe56:22, P67:1   **down Grafton Street**   I.e., north along Grafton Street. Lenehan continues to walk north, past Trinity College, through Westmoreland Street, over O'Connell Bridge, and along O'Connell Street until he reaches Rutland (now Parnell) Square.

C56:33, pe56:31, P67:11   **turned to the left**   Lenehan turns west into Great Britain (now Parnell) Street; see *Dub* C11:32n.

C56:34, pe56:32, P67:12   **Rutland Square**   Now Parnell Square; see *Dub* C49:10n.

C57:3, pe56:35, P67:14–15   *Refreshment Bar*   Unidentified, though the name and the scene which follows suggest a lower-class "quick lunch counter," no alcoholic beverages.

C57:11, pe57:8, P67:23   **curates**   Literally clergymen who assist a vicar or a rector in the celebration of the Mass, thus, slang for bartenders.

C57:16, pe57:13, P67:28 **Three halfpence** The implication is that the "plate of peas" (baked or boiled dried peas or peabeans) is the cheapest and most filling meal the impecunious Lenehan can afford.

C57:19, pe57:16, P67:31 **his air of gentility** I.e., in spite of his indigence, Lenehan's accent and manner mark him as middle-class and thus as suspect from a lower-class point of view.

C57:34, pe57:32–33, P68:13 **pulling the devil by the tail** In financial difficulties or always just on the verge of being in serious trouble.

C58:12, pe58:9, P68:26 **with a little of the ready** With cash on hand.

C58:15, pe58:12, P68:29 **Capel Street** Lenehan turns south into Capel Street, walks to Grattan Bridge over the Liffey and thence into Parliament Street, which approaches City Hall and the Dublin Castle complex from the north.

C58:15, pe58:12–13, P68:30 **the City Hall** Just south of the Liffey in central Dublin, the seat of the city's municipal government, the Dublin Corporation, a parliamentary body of twenty aldermen and sixty councilors elected from the city's twenty wards.

C58:16, pe58:13, P68:30 **Dame Street** See *Dub* C45:13n. Lenehan walks east in the general direction of the place appointed for his meeting with Corley.

C58:16, pe58:14, P68:31 **George's Street** Great George Street South enters Dame Street from the south. When Lenehan leaves his friends, he walks south along George Street to Exchequer Street, which enters from the east.

C58:23, pe58:21, P69:3–4 **Westmoreland Street** Not far to the east, runs from the west front of Trinity College north to O'Connell Bridge over the Liffey.

C58:25, pe58:22, P69:5 **Egan's** John J. Egan ran a pub called The Oval at 78 Abbey Street Middle, off O'Connell Street just north of the Liffey and not far from the newspaper offices where the racing forms with which Lenehan is associated in *Ulysses* were published.

C58:27, pe58:25, P69:8 **Holohan** Appears as a character in "A Mother," *Dubliners*, is mentioned in the Hades and Aeolus episodes in *Ulysses*, pp. 73 and 135, and appears in Circe, pp. 491 and 571.

C58:30, pe58:29, P69:11 **the City Markets** On the east side of Great George Street South, a block south of Dame Street. Lenehan turns east and walks along the northern side of the Markets through Exchequer and Wicklow Streets to Grafton Street.

C58:31, pe58:29, P69:12 **Grafton Street** See *Dub* C45:20–21n. Lenehan continues south on Grafton Street, which gives into Stephen's Green West.

C58:34, pe58:32-33, P69:16 **College of Surgeons** The Royal College of Surgeons, 123 Stephen's Green West. The College was charged with overseeing the education, qualifications, and conduct of surgeons in Ireland.

C59:3, pe58:35-36, P69:19 **the corner of Merrion Street** See *Dub* C55:9n.

C59:30, pe59:29, P70:14 **Baggot Street** See *Dub* C50:32-33n and C55:9n.

C60:20, pe60:19, P71:7 **Ely Place** Runs south to a dead-end from Baggot Street where Baggot Street gives into Merrion Row. One nineteenth-century guidebook described it as "a quiet and fashionable *cul-de-sac* with the reputation of having housed the very famous of Dublin's history."

C60:29, pe60:28, P71:17 **A small gold coin** A sovereign (£1 or twenty shillings), the girl's wages for at least six or seven weeks.

"The Boarding House"

"The Boarding House" was fifth in order of composition; the manuscript is dated 1 July 1905.

C61:3, pe61:3, P71:19 **Mrs. Mooney** Is the subject of scurrilous gossip in the Cyclops episode of *Ulysses*, p. 314.

C61:6, pe61:7, P71:24 **Spring Gardens** Off North Strand Road between the Royal Canal and the River Tolka on the northeastern outskirts of metropolitan Dublin.

C61:9, pe61:10, P71:27 **take the pledge** Take an oath that he would give up drinking.

C61:14-15, pe61:15-16, P72:3-4 **She went to the priest and got a separation** British law made few provisions (adultery, desertion for an extended period) for divorce, but Irish Roman Catholics were forbidden by Church Law to take advantage even of those minimal provisions. The only recourse for Irish Catholics caught in impossible marriages was a legal separation backed by (and in effect secured by) the Church's authority.

C61 : 17, pe61 : 18, P72 : 6 **sheriff's man** A process server and piece-work errand boy in the bailiff's office.

C62 : 3, pe62 : 2, P72 : 13 **Hardwicke Street** In the northeastern quadrant of Dublin, lined with a mixture of modest middle-class dwellings and tenements in 1900.

C62 : 5, pe62 : 4, P72 : 15–16 **Liverpool and the Isle of Man** Steam packet lines between Dublin and Liverpool were a major link between Ireland and England. The Isle of Man, directly west of Liverpool, was a port of call on this run. Liverpool and the Isle of Man were supposed to be the homes of an extraordinarily rowdy citizenry.

C62 : 6, pe62 : 5, P72 : 16 *artistes* **from the music halls** Mrs. Mooney's boarding house is obviously "for men only," but both male and female music hall *artistes* were assumed (in 1900) to be living on the permissive fringes of middle-class morality.

C62 : 10, pe62 : 9, P72 : 21 *The Madam* Also slang for the proprietress of a house of prostitution.

C62 : 16, pe62 : 15, P72 : 27 **Jack Mooney** Is mentioned three times in *Ulysses*: in the Hades episode, p. 172; in Wandering Rocks, p. 246; and in Cyclops, p. 314.

C62 : 16–17, pe62 : 16, P72 : 28 **a commission agent in Fleet Street** A commission agent transacts business for others on a commission or percentage basis. Fleet Street in central Dublin just south of the Liffey was in an office district for solicitors and a variety of agents. Since Jack Mooney is "a hard case," it may be that he is well-suited to assist in the debt-collection side of a commission agency.

C62 : 25, pe62 : 25, P73 : 3 **vamped** Improvised.

C62 : 26, pe62 : 26, P73 : 4 **Polly Mooney** Also the subject of ribald gossip in the Cyclops episode of *Ulysses*, pp. 303 and 314.

C62 : 28–30, pe62 : 28–30, P73 : 6–8 *I'm a . . . naughty girl. / You needn't sham: / You know I am.* The song as quoted in Zack Bowen, *Musical Allusions in the Works of James Joyce* (Albany, N.Y., 1974) pp. 16–17:

Stanza I:
  I'm an imp on mischief bent,
  Only feeling quite content
  When doing wrong!
  When doing wrong!
  Sometimes when I've *had* the fun
  I repent of what I've done,
  But not for long!
  But not for long!
  On my mistress tricks I play,

Telling her what love should say,
Whispering what love should do;
She believes and does it too!
I'm a naughty girl
You needn't sham;
You know, I am!
Rome is in a whirl,
Because they're all afraid
Of this naughty little maid!

Chorus:
She's a naughty girl!
We know it well
And mean to tell!
She's a bad one
If we ever had one:
Oh, she's a very very naughty little girl!

Stanza II:
At the Roman Clubs, no doubt,
Funny tales you hear about
My goings on!
Your goings on!
If I like to sit and chat,
What can be the harm in that
Though daylight's gone?
Though daylight's gone!
If some youth with manners free
Dares to snatch a kiss from me,
Do I ask him to explain?
No I kiss him back again!

I'm a naughty girl, etc.

C62 : 32–33, pe62 : 32–33, P73 : 10–11 **eyes . . . with a shade of green**
See *Dub* C23 : 26n and cf. the Irish children's street rhyme, "Green eyes
and coppered hair, / My mother wouldn't trust you."

C63 : 2, pe63 : 1, P74 : 10 **corn-factor** One who buys corn from the
farmer and sells it to merchants, an agent or broker.

C63 : 30, pe63 : 31, P74 : 10 **George's Church** St. George's (Church of
Ireland, Protestant) on Temple Street, just around the corner from
Hardwicke Street in the northeast quadrant of Dublin.

C64 : 22, pe64 : 23, P75 : 5 **Mr. Doran** *Doran* in Irish means an exile or
a stranger. In *Ulysses* Bob Doran is mentioned as "on one of his peri-
odical bends" (p. 74); he is sighted in the Lestrygonians episode, is on
stage in Cyclops, and appears briefly in Circe.

C64:23, pe64:23, P75:5–6 **short twelve at Marlborough Street** The noon Mass, the shortest of the day (about twenty minutes), at the Church of the Conception, the Roman Catholic pro-cathedral, a short walk south from the boarding house. A pro-cathedral is a temporary cathedral, a sore point with Dublin Catholics because the Church of Ireland occupied both Christ Church and St. Patrick's, Dublin's great medieval cathedrals (and still does).

C64:32, pe64:33, P75:16 **reparation** In the secular sense of making financial restitution for a wrong committed and in the religious sense of acting in such a way as to atone for a sin. During confession the confessor enjoins "penance" on "penitents, in satisfaction for their sins . . . . Satisfaction is reparation of the injury and insult offered to God by sin, and of the injustice done to our neighbor" (*Maynooth Catechism*, p. 60).

C65:10, pe65:10, P75:30–31 **Bantam Lyons** Appears as a character in "Ivy Day in the Committee Room," *Dubliners*, and is mentioned or appears in eight of the episodes of *Ulysses*, beginning with Lotus Eaters, pp. 74 and 85–86.

C65:14–15, pe65:14–15, P75:35 **a great Catholic wine-merchant's office** Apparently fictional.

C65:17, pe65:17, P76:3 **screw** Salary.

C65:20, pe65:20, P76:5 **pier-glass** A large high mirror, usually attached to the wall, often in the space, the "pier," between two windows.

C65:29, pe65:29, P76:16 **confession** See *Dub* C13:13–14n. The implication is that Doran has gone to confession on Saturday evening to seek advice as well as absolution because he is guilty of a mortal sin ("impurity," see *Por* 144:16n) and has come to a crisis of worry about it.

C65:32, pe65:33, P76:20–21 **reparation** See *Dub* C64:32n.

C66:11, pe66:10–11, P76:35 **Reynolds's Newspaper** *Reynolds Weekly Newspaper*, a radical London Sunday newspaper, started in 1850 as a fourpenny record of social and political scandals. From a conservative point of view, its politics were "rude," and *Reynolds* was characterized as "a formidable spokesman for the most irreconcilable portions of the community."

C66:12, pe66:11–12, P77:1 **his religious duties** As a communicant in the Church, Doran would be expected to attend Mass every Sunday and on Holy Days of Obligation, to fast and abstain on the days appointed by the Church, to confess his sins at least once a year, to receive Holy Communion during Easter time, to contribute to the support of the Church, and to observe the laws of the Church concerning marriage.

C68:6, pe68:6, P78:35 *Bass* A strong, brown ale, brewed by Bass, Ratcliff, and Gretton, Ltd., Burton-on-Trent, Staffordshire, England.

C68:9, pe68:10, P79:5 **the return-room** A small room added onto the wall of a house and projecting out from it.

C68:25–26, pe68:29, P79:23 **amiable** In the usual sense of agreeable, pleasantly disposed, but also in the obsolete sense of amorous.

"A Little Cloud"

"A Little Cloud," fourteenth in order of composition, was completed by mid-1906.

C70:1, pe70:1, P80:1 (title) **A Little Cloud** In I Kings the Israelites under Ahab turn from the worship of the Lord to the worship of Baal. Elijah prophesies that as a consequence, "There shall not be dew nor rain these years, but according to my word" (I Kings 17:1). After two wasteland years, Elijah returns to confront Ahab, to demonstrate the spiritual impotence of the prophets of Baal (who are slain), to restore faith in the Lord among the Israelites, and to bring rain, "according to his word." The first news of the coming of rain is brought by Elijah's servant, "Behold, there ariseth a little cloud out of the sea, like a man's hand" (I Kings 18:44).

C70:2–3, pe70:3, P80:8 **North Wall** See *Dub* C40:23n.

C70:3, pe70:4, P80:8–9 **Gallaher** Ignatius Gallaher, a reporter, is identified by J. J. O'Molloy (a character in the Aeolus episode in *Ulysses*) as an employee of the Irish-born English publisher Alfred C. Harmsworth on either the *London Daily Mail* or the *London Evening News* (p. 139). He is recalled in the Hades episode, p. 88, and a notable story is told about him in Aeolus, pp. 135ff.

C71:1, pe70:22, P80:27 **the King's Inns** The Irish counterpart of the Inns of Court in London, located in a small park north of the Liffey in central Dublin. The Inns housed the legal societies that admitted persons to the bar, together with a Law Library, the Deeds Registry Office, Stamp Office, and Local Registry of Title Office.

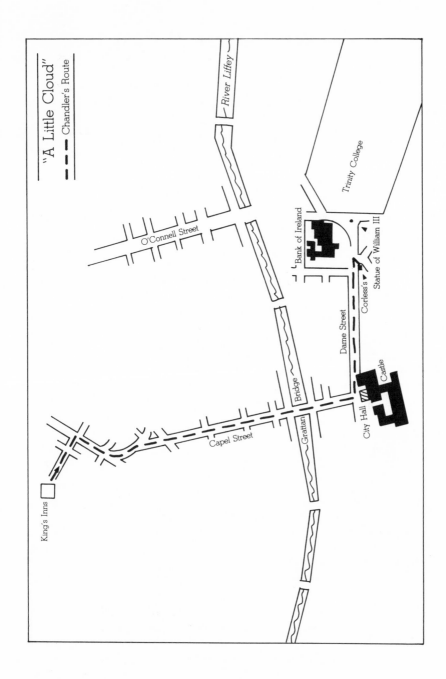

"A Little Cloud"
----- Chandler's Route

King's Inns

Capel Street

O'Connell Street

River Liffey

Grattan Bridge

Dame Street

Bank of Ireland

Trinity College

Corless's

Statue of William III

City Hall

Castle

C71:26, pe71:28, P81:27–28   **Henrietta Street**   Runs east-southeast from the eastern entrance to King's Inns. In 1900 it was lined with poor tenements.

C71:32–33, pe71:35–36, P82:1–2   **the gaunt spectral mansions in which the old nobility of Dublin had roystered**   Many of Dublin's slumdwellers lived in "the worn-out shells of Georgian mansions," as many of the Dublin poor still do (F. S. L. Lyons, *Ireland Since the Famine* [London, 1973], p. 277, quoted in Introduction, above, p. 15).

C72:1, pe72:1, P82:2   **memory of the past**   A song, also entitled "There Is a Flower That Bloometh," from act three of the opera *Maritana* (1845), libretto by Edward Fitzball (1792–1873), music by the Irish composer William Vincent Wallace (1813–65).

> There is a flower that bloometh
> When autumn leaves are shed.
> With the silent moment it weepeth,
> The spring and summer fled.
> The early frost of winter
> Scarce one tint hath overcast.
> Oh, pluck it ere it wither,
> 'Tis the memory of the past!
>
> It wafted perfume o'er us
> Of sweet, though sad regret
> For the true friends gone before us,
> Whom none would e're forget.
> Let no heart brave its power,
> By guilty thoughts o'ercast,
> For then, a poison flow'r
> Is—the memory of the past!

C72:3, pe72:3, P82:4   **Corless's**   The Burlington Hotel, Restaurant, and Dining Rooms, 26–27 St. Andrew's Street and 6 Church Lane in central Dublin south of the Liffey. By 1904 the hotel was owned and managed by the Jammet Brothers, who had taken over from Thomas Corless. Some Dubliners called it Jammet's; others went on calling it Corless's.

C72:11, pe72:11–12, P82:13   **alarmed Atalantas**   Atalanta, a mythological Greek princess, was exposed by her father, who wanted only male children. She was suckled by a bear and eventually found and raised by a party of hunters. She was distinguished for beauty and for a masculine fleetness of foot. An oracle warned her against marriage, so she tested her suitors by challenging them to a footrace and then by overtaking them in the race and spearing them in the back. She was finally defeated (and married) by Hippomenes, who distracted her during the race by dropping three golden apples Aphrodite had given him for the purpose. But Hippomenes forgot to thank Aphrodite, who then arranged for the newlyweds to profane a temple in their passion and to be turned into lions as a punishment.

C72:21, pe72:22, P82:24   **to the right towards Capel Street**   I.e., he turns south-southwest into Bolton Street, which gives into Capel Street. Little Chandler is walking south toward Grattan Bridge over the Liffey.

C73:3, pe73:2, P83:6   **Half time**   I.e., the period between the halves of a game of football, soccer, etc., a time for rest and for discussion of revised tactics for the second half of play.

C73:4, pe73:3, P83:7   **my considering cap**   Silas Wegg, one of the "birds of prey" in Dickens's novel *Our Mutual Friend* (1865) is a "man of low cunning" who temporarily acquires an apparent "mastery over [a] man of high simplicity." In chapter 15, as part of his plot to exploit his victim seems about to succeed, Wegg says, "Let me get on my considering cap, sir."

C73:5, pe73:4, P83:8   **That was Ignatius Gallaher all out**   P. W. Joyce (p. 38) cites this as Irish-English with the example: "He's not as bad as that *all out*"—i.e., he has his failings, but . . . .

C73:12, pe73:11, P83:15–16   **Grattan Bridge**   Over the Liffey in central Dublin. Little Chandler crosses from Capel Street on the north bank into Parliament Street on the south bank.

C73:24, pe73:24, P83:29   **nearer to London**   Little Chandler's route does take him east and south, toward the fashionable world of Corless's (The Burlington Hotel). When he arrives there, he will be almost a mile "nearer to London" than he was at King's Inns.

C74:4, pe74:2, P84:8–9   **the Celtic school**   A label under which English critics, taking their lead from Matthew Arnold's *Study of Celtic Literature* (London, 1867), had grouped late nineteenth-century Irish poets, particularly those who indulged a vague and dreamy melancholy and who were interested in a revival of the Irish cultural past, its language, folklore, and mythology. W. B. Yeats's early poems, plays, and stories and the poetry of A. E. (George William Russell) could be regarded as characteristic of what the labels "Celtic School" or "Celtic Twilight" meant (see *Por* C225:28–31n).

C74:30, pe74:30, P85:2   **Lithia**   Bottled spring water.

C75:7, pe75:5, P85:13   **orange tie**   Orange is not regarded as a color sympathetic to the green of Ireland (see *Dub* C165:27n).

C75:17–18, pe75:16, P85:25   **dear dirty Dublin**   A phrase coined by the Irish woman of letters, Lady Sydney Morgan (1780–1859).

C75:30, pe75:29, P86:3   **O'Hara**   Possibly Matthew O'Hara, a newspaperman on *The Irish Times* who offered Joyce a bit of help in 1902–03; see Richard Ellmann, *James Joyce* (New York, 1959), pp. 123, 132.

C75:32, pe75:32, P86:7   **Hogan**   Apparently fictional.

C75:32, pe75:32, P86:7   **sit**   I.e., situation or position.

C75:33, pe75:33, P86:8   **Land Commission**   The Irish Land Commission Court, which managed the transfer of farm lands from landlords to tenants. Until the land reforms of the late nineteenth century, Ireland had been dominated by a relatively small number of great landowners who had almost feudal power over their tenants. The Land Purchase Bills of 1891, 1896, and 1903 provided for the tenants' purchase of their farms from the landlords through the backing of British credit. The amounts of money involved (together with the bonuses paid after 1903 to encourage landlords to sell) made the Commission a notorious porkbarrel.

C76:10, pe76:7, P86:19   **the Isle of Man**   In spite of the prejudice that lower-class Manxmen were a rough lot (see *Dub* C62:5n), the Isle was regarded in Dublin as a quiet tourist trip for the unadventurous.

C76:28, pe76:26, P87:3   **the Moulin Rouge**   One of the great Paris music halls. The entertainment was regarded as risqué by sober British tourists. Baedeker's (1907) warned its readers that "the society is very mixed," a code way of suggesting that the music halls were not unqualifiedly "suitable for ladies."

C76:30, pe76:28, P87:5   **the Bohemian cafés**   Baedeker's (1907) lists these (p. 42) as "Cabarets Artistiques" and notes that they descend from cabarets located in Montmartre and formerly frequented by literary men and artists. Baedeker's says the entertainments presuppose "a considerable knowledge of colloquial French" and "are scarcely suitable for ladies."

C77:18, pe77:14, P87:28   **a catholic gesture**   With a small *c*, a gesture signifying universality, but a devout Catholic might very well make the Catholic gesture of crossing himself to defend himself against the thought of so much immorality and temptation in the world.

C77:20, pe77:17, P87:31   **one of the students' balls**   Baedeker's (1907) lists several "which take place all year round and may be regarded as one of the specialities of Paris." Some are "noted as a resort of students," and all are covered by the injunction: "It need hardly be said that ladies cannot attend these balls." Gallaher is right about "the *cocottes*": Baedeker's notes that "many of these entertainments [are] 'got up' for the benefit of strangers, numbers of the supposed visitors being hired as decoys by the lessee of the saloon" (p. 42).

C77:21, pe77:18, P87:32   *cocottes*   French: gay women, prostitutes.

C78:4, pe78:2, P88:17   *François*   Gallaher's attempt at a colloquial Parisian manner with the waiter or barman.

C78:10, pe78:9, P88:24   **rum**   Gypsy slang: queer, odd (in a derogatory sense).

C78:20, pe78:19–20, P88:35   **the secrets of religious houses on the Continent**   The suspicion of sexual license and orgies in "religious houses" was a staple of the Victorian pornographic imagination; it also came in handy as anti-Roman Catholic propaganda.

C78:22–23, pe78:22, P89:2–3   **a story about an English duchess**   Upper-class licentiousness was another old standby for the Victorian pornographic imagination.

C80:3, pe80:4, P90:24   *parole d'honneur*   French: word of honor.

C80:8, pe80:10, P90:30   **an a.p.**   An author's proof, the proof sent to an author for emendation and approval after the compositors' errors have been corrected and before the work is sent to the press. If indeed an a.p. has been forwarded from London to Gallaher in Dublin, Gallaher must be a journalist of some importance.

C80:11, pe80:13, P90:33   *deoc an doruis*   Irish: (literally) a doordrink; one for the road.

C82:14, pe82:17, P93:11   **Bewley's**   There were several Bewleys, but the nearest to The Burlington would have been Samuel Bewley and Company, tea and coffee merchants, 6 Dame Street (just around the corner).

C82:27, pe82:30, P93:26   **ten and elevenpence**   An expensive and generous gift, undoubtedly more than Little Chandler and family could readily afford.

C83:20, pe83:24–25, P94:23   **on the hire system**   On the installment plan.

C83:31–34, pe84:1–4, P95:1–4   *Hushed are the winds . . . dust I love*   The first stanza of Byron's "On the Death of a Young Lady, Cousin of the Author, and Very Dear to Him" (1802), the opening poem of Byron's *Hours of Idleness* (1807).

C84:13, pe84:17, P95:18   *That clay where once . . .*   The balance of the poem (stanzas two through six):

> Within this narrow cell reclines her clay,
>   That clay, where once such animation beam'd:
> The King of Terrors seized her as his prey;
>   Not worth, nor beauty, have her life redeem'd.
>
> Oh! could that King of Terrors pity feel,
>   Or Heaven reverse the dream decrees of fate!

Not here the mourner would his grief reveal,
Not here the muse her virtues would relate.

But wherefore weep? Her matchless spirit soars
Beyond where splendid shines the orb of day;
And weeping angels lead her to those bowers
Where endless pleasures virtue's deeds repay.

And shall presumptuous mortals Heaven arraign,
And, madly, godlike Providence accuse?
Ah! no, far fly from me attempts so vain; —
I'll ne'er submission to my God refuse.

Yet is remembrance of those virtues dear,
Yet fresh the memory of that beauteous face;
Still they call forth my warm affection's tear,
Still in my heart retain their wonted place.

C85:17, pe85:19, P96:24–25   **Lambabaun**   Irish dialect: lamb-baby, lamb-child.

C85:18, pe85:20, P96:25   **lamb of the world**   In contrast to John the Baptist's epithet for Jesus, "the Lamb of God" (John 1:29); cf. Jesus's answer to Pilate: "My kingdom is not of this world" (John 18:36).

"Counterparts"

"Counterparts" was sixth in order of composition, finished by mid-July 1905 (shortly after "The Boarding House").

C86:2, pe86:3, P97:2   **Miss Parker**   Apparently fictional.

C86:3, pe86:3, P97:3   **tube**   Intercommunication device.

C86:3–4, pe86:4, P97:4   **North of Ireland accent**   Marks the speaker as unsympathetic from Catholic Dublin's point of view because in all probability he would be in favor of Protestantism and English rule.

C86:5, pe86:5, P97:5   **Farrington**   Works as a scrivener or copy clerk, copying legal documents in handwriting because typewritten copies were not accepted as legally valid copies of legal documents in the early twentieth century. The first syllable of Farrington's name has the same sound as the Irish word *fear*, which means man, husband.

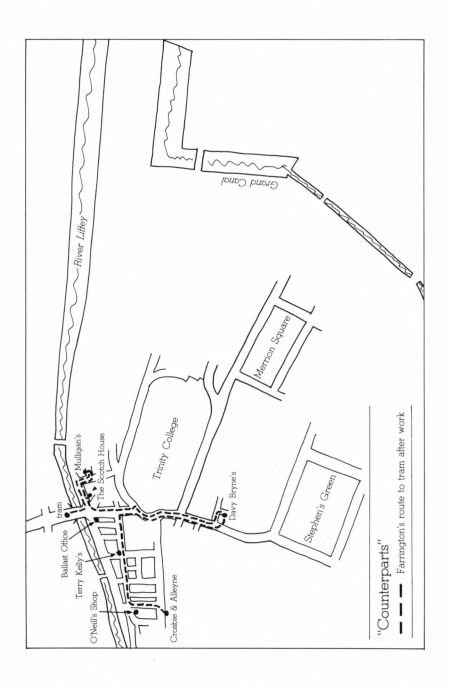

"Counterparts"

- - - Farrington's route to tram after work

River Liffey

Grand Canal

Merrion Square

Trinity College

Stephen's Green

Davy Byrne's

Mulligan's

The Scotch House

tram

Ballast Office

Terry Kelly's

O'Neill's Shop

Crosbie & Alleyne

C86:8, pe86:8, P97:8   **Mr. Alleyne**   C. W. Alleyne, a solicitor, had offices at 24 Dame Street (on the corner of Eustace Street) in central Dublin just south of the Liffey (*Thom's* 1904, p. 1468). No Crosbie is in evidence in *Thom's*, though Crosbie and Alleyne, solicitors, show up again in *Ulysses*, p. 91. Cf. Ellmann, pp. 14–15, 39.

C87:9, pe87:7–8, P97:29–98:1   **Bodley and Kirwan**   Unknown or fictional, unless Joyce had in mind the well-known and affluent Dublin developer-builder, Michael Kirwan.

C87:11, pe87:9, P98:2   **Mr. Shelley**   The chief clerk, apparently fictional.

C87:16, pe87:14, P98:7   **Mr. Crosbie**   See *Dub* C86:8n.

C88:30, pe88:30, P99:29   **the snug of O'Neill's shop**   Farrington walks north up Eustace Street from Dame Street to the corner of Essex Street East where J. J. O'Neill, tea and wine merchant, had a pub at 28 Essex Street. A snug is a small room or parlor behind the bar for private parties.

C88:33, pe88:33, P99:29   **g.p.**   Glass of porter (with a thoroughly tired pun on general practitioner). A glass is half a pint.

C89:1, pe88:34, P99:30   **curate**   See *Dub* C57:11n.

C89:2, pe88:35, P99:31   **a caraway seed**   To disguise his breath.

C89:11, pe89:8–9, P100:6   **Miss Delacour**   Apparently fictional.

C91:1, pe90:33, P102:1   **Leonard**   Paddy Leonard appears as a character in *Ulysses*; he is first mentioned on p. 90. He is on stage toward the end of Lestrygonians and appears briefly in Circe.

C91:2, pe90:33, P102:1   **O'Halloran**   No other appearances.

C91:2, pe90:33, P102:2   **Nosey Flynn**   Appears as a character in the Lestrygonians episode of *Ulysses* where, on p. 171, he is discovered at midday "in his usual corner of Davy Byrne's" (see *Dub* C93:20–21n).

C91:13, pe91:9, P102:14   **manikin**   Little man, dwarf, pigmy.

C92:11, pe92:9–10, P103:14   **little Peake**   Is mentioned as having been employed in Crosbie and Alleyne's in *Ulysses*, p. 91.

C92:31, pe92:30–31, P104:1–2   **Terry Kelly's pawn-office in Fleet Street**   Terence Kelly, pawnbroker (and justice of the peace), 48 Fleet Street. Fleet Street is parallel to and just northeast of Dame Street.

C92:33, pe92:31, P104:1   **dart**   Scheme or plan.

C92:34, pe92:34, P104:4   **Temple Bar**   Farrington walks north along Eustace Street from the offices in Dame Street, then east through Temple Bar, which gives into Fleet Street.

C93:3, pe92:37, P104:7   **A crown**   Five shillings.

C93:4, pe93:1, P104:8   **six shillings**   A sizeable sum for a night of pub-crawling. A glass (one half pint) of porter cost Farrington 1 d. in O'Neill's shop; a comparable glass of beer today would cost the equivalent of 45¢ to 50¢ in a Dublin pub. So Farrington's six shillings would be worth between $30 and $35 in modern pub exchange. But that leaves out of account the fact that Farrington's six shillings would probably represent one-fifth to one-fourth of his weekly wage (most of which would have to have been committed to his family's subsistence). His night's carousal would have been much more of a lien on his weekly wage than a comparable expenditure by a modern office worker would be.

C93:6–7, pe93:4, P104:11–12 **Westmoreland Street** Farrington turns south out of Fleet Street and walks along Westmoreland Street, which gives into College Green across the front of Trinity College and thence into Grafton Street. From Grafton Street he turns east into Duke Street.

C93:20–21, pe93:19–20, P104:27 **Davy Byrne's** David Byrne, wine and spirit merchant, 21 Duke Street, between Grafton and Dawson Streets.

C93:25, pe93:24, P104:32 **tailors of malt** Measures of whiskey.

C93:27, pe93:26, P104:34 **Callan's of Fownes's Street** Unknown or fictional, though there was a solicitor's office, Callan and Murphy, nearby in St. Andrew's Street.

C93:28, pe93:27–28, P105:1 **liberal shepherds in the eclogues** Virgil's (70–19 B.C.) ten bucolic or pastoral poems, *Bucolica* (41–39 B.C.). The shepherds are portrayed as living the simple epitome of the pastoral, kindly, rustic life. They are mild in speech, hospitable and generous, and—though suffering from the deprivations consequent on civil wars—not reduced to citified cruelty.

C94:3, pe94:1, P105:12 **nabs** Or "nab," in northwestern Ireland, "a knowing old-fashioned little fellow" (P. W. Joyce, p. 297).

C94:11, pe94:8, P105:20 **corner of Duke Street** The men have walked west from Davy Byrne's pub to the intersection of Duke and Grafton streets. Higgins and Flynn turn south; Farrington and company walk north.

C94:11, pe94:9, P105:21 **bevelled** Pushed or moved.

C94:14, pe94:11, P105:23–24 **the Ballast Office** On the west side of Westmoreland Street, on the corner of Aston's Quay (part of the south bank of the Liffey). The building housed the Dublin Port and Docks Board and was headquarters for the supervision of Dublin Harbour and its works. It was destroyed by fire in May 1921.

C94:14–15, pe94:12, P105:24 **the Scotch House** A pub, James Weir and Company, Ltd., tea dealers, wine and spirit merchants, 6–7 Burgh Quay, on the south bank of the Liffey just east of the Ballast Office.

C94:20, pe94:18, P105:30 **the Tivoli** At 12 and 13 Burgh Quay, just east of the Scotch House. Formerly the Lyric Theatre of Varieties, it offered music-hall and vaudeville entertainment.

C94:22, pe94:20, P105:32–33   **Irish and Appollinaris**   Irish whiskey and Appollinaris, an effervesent alkaline mineral water from a spring at Neuenarh in Germany.

C94:32, pe94:30, P106:10   **chaffed**   Kidded.

C94:34, pe94:32–33, p106:12   **Mulligan's in Poolbeg Street**   A pub, James Mulligan, grocer, wine and spirits merchant, 8 Poolbeg Street. The street is a short block south of and parallel to Burgh Quay.

C95:1, pe94:34, P106:13   **When the Scotch House closed**   The Scotch House had "a six day or Early Closing License," which meant that it closed earlier in the evening than fully licensed pubs, which closed at 11 P.M.

C95:3, pe94:36, P106:15   **small hot specials**   Hot toddies, a mixture of whiskey and sweetened water.

C96:27, pe96:26, P108:11   **Pony up**   Pay up. Also a pun, since pony is a small liquor glass.

C96:28, pe96:27, P108:12   **smahan**   Irish: a taste.

C96:29–30, pe96:28–29, P108:13–14   **O'Connell Bridge**   Farrington has walked back to the Ballast Office (at the southern end of the Bridge) and crossed to the north bank of the Liffey into O'Connell Street, where he will board the tram.

C96:30, pe96:29, P108:14   **Sandymount tram**   Sandymount was a suburban village on Dublin Bay three miles east-southeast of the center of Dublin. Farrington goes only to the northwestern outskirts of Sandymount.

C97:10, pe97:5, P108:27   **Shelbourne Road**   Just south of the Grand Canal but still within the limits of metropolitan Dublin, in a district of lower-middle-class homes and tenements.

C97:11, pe97:7, P108:29   **the barracks**   Beggar's Bush Infantry Barracks, on the west side of Shelbourne Road, was part of the British Army's Southern Dublin Division of the Dublin Military District.

C97:25, pe97:21, P109:9   **the chapel**   In Irish usage a chapel is a Roman Catholic Church; a church is Protestant, Church of Ireland.

C98:23, pe98:16, P110:5   **a *Hail Mary***   The Angelical Salutation, "Hail, Mary, full of grace, the Lord is with thee. Blessed art thou among women, and blessed is the fruit of thy womb, Jesus. Holy Mary, Mother of God, pray for us sinners, now, and at the hour of our death. Amen." This prayer would be typical of the sort of "penance" enjoined on the boy "in satisfaction for his sins" (see *Dub* C64:32n). But the child's offer also implies a bargain: a prayer that his father will not suffer the spiritual punishment consequent on his drunkenness and anger.

"Clay" was fourth in the order of composition; completed in January 1905, it was retouched, though not extensively reworked, in 1906. Apparently it was in its final form by the end of that year.

C99:1, pe99:1, P110:8 (title)   **Clay**   All Hallow's Eve more or less coincides with the beginning of one of the pagan Celtic half-years (May and November). In Celtic ritual, divination games, with their glimpses into the future, were traditional at those seasons; much simplified versions of some of those games are still popular in Ireland on Halloween. In the saucer game the saucers contain various items: a ring, a prayerbook, water, clay, etc. The person touching the ring would be married in the coming year; the person touching the prayerbook would enter a convent; the water meant continued fruitfulness, life; the clay, death. Genteel Victorian and Edwardian versions of the game usually omitted the saucer of clay. See Sir James G. Frazer, *The Golden Bough*.

C99:2, pe99:2-3, P110:9   **the matron had given her leave**   Maria lives and works, apparently as a scullery maid, at the *Dublin by Lamplight* institution. She is not an "inmate" but an employee, free to come and go, though she needs permission to leave her job early. *Dublin by Lamplight*, located at 35 Ballsbridge Terrace in Ballsbridge, was a Protestant institution for "fallen women"—its motto: "That they may recover themselves out of the snares of the devil" (II Timothy 2:24); i.e., it was an institution for the rehabilitation of drunkards and "occasional prostitutes." It was supported "by voluntary contributions and by the inmates' own exertions . . . [in the] excellent laundry attached" (*Thom's* 1904, p. 1386). Women who were sentenced to prison in Dublin for vagrancy, public drunkenness, or occasional prostitution could have their sentences commuted or shortened if they agreed to enter this or a similar "Magdalene institution."

C99:7, pe99:8, P110:14   **barmbracks**   Speckled cakes traditionally used in another divination game on Halloween; see *Dub* C99:1n. When the cakes were prepared for divination, they would contain a ring and a nut. Whoever got the ring would be married first; whoever got the nut would marry a wealthy widow or widower unless the nut were empty, in which case the person would remain unwed.

C99:17, pe99:18, P110:26   **Maria, you are a veritable peace-maker**   From Jesus's Sermon on the Mount (Matthew 5:9), "Blessed *are* the

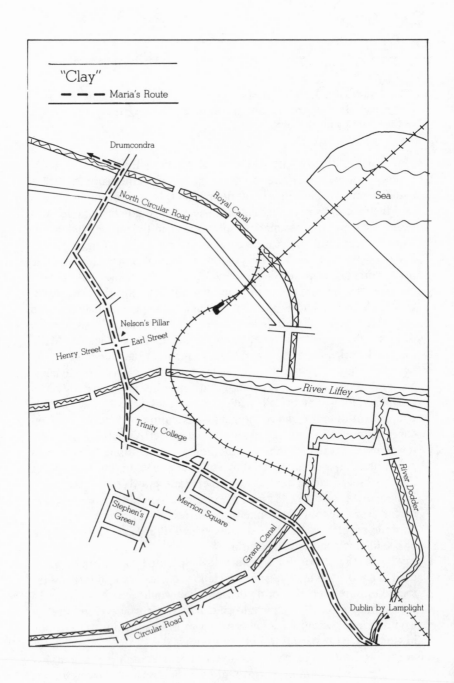

"Clay"

– – – Maria's Route

Drumcondra

North Circular Road

Royal Canal

Sea

Nelson's Pillar

Henry Street   Earl Street

Trinity College

River Liffey

River Dodder

Stephen's Green

Merrion Square

Grand Canal

Circular Road

Dublin by Lamplight

peace-makers: for they shall be called the children of God." From the Donlevy *Catechism*, p. 191: "Q. Who are the *peace-makers?* A. Those who subdue their passions so well, that they are at peace with God, with their neighbour, and with themselves; and that endeavour to make peace among others; and who, upon that account, are called the children of God and co-heirs with Christ in heaven."

C99:18, pe99:19, P110:27   **the Board ladies**   I.e., members of the Board of Governors of the Dublin by Lamplight institution; see *Dub* C99:2n.

C100:1–2, pe99:21–22, P111:1–2   **the dummy who had charge of the irons**   The pressing irons for the laundry would have been heated on a stove and would have had to be watched constantly so that they could be supplied at·the right temperature to those doing the ironing.

C100:4, pe100:2, P111:5–6   **Ballsbridge**   One and three-quarter miles southeast of the center of Dublin.

C100:5, pe100:3, P111:6   **the Pillar**   Nelson's Pillar, in honor of Admiral Horatio Lord Nelson (1758–1805). Erected in 1808, it stood in the middle of O'Connell Street in front of the General Post Office. The 134 foot monument was a mid-Dublin landmark and the hub-terminal for many of Dublin's tram lines. The Pillar was demolished by Irish patriots in 1966 on the 50th anniversary of the Easter 1916 Rebellion.

C100:5, pe100:3–4, P111:7   **Drumcondra**   A rural village cum suburb of Dublin, one and one-half miles north of the General Post Office and Nelson's Pillar.

C100:8, pe100:6–7, P111:10   *A Present from Belfast*   Suspect as more British than Irish; see *Dub* C36:10n and C86:3–4n.

C100:11, pe100:9, P111:13   **Whit-Monday**   The bank holiday following Whitsunday, the seventh Sunday after Easter, when the descent of the Holy Spirit in the form of "cloven tongues as of fire" on the Apostles is commemorated in the Feast of the Day of Pentecost; see Acts 2:1–6.

C100:11, pe100:10, P111:13   **two half-crowns**   Five shillings, a considerable sum of money for Maria.

C100:23, pe100:23, P111:27   **the *Dublin by Lamplight* laundry**   See *Dub* C99:2n.

C100:31, pe100:31–32, P112:2   **tracts on the walls**   Placards with Protestant exhortations (for the moral and spiritual benefit of the inmates).

C101:5–6, pe101:5–6, P112:11–12   **hot tea, already mixed with milk and sugar**   A notably vulgar and ungenteel way of serving tea, typical of prisons, the military, etc.

C101:9, pe101:10, P112:16   **ring**   See *Dub* C99:1n and C99:7n.

C101:10–11, pe101:11, P112:17   **Hallow Eves**   31 October, the evening preceding All Hallows' (All Saints' Day), 1 November.

C101:12, pe101:13, P112:14   **her grey-green eyes**   See *Dub* C23:26n.

C101:25, pe101:26, P112:33–34   **a mass morning**   1 November, All Saints' Day, was a Holy Day of Obligation (see *Dub* C66:12n). As a devout Catholic, Maria would attend Mass as "the Christian community rejoices with the Angels and Saints." The Gospel in this Mass is from the Sermon on the Mount, Matthew 5:1–12; see *Dub* C99:17n.

C102:12, pe102:13, P114:23–24   **Downes's cake-shop**   Sir Joseph Downes, confectioner, 6 Earl Street North, a few steps east from Nelson's Pillar.

C102:21, pe102:23, P113:33   **a shop in Henry Street**   Maria would have had her choice of at least three confectioners in Henry Street, which continues Earl Street beyond Nelson's Pillar to the west.

C102:28, pe102:31, P114:6   **Two-and-four**   Two shillings, four pence, an extravagance Maria could ill afford on her weekly income, which would have been more like an allowance than a salary.

C103:9, pe103:10, P114:21   **the Canal Bridge**   Maria gets out at Binn's Bridge, which carries Dorset Street Lower over the Royal Canal into Drumcondra Road Lower on the northern outskirts of metropolitan Dublin.

C103:11, pe103:12, P114:24   **along the terrace**   Maria apparently turns west along the north bank of the Royal Canal into what is now called Whitworth Street.

C103:13, pe103:14, P114:26   **when he has a drop taken**   Colloquial for: when he is pleasantly inebriated.

C105:1, pe104:37, P116:18   **saucers**   See *Dub* C99:1n.

C105:22, pe105:23, P117:6   **Miss McCloud's Reel**   A traditional Irish fiddle tune, commonly played in the key of G.

C106:2, pe106:1–2, P117:22   *I Dreamt that I Dwelt*   The hit tune from Balfe's *The Bohemian Girl*; see *Dub* C39:3n. The opera's heroine, Arlene, sings the song in act II when she recalls in a dream the luxury of her pre-gypsy existence.

C106:12, pe106:12, P117:32   **her mistake**   Maria mistakenly repeats the first verse instead of singing the second verse:

I dreamt that suitors sought my hand,
That knights on bended knee,
And with vows no maiden heart could withstand,
They pledged their faith to me.

And I dreamt that one of that noble band,
Came forth my heart to claim,
But I also dreamt, which charmed me most
That you loved me all the same.

The "you" in the last line is Arlene's true love, a Polish count disguised as a gypsy.

"A Painful Case"

"A Painful Case" was the seventh story in order of composition (July 1905), but it was repeatedly retouched in 1906.

C107:2, pe107:2, P118:8   **Duffy**   The Irish root of this name, *dub* or *duff*, suggests dark, black, dusk.

C107:2, pe107:3, P118:8   **Chapelizod**   A village astride the River Liffey, three miles west of the center of Dublin and at the southwestern corner of Phoenix Park. The village derives its name from Iseult's chapel, and some Irish versions of the Tristan and Iseult story say that it was here that they consummated their ill-fated love. Phoenix Park is also involved in the legend as the site of the Forest of Tristan, into which Tristan retreated in despair and madness (occasioned by the impossibility of his love and the double bind of his oath of allegiance to King Mark and Iseult's betrothal to the king).

C107:6, pe107:7, P118:13   **the disused distillery**   By 1900 it was in use again as the Phoenix Park Distillery, though it had fallen into a disuse notable to the Joyce family in the late 1870s because John Joyce had had an interest in the distillery out of which he was cheated; see Ellmann, pp. 14–15.

C107:7, pe107:8, P118:14   **the shallow river**   The Liffey, an estuary in central Dublin, is a shallow river as it passes through Chapelizod.

C107:11, pe107:12, P118:18   **four cane chairs**   The stage directions for act II of Hauptmann's *Michael Kramer* (see *Dub* C108:4n below) describe the "cleanliness" and "order" of Kramer's studio and specify, "Two simple cane chairs complete the furnishing of the room" (*The Dramatic Works of Gerhart Hauptmann*, ed. Ludwig Lewisohn [New York, 1914], 3:454).

C107:12, pe107:13, P118:20   **a double desk**   A desk-like portfolio with a slanted surface on which to write and, beneath a hinged top, a shallow compartment in which to store papers and writing materials.

C107:19, pe107:21, P118:27   **a complete Wordsworth**   Wordsworth was regarded at the beginning of the twentieth century as a safe and essentially undaring romantic poet, acceptable to the academic establishment and, from an avant-garde point of view, suspect as too unembittered and too conformist to the established Church and to the authority of the state.

C108:1, pe107:22, P118:28–29   ***Maynooth Catechism***   *The Catechism Ordered by the National Synod of Maynooth.* (Dublin, 1883). This was the standard text for Roman Catholic religious instruction in Ireland at the turn of the century (see p. 11 above). The Royal College of St. Patrick at Maynooth, fifteen miles west of Dublin, is the clerical center of Catholic Ireland.

C108:4, pe108:2–3, P119:3   **Hauptmann's *Michael Kramer***   Gerhart Hauptmann (1862–1946), German dramatist, novelist, and poet. *Michael Kramer* (1900) is a four-act naturalistic play that focuses on the conflict between a hopelessly uncompromising father and a hopelessly compromised son. The father, Michael Kramer, is described in act I by a former pupil, who recalls that, faced with Kramer's "unflaggingly loyal seriousness in the service of art, the outside world seems . . . entirely frivolous." Kramer struggles against debased public taste, against the corrupt and compromising politics of academic art, and against what he regards as "the vulgar soul" of his son, Arnold, who is characterized as "sickly," "slightly deformed," and dissipated. He is talented as an artist but "doesn't profit" from his father's "seriousness," which he abhors and fears. He is caught up in the "frivolous" world of a Bohemian café (and an unrequited fixation on the owner's daughter), where he is despised, mocked, and finally driven out (at the end of act III) into a suicide, spurred immediately by public humiliation and comprehensively by his father's intransigence. In act IV, after the son's death, Michael Kramer takes the full impact of the son's wasted life and recognizes that, in his inexorable demand for artistic dedication and moral rectitude, he may have "maltreated" his son (*Works of Hauptmann*, 3:537). Kramer wonders whether he has failed in life to give the warmth and love that would have redeemed his son—a warmth and love he can proffer only after death, in death. The play's central irony is that Kramer's attempt to save his son has sealed the son's doom and that the intensity of Kramer's commitment to high art has, until his self-recognition at the play's end, rendered his life as ster-

"A Painful Case"

Dublin Bay

River Liffey

Phoenix Park

(Fifteen Acres)

Magazine Hill

Wellington Monument

Chapelizod

Chapelizod Gate

Chapelizod Rd.

Conyngham Rd.

Park Gate

Islandbridge

Kingsbridge Station

railroad

Lucan Rd.

River Liffey

Grand Canal

Navan Rd.

Royal Canal

Cabra Rd.

N. Circular Rd.

Rutland (now Parnell) Square

The Rotunda

G.P.O.

The Castle

Gt. George St.

Trinity College

St. Stephen's Green

Merrion Square

Earlsfort Terrace

Baggot St. Lr.

Baggot St. Up.

Royal City of Dublin Hospital

Grand Canal

Ballsbridge

River Dodder

Donnybrook

Sydney Parade station

ile as the lives of the "vulgar souls" and "Philistines" against whom he has struggled.

C108:8, pe108:7, P119:8   **Bile Beans**   A patent medicine for bilious (embittered) conditions. The standard advertising formula: "Bile Beans for Biliousness are purely vegetable and are a certain cure for headache, constipation, piles, pimples, blood impurities, bad blood, skin eruptions, liver troubles, bad breath, indigestion, palpitation, loss of appetite, flatulence, dizziness, buzzing in the head, debility, sleeplessness, nervousness, anaemia, and all female ailments." See *Dub* C112: 15–16n.

C108:16, pe108:14, P119:15   **saturnine**   In medieval terms, born under the influence of Saturn, the watery planet, and hence heavy, grave, gloomy, dull (the opposite of mercurial). The saturnine man suffers from an excess of bile and tends toward a melancholia which can be alleviated by music.

C108:17, pe108:.15, P119:16   **the brown tint of Dublin streets**   See *Dub* C29:7n.

C108:28, pe108:28, P119:30   **a stout hazel**   In Celtic mythology the Hazel is "the poet's tree," simultaneously bearing the nut of wisdom and the flower of beauty. Ancient Irish ollaves (poet-priests) traditionally carried hazel wands (Robert Graves, *The White Goddess*, pp. 151–52, 166).

C108:29–30, pe108:29–30, P119:31–32   **cashier of a private bank in Baggot Street**   There were a number of small branch banks and private banks in Baggot Street (the southeasterly extension of Stephen's Green North) in 1900. A cashier was an important bank officer, responsible not only for the handling of the bank's monies but also for the employees who handled money and were subordinate to him.

C108:31, pe108:31, P119:33   **Dan Burke's**   Daniel Burke and Company, wine merchants, ran a pub which served light meals at 50 Baggot Street Lower (and several other pubs in Dublin).

C108:33–109:2, pe108:34–35, P120:1–3   **an eating-house in George's Street . . . Dublin's gilded youth**   There are two George's Streets in Dublin, one north and one south of the Liffey. George's Street North was lined with well-to-do homes (and no eating houses) in 1900. Great George's Street South was the main north-south axis of a commercial district (hardly a resort for the fashionable) with several modest eating houses, and besides, it lay on Mr. Duffy's route from Baggot Street to Chapelizod. "Gilded youth" is a translation of the French *Jeunesse Dorée*, gangs of young men who, during the French Revolution, broke into prisons in the provinces and massacred the Jacobin prisoners.

C109:5, pe109:3, P120:6   **Mozart's music**   Late-nineteenth-century "appreciations" of Mozart's music (and personality) tend to emphasize "the buoyant nature which seemed to override misfortune and intrigue and to laugh at poverty" (*The New International Encyclopedia* [New York, 1903], 14:84b). Cf. *Dub* C108:16n.

C109:18, pe109:16, P120:20   **the Rotunda**   A group of buildings in the southeast corner of then Rutland (now Parnell) Square in northeast-central Dublin. The buildings housed a theatre, a concert hall, and assembly rooms, the proceeds from the uses of which partially supported a highly regarded maternity hospital.

C110:4–5, pe110:1–2, P121:7–8   **a concert in Earlsfort Terrace**   The Terrace is the southerly extension of Stephen's Green East. The Dublin International Exhibition Building was located on the west side of Earlsfort Terrace. At the beginning of the twentieth century the building was used for concerts, meetings, etc. It was later included in University College, Dublin, which was then located in Stephen's Green South.

C110:8, pe110:5–6, P121:12   **Mrs. Sinico**   Emily Sinico's death and funeral are recalled three times by Bloom in *Ulysses* (pp. 114, 695 and 711).

C110:33, pe110:32, P122:4–5   **Irish Socialist Party**   Sidney Webb, *Socialism in England* (London, 1894), remarks: "Ireland has not proved a successful field for avowed and conscious social propaganda" (p. 61). The Irish were, during this period, far more interested in land reform than in wage reform; in addition, the Roman Catholic clergy regarded socialism as "simply irreligion and atheism" (Cardinal Logue; see *Por* C33:18–19n). "The Socialist Party of Ireland" was thus a small series of study groups, vaguely committed to "every improvement in the mode of life"—but with little or no political power or presence in the late nineteenth century. The one possible exception was Michael Davitt (see pp. 21–22) who is reputed to have been the only prominent Irish politician to affirm openly (but not in name) the doctrines of socialism. This is all, of course, before the advent of the socialist James Connolly (1868–1916) and the labor leader James Larkin (1876–1947) in the early twentieth century.

C111:15, pe111:14, P122:22   **her little cottage outside Dublin**   Mrs. Sinico lives in Sydney Parade Avenue, a street in a modestly well-to-do, middle-class section of the village of Merrion on Dublin Bay, three miles south-southeast of the General Post Office in Dublin.

C112:4, pe112:2, P123:12   **Parkgate**   The southeastern (and main) entrance to Phoenix Park. The Park's 1760 acres lie north of the Liffey in western Dublin. The Phoenix, a mythical bird, consumed by fire once a millennium yet reborn of its own ashes, is a traditional symbol variously of Christ and of the regenerative power of passionate love. For the Irish the Phoenix was also a symbol of the rebirth of Ireland as an independent (and ideal) nation; see *Dub* C107:2n. The name Phoenix is actually an English substitute for the Irish name of the region, *Fionnusige* (Fair Water).

C112:15–16, pe112:15–16, P123:26–27   **Nietzsche: Thus Spake Zarathustra and The Gay Science**   Friedrich Nietzsche (1844–1900), German philosopher, critic, and poet, *Also Sprach Zarathustra* (1883–84) and *La Gaya Scienza* (1881–82). Nietzsche preached the doctrine of the Superman, who, of necessity, is a god unto himself since "God is Dead." In the light of this doctrine, the disciple who wants to aid the advance of humanity toward Superman status should turn his back on the "marketplace" and the "rabble" and commit himself to the discipline and order of a hermit's existence. His goal is "to create beyond himself," to realize life as "a wellspring of delight," uncontaminated by the rabble and its petty preoccupations with repressive morality and fashionable pursuits. The true disciple has no need for public response or for a woman's supportive love. He writes proverbs "in blood" not for the many but for the few who, like himself, await and seek to abet the evolutionary coming of the Superman.

C112:19–22, pe112:19–22, P123:30–33   **Love between man and man . . . must be sexual intercourse**   Cf. Nietzsche, *Thus Spake Zarathustra*, I:xiv (trans. Thomas Common [New York, 1917], p. 72), "The Friend":

> Art thou a slave? Then thou canst not be a friend. Art thou a tyrant? Then thou canst not have friends.
>
> Far too long hath there been a slave and a tyrant concealed in woman. On that account woman is not yet capable of friendship; she knoweth only love.
>
> In woman's love there is injustice and blindness to all she doth not love. And even in woman's conscious love there is still always surprise and lightning and night, along with the light.
>
> As yet woman is not capable of friendship: women are still cats, and birds. Or at the best, cows.
>
> As yet woman is not capable of friendship. But men, ye men, who of you are capable of friendship?

C112:30, pe112:30, P124:6   **paragraph**   I.e., a news story.

C113:9, pe113:7, P124:19   **the buff Mail**   The *Dublin Evening Mail*, a right-wing, pro-English daily newspaper, "buff" because it was printed on light brown paper.

C113:9–10, pe113:8, P124:20   **reefer overcoat**   A close-fitting, double-breasted jacket or short coat of thick cloth.

C113:10–11, pe113:9, P124–21   **the Parkgate to Chapelizod**   From Parkgate at the eastern end of Phoenix Park Mr. Duffy would walk west between the south side of the park and the north bank of the Liffey along Conyngham and Chapelizod Roads. His walk home after his evening meal in Great George's Street South would have been three and one half miles, two of them along the walled southern perimeter of Phoenix Park—a damp, bleak, and lonely walk except on pleasant summer evenings.

C113:17, pe113:16, P124:29   **the prayers** *Secreto*   *Secreto*, Latin: set apart. In the Mass the "Prayer over the Offerings, the variable prayer, or prayers in collect form that immediately precede the preface [the solemn prayer of Thanksgiving . . . at the beginning of the Canon of the Mass], the celebrant says [the *Secreto*] in a low voice" (*Layman's Missal*, p. xlviii).

C113:19, pe113:18, P124:25   **Sydney Parade**   The railroad station in the suburban village of Merrion was (and is) located in Sydney Parade Avenue; see *Dub* C111:15n.

C113:21, pe113:20, P124:27   **the City of Dublin Hospital**   Royal City of Dublin Hospital in Baggot Street Upper, a charitable institution which received accident and emergency cases "at all hours, without recommendation." The hospital was located just south of the Grand Canal on the southeastern outskirts of metropolitan Dublin, a mile and a half northwest of Sydney Parade Station, where the accident took place.

C113:21ff, pe113:20ff, P124:27ff   **the Deputy Coroner . . . Mr. Leverett**   Unknown and presumably fictional, as are the other public and railroad officials in the following pages (James Lennon, P. Dunne, Police Sergeant Croly, Dr. Halpin and Mr. H. B. Patterson Finlay). In *Ulysses*, when Joyce had occasion to mention minor public officials, he frequently chose to use their proper names.

C113:27, pe113:26, P125:6   **Kingstown**   Now Dun Laoghaire; see *Dub* C43:17n.

C115:7, pe115:5, P126:20   **a League**   I.e., a temperance league, to enter which Mrs. Sinico would have had to take an oath that she would never drink again.

C115:18, pe115:17, P126:33   **the Lucan road**   Along the south bank of the Liffey, from Chapelizod to the village of Lucan, four miles to the west.

C115:29–30, pe115:30–31, P127:12   **one of the wrecks on which civi-**

lization has been reared   Echoes vintage Nietzsche; see *Dub* CI12: 15–16n.

CI16:8, peII6:7–8, P127:23–24   the public-house at Chapelizod Bridge   The Bridge Inn (now Murphy's) just south of the bridge which links the north and south ends of Chapelizod over the River Liffey.

CI16:12, peII6:12, P127:28   County Kildare   Just west and southwest of County Dublin.

CI16:19, peII6:19, P127:35   the *Herald*   *The Evening Herald*, another Dublin evening newspaper.

CI17:1, peII6:35–36, P128:17–18   entered the Park by the first gate   Chapelizod Gate into Phoenix Park is 500 yards east of Chapelizod Bridge along the south side of the park.

CI17:9, peII7:7, P128:25   Magazine Hill   Or Thomas's Hill on the south side of Phoenix Park overlooking the Liffey. It was topped by a "Magazine Fort," constructed in the eighteenth century. Mr. Duffy has walked over a mile through the park.

CI17:22, peII7:21–22, P129:5   Kingsbridge Station   Now Séan Heuston Station, just south of the Liffey and opposite the eastern end of Phoenix Park. It was the terminus of the Great Southern and Western Railroad, which served the south (Cork) and southwest of Ireland.

"Ivy Day in the Committee Room"

"Ivy Day in the Committee Room" was the eighth story in order of composition, virtually in its final form by late August 1905.

The story takes place after Queen Victoria's death in 1901 and before King Edward VII's (b. 1841, king 1901–10) visit to Ireland, 21 July–1 August 1903; therefore, the story takes place on 6 October 1902.

The characters in the story represent the spectrum of Irish political opinion in 1902, from the working-class Colgan (offstage) and the dedicated Parnellite Hynes on the left, to the left-leaning O'Connor, to the ambivalent center of Mr. Henchy and the offstage Tierney, to Lyons, right of center, to Crofton the conservative Orangeman on the far right (with the proviso that "left" and "right" are not very illuminating terms when applied to Irish politics in the post-Parnell decade; see Introduction, pp. 20–21 above, and *Dub* CI10:33n).

C118:1–3, pe118:1–2, P129:18–19 (title) **Ivy Day in the Committee Room** Ivy Day is observed on 6 October, on the anniversary of the death of Charles Stewart Parnell (1846–91). On that date his political sympathizers and admirers wore a leaf of ivy, an evergreen symbolic of regeneration. In Committee Room No. 15 of the House of Parliament in London Parnell was in effect deposed from his political leadership by the Split in the Irish Parliamentary Party delegation on Saturday, 6 December 1890. Parnell, the "Chief," was called by Timothy Michael Healy, one of his retainers (whom Joyce was to regard as his betrayer), "the uncrowned king of Ireland." See "An Outline of Irish History," pp. 21–22 above.

C119:1, pe118:22, P130:12 **Mr. Tierney** No Richard J. Tierney is listed as a Dublin publican (or otherwise) by *Thom's* 1900–1905, but the alderman for the Royal Exchange Ward in the early twentieth century was a publican, Joseph Delahunt, who had two establishments (at 42 and 92 Camden Street Lower), neither of which was called The Black Eagle. A publican who became a member of the Dublin Corporation was assumed to have a considerable business advantage because, presumably, his public house would be frequented by those in search of political favors and influence.

C119:10, pe119:8, P130:22 **MUNICIPAL ELECTIONS** The pending election is for membership in the Municipal Council, the parliamentary ruling body of the City of Dublin Corporation. Each of the city's twenty wards would elect an alderman and three town councilors. The Municipal Council would, in turn, annually elect a lord mayor and a high sheriff from among its members. (The two offices were as much honorary and ceremonial as they were administrative.) Franchise in Dublin was confined to male citizens over 21 who were £10 householders, i.e., those whose houses were listed on the tax rolls as being worth £10 or more in "annual rent." In 1901 there were 34,906 eligible voters out of a population of 290,638 in Dublin.

C119:11, pe119:9, P130:23 **ROYAL EXCHANGE WARD** In central Dublin south of the Liffey. The ward included Dublin Castle and the City Hall; i.e., it included the political power centers of Anglo-Irish Dublin.

C119:12, pe119:10, P130:24 **P.L.G.** Poor Law Guardian. The Poor Law Amendment Act of 1834 was designed "to make the parish the hardest taskmaster, so as to drive able-bodied men to seek honest work elsewhere and not hang in laziness on parish relief." The law was administered by Guardians elected by the ratepayers (the tax and tithe payers) of each parish. The Guardians were popularly regarded as oppressors of the poor, and the organization of Dublin into two Poor Law Unions (north and south) did little to change that reputation.

C119:15, pe119:14, P130:27–28   **Tierney's agent**   His campaign manager.

C119:18, pe119:17–18, P130:30–31   **the Committee Room in Wicklow Street**   The Nationalist Party's ward headquarters, apparently in one of the small office buildings in Wicklow Street, just south of the Liffey and east of the Castle in central Dublin. "Committee Room" also alludes to Committee Room 15 of the House of Parliament in London. See "An Outline of Irish History," pp. 21–22 above.

C119:20, pe119:19, P130:32–131:1   **the short day had grown dark**   On 6 October 1902 the sun would have set at 5:25 P.M. in Dublin.

C119:23, pe119:22–23, P131:4–5   **a leaf of dark glossy ivy**   Worn in memory of Parnell on this 6 October, the eleventh anniversary of his death.

C119:29, pe119:29, P131:11   **Christian Brothers**   See *Dub* C29:3n.

C120:4, pe120:3, P131:18   **cocks him up**   Slang for inflates his ego.

C120:8, pe120:7, P131:23   **a sup**   Archaic English for "one mouthful of liquid" (P. W. Joyce, p. 338).

C120:20, pe120:20, P132:1   **Freemason's meeting**   The Masons were reputed to conduct their meetings in cabalistic secrecy; see *Dub* C32:21n.

C120:23, pe120:23, P132:4   **Hynes**   Joe Hynes appears as a character in the Aeolus and Cyclops episodes and is recalled elsewhere in *Ulysses*.

C121:4, pe121:4, P132:21   **Has he paid you yet**   I.e., for canvassing for votes.

C121:15, pe121:15, P132:33   **tinker**   In Ireland, a gypsy. Gypsies in Ireland were (and are) notorious for their apparent indigence; for beggary, cunning, and petty thievery; and for a shiftless, nomadic way of life. See John Millington Synge's (1871–1909) play, *The Tinker's Wedding* (1907).

C121:16, pe121:17, P132:34   **Colgan**   Unknown, except that he has an Irish name; cf. *Dub* C131:3–4n and C131:15–16n. Presumably Colgan is a candidate of the United Irish League, politically well to the left of Nationalists of Tierney's stripe; see *Dub* C110:33n.

C121:20, pe121:21, P133:3   **Corporation**   The Dublin Corporation is the ruling body of the city, including the lord mayor, the sheriffs, the aldermen and councilmen, their various committees and the bureaucracies which answer to those committees.

C121:21, pe121:22, P133:4   **shoneens**   A shoneen is "a *gentleman* in a small way: a would-be gentleman who puts on superior airs. Always used contemptuously" (P. W. Joyce, p. 321).

C121:21–22, peI21:23, P133:5   **with a handle to his name**   I.e., with some sort of title.

C121:25, peI21:26–27, P133:9–10   **hunker-sliding**   To hunker-slide is "to slide on ice sitting on the hunkers [on one's heels] . . . instead of standing up straight: hence to act with duplicity: to shirk work" (P. W. Joyce, p. 275).

C121:26, peI21:27, P133:10–11   **to represent the labour classes** Precious few members of the "labour classes" were enfranchised to vote in Dublin, 1902; see *Dub* C119:10n.

C121:30–31, peI21:32–33, P133:15–16   **all kicks and no halfpence** All the physical discomfort (of labor) for none of the financial reward.

C121:34, peI21:36–37, P133:19–20   **a German monarch**   Edward VII of England (b. 1841, king 1901–10), a direct descendant through his mother, Queen Victoria, and his father, Prince Albert, of German princely families. Victoria was the granddaughter of George III of England and the daughter of Princess Victoria of Saxe-Coburg-Gotha. Albert was the son of the Duke of Saxe-Coburg-Gotha. Victoria and Albert maintained close ties with Germany, as did Edward VII.

C122:2, peI22:2–3, P133:22–23   **they want to present an address of welcome**   To give an address of welcome was (from an Irish nationalist point of view) to imply loyalty to the Crown and acceptance of British rule. In 1902 Edward VII canceled a proposed visit to Ireland because his advisors anticipated an unfavorable reception. When he did visit Ireland, 21 July through 1 August 1903, the reception was mixed. He arrived at Kingstown (Dun Laoghaire) on Tuesday, the 21st, where he was greeted with an address of welcome by the Kingstown Urban District Council. The Dublin Corporation had (by three votes) refused to authorize the customary address of welcome; the Dublin County Council voted (1 July 1903) to present an address but at the last minute hid behind the Urban District Councils. The Councils of Pembroke, Rathmines, and Blackrock (districts just south of the city of Dublin) combined to present an address when the Royal Progress paused just south of the Dublin City limits. That address had the appearance of a formal welcome to the city and enabled Dublin to have its refusal and at the same time to be praised for having received the king "enthusiastically" in the conservative *Irish Times*, 22 July 1903.

C122:6, peI22:6, P133:26   **the Nationalist ticket**   I.e., the Irish Parliamentary or Home Rule Party. After the death of Parnell, the party was divided against itself under the titular leadership of John Redmond (1856–1918); see *Dub* C43:15n.

C122:10, peI22:10, P133:31   **spondulics**   U.S. slang: funds, money.

C122:18, pe122:18, P134:4   **Musha**   An Irish interjection connoting strong feeling.

C122:30, pe122:30, P134:16   **serve**   Canvass for votes.

C122:30, pe122:30, P134:16   **Aungier Street**   South of the Castle in central Dublin.

C122:33, pe122:34, P134:20   **Grimes**   Apparently fictional. No Grimes is listed in Aungier Street by *Thom's* 1901–04.

C123:6, pe123:4, P134:28   **Father Burke's name**   Apparently fictional.

C123:13, pe123:12, P135:1   **shoeboy**   I.e., Tierney. Shoeshine boy is slang for a low or cringing flatterer (because the boy appears to be about to kiss his customer's foot as he kneels to shine the shoes).

C123:21, pe123:21, P135:10   **Mr Fanning**   "Long" John Fanning, Joyce's fictional name for the subsheriff of Dublin, the more or less tenured administrative officer as against the influential but essentially ceremonial position of high sheriff (who had a one year term). Fanning appears as a character in "Grace," *Dubliners*. In *Ulysses* he is mentioned several times and is on stage in The Wandering Rocks episode, pp. 247–48.

C123:23, pe123:24, P135:15   **Mary's Lane**   A street of poor shops and tenements just north of the Liffey in central Dublin.

C123:27, pe123:27–28, P135:17   **the houses**   Public houses or bars. Opening and closing times were fixed by law and were rather strictly policed. No house could open on Sunday before early afternoon.

C123:27, pe123:28, P135:18   **moya**   Irish: gentle, mild, demure, affected; almost always said in irony.

C123:28–29, pe123:29–30, P135:19   **a tricky little black bottle**   I.e., the elder Tierney improved his second-hand clothing business by the illegal sale of drinks of whiskey during hours when the pubs were not open.

C123:34, pe123:35, P135:26   **stump up**   Pay up, or hand over the money; after "to stump" which means "to bring to a halt."

C124:17, pe124:17, P136:9   **'Usha**   Musha, see *Dub* C122:18n.

C124:23, pe124:27, P136:19   **twig**   Catch on, understand.

C124:24, pe124:28, P136:20   **a decent skin**   A decent fellow (in the sense that he gets by, skins by), but skin is also slang for a fraud, a cheat, a sharper—as in skin game.

C125:5, pe125:5, P136:35   **these hillsiders and fenians**   The Irish Republican Brotherhood, organized in 1858 by James Stephens (1824–1901), was committed to the achievement of Irish independence through terrorist tactics and violent revolution (rather than parliamentary or

constitutional reform). Members of the Brotherhood called themselves
Fenians after the Fianna of Irish legend, a standing force of warriors led
by Finn MacCool in the third century A.D. The British press carica-
tured them as hiding out in hillside retreats and therefore called them
the hillside men or hillsiders.

C125:8, pe125:8, P137:3–4   **in the pay of the Castle**   I.e., spying on
Irish nationalists for the British. The Castle housed the offices of the
chief secretary for Ireland (the British official responsible to the Cabinet
and Parliament for the government of Ireland) and the law-enforce-
ment offices of the Crown (the Royal Irish Constabulary). In context
Henchy's accusation seems farfetched, but in practice the Castle did
have an extensive net of paid informers in Irish political movements;
see *Por* 202:8n.

C125:12–13, pe125:12–13, P137:9   **a certain little nobleman with a
cock-eye**   Unknown.

C125:16, pe125:16, P137:12   **Major Sirr**   Henry Charles Sirr (1764–
1841), an Irishman who served the British as town major of Dublin
during the Rebellion of 1798. He was active in arresting the leaders of
the rebellion, among them Lord Edward Fitzgerald (1763–98), who
was mortally wounded while being captured. Sirr was notorious for his
ruthless use of informers and for the brutality of the police he led.

C126:9, pe126:7, P138:5   **the *Black Eagle***   The fictional Tierney's
apparently fictional pub.

C126:29, pe126:28, P138:26   **Kavanagh's**   James Kavanagh, justice of
the peace, tea, wine, and spirit merchant, 27 Parliament Street (at the
intersection of Essex Gate). Kavanagh's pub was located just north of
the City Hall and the Castle and was a gathering place for Dublin politicians and for those in search of political favors.

C126:31, pe126:30, P138:28   **a black sheep**   The implication is that
Father Keon has "wandered" from his vocation in the priesthood and
has been "deprived of jurisdiction" (silenced) by his bishop; thus he
can no longer say Mass or hear confession but lives ambiguously between the priesthood and the laity. Apparently he has not behaved
scandalously enough to be excommunicated or courageously enough to
attempt reentry into life as a lay person. See *Dub* C10:8–9n and *Por*
C160:3n.

C126:33, pe126:33, P138:31   **how does he knock it out?**   How does
he make a living?

C127:1, pe126:35, P138:33   **chapel**   See *Dub* 97:25n.

C127:11, pe127:10, P139:9   **goster**   Irish dialect: bluster, bully, brag,
gossip.

C127:11, pe127:10, P139:10   **Alderman Cowley**   Not listed in *Thom's* as a member of the Municipal council in 1900–04, but he is also cited as a member in *Ulysses*, p. 246.

C127:16, pe127:15, P139:15   **Yerra**   After the Irish *aire*, "take care, look out, look you" (P. W. Joyce, p. 61).

C127:16, pe127:16, P139:16   **hop-o'-my-thumb**   A diminutive person. In one of Charles Perrault's (1628–1703) *Mother Goose Stories*, Hop-o'-my-thumb is the minute hero who by his cleverness and ingenuity saves his full-sized brothers and himself from an ogre.

C127:20, pe127:19, P139:20   **Suffolk Street corner**   A short block north of the ward committee room in Wicklow Street.

C127:28–29, pe127:28–29, P139:29–30   **Driving out of the Mansion House . . . in all my vermin**   The Mansion House in Dawson Street in east-central Dublin south of the Liffey is the official residence of the lords mayor of Dublin. On state occasions the lord mayor wore ermine-trimmed robes and rode in an ornate horse-drawn coach.

C128:8–9, pe128:6–7, P140:8–9   *a Lord Mayor . . . pound of chops*   Timothy Charles Harrington (1851–1910) was lord mayor of Dublin from 1901 through 1904. He came from a lower-class background and was well-known for his simple tastes and for his unswerving loyalty to Parnell.

C128:10, pe128:8, P140:10   **Wisha**   A mild Irish expression of surprise.

C128:27–28, pe128:27, P140:30   **O'Farrell's**   Unknown in the vicinity, apparently fictional.

C129:6–7, pe129:4, P141:10   **tinpot way**   I.e., tinker's way: wretched, inferior, paltry; see *Dub* C121:15n.

C129:24, pe129:21, P141:27   **the thin edge of the wedge**   The thin edge of the splitting wedge makes the initial opening in the log, and then the tapered, thick body of the wedge is driven in to split the log.

C129:32, pe129:30–31, P142:2–3   **Dawson Street**   A north-south street of shops and offices (and the Mansion House) between the south side of Trinity College and the north side of Stephen's Green. Only half of the street was in the Royal Exchange Ward.

C129:33, pe129:31, P142:3   **Crofton**   The fictional Crofton, an Orangeman (from Ulster), Protestant, Conservative, and pro-British is mentioned in "Grace," *Dubliners*, and appears as a character in the Cyclops episode in *Ulysses*, pp. 336–45.

C130:13, pe130:11, P142:19   **Did the cow calve?**   When a cow calves, it begins to give milk.

C130:14, pe130:12, P142:20   **Lyons**   See *Dub* C65:10n.

C131:3–4, pe130:35–36, P143:10   **Wilkins, the Conservative**   Unknown and probably fictional, but his name is not Irish.

C131:4, pe130:36, P143:11   **the Conservatives**   The Irish Conservative Party was allied with the Conservative (Tory) Party in England. During the 1890s, when the Conservatives were in power in Parliament, they compromised on the Irish question by continuing and promoting land reform, but they insisted on Union and regarded Home Rule as "marching through rapine and ruin to the dismemberment of Empire."

C131:15–16, pe131:11–12, P143:22–23   **Parkes . . . Atkinson . . . Ward**   Unknown as voters qualified in the Royal Exchange Ward and probably fictional, though the point is that their names are English, not Irish.

C131:17, pe131:13, P143:24   **toff**   British slang; a dandy, an affected gentleman.

C131:19–20, pe131:16, P143:27   *a big ratepayer*   A big payer of property taxes; i.e., he owns a lot of real estate in the city and is not about to do anything to upset the propertied class.

C131:23, pe131:19, P143:31   *Poor Law Guardian*   See *Dub* C119: 12n.

C131:25, pe131:22, P143:33   **the address to the King**   See *Dub* C122:2n.

C132:2, pe131:33, P149:9–10   **Didn't Parnell himself . . .**   When Edward VII, then Prince of Wales, visited Ireland in 1885 Parnell advised all "independent and patriotic people of Ireland" not to respond to the presence of the prince and princess. But Parnell was also involved in a complex balance of power maneuver between the two major English parties, so he took the calculated political risk of asking the Irish to help his game by avoiding all acts of discourtesy, and for the most part, though uncomprehending of British Parliamentary politics, they did.

C132:8–9, pe132:4–5, P144:17   *The old one never went to see these wild Irish*   Queen Victoria (b. 1819, queen 1837–1901). In point of fact Queen Victoria did visit Ireland four times during her reign: in 1849, 1853, 1861, and 1900. In April 1900 she came "in reply to an address of welcome from the Dublin Corporation"; she spent the month in residence at the Vice Regal Lodge in Phoenix Park, Dublin, and was so enthusiastically received that one Irish critic called the public response "idolatrous and utterly unworthy of a free, not to say ill-used, nation." Since the action of this story takes place in 1902, it is strange that the queen's last visit has slipped Mr. Henchy's mind.

C132:13–14, pe132:11, P144:23   **King Edward's life, you know, is not**

the very . . .   King Edward's behavior with married women while he was Prince of Wales was common gossip and was publicly exposed in a divorce trial, as was Parnell's relationship with Mrs. O'Shea.

C133:1–2, pe132:34–35, P145:10–11   **because he was a gentleman**   I.e., Conservatives respected Parnell because he was really one of them, a member of the Anglo-Irish Protestant, land-owning establishment. But from the point of view of many of his gentlemanly English contemporaries Parnell was anathema—a renegade, a traitor to his class.

C133:15, pe133:11, P145:24   **the Chief**   Parnell.

C134:7, pe134:3, P146:16   ***Our Uncrowned King***   An appellation for Parnell, apparently coined by Timothy Michael Healy.

C134:20, pe134:16, P146:29   ***green flag***   Green is the national color of Ireland. It is interesting to note that Parnell (who was a very superstitious man) had a superstitious aversion to green that caused him many unpleasant and embarrassing moments.

C134:27–30, pe134:23–26, P147:7–10   ***Shame on the coward . . . fawning priests***   As a result of the divorce trial and the subsequent scandal, Parnell was deserted by Gladstone and his allies in the British Liberal Party, by the majority of his political supporters in Ireland, and he was condemned from the pulpit by the Irish Roman Catholic hierarchy. The references are also biblical: to the Roman soldiers who mocked the condemned Jesus as "King of the Jews" and beat him (Matthew 27:27–30) and to Judas's kiss-betrayal of Jesus to "the chief priests and elders of the people" (Matthew 26:47–49).

"A Mother"

"A Mother" was the tenth story in order of composition; it was finished in September 1905.

C136:2, pe136:2, P136:19   **Holohan**   Appears as an offstage character in "Two Gallants" and in *Ulysses*; see *Dub* C58:27n.

C136:2, pe136:3, P148:19–20   ***Eire Abu***   Irish: ripe or mature Ireland; the name places the society in the ranks of the "Irish Revival"; see *Dub* C137:25n.

C137:4, pe137:3, P149:14 **a bootmaker on Ormond Quay** The Quay is on the north bank of the Liffey in central Dublin. A bootmaker should not be confused with a cobbler; bootmaking is an honored middle-class profession in England and Ireland.

C137:10, pe137:9–10, P149:20–21 **he went to the altar every first Friday** I.e., he was practicing a nonliturgical devotion in response to the promises made to then Blessed (now Saint) Margaret Mary Alacoque in her visions of the Sacred Heart. See *Dub* C37:13–14n.

C137:17, pe137:17, P149:28 **a society** One of a number of insurance companies often called "Friendly Societies," which offered policies for funeral expenses, wedding expenses, etc.

C137:21, pe137:21, P149:33 **the Academy** The Royal Academy of Music, founded in 1848 and located at 6 Merrion Square, a fashionable address in southeastern Dublin. The *Official Guide to Dublin* (Dublin, n.d.) remarks that it is an institution "which contributed greatly to the rise of Dublin as a noted teaching center" and further that the Academy was "particularly enhanced by the work of Commendatore Esposito." Michele Esposito (1855–1929), Italian pianist, composer, and teacher, taught at the Academy and gave concerts in Dublin. In 1899 he succeeded in establishing a resident symphony orchestra, the Dublin Orchestral Society. An "Irish" symphony by this Italian composer won the Feis Ceoil prize in 1902; see *Dub* C142:32n.

C137:24, pe137:26, P150:3 **Skerries . . . Howth . . . Greystones** Three villages on the Irish Sea, popular as summer resorts during the nineteenth century. Skerries is eighteen miles north of Dublin and was the most fashionable of the three. Howth, nine miles northeast of Dublin, and Greystones, fourteen miles south, were at the time small fishing villages whose populations as much as trebled during the summer months.

C137:25, pe137:17, P150:4 **the Irish Revival** During the 1890s a number of organizations and committees emerged in Ireland dedicated to the revival of things Irish and cultural (language, literature, mythology, folklore, art, music, sports, etc.). The revival movement was as covertly political as it was overtly cultural. The key gesture was the movement to revive the Irish language, spearheaded by the Gaelic League, which was founded in 1893; its avowed aim was, in Douglas Hyde's phrase, "the de-anglicization of Ireland."

C137:26, pe137:28–29, P150:5–6 **to take advantage of her daughter's name** I.e., Kathleen, since Kathleen ni Houlihan is a traditional symbol of Ireland (see Yeats's play, *Cathleen Ni Houlihan*, 1902). But Kathleen Kearney may also owe her name to a song by the Irish writer, Lady Sydney Morgan (1783–1859), "Kate Kearney":

O, did you not hear of Kate Kearney?
She lives on the banks of Killarney,
From the glance of her eye shun danger and fly,
For fatal's the glance of Kate Kearney!
For that eye is so modestly beaming,
You'd ne'er think of mischief she's dreaming,
Yet oh, I can tell how fatal's the spell
That lurks in the eye of Kate Kearney!

O, should you e'er meet this Kate Kearney,
Who lives on the banks of Killarney,
Beware of her smile, for many a wile
Lies hid in the smile of Kate Kearney.
Though she looks so bewitchingly simple,
There's mischief in every dimple;
Who dares inhale her mouth's spicy gale
Must die by the breath of Kate Kearney.

Kathleen Kearney is mentioned with contempt by Molly Bloom in *Ulysses* (pp. 748 and 762).

C137:30, pe137:33, P150:10   **pro-cathedral**   See *Dub* C64:23n.

C137:31–32, pe137:34, P150:11–12   **the corner of Cathedral Street** The Metropolitan Pro-Cathedral is on the corner of Marlborough and Cathedral Streets.

C137:33, pe137:35–36, P150:13   **Nationalist**   See *Dub* C43:15n.

C138:5–6, pe138:7, P150:20–21   **language movement**   See *Dub* C137:25n.

C138:10, pe138:15–17, P150:26   **the Antient Concert Rooms**   At 42 Brunswick Street Great (now Pearse Street) in southeastern-central Dublin, a hall where privately sponsored concerts (and various sorts of meetings) were held.

C138:14–15, pe138:15–17, P150:30–31   **a contract . . . eight guineas**   The payment would not have been exorbitant for four performances had Kathleen Kearney been an experienced performer. As it stands the contract indicates Mrs. Kearney's pretension for her daughter in both the amount of money itself (eight pounds, eight shillings) and the fact that it is expressed as the fashionable "guinea" rather than flatly as eight pounds. In the argument about the payment of the contracted fee later in the story the weight of tradition is against the Kearneys. Theatrical and musical contracts of this quasi-amateur sort were regarded (and still are to a certain extent in England and Ireland) as more promising than binding, provided the person was not an established star. The promise was that the contracted fee would be paid if the concert was a financial success; if not, the performers would share whatever proceeds there were after expenses had been paid. Mrs. Kearney's attitude is in violation of this unstated assumption about the improvisatory nature of economic agreements in the theatrical and concert worlds.

C138:32, pe138:34, P151:14 **charmeuse** A French adjective: bewitching, fascinating, alluring—in context, an advertising word or slogan.

C138:32, pe138:34, P151:14 **Brown Thomas's** Brown, Thomas and Company, silk mercers, general drapers, and milliners in Grafton Street, a fashionable shop which advertised itself in 1904 as having been famous for "the best quality" of Irish laces and linens for one hundred years.

C139:1, pe138:37, P151:17 **two-shilling tickets** Not the best seats in the house, but certainly good seats.

C139:18, pe139:18–19, P152:2–3 **his accent was flat** A lower-class Dublin accent has frequently been described as "flat."

C140:19, pe140:18–19, P153:6–7 **the house was filled with paper** I.e., by the recipients of free tickets.

C141:12, pe141:11, P154:1 *Cometty* In imitation of Fitzpatrick's "flat" accent.

C141:23–24, pe141:23, P154:14 **the General Post Office** On O'Connell Street in central Dublin just north of the Liffey. It has an imposing Greco-Roman Revival façade (1814–18) and was once regarded as the geographical center of Dublin, City and County—all distances were quoted in miles from the G.P.O., etc.

C142:13, pe142:12, P155:6 **the dear knows** A mild Irish oath. See *Por* C225:17n.

C142:23–24, pe142:22–23, P155:16–17 **the part of the king in the opera of *Maritana*** Libretto by Edward Fitzball, music by William Vincent Wallace (1845); see *Dub* C72:1n. "Rousing" and "sentimental," the piece has all the stock theatrical bravado of the mid-nineteenth-century light-opera tradition. The king is the principal bass role in this elaborate Spanish love intrigue. See *Dub* C199:10n.

C142:24, pe142:23, P155:17 **Queen's Theatre** One of the three major theatres in Dublin at the turn of the century. The Theatre Royal was primarily used for dramatic presentations, the Gaiety for the more socially prominent musical events, and the Queen's for the productions that fit neither category.

C142:29, pe142:28, P155:23 *yous* I.e., in his countryman's accent he adds an *s* to "you."

C142:32, pe142:31, P155:26 *Feis Ceoil* Irish: Festival of Music, the annual Dublin music competition, founded in 1897 to promote Irish music.

C144:12, pe144:11, P157:10 **eight guineas** See *Dub* C138:14–15n.

C144:27, pe144:26, P157:25 **The *Freeman* man** The reviewer for the *Freeman's Journal*; see *Dub* C16:12n.

C144:27, pe144:26, P157:25–26 **Mr. O'Madden Burke** Appears as a character in the Aeolus episode (pp. 131ff.) and is mentioned elsewhere in *Ulysses*.

C144:30, pe144:29, P157:29 **the Mansion House** See *Dub* C127: 28–29n.

C145:14, pe145:12, P158:15 **Mr. Hendrick** Apparently fictional, though the Hendricks were a well-known family of Dublin undertakers.

C146:22, pe146:21, P159:27 **Mrs. Pat Campbell** An English actress (1876–1940), friend of George Bernard Shaw. She toured extensively in the provinces and abroad and was noted for her wit.

C147:10, pe147:7, P160:16 *Killarney* A ballad from *Innisfallen*, by Michael William Balfe; see *Dub* C39:3n:

> By Killarney's lakes and fells,
> Em'rald isles and winding bays,
> Mountain paths, and woodland dells,
> Mem'ry ever fondly strays;
> Bounteous nature loves all lands;
> Beauty wanders ev'ry where;
> Footprints leaves on many strands;
> But her home is surely there!
> Angels fold their wings and rest!
> In that Eden of the west,
> Beauty's home, Killarney,
> Ever fair, Killarney.

"Grace"

"Grace" was the twelfth story in order of composition; it was written between October and December 1905. See Preface, p. ix above for a joke about the story's indebtedness to Dante's *Divine Comedy*.

C150:1, pe150:1, P163:16 (title) **Grace** The *Maynooth Catechism* defines grace as "a supernatural gift bestowed upon us by God for our salvation" (p. 24) and refines the definition into two kinds of grace: "Sanctifying grace is that grace which makes the soul holy and pleasing to God . . . . Actual grace is that which helps us to do good works, and to avoid sin" (p. 25). In the world of commerce grace is the extra time allowed a debtor to enable him to settle his debts.

C150:10, pe150:11, P163:27 **curates** Bartenders; see *Dub* C57:11n.

C152:20, pe152:20, P165:35 **Mr. Power** Jack Power appears as a character in the Hades, Wandering Rocks, and Cyclops episodes in *Ulysses*.

C153:4, pe153:3, P166:20 **Grafton Street** See *Dub* C45:20–21n.

C153:5, pe153:4, P166:21 **an outsider** A two-wheeled horse-drawn vehicle with back-to-back seats perpendicular to rather than parallel to the axle.

C153:8, pe153:7, P166:24 **Kernan** Tom Kernan appears as one of the more important minor characters in *Ulysses*, in the Hades, Wandering Rocks, and Sirens episodes.

C153:16, pe153:16, P166:34 **Westmoreland Street** See *Dub* C93:6n.

C153:17, pe153:17, P166:35 **Ballast Office** See *Dub* C94:14n.

C154:5, pe154:4–5, P167:25 **the great Blackwhite** Unknown, but apparently a legendary (or real) supersalesman.

C154:7–8, pe154:7, P167:28 **Crowe Street** Off the north side of Dame Street just south of the Liffey in central Dublin.

C154:8–9, pe154:8, P167:29 **the name of his firm** In *Ulysses* the fictional Kernan has an office at 5 Dame Street (just around the corner from Crowe Street) and works as an agent for the real London tea firm of Pulbrook, Robertson, and Company (p. 239).

C154:9, pe154:9, P167:30 **E.C.** Was the mailing code for the commercial district in central London.

C154:16–17, pe154:17, P168:4 **Royal Irish Constabulary Office in Dublin Castle** The R.I.C. was what Gladstone called a "semi-military police," an armed police under the direct control of the (British) lord lieutenant of Ireland—and armed, as against the tradition of unarmed police in England. This British police presence is not to be confused with the Dublin Metropolitan Police, whose constable Mr. Power dismisses earlier in the story. To an extent the R.I.C. modeled itself after Scotland Yard, but the R.I.C.'s function was much more political than the Yard's. The R.I.C. was charged with the control and suppression of Irish dissidents and thus in effect with the maintenance of British overlordship in Ireland. See *Dub* C125:8n.

C154:24, pe154:25–26, P168:12   **the Glasnevin road**   Glasnevin was a village two miles north of the General Post Office, Dublin. There was no "Glasnevin Road," but the sequence of roads that led from the outskirts of Dublin to the village was often so called.

C154:30–31, pe154:31–32, P168:19–20   **He was surprised at their manners and at their accents**   I.e., Mr. Power perceives them to be from a lower class background than his association with the father had led him to expect.

C154:33–34, pe154:36, P168:23   **that's the holy alls of it**   A literal translation of an Irish saying, the sense of which is: that is the holy and eternal (truth) of it.

C155:14, pe155:14, P169:3.   **Fogarty's**   Possibly P. Fogarty, grocer and tea, wine and spirits merchant, 35 Glengarrif Parade, off North Circular Road on the then northern outskirts of metropolitan Dublin. He is mentioned as Kernan's disappointed creditor in *Ulysses*, p. 99.

C155:19, pe155:19, P169:8   **Martin**   Martin Cunningham appears as an important minor character in *Ulysses*; he is mentioned frequently and appears in the Hades, Wandering Rocks, Cyclops, and Circe episodes.

C156:6, pe156:6–7, P169:32   **the Star of the Sea Church in Sandymount**   Star of the Sea (*Stella Maris*) is an appellation of the Virgin Mary. The Church stands at the corner of Leahy's Terrace and Sandymount Road in Sandymount, a suburban village on the coast about a mile south of the mouth of the Liffey.

C156:15–16, pe156:16–17, P170:7–8   **Glasgow ... Belfast**   The two Protestant cities suggest that, like their father, the Kernan sons were essentially Protestant in their orientation, Catholics in name only.

C156:25, pe156:26–27, P170:18   **to the end of Thomas Street**   From Crowe Street, where Kernan's business is located, it is a mile to Thomas Street, which is in west-central Dublin south of the Liffey. The Guinness Brewery is located in Thomas Street and visitors to the brewery in Kernan's day were given a free glass of stout.

C157:4, pe157:4, P170:32   **Mr. M'Coy**   Appears as a character in *Ulysses*. He is frequently recalled by other characters and is on stage in the Lotus Eaters, Wandering Rocks, and Circe episodes.

C157:9, pe157:10, P171:3   **the pale**   Sometimes called the English pale, the area around Dublin (thirty miles along the coast and twenty miles inland) to which English dominion in Ireland was more or less confined in the fourteenth and fifteenth centuries. To be "in the pale" meant to be in the area under stable authority, safe among (English) friends and protected from the "wild Irish."

C158:4–5, pe158:4–5, P171:35 **the Sacred Heart** See *Dub* C37: 13–14n.

C158:8, pe158:8, P172:3 **the banshee** An Irish nature spirit, which takes the form of an old woman who keens and chants dirges when a death is about to occur.

C158:22–23, pe158:23, P172:19 *The Irish Times* A Dublin daily newspaper; its editorial policy was consistently, though not stridently, conservative and anti-violence.

C158:23, pe158:23–24, P172:20 *The Freeman's Journal* See *Dub* C16:12n.

C158:25, pe158:25–26, P172:22 **the office of the Sub-Sheriff** The office was responsible for process serving, for evictions of tenants who did not pay their rents, for expropriation of personal property for non-payment of debts, etc.

C159:24, pe159:23, P173:23 **bona fide travellers** The laws governing the times when alcoholic beverages could be served in public houses were subject to certain exceptions for those who could prove they were traveling and thus would not be able to "dine" (drink) during the legal hours.

C159:28–29, pe159:28, P173:28 **the Liffey Loan Bank** Apparently fictional, but not without its usurious Dublin precedents.

C160:16, pe160:14, P174:17 **peloothered** Drunk; an uncertain Anglicization of the Irish *phloothered*.

C160:18, pe160:16. P174:19 **True bill** If a bill of indictment returned by a grand jury is endorsed "true bill," the endorsement means that the jury thinks there is enough evidence of guilt in the case to warrant its being brought to trial.

C160:32, pe160:33, P175:2 **bostooms** Or bosthoon, Irish: a flexible rod or whip composed of a number of green rushes laid together, often made by children in play; figuratively (and in contempt) a soft, worthless, spiritless fellow.

C161:10, pe161:10, P175:15 **omadhauns** Irish: stupid people, simpletons, fools.

C161:20, pe161:21, P175:28 **yahoos** Beasts in human form whose depravity is contrasted with the sterile behavior of rational horses, the Houyhnhnms, in book IV of Swift's *Gulliver's Travels* (1726).

C162:17, pe162:17, P176:25 **M'Auley's** A pub, Thomas M'Auley, grocer and wine merchant, 39 Dorset Street Lower, about a block northwest of the Jesuit Church of Saint Francis Xavier in Gardiner Street Upper where the retreat is to be held.

C162:34, pe162:36–37, P177:10–11 **to make a retreat** See *Dub* C32:3–4n.

C163:22, pe163:24, P178:2   **Jesuits**   The Society of Jesus, a religious order of the Roman Catholic Church, founded in 1540 by St.·Ignatius of Loyola (1491–1556), who was elected its first general. Members of the Order were to be bound not only by the three usual vows of religious orders (poverty, chastity, obedience) but also by a vow to go as missionaries wherever the pope might send them. Traditionally, Jesuit training is rigorous and intellectually thorough, with a heavy emphasis on subjugation of the individual will in obedience. The general of the order (*Dub* C163:27, pe163:29, P178:7) is elected for life, with powers that are not absolute (as sometimes popularly believed) but strictly limited by the Constitution of the Order. Within these limitations the general is responsible directly and only to the pope. Administrative and executive officers of the Order are appointed for limited terms by the general. While the Order was "never once reformed" (*Dub* C164:1–2, pe164:1–2, P178:17) in the strict sense of the word, it was subjected to political suppression (1764ff.) and finally to papal suppression (1772). Gradual reestablishment of the Order began in 1792 and climaxed in complete rehabilitation in 1814. The Order has a high reputation for the intellectual standards set and maintained by its members and for the success of its missionaries. St. Ignatius regarded education as a special ministry, and the Order is particularly zealous in and noted for its commitment to education.

C164:5, pe164:5, P178:21   **their church**   The Church of Saint Francis Xavier in Gardiner Street Upper was noted for its well-heeled and fashionable congregation.

C164:27, pe164:29, P179:11   **Purdon**   Purdon Street was one of the central streets in Dublin's red light district at the beginning of the twentieth century. Joyce called the district "Nighttown" and set the action of the Circe episode of *Ulysses* there.

C165:7, pe165:9, P179:27   **Father Tom Burke**   Thomas Nicholas Burke (1830–83), an Irish Dominican, much admired as an orator and familiarly known as "Father Tom." His crusading emphasis was as much if not more political than it was religious. He was famous not only in Ireland but also in England and in the United States, particularly for a series of lectures, "English Misrule in Ireland," and for a detailed defense of the Irish cause, *Ireland's Case Stated* (Dublin, 1873).

C165:19, pe165:22, P180:7   **pit**   Kernan uses the theatrical term instead of the church term "body" or "nave."

C165:24–25, pe165:27–28, P180:13   *The Prisoner of the Vatican*   Victor Emmanuel II (1820–78), first king of Italy (1861–78), defeated the papal army in 1859 and stripped the pope of his temporal power and possessions, finally taking even Rome, which was declared the new capital of a united Italy. Pope Pius IX (b. 1792, pope 1846–78) was thus left in possession of only Vatican City—in effect a prisoner within his own city walls, so he and his successor, Leo XIII, were both styled "the prisoner of the Vatican."

C165:27, pe165:30, P180:15 **an Orangeman** In general, Protestant and politically pro-English. The Orangemen were originally rich and influential Ulster Protestants who were dedicated to the defense of Protestant ascendancy in Ireland. In the late eighteenth century they were called the Peep-of-Day Boys after their predilection for dawn attacks on Catholic households; they were formed into Orange Lodges, named for William of Orange, William III of England (b. 1650, king 1689–1702), whose reign is associated with a vigorous assertion of Protestant supremacy in Ireland.

C165:29, pe165:33, P180:18 **Butler's in Moore Street** A pub, Patrick Butler, wine and spirit merchant, 1 & 2 Moore Street in central Dublin north of the Liffey.

C166:22, pe166:25–26, P181:12–13 **to tie himself to second-class distillers and brewers** I.e., in exchange for financial support Fogarty contracted to sell only his second-class supplier's products. The better pubs tried to keep themselves free (as "free houses") to buy from a number of suppliers and to serve what they pleased and/or what their customers wanted.

C167:5, pe167:7, P181:33 **Leo XIII** Gioachino Pecci (1810–1903), Pope Leo XIII (1878–1903). He was noted for his learning, holiness, and statesmanship and was regarded as "one of the most notable Popes in recent history." In politics he was essentially conservative. He preached against international socialism and in favor of the political *status quo*; somewhat to the consternation of the Irish he was not sympathetic to Irish Nationalist aspirations. One of his primary concerns was the restoration of Christian unity, not only in "the union of the Latin and Greek Churches" (*Dub* C167:6–7, pe167:8–9, P182:1), but also in reunion with the English-speaking churches. It was this latter interest (as well as his political conservatism) that determined his coolness to the Irish "cause" against the English. He was a great advocate of the study of the philosophy of St. Thomas Aquinas—and in some ways a liberal scholar: he provided large sums of money for the Vatican observatory and in 1883 opened the Vatican archives "to all properly qualified scholars" with the assertion that the Church had nothing to fear from "the study of the facts of history." The composition of Latin poetry was one of his favorite relaxations.

C167:8–9, pe167:11–12, P182:3–4 **one of the most intellectual**

men in Europe   Something of an overstatement, considering the
competition.

C167:10–11, pe167:15–16, P182:7   **His motto . . . as Pope**   Strictly
speaking, the popes do not have official mottoes. But in what is now
regarded as a sixteenth-century forgery, *The Prophecy of the Popes*, St.
Malachy of Armagh (1094–1148) was supposed to have had revealed to
him mottoes appropriate for each of the 111 successors to Pope Celes-
tine II, who was elected in 1143. Leo XIII's motto would thus be
Lumen in Coelo, Latin for "Light in Heaven."

C167:17, pe167:22, P182:14   **Pius IX**   Count Giovanni Maria Mastai-
Ferretti (1792–1878), Pope Pius IX (1846–78). He began his career as
an ardent advocate of social, political, and religious reforms, but during
his pontificate a series of revolutions virtually stripped the Papacy of its
territorial powers in Italy and modified his political attitudes. His ecclesiastical administration was active, producing a series of crises by its
radical assertions of the Church's right to independent action. In 1854
he issued a decree propounding as a doctrine of the Church the dogma
of the Immaculate Conception of the Blessed Virgin Mary (until that
time, a matter of pious faith). In 1869 he convened the Vatican Council
for the first time since the Council of Trent (1545–63), and the Council,
amidst some controversy in both the Catholic and Protestant worlds,
decreed the doctrine of Papal Infallibility; the doctrine holds that the
pope, when he speaks in his official (*ex cathedra*) capacity, is not subject
to error.

C167:17, pe167:22, P182:14   **Pius IX . . . motto**   According to *The
Prophecy of the Popes* it would have been *Crux de Cruce*; Latin: literally,
cross from a cross; figuratively, suffering from the cross.

C167:29–30,   pe167:34–35,   P182:31–32   **penny-a-week   school**
Schools "conducted by a private teacher who lived on the fees paid by
his pupils . . . spread all over the country during the eighteenth century and the first half of the nineteenth" (P. W. Joyce, p. 150). P. W.
Joyce (1827–1914) regarded these schools as an outgrowth of the
Hedge-schools (clandestine schools that circumvented the early eighteenth-century Penal Laws and their all but prohibition of education
for Catholics). He says (with praise) that he attended several of these
penny-a-week schools and that "they were finally broken up by the
famine of 1847" (p. 151), and, of course, by the advent of the National
Schools: primary, 1834ff.; intermediate, 1859ff.; see *Dub* C20:29n.

C167:32, pe167:37, P182:32   **with a sod of turf under his oxter**   I.e.,
he brought his contribution to the daily fuel supply. "Oxter" is dialect
English for armpit or the space between the inside of the upper arm and
the body.

C168:4–5, pe168:7–8, P183:5 **one of Pope Leo's poems was on the invention of the photograph** Leo XIII's Latin poem as translated by Robert M. Adams, "The Art of Photography" (1867), in his *Surface and Symbol* (New York: Oxford University Press, 1962), p. 179:

Drawn by the sun's bright pencil,
How well, O glistening stencil,
You express the brow's fine grace,
Eyes' sparkle, and beauty of face.

O marvelous might of mind,
New prodigy! A design
Beyond the contrival
Of Apelles, Nature's rival.

Apelles, a Greek painter of the fourth century B.C. was supposed to have painted grapes so realistically that the birds came to peck at them.

C168:14, pe168:16–17, P183:14 *Great minds are very near to madness* A misquotation of Dryden's line: "Great wits are sure to madness near allied" (*Absalom and Achitophel*, part 1, 1:163).

C168:19, pe168:21, P183:20–21 **some of the popes** At times, particularly during the Renaissance, papal conduct has been somewhat lurid by contrast with the traditional Christian vows of poverty, chastity, and obedience.

C168:21–22, pe168:23–24, P183:23 **up to the knocker** Up to the expected standard.

C168:27, pe168:29, P183:28 *ex cathedra* Latin: literally, from the chair. When the pope speaks *ex cathedra* (i.e., in discharging the office of pastor and doctor to all Christians), he is considered infallible.

C168:33, pe168:35, P183:34 **infallibility of the Pope** Formally decreed by the Vatican Council of 1870; see *Dub* C167:17n.

C169:16, pe169:18, P184:19 **a German cardinal** Johann Döllinger (1799–1890), not a cardinal, nor a member of the Vatican Council of 1869–70, but a priest, politician, historian, theologian, and educator, whose active opposition to the doctrine of infallibility resulted in his excommunication in 1871.

C169:18, pe169:20, P184:21 **a sure five** I.e., a sure thing, after an arrangement of billiard balls which all but guarantees the player a five-stroke, the top score for a single stroke in billiards.

C169:21, pe169:23, P184:24 **John MacHale** (1791–1881), archbishop of Tuam in Ireland (1835–76), and a hero in the Irish struggle against British domination. He succeeded in 1850 in getting the Vatican to sever diplomatic relations with England. He resisted the doctrine of Papal Infallibility until it was approved by the Vatican Council. He was not present or voting on 18 July 1870 when Papal Infallibility was decreed, but he immediately subjugated his will to that of the pope and preached infallibility.

C169:24, pe169:26, P188:27   **some Italian or American**   On 18 July 1870, during the fourth session of the Vatican Council, only two dissenting ballots were cast against the doctrine of Papal Infallibility. The dissenters were Bishop Riccio of Italy and Bishop Fitzgerald of Arkansas. After the balloting, they switched their votes and accepted the doctrine as dogma.

C169:28–170:3, pe169:31–170:4, P184:32–185:9   **There they were at it . . . the Pope spoke**   Archbishop MacHale was against the immediate decree of the doctrine of Infallibility, but this story is a dramatic and highly inaccurate version of his resistance and final acceptance. He was not in attendance at the Vatican Council when the Council voted the decree; he was in Ireland, but when informed that the doctrine was decreed as dogma he is supposed to have accepted with a simple "so be it."

C170:5, pe170:6–7, P185:11–12   **He left the church**   But not of his own volition. Döllinger was excommunicated for his refusal to accept the doctrine of Papal Infallibility in April 1871. He continued an influential career as educator, though he ceased to teach theology and concentrated instead on ecclesiastical history; see *Dub* C169:16n.

C170:17, pe170:20, P185:25   **Sir John Gray's statue**   stands in O'Connell Street in Dublin. Gray (1816–75) was a Protestant Irish patriot, editor, and proprietor of *The Freeman's Journal* (see *Dub* C16:12n). He was also Dublin town councilor and a member of Parliament. Archbishop MacHale did attend the unveiling of the statue to the Protestant Gray, and his presence was remarked as a sign of increasing religious tolerance.

C170:17–18, pe170:21, P185:26   **Edmund Dwyer Gray**   The son (1845–88) of Sir John Gray, he owned and edited *The Freeman's Journal* in his turn and was also active in politics; though he could hardly have been characterized as a patriotic firebrand, he was pro-Home Rule. Kernan misremembers the unveiling, however, because Edward Dwyer Gray, while present, did not speak until a public meeting later in the evening.

C170:25, pe170:28, P185:33   *taped*   Measured, sized up.

C171:12, pe171:14, P186:22   **Get behind me, Satan**   Matthew 16: 21–23:

From that time forth began Jesus to show unto his disciples, how that he must go into Jerusalem, and suffer many things of the elders and chief priests and scribes, and be killed, and be raised again the third day. Then Peter took him, and began to rebuke him, saying, Be it far from thee, Lord; this shall not be unto thee. But he turned and said unto Peter, Get thee behind me, Satan: thou art an offence unto me: for thou savourest not the things that be of God, but those that be of men.

C171:17–18, pe171:19–20, P186:28–29   **renew our baptismal vows** I.e., the individual remakes the vows which his godparents made for him when he was baptized.

C172:3, pe172:3, P187:14   **the Jesuit Church in Gardiner Street**   See *Dub* C164:5n.

C172:13–14, pe172:14, P187:26   **speck of red light**   The sanctuary light indicates the presence of the Blessed Sacrament.

C172:20, pe172:21, P187:34   **quincunx**   An arrangement of five points, one at each of the four corners of a square and one in the center, associated with the pattern of wounds which Jesus received on the cross. Cf. the *Maynooth Catechism*: "Another motive to excite sorrow for our sins, is to consider that the Son of God died for our sins, and that *we crucify Him again* as often as we offend Him" (p. 59).

C172:26, pe172:27–28, P188:6–7   **Mr. Fanning, the registration agent and mayor maker**   As subsheriff, Fanning would have been in charge of the registration of voters in Dublin and would have overseen the Municipal Council's annual election of the lord mayor; see *Dub* C123:21n.

C172:29–32, pe172:31–35, P188:10–14   **Michael Grimes . . . Dan Hogan's nephew . . . Mr. Hendrick . . . poor O'Carroll**   These seem to be fictional or "almost" names rather than the real thing as they might well have been in *Ulysses*. For Hendrick see *Dub* C145:14n.

C173:21–24, pe173:24–27, P189:4–8   ***For the children of this world . . . into everlasting dwellings***   Luke 16:8–9, the conclusion or "point" of Jesus's parable of the unjust steward; the balance of the parable (Luke 16:1–9; passage quoted in "Grace" in italics):

> There was a certain rich man, which had a steward; and the same was accused unto him that he had wasted his goods. And he called him and said unto him, How is it that I hear this of thee? give an account of thy stewardship; for thou mayest no longer be steward. Then the steward said within himself, What shall I do? for my lord taketh away from me the stewardship: I cannot dig; to beg I am ashamed. I am resolved what to do, that, when I am put out of the stewardship, they may receive me into their houses. So he called every one of his lord's debtors unto him, and said unto the first, How much owest thou unto my Lord? And he said, An hundred measures of oil. And he said unto him, Take thy bill, and sit down quickly, and write fifty. Then said he to another, And how much owest thou? And he said, An hun-

dred measures of wheat. And he said unto him, Take thy bill, and write fourscore. And the lord commended the unjust steward, because he had done wisely: *for the children of this world are in their generation wiser than the children of light. And I say unto you, Make to yourselves friends of the mammon of unrighteousness; that, when ye fail, they may receive you into everlasting habitations.*

C174:28–30, peI74:30–32, PI90:15–17   **Well I have looked . . . set right my accounts**   Almost approaches parody of "The Examination of Conscience and Firm Purpose of Amendment," which Irish Catechisms counsel as preparation for the Sacrament of Penance (Confession). For example: "Q. What is the best method to prepare for a good confession? A. The best method to prepare for a good confession is, first, earnestly to beg of God the grace to make a good confession; secondly, to examine carefully our conscience; thirdly, to make acts of Faith, Hope, and Charity; and fourthly, to excite ourselves to a sincere contrition for our sins" (*Maynooth Catechism*, p. 58).

"The Dead"

"The Dead" was the last of the stories in order of composition; it was completed in 1907.

Since the Misses Morkan's party is after "New Year's Eve" (C185:13, peI85:17, P201:16–17) but still during "Christmas time," it must be between the 1st and 6th of January (because the 6th is Twelfth Night, the Feast of Epiphany, the last day of "Christmas"). And since Pope Pius X's November 1903 *Motu Proprio* (see *Dub* C194:21–22n) is a topic for heated discussion, it may very well be early 1904, between Saturday, 2 January, and Wednesday, 6 January.

C175:1, peI75:1, PI90:18 (title)   **The Dead**   Cf. Thomas Moore's song, "Oh, Ye Dead!" from *Irish Melodies*:

Oh, ye Dead! oh, ye Dead! whom we know by the light you give
From your cold gleaming eyes, though you move like men who live.
Why leave you thus your graves,
In far off fields and waves,
Where the worm and the sea-bird only know your bed,
To haunt this spot where all

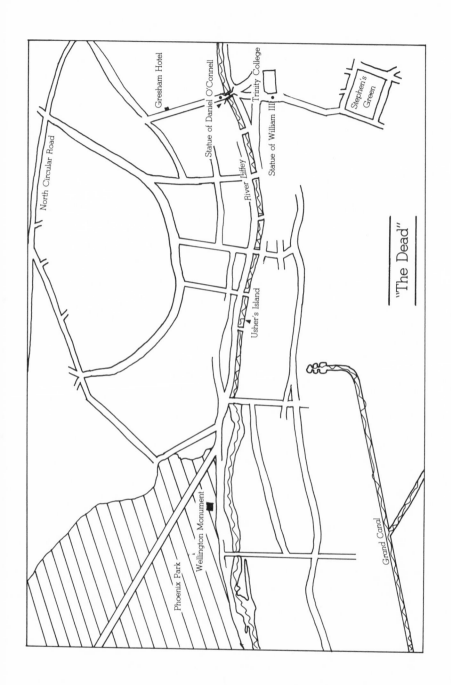

North Circular Road

Gresham Hotel

Statue of Daniel O'Connell

Trinity College

River Liffey

Statue of William III

Stephen's Green

Usher's Island

Phoenix Park

Wellington Monument

Grand Canal

"The Dead"

Those eyes that wept your fall,
And the hearts that wail'd you, like your own, lie dead?

It is true, it is true, we are shadows cold and wan;
And the fair and the brave whom we lov'd on earth are gone,
But still thus ev'n in death,
So sweet the living breath
Of the fields and the flow'rs in our youth we wander'd o'er
That ere, condemn'd, we go
To freeze 'mid Hecla's snow,
We would taste it awhile, and think we live once more!

(Hecla is a volcano in Iceland.)

C175:2, pe175:2, P190:19   **Lily**   An attribute of the Archangel Gabriel, who announced the coming of Jesus to Mary (Luke 1:26–38) and who will also announce the second coming of Christ. The lily serves as a symbol of death and rebirth at funerals and in the ceremony that celebrates the Resurrection at Easter. See *Dub* C176:26n.

C175:7, pe175:8, P190:25   **It was well for her**   See *Dub* C32:11n.

C176:2–3, pe176:2, P191:13   **Stoney Batter**   A street of small shops, tenements, and a few middle-class homes, part of a main thoroughfare to the northwest from west-central Dublin north of the Liffey.

C176:4, pe176:4, P191:15   **Usher's Island**   A section of the Quay on the south bank of the Liffey west of the center of Dublin. The real-life counterparts of the Morkans lived at 15, Usher's Island, a building in part occupied in 1904 by M. Smith & Son, forage contractors, seed and commission merchants, and W. J. Smith, corn merchant. Usher's Island was (and is) a fairly bleak section of the quayside, just east of the industrial sprawl of Guinness's Brewery.

C176:8–9, pe176:8–9, P191:20–21   **the organ in Haddington Road**   She was organist at Saint Mary's Roman Catholic Church in Haddington Road, on the southeastern outskirts of metropolitan Dublin.

C176:9, pe176:8–9, P191:21   **the Academy**   See *Dub* C137:21n.

C176:11, pe176:11, P191:23   **Antient Concert Rooms**   See *Dub* C138:10n.

C176:12, pe176:12, P191:24   **the Kingstown and Dalkey line**   Kingstown (now Dun Laoghaire) and Dalkey, on the southeast headland of Dublin Bay, six and eight miles southeast of the center of Dublin, comprised a fashionable rural-suburban residential district at the beginning of the twentieth century.

C176:14, pe176:15, P191:27   **Adam and Eve's**   Popular name for the Franciscan Church of St. Francis of Assisi in Merchant's Quay, the south bank of the Liffey just east of Usher's Island.

C176:19, pe176:20, P191:32   **three-shilling tea**   Since the price of tea was usually quoted by the quarter pound and the inexpensive quarter pound was eight or nine pence, this tea at 36 pence per quarter pound would have been an expensive, choice tea.

C176:26, pe176:27, P192:6   **Gabriel**   Hebrew, "Man of God," one of the seven Archangels. In Christian tradition Gabriel is charged with the ministration of comfort and sympathy to man. In the New Testament he appears to Zacharias (Luke 1:11–20) to announce the birth and mission of John the Baptist, and, in Luke 1:26–38, he appears to the Virgin Mary to announce the birth of Jesus, the Messiah. Gabriel Conroy may also owe his name to the hero of Bret Harte's (1836–1902) novel, *Gabriel Conroy* (1875). Harte describes his hero as "an uncouth but gentle giant, of superb physique, but modest and diffident in manner and perfectly simple and sincere in character." He escapes from Starvation Camp in the Sierras (California) with his little sister Olly and takes a squatter's claim at One Horse Gulch, where he finds a little gold and where he earns a reputation as a nurse for the sick. Mme. Devarges, a divorcée and adventuress, learns of the presence of silver on Gabriel's claim and, assuming the name of Grace (a variant of Gretta?) Conroy (Gabriel's sister, who is the real owner of the property by inheritance from Dr. Paul Devarges) begins proceedings against Gabriel, but, being saved by him from drowning, changes her mind and marries him instead. The silver is found, and Gabriel becomes rich. He is accused of killing his wife's former suitor and accomplice, Victor Ramirez, and does all in his power to sacrifice himself in order to save his wife, whom he believes to be the guilty person; but on the testimony of Henry Perkins, alias Henry Devarges, he is acquitted. Gabriel had married primarily to give his little sister a female companion, but the birth of a child draws him toward his wife, who has loved him for some time although her original motives in marrying him were purely selfish.

Thus outlined, the characters and plot of Harte's novel do not seem as relevant to Joyce's allusion as do the novel's opening paragraphs with their description of snow:

Snow. Everywhere. As far as the eye could reach—fifty miles, looking southward from the highest white peak—filling ravines and gulches, and dropping from the walls of cañons in white shroud-like drifts, fashioning the dividing ridge into the likeness of a monstrous grave, hiding the bases of giant pines, and completely covering young trees and larches, rimming with porcelain the bowl-like edges of still, cold lakes, and undulating in motionless white billows to the edge of the distant horizon. Snow lying everywhere over the California Sierras on the 15th day of March 1848, and still falling.

It had been snowing for ten days: snowing in finely granulated powder, in damp spongy flakes, in thin, feathery plumes, snowing from a leaden sky steadily, snowing fiercely, shaken out of purple-black clouds in white flocculent masses, or dropping in long level lines, like white lances from the tumbled and broken heavens. But always silently!

Gabriel Conroy is mentioned twice in *Ulysses* (pp. 125 and 377); his wife Gretta is mentioned once (p. 69).

C176:27, pe176:29, P192:8   **screwed**   British slang: drunk.

C177:5, pe177:5, P192:22   **snow**   *The Official Guide* of the Irish National Tourist Publicity Organization remarks, "Snow is relatively infrequent except in the mountains, and when it does occur, it is rarely of serious importance." February is the coldest month of the year in Dublin; the mean temperature of that "cold" month is about 40° F. See *Dub* C176:26n.

C179:9, pe179:10, P194:32   **Robert Browning**   In the closing decades of the nineteenth century Robert Browning (1812–89) was regarded as a difficult and obscure avant-garde poet.

C179:11–12, pe179:12, P194:35   **the Melodies**   *Irish Melodies*, a collection of poems, published in installments (1807–34), written by Thomas Moore (see *Dub* C25:8n). Many of the songs contain new words set to old melodies. "Every Irish household" worthy of the name had a copy.

C179:34, pe179:36, P195:25   **the Port and Docks**   The Dublin Port and Docks Board was charged with the management of the facilities of the Port of Dublin, with the regulation of shipping, and with the collection of customs.

C180:1, pe180:1, P195:26   **to take a cab back**   If the story is set in January 1904, the last train from Dublin to Monkstown would have departed from Westland Row Station at 11:15 P.M.

C180:2, pe180:2, P195:27   **Monkstown**   In 1904 an attractive and relatively affluent village on the south side of Dublin Bay, five miles southeast of the center of Dublin.

C180:6, pe180:7, P195:32   **Merrion**   A village on Dublin Bay, three miles south-southeast of the center of Dublin.

C180:17–18, pe180:19, P196:9   **stirabout**   See *Dub* C9:18–19n.

C180:26, pe180:27, P196:17   **Goloshes**   Made of India rubber or the less elastic gutta-percha. They were first introduced into Great Britain from America in 1847, but it was not until the end of the century that they became fashionable and popular.

C181:12–13, pe181:12–13, P197:7   **Christy Minstrels**   Organized in Buffalo, New York, c. 1843, they flourished throughout the second half of the nineteenth century. The Christy Minstrels gave the minstrel show its stereotype, the semicircular arrangement of the performers in the "first part," with the interlocutor in the middle and the endmen, with bones and tambourines, on the outside. The "second part" or "olio" consisted of variety acts not unlike vaudeville. By 1900 the Christy Minstrels had been so much imitated that the name had become synonymous with the minstrel show and its blackface imitation of southern Negro dialect and song.

C181:17, pe181:18, P197:12   **the Gresham**   Was and still is a fashionable hotel in then Sackville, now O'Connell Street, in east-central Dublin north of the Liffey. That the Conroys can stop there indicates financial well-being.

C182:20, pe182:23–24, P198:19   **Mr. Browne**   George Browne, the first Protestant archbishop of Dublin (1536ff.) was politically shrewd enough to survive the accession of Mary I (and the consequent restoration of the Roman Catholic Church in England and Ireland), but eventually the fact that he had a wife and children cost him his archbishopric. Ellmann notes that a first cousin of Joyce's mother "married a Protestant named Mervyn Archdale Browne, who combined the profession of music teacher with that of agent for a burglary insurance company" (p. 255). See *Dub* C29:7n.

C183:19–20, pe183:23–24, P199:19–20   **the famous Mrs. Cassidy . . . Mary Grimes**   Unknown, but possibly a pair of stock Dublin comic characters like the Pat and Mike of Irish jokes.

C183:23, pe183:27, P199:23–24   **a very low Dublin accent**   Class distinctions and the accents which revealed them could be used (as in this case) for the purposes of low and potentially shocking humor; see *Dub* C139:18n.

C184:9, pe184:14, P200:12   **Mr. Bartell D'Arcy**   An offstage character (as Bartell d'Arcy) in *Ulysses*.

C185:13, pe185:17, P201:16   **the pledge**   I.e., a religious oath to give up drinking.

C186:1–2, pe186:5, P202:5   **her Academy piece**   I.e., a piece designed to display her technical skills and thus her qualifications as a piano teacher; see *Dub* C137:21n.

C186:16–17, pe186:21, P202:22   **the balcony scene in *Romeo and Juliet***   An illustration of act II, scene ii, of Shakespeare's tragedy; Juliet is above on the balcony, Romeo below in the garden.

C186:17–18, pe186:22, P202:22   **the two murdered princes in the Tower**   Richard III of England (b. 1453, king 1483–1485) was reputed to have ordered or at least countenanced the murder (by smothering) of his two nephews, the sons of his older brother, Edward IV. The older of the princes, King Edward V, was under the control of

Richard, then duke of Gloucester, Protector of the Realm; the younger
was Prince Arthur. Before their deaths the two princes had been set
aside as "the fruit of an unlawful marriage" in favor of Richard III's
accession to the throne and had been imprisoned in the Tower of
London. Illustrations of this theme sentimentally depict the apparently
sleeping, actually dead princes as babes-in-the-woods (in a nest of
straw).

C186:22, pe186:27, P202:26   **tabinet**   Or tabbinett, a fabric like poplin with a watered surface.

C186:28, pe186:33, P202:33   **the pierglass**   See *Dub* C65:20n.

C186:29–30, pe186:34, P203:1   **Constantine**   After the Roman emperor, Constantine the Great (b. 270 A.D.? emperor 306–37), a sympathetic, if mildly religious, Christian. The first of the Christian em-
perors, he is credited with having made the Roman Empire safe for
Christianity.

C186:33, pe187:2, P203:5   **Balbriggan**   A town on the Irish Sea twenty miles north of Dublin.

C187:1, pe187:4, P203:7   **the Royal University**   Not an institution of
learning but an examining and degree-granting institution in Dublin,
established by the University Education Act of 1879 and organized in
1880. It reflected English (Protestant) academic standards and effectively determined the curricula of its member institutions (including
Catholic University College, Dublin) by the examinations it set.

C187:22–23, pe187:25–26, P203:31   **large brooch . . . an Irish device and motto**   The revival of interest in the Irish cultural heritage in
the 1890s was the occasion for the appearance of reproductions of Celtic
brooches and other artifacts.

C187:33–34, pe188:2, P204:8   *The Daily Express*   An Irish newspaper published in Dublin (1851–1921), essentially conservative and
opposed to Irish aspirations to nationhood. Its announced editorial policy involved "the development of industrial resources" and a reconcil-
iation of "the rights and impulses of Irish nationality with the demands
and obligations of imperial dominions."

C188:5, pe188:7, P204:14   **a West Briton**   An Irishman whose allegiance is toward England and who therefore accepts Ireland's status as a
provincial "West of England."

C188:14–15, pe188:17–18, P204:24–26   **Hickey's on Bachelor's . . .
O'Clohissey's**   Michael Hickey, bookseller, 8 Bachelor's Walk (the
north quayside of the Liffey, just west of O'Connell Bridge); George
Webb, bookseller, 5 Crampton Quay (on the south bank of the Liffey,
west of O'Connell Bridge, often called Aston's Quay, which actually
continues it east to the bridge); Edward Massey, bookseller, 6 Aston's

Quay; M. Clohissey, bookseller, 10 & 11 Bedford Row (just around the corner and south of the intersection of Aston's Quay and Crampton Quay).

C188:19, pe188:22, P204:30 **at the University** Not that they attended the same university; the implication is that Gabriel has attended University College, Dublin, and that Miss Ivors' career has been parallel at a similar institution for young women. University College, Dublin, was founded as Catholic University by John Henry Cardinal Newman (1801–90) in 1853 and reorganized as University College in 1879–80, when its curriculum was coordinated with the Royal University; see *Dub* C187:1n. From 1883 to 1909 University College, Dublin, was run by the Jesuits.

C188:27–28, pe188:30–31, P205:4 **the University question** The tangled, and in the early twentieth century still unresolved, question of how to provide the Irish with the opportunity for a university education comparable to that of the great Protestant English universities of Oxford and Cambridge (and Trinity College, Dublin), but an education Irish and Catholic in character and atmosphere. Until 1871, candidates for matriculation in English universities (and at Trinity College) were required to pass religious (Protestant) examinations, but even after that requirement was dropped, the cultural climate which had dictated the examinations at the universities continued to prevail. As early as 1845, a British prime minister (Sir Robert Peel), apparently to distract the Irish from their preoccupation with Home Rule, had offered to establish a nonsectarian (and essentially British) Queen's University in Dublin. The offer was rejected by the Irish Catholic hierarchy, which then attempted to found its own university, Catholic University, Dublin (1850), subsequently under the leadership of Newman (see *Dub* C188:19n). But the experiment languished because Catholic University did not have degree-granting powers and thus could not advance its students toward careers. When the Royal University was established, Catholic University was reorganized as University College, Dublin, but the curricula imposed by the Royal University were so undemanding as to be almost ludicrous, and the specifically Catholic and Irish courses of education were relegated to non-credit (virtually extracurricular) status. The result was a continuing non-answer to the "university question" in Catholic Ireland.

C188:32–33, pe188:36, P205:10 **the Aran Isles** Off Galway on the west coast of Ireland. The properly patriotic Irish Revivalist regarded the Isles as an Irish utopia since the natives still spoke Irish and lived in what was sentimentally regarded as true Irish fashion (i.e., in eighteenth-century poverty and superstition).

C189:2, pe189:2–3, P205:13   **Kathleen Kearney**   From "A Mother,"
Dubliners; see *Dub* C137:26n.

C189:4, pe189:4, P205:14   **Connacht**   The northwestern province of
Ireland; it includes County Galway, Gretta Conroy's home county.

C192:5, pe192:7, P208:26   **the park**   Phoenix Park, only a half mile to
the west of Usher's Island; see *Dub* C112:4n.

C192:7, pe192:9, P208:28   **Wellington Monument**   An obelisk just
inside the eastern (main) entrance to Phoenix Park. *Black's Guide to
Ireland* (Edinburgh, 1888) remarks that it was "erected in 1817 by his
[Wellington's] fellow-townsmen of Dublin, to testify their great esteem
for him as a military commander" (p. 30). However, the Dublin-born
Arthur Wellesley (1769–1852), Duke of Wellington, was regarded by
the Irish as another personification of stiff-necked English conservative
attitudes toward Ireland.

C192:10, pe192:12, P208:31   **the Three Graces**   In Greek mythology,
the daughters of Zeus and Eurynome: Agalaia (Brilliance), Euphrosyne
(Joy), and Thalia (Bloom)—the inspirers of those qualities which give
charm to nature and to wisdom, love, social intercourse, etc.

C192:10, pe192:12, P208:31   **Paris**   In Greek mythology, one of the
sons of Priam, king of Troy. He is called upon to judge a beauty contest
among the three principal goddesses of Olympus (Hera, Athena, and
Aphrodite). He chooses Aphrodite, who rewards him with Helen of
Troy and, as a consequence, rewards his family with the Trojan War
and destruction.

C193:1–2, pe193:2, P209:25   **Arrayed for the Bridal**   A lyric by
George Linley to music from Vincenzo Bellini's opera, *I Puritani* (*The
Puritans*, 1835). The song is a free and sentimentalized English version
of the song "A Chaplet of Roses" in act I of the opera. The opera is set
in England after the execution of Charles I and just before Cromwell's
successful termination of the Civil War. A Puritan father wants to
marry his daughter, the heroine, to a Puritan colonel; she prefers a Cavalier (Royalist) lord. The Puritan father also has command of a fortress
and is charged with the care of an important prisoner, Henrietta of
France, Charles I's widow. The heroine wins her father's grudging approval of her Cavalier fiancé—and just as she is "arrayed for the bridal"
(and inspires the song), she drapes her bridal veil playfully over Henrietta's head; the Cavalier fiancé sees in this playful moment the possibility of spiriting his queen away to safety disguised as his bride.
Linley's version of the song:

Arrayed for the bridal, in beauty behold her,
A white wreath entwineth a forehead more fair;

I envy the zephyrs that softly enfold her, enfold her,
And play with the locks of her beautiful hair.
May life to her prove full of sunshine and love,
    full of love, yes! yes! yes!
Who would not love her
Sweet star of the morning! shining so bright,
Earth's circle adorning, fair creature of light,
Fair creature of light.

C194:9–10, pe194:10, P211:1–2   **never would be said**   I.e., gainsaid; an almost obsolete dialect use of the verb *to say*, meaning: to advise, direct, check.

C194:21–22, pe194:24–25, P211:16–17   **for the pope to turn out the women out of the choirs**   A controversy aroused by Pius X's (b. 1835, pope 1903–14) *Motu Proprio* (papal rescript, "of his own accord," i.e., not on the advice of cardinals or others): *Inter Sollicitudines* (with solicitude), 22 November 1903: ". . . singers in churches have a real liturgical office, and . . . therefore women, as being incapable of exercising such office, cannot be admitted to form part of the choir or of the musical chapel. Whenever, then, it is desired to employ the acute voices of sopranos and contraltos, these parts must be taken by boys, according to the most ancient usage of the church."

C195:3, pe195:5, P211:34   **Father Healey**   No priest of this name was listed as attached to Adam and Eve's at the beginning of this century.

C195:19, pe195:21, P212:16   **To take a pick itself**   I.e., "won't you even have a bite." P. W. Joyce explains "that in the common colloquial Irish the usual word to express both *even* and *itself*, is *féin*." Thus an Irish sentence which would correctly be "rendered 'if I had even that much'" will be translated ("because the people don't like *even*") as "if I had that much *itself*" (pp. 36–37).

C196:3, pe196:3, P212:34   **Beannacht libh**   Irish: farewell, my blessing go with you.

C196:13, pe196:14, P213:10   **stage to let**   Theatre slang: it is as though the theatre were for rent; the audience is seated but there are no performers.

C198:18, pe198:19, P215:20   **Theatre Royal**   See *Dub* C142:24n.

C198:22–23, pe198:23–24, P215:25–26   **a Negro chieftain singing in the second part of the Gaiety pantomime**   On 16 June 1904 the Theatre Royal (not the Gaiety) advertised a double feature, the first half of which was "an American Eccentric Comedy-Oddity . . . funnier than a pantomime." The second half of the program was a song and dance recital by the American Negro impersonator, Eugene Stratton (Eugene Augustus Ruhlmann, 1861–1918). See *Ulysses*, p. 92.

C199:2, pe199:3, P216:5   **Mignon**   One of the most popular of nine-teenth-century French operas (1886), by Ambroise Thomas (1811–96). The opera was based, at least by assertion, on Goethe's *Wilhelm Meister* (1796); it focuses on the fortunes of Mignon, a gypsy girl, who is finally revealed as being of noble birth. In the course of the opera Mignon loses her wits through the suffering of unrequited love and the shock of being trapped in a burning castle. Miraculous coincidence restores sanity and resolves all at the opera's end.

C199:3, pe199:4, P216:6–7   **poor Georgina Burns**   Unknown.

C199:5–6, pe199:6–8, P216:9–10   **Tietjens, Ilma de Murzka, Campanini, the great Trebelli, Giuglini, Ravelli, Aramburo**   Therese Tietjens (1831–77), a German dramatic soprano, went to London in 1858 and was popular there and on tour in the British Isles until her death. Ilma de Murzka (1836–89) was a dramatic soprano whose success on tour was worldwide before her death by suicide. Italo Campanini (1846–96) was an operatic tenor of considerable note in his time; his most famous role was in *Lucrezia Borgia* (a great favorite with the Dublin audience). Zelia Trebelli (1838–92) was a French mezzo-soprano who was extraordinarily popular in London. The career of Antonio Giuglini (1827–65), an Italian operatic tenor who sang in London after 1857, was ended by insanity in 1864. Antonio Aramburo, a Spanish tenor, made his debut in Milan in 1871. He is reputed to have had a voice of perfect timbre and was successful on tour in Europe and in South America. Ravelli flourished in the 1880s as an operatic tenor in the Naples Opera Company. He was famous for his hatred of soprano Minnie Hauk, who once choked his high B flat with a too comprehensive embrace, and his expression of rage, being understood by the audience as a tremendous outburst of dramatic enthusiasm, was loudly applauded.

C199:8, pe199:10, P216:12–13   **the old Royal**   Destroyed by fire in 1880 and subsequently replaced by a new Theatre Royal; see *Dub* C142:24n.

C199:10, pe199:12, P216:14–15   **Let me like a Soldier fall**   The hero (tenor) of the opera *Maritana* (see *Dub* C142:23–24n) is condemned to die as a result of the villain's complex plotting. The hero's death is to be by hanging (ignominious), but the villain arranges to switch the sentence to death before a firing squad (the honorable soldier's death), provided the hero marry Maritana first! The hero, Don Caesar de Bazan, proclaims his pleasure:

Yes! let me like a Soldier fall,
Upon some open plain;

This breast expanding for the ball,
To blot out every stain.
Brave, manly hearts, confer my doom,
That gentler ones may tell,
However forgot, unknown my tomb,
I like a Soldier fell,
Howe'er forgot, unknown my tomb,
I like a Soldier fell!

C199:15, pe199:17, P216:20 *Dinorah* Popular name for *Le Pardon de Poërmel* (1859), French opera in three acts, libretto by Jules Bertier and Michel Carré, music by Giacomo Meyerbeer (1791–1864). The opera was particularly popular with florid sopranos since throughout most of the opera the heroine, Dinorah, wanders about demented by the loss of her lover and by the coincidence of other disasters, such as the thunderbolt that strikes her house as she is about to be married. The plot is a gothic web of sorcerers and treasure with a curse on it. At the climax of the opera, Dinorah plunges into a raging torrent and is rescued both physically and mentally by her former fiancé.

C199:15, pe199:17–18, P216:20 *Lucrezia Borgia* Italian opera in a prologue and two acts (1833), libretto by Felice Romani from Victor Hugo's play *Lucrèce Borgia*, music by Gaetano Donizetti (1797–1848). This opera was another favorite vehicle of the florid soprano, largely because the title role gives such scope for flamboyant performance. Lucrezia is portrayed as the arch-poisoner, and the opera climaxes in a banquet scene with a mass poisoning revealed by Lucrezia's announcement that coffins have been provided for all the guests.

C199:22, pe199:24, P216:27 **Caruso** Enrico Caruso (1874–1921), Italian dramatic tenor, whose name was by 1910 a household word for the great opera star. He first attracted attention in Naples in 1896; after a series of tours, including London (1903), he went to New York (1904), where he was destined to become the chief attraction of the Metropolitan Opera House Company.

C199:32, pe199:35, P217:5 **Parkinson** Probably fictional, although there was at least one theatrical Parkinson. In the Theatre Collection of the Lincoln Center Library in New York there are two letters from Henry Carres Parkinson to a friend, both dated London, 1879. What evidence there is suggests that Parkinson was a performer in comedies with incidental music and in pantomimes; it certainly does not imply that he sang in opera.

C200:17, pe200:19, P217:26–27 **I'm all brown** See *Dub* C29:6n. Bernard Benstock suggests that Browne's remark may be the punch line of an off-color joke.

C200:25, pe200:27, P218:1-2 **Mount Melleray** In County Waterford in southeastern Ireland, the site of a Cistercian (Trappist) abbey, founded in 1832 by Irish monks expelled from France in 1822. The abbey guest house dispensed hospitality technically without charge and was known as a refuge for well-heeled alcoholics in need of a cure.

C200:27, pe200:30, P218:4-5 **never asked for a penny-piece** The monks' hospitality was free, but in practice the abbey's guests were expected to and did make donations to the abbey.

C201:6, pe201:6, P218:17 **the rule of the order** The Trappists, a branch of the Cistercian Order, are well-known for the rigors of their rule; they do observe the rule of perpetual silence; the Trappist day does begin with Matins at 2 A.M.; but the Trappist Rule does *not* dictate that the monks sleep in their coffins, rather that they sleep in their habits, removing only their shoes, and "the dead are to be buried in their habits without coffins." The story of the coffin-bed is a not unusual lay embellishment of the rules of religious orders thought to be rigorous.

C202:10, pe202:10, P219:24-25 **The Wellington Monument** See *Dub* C192:7n.

C202:12, pe202:11-12, P219:26 **Fifteen Acres** A large open field in the south-central section of Phoenix Park; it was the site of frequent military reviews and formal maneuvers.

C203:33, pe203:32-33, P221:18 **the world will not willingly let die** After Milton in *The Reason of Church Government* (1641), Introduction, book ii: "By labour and intent study (which I take to be my portion in this life), joined with the strong propensity of nature, I might perhaps leave something so written to after times as they should not willingly let it die."

C204:16, pe204:14-15, P222:2 **the Three Graces** See *Dub* C192:10n.

C204:26, pe204:24, P222:11 **Paris** See *Dub* C192:10n.

C205:17-20/25-26, pe205:15-18/24-25, P223:4-7/13-14 *For they are jolly . . . tells a lie* Traditional drinking song after the eighteenth-century French popular song "Malbrouk s'en va" ("Marlborough Has Left"). The Duke of Marlborough (1650-1722) was a brilliant and successful English general (at the expense of the French).

C206:11, pe206:12, P224:3 **laid on** Supplied by plan.

C207:26-27, pe207:29, P225:20 **a military review in the park** At the Fifteen Acres in Phoenix Park; see *Dub* C202:12n.

C207:33, pe207:35, P225:26-27 **Back Lane** A street in a rundown area in central Dublin south of the Liffey.

C208:7, pe208:7-8, P225:34 **King Billy** William of Orange, King William III of England (b. 1650, king 1689-1702). Protestant William

won the Battle of the Boyne in 1690 and went on to thoroughly suppress yet another Irish bid for independence. His reconquest of Ireland
in effect turned the country into a penal colony. He is consequently remembered with a cordiality similar to that accorded Cromwell as a
great oppressor. A frequently vandalized and much mocked equestrian
statue of King William stood in College Green in front of Trinity College at one of the busiest intersections in Dublin.

C209:14, pe209:13, P227:7   **Trinity College**   I.e., they are to drive
east about three quarters of a mile.

C210:9, pe210:7–8, P228:3   *Distant Music*   From Charles Dickens,
David Copperfield (London, 1849–50), chapter LX. Copperfield, having just returned from three years abroad and having begun to establish
himself as a writer, visits Agnes Wickfield, whom he has loved "as a
sister" and whom he is subsequently to marry. Copperfield has been
thinking about his first wife, Dora, who was sweet and appealing but
childishly inadequate to marriage. Agnes speaks to Copperfield about
"Dora's grave," and Copperfield muses:

> With the unerring instinct of her noble heart, she touched the chords of my
> memory so softly and harmoniously, that not one jarred within me; I could
> listen to the sorrowful, distant music, and desire to shrink from nothing it
> awoke. How could I, when, blended with it all, was her dear self, the better
> angel of my life?

C210:19, pe210:17, P228:13   **the old Irish tonality**   Early Irish music
was based on a five-tone scale; later (some time before the seventeenth
century) a sixth and seventh tone were added. Attempts to translate the
old scales into the eight-tone octave of the modern diatonic scale usually have strange intervals and rather uncertain results.

C210:23–25, pe210:22–24, P228:18–20   *O, the rain falls . . . lies
cold*   From "The Lass of Aughrim," a western Ireland version of
"The Lass of Lochroyan [or Loch Royal]," Child Ballad #76. The lass,
peasant-born, is seduced and abandoned by a lord. With her child in
her arms she seeks the lord in his castle and is turned away by the lord's
mother, who imitates her son's voice through the closed door. The
quoted lines are a variant of the lass's complaint as she stands in the
rain. Rejected, the lass puts to sea, and she and her child are drowned.
But the lord meanwhile has dreamt of her arrival, gets the truth from
his mother, and pursues the lass, only to witness the drowning. The
ballad closes with the lord's lament and with the curse he calls down on
his mother. Aughrim is a small village in the west of Ireland, about
thirty miles east of Galway.

The words of the song (incomplete) which Nora Joyce could recall and which she sang to Joyce (quoted by Richard Ellmann in *James Joyce* [New York: Oxford University Press, 1959], p. 295):

> If you'll be the lass of Aughrim
> As I am taking you mean to be
> Tell me the first token
> That passed between you and me.

> O don't you remember
> That night on yon lean hill
> When we both met together
> Which I am sorry now to tell.

> The rain falls on my yellow locks
> And the dew it wets my skin;
> My babe lies cold within my arms:
> Lord Gregory let me in.

C211:22–23, pe211:20–21, P229:18–19   **We haven't had snow like it for thirty years**   See *Dub* C177:5n.

C212:10, pe212:9, P230:8   *The Lass of Aughrim*   See *Dub* C210:23–25n.

C213:2, pe212:36, P231:2   **the palace of the Four Courts**   A large eighteenth-century building that houses the courts of Ireland, on the north bank of the Liffey between Usher's Island (where the Morkans live) and east-central Dublin (where the Conroys are to spend the night at the Gresham Hotel).

C214:17, pe214:15, P232:22   **Winetavern Street**   Intersects the quayside on the south bank of the Liffey about three hundred yards east of Usher's Island.

C214:25, pe214:24, P232:31   **O'Connell Bridge**   Over the Liffey just east of the center of Dublin; it gives north into O'Connell Street, where the Gresham Hotel is located.

C214:31, pe214:30, P233:2   **the statue**   The pedestaled statue that stands in the northern approach to O'Connell Bridge is of Daniel O'Connell (1775–1847), the Irish political leader known as "The Liberator" because he successfully agitated for the 1829 repeal of the laws that limited the civil and political rights of Catholics. As leader, his chief political weapon was "moral force" within the limits of constitutional procedures, though his followers pressed him to use illegal and violent means. His agitations for repeal of the Act of Union, which had dissolved the Parliament of Ireland into the Parliament at Westminster in 1800, were carried out in a series of "monster meetings" (1841–43) which he organized to demonstrate Irish unanimity and which were interrupted when he was tried and sentenced to one year in prison for "seditious conspiracy." The end of his career was marred not only by his failing health but also by mounting dissension between the constitutional moderates and the New Irelanders within his own party.

C217:19–20, pe217:18–19, P235:29–30 **at Christmas, when he opened that little Christmas-card shop** Traditionally, Christmas cards in the British Isles were sold in temporary shops opened specifically for the purpose and usually devoted to a charity.

C217:20, pe217:19, P235:30 **Henry Street** In 1900 a street of modestly prosperous small shops in central Dublin north of the Liffey; see *Dub* C102:21n.

C219:5, pe219:4, P237:16 **Michael** Hebrew: "Who is like God?" In Christian tradition Michael is the archangel of the Church Militant. He is mentioned in the Bible as disputing with Satan about the body of Moses (Jude 9) and as warring against the dragon, Satan, and his forces in the upper regions (Revelation 12:7–9). He also keeps watch and records the deeds of all men in the heavenly books.

C219:13, pe219:12, P237:24–25 **go out walking with** Irish colloquialism for "we were dating." The implication is that they met and walked in full view of their neighbors and thus were chaperoned.

C219:28, pe219:28, P238:8 **the gasworks** A utilities plant where gas for lighting and heating was manufactured from coal. One of the chief byproducts was air pollution, and the work was notoriously dirty and unhealthy.

C220:12, pe220:10, P238:23 **great** "Intimate, closely acquainted . . . (All over Ireland)" (P. W. Joyce, p. 268). The connotation of the word is the intimacy of friendship rather than of "love."

C220:18, pe220:16, P238:30 **I think he died for me** In Yeats's play, *Cathleen ni Houlihan* (1902), Cathleen, the Poor Old Woman, is the embodiment of Ireland who, though old and withered, appears young and beautiful to the true patriots. She is asked about a martyr-patriot, "yellowed-haired Donough that was hanged in Galway," and she responds, "He died for love of me: many a man has died for love of me." The skeptical father regards this as evidence that "her wits [are] astray," because he can only see an old woman, but the ardent son, Michael, is drawn toward her and will eventually follow her, presumably to his death in the Rebellion of 1798 (*Collected Plays* [New York, 1934], p. 82).

C220:32, pe220:31, P239:10 **Oughterard** A small village in the west of Ireland, seventeen miles west-northwest of Galway.

C221:16, pe221:13, P239:28 **Nuns' Island** The city of Galway on the west coast of Ireland is bisected by the Galway River which, with its attendant channels and canals, creates several semi-islands within the city. One of those islands is Nun's Island, named after the Convent of the Poor Clares, which is located on it. Nun's Island is also a street on which the convent opened in what was, in the late nineteenth century, an old and rundown section of the city.

C221:23, pe221:19–20, P239:35   **get his death**   "To get one's death" is a common expression in Irish, and it has passed directly into the English spoken in the west of Ireland.

C222:28, pe222:25, P241:10   **Arrayed for the Bridal**   See *Dub* C193:2n.

C223:29, pe223:25, P242:11   **Bog of Allen**   Twenty-five miles west-southwest of Dublin, originally an extensive area of bog, now partially reclaimed.

C223:30, pe223:26, P242:12   **Shannon**   A meandering river and estuary in the west of Ireland, west-southwest of Dublin.

NOTES FOR

A Portrait of the Artist
as a Young Man

(1916)

NOTE ON ABBREVIATIONS

The letters and numerals at the head of each annotated word or phrase indicate edition, page, and line.

C5:2   Viking Compass Edition, corrected by Chester G. Anderson and edited by Richard Ellmann (New York, 1964), page 5, line 2.

pe5:2   Penguin Books (New York, 1976), page 5, line 2.

P243:3   *The Portable James Joyce* (New York, 1968), page 243, line 3.

References to other notes in this volume are labeled *Dub* for *Dubliners* and *Por* for *A Portrait of the Artist as a Young Man*.

Readers of *Ulysses* are well aware of how the sustained analogy to *The Odyssey* structures Joyce's novel and of how that analogy informs us of the importance and significance of "trivial things"—importance and significance all but unavailable to the central characters in the fiction. Significances in *Ulysses* are also reenforced and rendered more subtle by sustained analogies to *Hamlet*, to Mozart's *Don Giovanni*, and to the Christian and Judaic liturgical calendars.

A *Portrait* is not informed by an analogy as complex and sustained as the analogy to *The Odyssey* in *Ulysses*, but there is the presence of Ovid's story of Daedalus and Icarus (see *Por* C5 : 2n) and the recurrent pattern of Daedalian (or rather Icarian) flight and fall, which seems to provide the overall structural rhythm of the novel.

Locally, the structure of the second section of chapter V (V : B), the episode in which Stephen awakes to compose a villanelle, is informed by a similar episode in Gabriele D'Annunzio's *Il Piacere* (1889); see the headnote to V : B below, pp. 260–61.

The narrative structure of *A Portrait* also shows some striking parallels to that of Ibsen's *Brand* (1866)—as Stephen's spirit may well owe something to what Joyce called "the will-glorification in *Brand*."[1] Brand asserts: "My infant soul grew up in loneliness" (act I, scene ii)[2], as Stephen has learned to "taste the joy of his loneliness" (chapter II : B). At the beginning of *Brand* II : ii, Brand refuses to become a parson on the note, "I have a greater duty laid on me" (p. 67), as Stephen will refuse a vocation in the priesthood. After his initial (and, as it turns out, temporary) refusal, Brand has a vision of a young woman, a vision which he regards as prophetic, just as Stephen encounters in the young woman in the tidal pool (IV : C) "the angel of mortal youth and beauty." Further, in II : ii, Brand's mother accuses him of taking unnecessary risks (pp. 72–73) as Stephen's mother is "hostile to the idea" of the university in IV : C and V : A; and Brand's mother wants Brand to improve the family's frayed fortune as Stephen foresees "a worldly voice would bid him raise up his father's fallen state by his labours" (II : C). Brand, to mollify his mother, promises, "And with a song, beside your pallet's foot, / [I] Will cool the burning fever in your blood" (p. 78), as Stephen has, in the interim between *A Portrait* and *Ulysses*, sung Yeats's song, "Who Goes with Fergus," to his mother to comfort her while she is on her deathbed.

Brand, in II : ii, reflects, "No ostentatious show of mighty works / Can stir the nation's conscience to repent" (p. 81), as Stephen wonders in V : C, "How he could hit their conscience . . . that they might breed a race less ignoble than their own?" At the end of II : ii Brand decides to become a parson and asserts: "My claim is 'nought or all'" (p. 82), a claim not all that different from Ste-

1. *The Critical Writings*, ed. Ellsworth Mason and Richard Ellmann (New York, 1959), p. 54.
2. This and all subsequent references to *Brand*, trans. G. M. Gathorne-Hardy (Seattle, 1966), p. 51.

phen's battle cry, "I will not serve," in V:C, and strikingly similar to Stephen's repeated "claim" in *Ulysses*, "All or not at all" (p. 49), and, "With me all or not at all" (p. 582). (Compare the no-compromise stance of Hauptmann's Michael Kramer, *Dub* C108:4n.)

In III:i, armed with his "awful slogan" (p. 94), Brand refuses to visit and absolve his dying mother (p. 92), as Stephen's slogan urges him to refuse to perform his Easter Duty (*Por* 239:1–2n) at the end of *A Portrait* and to refuse to pray at his mother's deathbed in the interim between *A Portrait* and *Ulysses*. Brand's mother observes that he is all "will" and no "love" (p. 90)—what Brand would call no "compromise" (p. 88). In *A Portrait* V:C Cranly asks Stephen three times whether he has ever felt love. Stephen avoids the question and defines his attempt "to love God" as "I tried to unite my will with the will of God, instant by instant." Brand's mother's last words are: "God's not inexorable like my son" (p. 105), and when the Doctor urges Brand "to be humane" (p. 105), Brand rejects "that limp and feeble word" with scorn (p. 105). At the end of *A Portrait* Stephen reports in his diary that his mother "prays . . . that I may learn in my own life . . . what the heart is and what it feels." Obviously, Mrs. Dedalus's prayer can be dismissed as the sentimental cliché which it is, but it can also be taken as an apt assessment of her son's state, an aptness that is reenforced if the analogy to *Brand* holds.

The analogy between the life-histories of Brand and Stephen may end there, with Stephen's future unforeclosed as against Brand's career, which continues toward closure: in act IV Brand's "all or nothing," "no compromise" stance causes the sacrificial deaths of his son and then his wife. In act V his crusade is to "build one vast cathedral of our land" (p. 186) and his refusal of even a "truce with compromise" (p. 189) results in his being abandoned by and then stoned by his parishioners. In the final scene, V:iii, Brand, on the mountain crest, has a climactic vision of Norway's materialism and cowardice. Briefly, Brand is imaged as Christ (p. 207), just before the avalanche wipes him out and the voice-over proclaims: "GOD IS LOVE" (p. 209).

If the analogy to *Brand* holds (and there are too many coincidences between the action of *Brand* II:ii and Stephen's career for the relationship not to be at least suggestive), then it is the last third of *Brand* (after the mother's death) that urges an emphasis on the difference between annotation and interpretation. Annotation can and does say: these are the parallels, and they stop *here*. The question for interpretation remains: is the last third of Brand's career an implicit outline of what Stephen's fate could be if he does not learn to love? And the answers to that question will depend not only on interpretive criticism of the internal coherence of *A Portrait* but also on interpretations of *Ulysses* and our perception of the interrelation between the two novels and beyond that on interpretation of the whole canon of Joyce's work, of its relation to biography and to the literary and cultural climates of his time and ours.

C5:2, pe5:2, P243:3 (epigraph)   *Et ignotas animum dimittit in artes* Latin: "And he sets his mind to work upon unknown arts." The passage in Ovid's *Metamorphoses*, VIII: 188, continues, "and changes the laws of nature." The lines are from the description of Daedalus's creation of wings for his (and his son Icarus's) escape from the Cretan Labyrinth and from Crete. Daedalus in Greek means "cunning artificer," and in Greek mythology Daedalus is the archetypical personification of the inventor-sculptor-architect. He is exiled from Athens because he has murdered his nephew Talus out of jealousy for Talus's extraordinary promise as an inventor. Daedalus goes to Crete, where he is attached to the court of King Minos. He constructs an artificial cow for Queen Pasiphaë so that she can fulfill her lust for a semi-divine bull, and then Daedalus constructs the Labyrinth to house the Minotaur, the half-bull-half-man offspring of the queen's affair. Minos then confines Daedalus and Icarus in the Labyrinth, but Daedalus contrives their escape by fashioning wings of wax and feathers. Icarus, in the excitement of being able to fly, flies too near the sun; his wings disintegrate and he falls into the sea. Daedalus escapes to Sicily, where he finds security and is able to live out his life creatively.

Ovid: Publius Ovidius Naso (B.C. 43–A.D. 18), Roman poet whose *Metamorphoses* are a compendium of the stories of miraculous transformations in Greek and Roman mythology, from the creation to the time of Julius Caesar, whose change into a star is the last story of the series.

Chapter I: Section A

C7:2, pe7:2, P245:2 **a moocow** Echoes "silk of the kine," in Irish idiom, the most beautiful of cattle, an allegorical epithet for Ireland. George Moore said to A. E. (George William Russell) about her: "Before the tumult she was." John Joyce, in a letter to his son James, 31 January 1931: "I wonder do you recollect the old days in Brighton Square [Rathgar, 1882–84], when you were Babie Tuckoo, and I used to take you out in the Square and tell you all about the moo-cow that used to come down from the mountain and take little boys across?" (*Letters of James Joyce* [New York, 1966], 3:212). Versions of this story are still current in Connemara in the west of Ireland: the supernatural (white) cow takes children across to an island realm where they are relieved of the petty restraints and dependencies of childhood and mag-

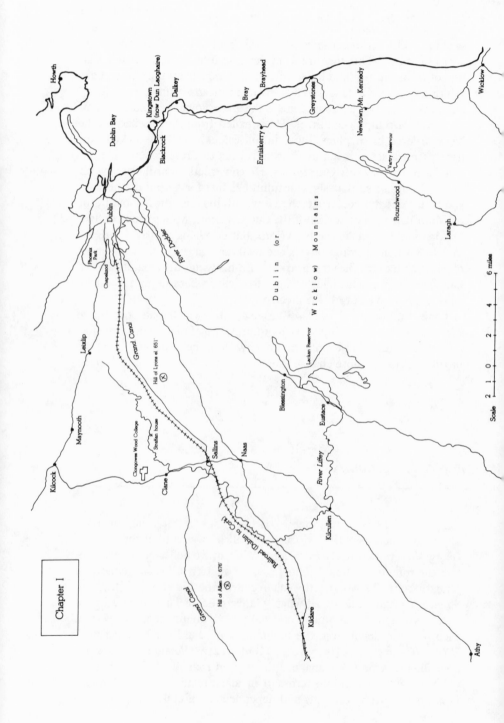

Chapter 1

Howth

Dublin Bay

Kingstown (now Dun Laoghaire)
Dalkey

Blackrock

Bray
Brayhead

Enniskerry

Greystones

Newtown Mt. Kennedy

Wicklow

Vartry Reservoir

Roundwood

Laragh

Dublin

Phoenix Park

Chapelizod

River Dodder

D u b l i n   (o r   W i c k l o w)   M o u n t a i n s

Leixlip

Grand Canal

Hill of Lyons el. 651'

Maynooth

Clongowes Wood College

Strafan house

Kilcock

Clane

Sallins

Naas

Blessington

Leckan Reservoir

Eustace

River Liffey

Kilcullen

Grand Canal

Hill of Allen el. 676'

Railroad (Dublin to Cork)

Kildare

Athy

Scale   2   1   0   2   4   6 miles

ically schooled as heroes before they are returned to their astonished parents and community.

C7:4, pe7:4, P245:4 **tuckoo** Suggests being tucked in bed, but "tuckin" (or "tuckout") is also Irish slang for a good meal, a feast.

C7:5, pe7:5, P245:5 **His father** Simon Dedalus appears as a character in the Hades, Aeolus, Wandering Rocks, Sirens, and Circe episodes in *Ulysses*; he is also frequently mentioned and recalled by other characters on that day, 16 June 1904.

C7:6, pe7:6, P245:6 **a glass** A monocle.

C7:13–14, pe7:14, P245:14 **His mother** Mary (May) Goulding Dedalus dies in the interim between *A Portrait* and *Ulysses* and is buried on 26 June 1903 (*Ulysses*, [New York, 1961], p. 695). On 16 June 1904 her importunate ghost still haunts Stephen, and she is variously recalled and mentioned by other characters.

C7:8, pe7:8, P245:8 **Betty Byrne** *Thom's Official Directory of the United Kingdom of Great Britain and Ireland* (Dublin, 1904) lists an Elizabeth Byrne as a grocer at 46 Main Street in Bray (where the Joyces lived at 1 Martello Terrace, 1887–92). Bray, "the Irish Brighton," is on the coast thirteen miles south-southeast of the center of Dublin.

C7:8, pe7:8, P245:8 **lemon platt** Candy made of plaited sticks of lemon-flavored barley-sugar.

C7:9–10, pe7:9–10, P245:9–10 *O the wild rose blossoms / On the little green place* From H. S. Thompson's song, "Lily Dale," chorus:

> "Oh! Lily, sweet Lily, dear Lily Dale,
> Now the wild rose blossoms
> O'er her little green grave,
> 'Neath the trees in the flow'ry vale."

C7:21, pe8:1, P245:23 **Dante** Childish for "Auntie"? Mrs. Riordan is also an offstage presence in *Ulysses* because in addition to her relation to Stephen and his family she lived in the City Arms Hotel when the Blooms were living there. According to *Ulysses* Mrs. Riordan lived in the Dedalus household from "1 September 1888 to 29 December 1891" (p. 680).

C7:23, pe8:4, P245:26 **press** Closet.

C7:24–25, pe8:5–6, P245:27–246:1 **Michael Davitt . . . Parnell** See "An Outline of Irish History," pp. 21–22 above. Since the names are linked here, it is worth noting that the split between the two political leaders (1882ff.) long predated the revelation of Parnell's relation to Mrs. O'Shea. Parnell's parliamentary moderation was suspect from Davitt's point of view, and when the Land League gradually dis-

solved (thanks to limited successes in land reform), Davitt switched
from advocating peasant-ownership to advocating a Henry George policy of land nationalization, a policy too radical for Parnell. Parnell did
not, however, directly repudiate Davitt and his policy but ignored the
policy and undermined Davitt's position.

C7:25, pe8:6, P246:1   **green**   See *Dub* C134:20n.

C7:25–26, pe8:7, P246:2   **cachou**   A candy made from cashew nuts.

C8:1, pe8:8, P246:4   **The Vances lived in number seven**   James
Vance and family (Protestants) lived at 4 Martello Terrace in Bray
(Richard Ellmann, *James Joyce* [New York, 1959], p. 25).

C8:7, pe8:14, P246:11–12   **the eagles will come and pull out his
eyes**   After Isaac Watts (1674–1748), Protestant hymnologist, in *Divine Songs Attempted in Easy Language for the Use of Children* (London,
1715; in facsimile, London, 1971), song XXIII, stanzas 2 and 3:

> Have you not heard what dreadful plagues
> Are threatened by the Lord,
> To him that breaks his father's law
> Or mocks his mother's word?
>
> What heavy guilt upon him lies!
> How cursed is his name!
> The ravens shall pick out his eyes
> And eagles eat the same.

The scriptural basis for Watts's "song" was Proverbs 30:17, "The eye
that mocketh at his father, and despiseth to obey his mother, the ravens
of the valley shall pick it out, and the young eagles shall eat it."

Chapter I: Section B

C8:17, pe8:24, P246:22   **the prefects**   Teachers who functioned as
housemasters and supervised the boys' activities outside the classroom.

C8:19, pe8:26, P246:24   **footballers**   In Irish football, an ancient Irish
game revived in the late nineteenth century. The game is played with
fifteen men on a side. Besides the familiar football goalposts at the ends
of the field there are outer point posts, which provide added oppor-
tunities for scoring. The teams line up for play in two parallel lines, the
opponents holding hands. The ball is then thrown into the center be-

tween the two lines; play begins at once and is continuous. Players advance the ball by kicking it or striking it with the hand. The ball cannot be thrown or carried. As played, the game is as open and rugged as rugby.

C8:25, pe8:32, P246:31   **the third line**   At Clongowes the students were divided into three groups by age: those under thirteen (including Stephen) were in the third line; from thirteen to fifteen, lower line; fifteen to eighteen, the higher line. The higher line was in turn divided into poetry and rhetoric; the lower, into second and first grammar; and the third, into elements and third grammar (see *Por* C12:17n).

C8:27–28, pe8:35–9:1, P247:1–2   **greaves in his number and a hamper in the refectory**   I.e., he has shin guards in his locker and a supply of food delicacies with which he can supplement the school meals.

C8:33, pe9:6, P247:7   **Stephen Dedalus**   Stephen, after the first Christian martyr, stoned to death outside the walls of Jerusalem, c. A.D. 34. He was a Jew educated in Greek and the dominant figure in Christianity before the conversion of Paul (who, as Saul, was one of the witnesses required by the law of Moses at the judicial execution by stoning of the martyr). For Dedalus (Daedalus), see *Por* C5:2n.

C9:9, pe9:15, P247:16   **a magistrate**   In the late nineteenth century there were sixty-four "resident magistrates" functioning as resident judges in every part of Ireland except Dublin. Magistrates were well-paid and traditionally portrayed as living the ideal life of the hunting-shooting-fishing country gentleman.

C9:21, pe9:28, P247:29   **the castle**   The central complex of buildings of Clongowes Wood College, a Jesuit school for boys regarded as the most fashionable Catholic school in Ireland. Clongowes Wood was the site of a medieval castle about four and one half miles north of Sallins (eighteen miles west-southwest of Dublin). In the seventeenth century the castle became a local center of Irish resistance to English rule and was consequently destroyed in 1642 by General George Monck, one of Cromwell's enforcers. In 1667, the grounds were acquired by the Browne family, and the castle was rebuilt. In 1814 the Brownes sold the castle to the Jesuit Order through the Rev. Peter Kenny, S.J., who founded the school and dedicated it to St. Aloysius Gonzaga (see *Por* C56:3–5n). The sale was in part owing to the good offices of Daniel O'Connell (see *Dub* C214:31n), since Father Kenny, as a priest in 1814, had only very limited legal rights and, as a Jesuit, no legal identity. Re the Jesuit Order, see *Dub* C163:22n.

C9:26, pe9:33, P248:1   **two fiveshilling pieces**   A generous sum which, depending on how it was spent, could be equal to as much as

$30 or $40 (1980)—particularly generous because there would have
been little for Stephen to spend it on.

C9:28, pe9:35, P248:3   **to peach on**   Slang: to inform on.

C9:29, pe9:36, P248:4   **the rector**   The administration of Clongowes
Wood College was organized in two divisions: academic affairs, under
the prefect of studies and masters; and housing, discipline, and recrea-
tion, under the minister and prefect of discipline. The rector was administrative head of the school, in charge of both divisions. He in turn
answered to the Rome provincial of the Irish Jesuits, who answered to
the general of the Order in Rome; see *Dub* C163:22n. The rector in the
1880s was the Rev. John Conmee, S. J. (1847–1910). He was subsequently prefect of studies at Belvedere College, Dublin, in the 1890s;
see *Dub* C20:25n. From 1898 until 16 June 1904 he was superior of the
residence at the Jesuit Church of Saint Francis Xavier in Upper Gardiner Street, Dublin. In August 1905 he was named Rome provincial of
the Irish Jesuits. Father Conmee takes his place as a character in *Ulysses* in the first section of The Wandering Rocks episode and is variously
recalled elsewhere in the novel.

C10:7–8, pe10:15, P248:21   **seventyseven to seventysix**   The implication is that it is early October.

C10:11, pe10:19, P248:25   **Hamilton Rowan**   Archibald Hamilton
Rowan (1751–1834), a friend and associate of Wolfe Tone's in the Society of United Irishmen, an organization dedicated to the achievement
of republican independence in Ireland. Rowan was convicted of "seditious conspiracy" in 1794 but escaped from the British troops escorting
him to prison and took refuge at Clongowes Wood Castle. Just as he
closed the library door, the troops are supposed to have opened fire. He
then is supposed to have thrown his hat onto the "ha-ha" from the library window to give the impression that he had leapt from the window
and escaped; meanwhile he hid in a secret room until he could be smug-
gled away to France. He was subsequently pardoned and allowed to return. A ha-ha is a bank or dry moat designed to keep cattle off the lawns
and gardens around a house without obstructing the view. The story of
the escape may very well be schoolboy apocrypha, though Rowan did
get away to France after his conviction.

C10:16, pe10:24, P248:30   **the community**   In this case, the faculty of
the College, the Jesuit priests who teach at the school and the scholastics (novices in the Jesuit Order who are serving as teaching
apprentices).

C10:18, pe10:25–26, P248:32   **Leicester Abbey**   The Abbey of Saint
Mary Pré (St. Mary of the Meadow) in England about one hundred
miles north-northwest of London. Cardinal Wolsey died there in 1530.

C10:19, pe10:27, P248:33–34 **Doctor Cornwall's Spelling Book** James Cornwall (1812–1902) and Alexander Allen (1814–42), *A Grammar for Beginners* (London, 1838); an introduction to the authors' advanced text, *An English School Grammar: With Very Copious Exercises and a Systematic View of the Formation and Derivation of Words* . . . . The texts were standard in primary and intermediate schools in Ireland, thanks to the English-oriented Intermediate Education Board for Ireland (1878ff.).

C10:22, pe10:29, P249:1 **Wolsey** Thomas, Cardinal Wolsey (1475?– 1530) archbishop of York, English churchman and statesman, one of Henry VIII's most powerful and guileful councilors. Wolsey's inability to carry out the king's "Great Matter" (to have the pope declare Henry's marriage to his first wife, Catherine of Aragon, void from the beginning) was eventually magnified into the occasion for his downfall. He died at the Abbey of Saint Mary Pré while he was being conveyed up to London to stand trial for high treason. (There would have been only one "abbot" in the Abbey.)

C10:29, pe10:37, P249:9 **square ditch** The lawns around the castle were protected from cattle by a ditch or ha-ha, but why "square" is not clear. The square was the school name for the urinal in the boys' lavatory.

C10:31, pe10:38, P249:10–11 **hacking chestnut** Prepared for use in a game in which the object is to knock two chestnuts suspended on strings against each other until one of them breaks.

C11:1, pe11:7, P249:18 **Mozambique Channel** Between the east coast of Africa and the island of Madagascar. Mozambique was Portuguese (i.e., Catholic) East Africa.

C11:2, pe11:8, P249:18–19 **the longest river in America** The central stem of the Mississippi is not as long as that of the Missouri, but technically the Mississippi can be said to include the Missouri and is thus the longest. Perhaps Mrs. Riordan would have opted for the Mississippi because it was discovered and explored by French and Spanish Catholics.

C11:2–3, pe11:8, P249:19–20 **the name of the highest mountain in the moon** Late nineteenth-century astronomy taught that the two highest mountain *ranges* on the moon (not single mountains, because measurements were not that precise) were the Dörfel and Leibnitz ranges, so named in 1791 by John Hieronymus Schröter after the German theologian (Protestant) and astronomer Georg Samuel Dörfel (1643–88) and Gottfried Wilhelm von Leibnitz (1646–1716), German philosopher, theologian, and mathematician. Leibnitz, who was not a Catholic but "a kind of eclectic, rationalistic" Christian, was held in high regard by Catholics for his attempts to reconcile the Protestant and Catholic communities in Hanover (*The Catholic Encyclopedia*, 16 vols. [New York, 1907–14], 9:135a).

C11:18, pe11:25, P250:5   **suck**   Low slang for a sycophant.

C11:20–21, pe11:28, P250:8   **the prefect's false sleeves**   The Jesuit gown (soutane) has two strips of cloth that hang from the shoulders down over the sleeves.

C11:23, pe11:30, P250:11   **the Wicklow Hotel**   6 to 8 Wicklow Street, just south of the Liffey in central Dublin.

C12:3–4, pe12:9–10, P250:29–30   **York! . . . Lancaster!**   The Jesuits believed that competition provided motivation for learning; hence, the boys are divided into teams with the names of the warring English houses in the Wars of the Roses (1445–85): Lancaster, the red rose, and York, the white rose. In the fifteenth century, Ireland enlisted under the losing banner of the white rose, and when the succession to the English throne had been determined by the Lancastrians, Henry VII undertook to reorganize Ireland for its pains; see Introduction, p. 17 above.

C12:10, pe12:16, P251:1   **a wax**   Slang for a rage, a passion.

C12:12, pe12:19, P251:4   **the red rose wins**   The dark rose before it had reddened "into bloom" (by means of "blood sacrifice") was a traditional symbol for conquered Ireland; see F. S. L. Lyons, *Ireland Since the Famine* (London, 1973), pp. 355–56.

C12:17, pe12:25, P251:10   **elements**   What the elements class of third line (see *Por* C8:25n) would study: spelling, grammar, writing, arithmetic, geography, history, and Latin.

C13:6, pe13:12, P252:3   **magistrates**   See *Por* C9:9n.

C13:25, pe13:31, P252:25   **Dalkey**   A village on the Irish Sea eight miles southeast of Dublin. It is on the railroad line which connects Bray (where Stephen's family lives) with Dublin.

C13:30, pe13:37, P252:31   **higher line**   See *Por* C8:25n.

C14:2, pe14:7, P253:5   **the little song of the gas**   The noise a gaslight makes.

C14:4, pe14:10, P253:8   **Tullabeg**   A hamlet 55 miles west of Dublin, where the Rev. Peter Kenny, S.J., the founder of Clongowes, founded another educational institution, St. Stanislaus's College. In 1886 St. Stanislaus's College was merged with Clongowes Wood College at Clongowes Wood. St. Stanislaus's College, Tullabeg, subsequently became the site of the Jesuit Novitiate in Ireland.

C14:7, pe14:13, P253:11   **do you kiss your mother**   One of the patron saints of youth, the Jesuit St. Aloysius Gonzaga (1568–91), is reputed to have been so chaste that he would not even raise his eyes to look at his mother, let alone kiss her.

C14:24, peI4:30, P253:29–30   **third of grammar**   I.e., he is in the class of studies just above Stephen's class; see *Por* C8:25n.

C15:29, peI5:35, P255:7   *Class of Elements*   See *Por* C12:17n and C8:25n.

C15:31–32, peI5:37–38, P255:9–10   *Sallins / County Kildare*   Sallins is a village on the main Dublin-Galway railroad line four and a half miles south of Clongowes Wood College in County Kildare, an inland county just west of County Dublin.

C16:1, peI6:6, P255:16   **a cod**   Slang for a joke.

C16:31, peI6:36–37, P256:16   **Parnell was a bad man**   I.e., after Parnell's relation to Mrs. O'Shea had been revealed in the divorce trial in 1890; see "An Outline of Irish History," pp. 21–22 above.

C16:35–36, peI7:4–5, P256:21   **Every day there was something in the paper about it**   I.e., the controversy over Parnell's continuing attempt to assert his leadership after the great split of December 1890 and before his death, 6 October 1891; see "An Outline of Irish History," pp. 21–22 above.

C17:3–4, peI7:9, P256:25   **in poetry and rhetoric**   The two highest grades at Clongowes; see *Por* C8:25n.

C17:12, peI7:17–18, P256:34   **prayers in the chapel**   Night prayers. The order of the day at Clongowes Wood College was quasi-monastic: "The day . . . began around six in the morning with a visit to the Blessed Sacrament, followed later by the celebration of Mass, and ended around nine in the evening with the school assembled in chapel for night prayers" (Kevin Sullivan, *Joyce among the Jesuits* [New York, 1958], p. 55).

C17:26, peI7:34, P257:16   **the marbles**   The chapel interior and its pillars were made of wood, but the pillars were painted to look like marble.

C17:30, peI7:38, P257:20   **the hob**   A shelf at the side or back of a fireplace.

C17:32, peI8:1, P257:22   **the responses**   See *Dub* C13:22n.

C17:33–36, peI8:2–5, P257:23–26   *O Lord, open our lips . . . make haste to help us!*   The opening lines of Matins in the Divine Office; the second and fourth lines are the responses; see *Por* C200:11n.

C18:6, peI8:11, P257:33   **Clane**   A parish and village one and one half miles south of the college. The Clongowes Wood College chapel was the parish church for Clane.

C18:18–22, peI8:24–28, P258:12–16   *Visit, we beseech Thee . . .*

Amen   The prayer just before the concluding lines of Compline (at bedtime), the last of the seven canonical hours in the Divine Office; see *Por* C200:11n.

C18:26, peI8:32–33, P258:20–21   **so that he might not go to hell when he died**   The "sin" involved (of neglecting his bedtime prayers) has been magnified all out of proportion by some combination of adult threat and childish imagination; see *Por* C93:5–6n.

C19:11–12, peI9:18–19, P259:10–12   **the black dog . . . with eyes as big as carriagelamps**   May have been borrowed from Hans Christian Andersen's (1805–75) fairy tale, "The Tinder Box," though the dogs in that short tale are benign.

C19:15, peI9:22, P259:15   **the ironingroom**   The room where armor had been stored and put on.

C19:18, peI9:25, P259:17   **a figure**   The Browne family owned Clongowes Wood in the eighteenth century; see *Por* C9:21n. Maximilian Ulysses, Count von Browne (1705–57), the Austrian-born son of an expatriated Irish Jacobite, became a marshal in the Austrian Army. He was killed at the Battle of Prague in 1757. The story is that on the day he fell his bloody ghost appeared to the servants in the castle at Clongowes Wood.

C19:36–37, pe20:3–4, P260:1–2   *Visit, we beseech Thee*   See *Por* C18:18–22n.

C20:2, pe20:7, P260:4   **the cars**   Long horse-drawn vehicles, which provided a relatively efficient system of road transport in rural Ireland; in the late nineteenth century the cars were still an important supplement to rail transport. They ran regular routes, were cheaper than the mail coaches, and could be chartered for special occasions (as in this context).

C20:8, pe20:12, P260:11   **Bodenstown**   The parish that includes Sallins; see *Por* C15:31–32n.

C20:9, pe20:13, P260:13   **the Jolly Farmer**   The name of an elementary piano piece by Robert Schumann (1810–56); it is #10 in his *Album for the Young*, Opus 68 (1848). Complete title: "The Jolly Farmer; Returning from Work."

C20:20–21, pe20:25, P260:26   **the Hill of Allen**   A hill 676 feet high, eight and a half miles west of Sallins. The train Stephen expects to take from Sallins to Dublin would not pass the hill en route.

C20:24, pe20:28, P260:29   **holly and ivy**   Traditional Christmas decorations. There are many medieval carols about the contention between the holly and the ivy (man and woman) over who should rule the Christmas feast.

C20:24, pe20:28, P260:30   **the pierglass**   See *Dub* C65:20n.

C20:31, pe20:36, P260:30   **a marshal now: higher than a magistrate**
For magistrate, see *Por* C9:9n; in his dream Stephen apparently con-
fuses military rank (see *Por* C19:18n) with rank in the Irish judiciary.

C21:21, pe21:25, P261:31   **mass**   See *Por* C17:12n.

C21:32, pe21:37, P262:7–8   **for cod**   I.e., as a joke or a tease.

C22:18, pe22:20, P262:32   **Father Minister**   Or vice-rector, the priest
in charge of all phases of school activity except studies; see *Por* C9:29n.

C22:21, pe22:24, P263:1   **Brother Michael**   A brother or "temporal
coadjutor" of the Jesuit Order, bound by vows but not subjected to the
rigorous education required for ordination as a Jesuit priest. As a
brother of the Order he would expect to be assigned housekeeping
tasks, etc.

C22:28, pe22:32, P263:10   **Hayfoot! Strawfoot!**   After the practice of
tying a wisp of hay to a rural recruit's left foot, a wisp of straw to his
right, to teach him how to march.

C23:11, pe23:13, P263:32   **the third of grammar**   The class of studies
just above Stephen's class; see *Por* C8:25n.

C24:2, pe24:2, P164:27–28   **a dead mass**   I.e., a Funeral Mass; the
Mass "says little about death but much about sleep and rest, resurrec-
tion and life, light and peace, with Christ who died and rose again"
(*The Layman's Missal* [Baltimore, Md., 1962], p. 1029).

C24:3, pe24:3–4, P264:29   **when Little had died**   Peter Stanislaus
Little (1874–90), a student at Clongowes Wood College, died there of
rheumatic fever and "fulminant pneumonia" after being caught in a
downpour on the Bog of Allen (see *Dub* C223:29n). He was buried in
the College cemetery.

C24:6, pe24:7, P264:32–33   **a cope of black and gold**   The color of
the priest's vestments for the Funeral Mass is black and gold; see *Dub*
C13:6n.

C24:10, pe24:11, P265:2–3   **the main avenue of limes**   The main avenue that leads to the castle at Clongowes Wood was flanked by rows of
linden (lime) trees.

C24:15–22, pe24:16–23, P265:7–14   ***Dingdong! . . . my soul away***
Anonymous nursery rhyme. Iona and Peter Opie quote this as "Scottish" (*The Language and Lore of Childhood* [Oxford, 1959], p. 34),
among several examples of the "ghoulism" which they say appeals to
children about ten years of age "when . . . they enter a period in which
the outward material facts of death seem extraordinarily funny" (p.
32).

C25:14, pe25:13, P266:9   **Athy**   A town in County Kildare, 43 miles
southwest of Dublin.

C26:6, pe26:7, P267:5   **a magistrate**   See *Por* C9:9n.

C26:13, pe26:15, P267:14   **the liberator**   Daniel O'Connell; see *Dub* C214:31n.

C26:16–18, pe26:18–20, P267:17–19   **blue coats . . . rabbitskin and drank beer**   From about 1816 to 1840 the Clongowes uniform for festivals was as described (plus corduroy trousers), according to the *Clongowes Record*, and beer was a staple in the daily diet.

C26:24, pe26:26, P267:25   **a legend**   I.e., the life of a saint.

C27:13, pe27:14, P268:22   **Parnell! Parnell! He is dead!**   Parnell died in England on 6 October 1891. His body was brought to Kingstown (Dun Laoghaire) on Sunday morning, 11 October, and thence to the Dublin City Hall, where it lay in state. Late in the afternoon there was a funeral procession to the site of his grave in Prospect Cemetery in Glasnevin (on the northern outskirts of metropolitan Dublin).

Chapter I: Section C

C27:29, pe27:31, P269:7   **boss**   "A kind of foot-stool with two ears, stuffed without a wooden frame. The term is childish and popular. Compare the word 'hassock'" (Joyce, *Letters*, 3:129).

C27:30, pe27:31, P269:8   **pierglass**   See *Dub* C65:20n.

C28:9–10, pe28:8–9, P269:22–23   **making a birthday present for Queen Victoria**   I.e., picking oakum, one form of hard labor in nineteenth-century British prisons.

C28:16, pe28:15, P269:30   **the Head**   Bray Head (791 feet), a stone hill facing the sea, just south of the village of Bray, which is on the coast thirteen miles south-southeast of Dublin.

C28:31, pe28:32, P270:12   **Christopher**   Unknown, quite possibly a fictional name for a real person, a hotel keeper engaged in the clandestine manufacture of explosives for Irish revolutionaries.

C28:34, pe28:35, P270:16   **champagne**   For explosives, as suggestive of their exhilarating effects?

C28:37, pe28:38, P270:20–21   **jack foxes**   Male foxes.

C29:24–26, pe29:26–28, P271:16–18   ***Bless us, O Lord . . . Amen***   A standard Catholic prayer to be recited before meals. Stephen could have learned it from the opening section of the *Maynooth Catechism* (p. 4).

C29:27, pe29:29, P271:19   **blessed themselves**   I.e., made the sign of the cross, touching the forehead, breast, left and right shoulders in sequence with the right forefinger.

C29:32, pe29:34, P271:24 **a guinea** Expensive items in fashionable shops were priced in guineas (one pound, one shilling) rather than in the more plebeian pounds.

C29:32, pe29:34, P271:24–25 **Dunn's of D'Olier Street** A fashionable poulterer, fishmonger, and game dealer, at 26 D'Olier Street, just southeast of O'Connell Bridge in central Dublin.

C29:36, pe30:1, P271:28 **Ally Dally** Dublin slang for the very best.

C30:1–2, pe30:2–3, P271:29–30 **Why did Mr Barrett . . . his pandybat a turkey?** A pandybat is a leather strap reenforced with whalebone used, for punishment, to strike schoolboys on the palms of their hands. Mr. Barrett, a scholastic (see *Por* C48:16n), calls it a "turkey" because it makes hands red, "turns them turkey." See *Dub* C22:32–33n.

C30:25, pe30:27, P272:22 **Dante covered her plate with her hands** Given the context and the role Mrs. Riordan is to play, the gesture is reminiscent of a gesture the celebrant makes toward the end of the Canon of the Mass just before the Consecration of the Host:

> During the 'Hanc igitur' the priest, who has joined his hands at the preceding 'Per eundem Christum Dominum nostrum. Amen', spreads them over the offerings. . . . This imposition of hands seems to have been introduced merely as a way of practically touching the sacrifice at this point, at which it is so definitely named in the prayer. [*The Catholic Encyclopedia* (1908), 3:263a]

The "Hanc igitur" begins: "This, then, is the offering that we, the servants of your altar, make to you . . . : Lord, please accept it. Order our days in your peace . . . ."

C31:4–5, pe31:5–6, P273:5–6 *I'll pay you your dues . . . house of God into a pollingbooth* Source unknown, but an obvious reference to the Irish Catholic clergy's condemnation of Parnell from the pulpit and its active intervention against Parnellite candidates after the split. Clerical pressure (including priests who organized and marched their parishioners to the polling places) defeated the Parnellite candidate in a Kilkenny by-election (24 December 1890), and from that time on there was, according to F. S. L. Lyons (*Parnell* [London, 1977], p. 549) "clerical intervention on the grand scale."

C32:3, pe32:2, P247:6 **the bishops and priests of Ireland have spoken** On the advice of Archbishop William J. Walsh of Dublin, the bishops of Ireland refrained from speaking out against Parnell over the divorce case (which ended on 17 November 1890) until after the Irish

parliamentarians had acted against Parnell's political leadership on
6 December 1890; see "An Outline of Irish History," pp. 21–22
above.

C32:10–11, pe32:10, P274:14–15. **Were we to desert him at the
bidding of the English people?** When the divorce trial (in which neither Parnell or Mrs. O'Shea contested the evidence of their liaison)
ended, the publicity aroused a public furor in England. Political leaders
brought pressure on Gladstone to the point where he felt his leadership
of the Liberal Party threatened, and, on 24 November 1890, he began
to press Parnell to withdraw from politics. Characteristically, Parnell
sidestepped, refused, and fought back. Gladstone then published the
ultimatum he had sent to Parnell, in effect demanding that the Irish
choose between Parnell and himself and, as F. S. L. Lyons puts it in
Ireland Since the Famine (London, 1973), p. 197, "between Parnell and
Home Rule." The Irish Nationalist M.P.s tried to reject Parnell and
drive him out of politics but managed only to split their party.

C32:16–20, pe32:15–19, P274:20–24 **Woe be to the man . . . my
least little ones** Jesus teaching his disciples to avoid occasions of
"scandal" and "offence" (Luke 17:1–2). Luke 17:3 continues, "Take
heed to yourselves: If thy brother trespass against thee, rebuke him;
and if he repent, forgive him."

C32:33, pe32:34, P275:4 **the pope's nose** The lap of the tail over the
anus of a dressed turkey looks like a Roman nose over a mouth (and the
pope is the bishop of Rome).

C33:18, pe33:19, P275:29 **Billy with the lip** The Reverend William
J. Walsh (1841–1921), archbishop of Dublin (1885–1921), was a member of several important government commissions and was instrumental in framing and publicizing the Irish Land Act of 1882. Since Parnell
was president of the Land League and one of the leading agitators for
land reform, this brought them into a cooperative working relationship. It was Archbishop Walsh who effectively blew the whistle on
the Pigott forgeries (see "An Outline of Irish History," pp. 21–22
above). When the divorce scandal first broke, he seemed reluctant to
condemn and held aloof until after the climax of the leadership crisis in
early December 1890; see *Por* C32:3n.

C33:18–19, pe33:20, P275:30 **the tub of guts up in Armagh** The
Reverend Michael Logue (1840–1924), archbishop of Armagh (1887–
1924). He was hardly an arch-conservative, nor was he as moderate-left
as Archbishop Walsh; he was afraid that the Parnellites were turning
into "a mere tail to the Radical party in England" (Lyons, *Parnell*, p.
620). Armagh (in what is now Northern Ireland) is the primatial city of
Ireland; Archbishop Logue became a cardinal in 1893.

C33:21, pe33:22, P275:33   **Lord Leitrim's coachman**   Lord Leitrim, the English landlord of practically a whole county in the west of Ireland, had a reputation as one of the worst absentee landlords. He was murdered while driving one day in 1877—presumably by Irish land-reform agitators. The story was that his Irish coachman "loyally" attempted to prevent the assault.

C34:27–28, pe34:28–29, P277:7–8   **county Wicklow where we are now**   County Wicklow is on the east coast of Ireland, south of County Dublin. Bray, "where we are now," is in the northeastern corner of County Wicklow; Arklow, the site of the story, is 29 miles south.

C35:12–13, pe35:10–11, P277:29–30   *O come all you Roman Catholics / That never went to mass*   Parodies the conventional opening to a *come-all-you* or Irish street ballad: "Come all you loyal [or gallant] Irish / And listen to my song"; see *Dub* C31:7–8n.

C35:23–25, pe35:21–23, P278:7–8   **a spoiled nun . . . from the savages**   According to Ellmann, Mrs. Riordan's real-life counterpart "had been on the verge of becoming a nun in America when her brother, who had made a fortune out of trading with African natives, died and left her 30,000 pounds" (p. 24), i.e., a wealth comparable to $750,000 to $1,000,000 (1980).

C35:25, pe35:24, P278:10   **chainies**   Damaged chinaware.

C35:30–31, pe35:29–30, P278:16   *Tower of Ivory . . . House of Gold*   Phrases applied to the Blessed Virgin Mary as gateway to the heavenly mansions in the Roman Catholic Litany of Our Lady, called "of Loretto." The section of the Litany from which the phrases are taken:

Mirror of Justice, pray for us.
Seat of Wisdom, pray for us.
Cause of our joy, pray for us.
Spiritual Vessel, . . .
Honourable Vessel, . . .
Vessel of singular devotion, . . .
Mystical Rose, . . .
Tower of David, . . .
Tower of Ivory, . . .
House of Gold, . . .
Ark of the Covenant, . . .
Gate of Heaven, . . .
Morning Star, . . .
Help of the infirm, . . .
Refuge of sinners, . . .
Comfort of the afflicted, . . .
Help of Christians, . . .

Mrs. Riordan's story, "protestants used to make fun of the litany," may be just a prejudicial story, but nineteenth-century Protestant attacks on Irish Catholics frequently focused on "idolatry" and "mariolatry"; the Donlevy and *Maynooth* Catechisms are, in a revealing way, very defensive on those points.

C36:1, pe35:36, P278:23   **tig**   A game like hide-and-go-seek.

C36:6, pe36:2, P278:28   **Arklow**   A town in County Wicklow on the coast of St. George's Channel, 39 miles south of Dublin.

C36:6–7, pe36:3, P278:29   **the chief**   Parnell.

C36:20, pe36:16–17, P279:9   *Priesthunter!*   Parnell was a Protestant and therefore suspect at the best of times, though his practice was to balance and to avoid confrontation with the Roman Catholic hierarchy. But once the hierarchy condemned him, he counterattacked with considerable vigor. Archbishop Thomas Croke (of Cashel) complained that Parnell took a special train through Ireland every week "to knock the bottom out of the priests" (Lyons, *Parnell*, p. 587).

C36:20–21, pe36:17, P279:9   *The Paris Funds!*   A treasury of political funds (largely from American subscriptions and investments in American securities) which Parnell and his associates kept on deposit in Paris so that the Nationalist Party's finances would not be vulnerable to British interference or confiscation. After the split in December 1890 Parnell was, on a legal technicality, still leader of the party and therefore entitled to control the Paris Funds and to use them for the political advantage of the Parnellite minority as against the majority. The financial advantage thus enjoyed by the Parnellite M.P.s was yet another source of bitter recrimination. Ugly rumor easily managed the step to the personal accusation that Parnell had used his control of the funds to finance his adventures with Mrs. O'Shea.

C36:21, pe36:17, P279:9   *Mr. Fox!*   At the divorce trial it was revealed that Parnell had communicated with Mrs. O'Shea under a number of assumed names, among them Mr. Fox. The assumed names implied that the relationship had been a good deal more clandestine than it actually was.

C36:21, pe36:17, P279:10   *Kitty O'Shea!*   The diminutive constitutes a far more insulting bit of name-calling in 1890–91 than it would in 1980.

C36:25, pe36:21, P279:14   **Tullamore**   A chewing tobacco manufactured in the town of Tullamore, fifty miles west of Dublin.

C37:19, pe37:15, P280:15   **Sergeant O'Neill**   Apparently fictional; no such name is listed as attached to the constabulary in Bray in the 1880s and 90s.

C37:24, pe37:20–21, P280:20 **Cabinteely road** A little-used road on an indirect, inland route from Bray to Dublin.

C37:28–29, pe37:26, P280:25 *God save the Queen* The (unofficial) British national anthem, apparently a recasting of a folk song. It appeared in England in 1745, when it was used as the rallying song of the House of Hanover (the English kings) during the second Jacobite rebellion. "King" and "Queen" are interchangeable: in this case Queen Victoria (b. 1819, queen 1837–1901) was on the throne.

C37:32, pe37:29, P280:28 **priestridden race** "Where in 1850 there were about 5000 priests, monks and nuns for a Catholic population of five million, in 1900 there were over 14,000 priests, monks and nuns to minister to approximately 3⅓ million Catholics . . ." (Lyons, *Ireland since the Famine*, p. 19).

C38:5, pe37:39, P281:3 **whiteboy** An agitator for land and tax reform, particularly for reform of church taxes (tithes), which were levied by the politically established, Protestant Church of Ireland on Protestants and Catholics alike and much resented by the Catholic community, which, of course, received none of the monies raised. Whiteboyism began during the reign of George III in the late eighteenth century. In the first half of the nineteenth century they concentrated on agitation (and threats of violence) against landlords who raised land rents and "blacklegs," peasants who were willing to pay higher rents. The whiteboys were so called because they wore white outer garments so that they could distinguish each other during their night raids and demonstrations.

C38:6–7, pe38:2, P281:5–6 **put his two feet under his mahogany** Literally, sit at his dining room table; figuratively, be received and entertained in his home.

C38:10–11, pe38:5–6, P281:9–10 *Touch them not . . . for they are the apple of My eye* After the prophecy of "the prayers of the Church of Christ" in Zacharias 2:8–9: "For thus saith the Lord of hosts: After the glory he hath sent me to the nations that robbed you: for he that toucheth you, toucheth the apple of my eye: for behold I lift up my hand upon them, and they shall be a prey to those that served them" (Douay Bible).

C38:21–22, pe38:16–17, P281:20 **Didn't the bishops . . . in the time of the union** In 1799 the British Government, spurred by the Rebellion of 1798 and the threats of French intervention in Ireland, determined to dissolve the Irish Parliament, which sat in Dublin, and to merge it with the British Parliament in London. Constitutionally, this necessitated that the Irish Parliament vote itself out of existence;

there was considerable resistance in Ireland, since the Irish regarded "Union" as a radical diminution of their quasi-independence. British policy won the day (1800) by dividing and conquering with bribery, skulduggery, and corruption. Jonah Barrington, an eyewitness anti-Unionite, remarks, "The Bishops yielded up their conscience to their interests and but two of the spiritual Peers could be found to uphold the independence of their country, which had been so nobly attained and so corruptly extinguished" (*The Rise and Fall of the Irish Nation* [New York, 1845], p. 371). Barrington is referring to the Church of Ireland bishops (peers), but many Catholic bishops were also pro-Union. The bribe offered to the Catholic bishops for their moral support was Catholic Emancipation; the bribe was not honored for 29 years. The effect of the Act of Union was that political (and with it economic) power was displaced from Dublin to London, which in Ireland meant a radical increase in absentee landlordism and in the exploitation of land and peasants.

C38:22, pe38:17, P281:21   **bishop Lanigan**   James Lanigan (d. 1812), Roman Catholic bishop of Ossory. From W. J. Fitzpatrick, *Irish Wits and Worthies* (Dublin, 1873), p. 336:

> An amusing anecdote is told of Bishop Lanigan, who at the time of the Union made a pilgrimage to St. Patrick's Hall in Dublin Castle with a complimentary address to the Viceroy, Lord Cornwallis. The antagonism of the Catholic hierarchy and laity had been silenced by diplomatic promises of prompt emancipation, meant to be broken like the piecrust with which his excellency feasted the deputations. . . . One of Cornwallis's eyes was smaller than the other and had acquired a rapid, uninterrupted winking motion, which he is said to have turned to profitable account in his negotiations with political jobbers on the great question of the Union. Bishop Lanigan, who had never seen Lord Cornwallis, composed in the remote seclusion of Ossory the compliments with which he meant to ply him personally. The Viceroy was sitting on his throne when Dr. Lanigan, at the head of his clergy, sonorously proceeded to read the address: "Your Excellency has always kept a *steady* eye upon the interests of Ireland."

Fitzpatrick remarks that Lanigan was an exemplary prelate but a bad politician and a worse diplomat.

C38:23, pe38:18, P281:22   **Marquess Cornwallis**   Charles, first marquess and second earl (1738–1805), English general and statesman, the general who surrendered to Washington at Yorktown (1781); governor of India (1786–93); appointed lord lieutenant of Ireland in 1798, where he was instrumental in putting down the Rebellion of that year and, subsequently, in implementing the British policy of Union. Cornwallis resigned in 1801 when George III refused to assent to Catholic Emancipation; i.e., Cornwallis resigned because the promises he had conveyed to the Irish Catholic community had been dishonored.

C38:23–25, pe38:18–20, P281:22–24 **Didn't the bishops and priests . . . for Catholic emancipation** The Catholic Emancipation Bill (1829) completed the enfranchisement of the Catholic population of Great Britain and Ireland. Until that time Catholics had been excluded from office in Parliament, government, and the military, and had been restricted in the practice of their religion and in religious education. Agitation for emancipation had been constant for more than one hundred years before its achievement. The Catholic bishops and priests did not exactly "sell out" after emancipation had been achieved, but they were far more vigorous in their support of Daniel O'Connell's campaign for emancipation (see *Dub* C214:31n) than they were in support of his subsequent, unsuccessful campaign for repeal of the Act of Union.

C38:25, pe38:21, P281:25 **the fenian movement** I.e., the Irish Republican Brotherhood. A majority of the Irish Catholic clergy did condemn the Brotherhood's advocacy and practice of violent revolution; see *Dub* C125:5n. Cf. the *Maynooth Catechism* (p. 37):

> Q. What are the duties of subjects to the temporal powers?
> A. The duties of subjects to the temporal powers are, *to be subject to them, and to honour and obey them, not only for wrath, but also for conscience' sake; for so is the will of God* (I Pet. and Rom. xiii) . . . . The Scripture also requires us to show respect to those who rule over us, *to pray for kings, and for all who are in high station, that we may lead a quiet and peaceable life* (I Tim. ii) [italics in text].

C38:27, pe38:22–23, P281:27 **Terence Bellew MacManus** Irish patriot (1823–60) and follower of Daniel O'Connell in the agitations of 1840–48. After he died in exile in San Francisco, his body was brought back to Ireland, and, in spite of the opposition of the archbishop of Dublin (see *Por* C38:31n) and other leaders of the Church, he was buried in Prospect Cemetery, Glasnevin, 10 November 1861. The funeral became the occasion for a large nationalist demonstration.

C38:31, pe38:27, P281:31–32 **Paul Cullen** (1803–78), archbishop of Dublin (1852–78). He became a cardinal in 1866 and subsequently apostolic delegate (ruler of the Catholic Church in Ireland). He did condemn the Irish Republican Brotherhood (the Fenians) and other agitators for Home Rule and land reform. He advocated support of the British government and was popularly regarded as one who sought favors from the British for himself and his friends.

C39:32, pe39:30, P283:3 **My dead king** Parnell, "the uncrowned King of Ireland"; see *Dub* C134:7n.

Chapter I: Section D

C40:3, pe39:36, P283:9 **the Hill of Lyons** A landmark at 657 feet, six miles east of Clongowes Wood College and eleven miles west of the center of Dublin; i.e., they were attempting to run away to Dublin.

C40:5, pe40:2, P283:11 **the minister** See *Por* C22:18n.

C40:5, pe40:2, P283:12 **a car** Not clear: possibly an outside car (*Dub* C153:5n) or one of the scheduled cars (*Por* C20:2n). The difference: if an outside car, the students are using their affluence in the attempt to escape; if one of the cars, they are trying to escape incognito, hidden among other travelers.

C40:11, pe40:8, P283:18 **fecked** To feck is a dialect variant of to fetch, obsolete for to steal.

C40:16, pe40:13, P283:24 **scut** "The tail of a hare or rabbit: often applied in scorn to a contemptible fellow—'He's just a scut and nothing better'" (P. W. Joyce, *English as We Speak It in Ireland* [Dublin, 1910], p. 318). P. W. Joyce claims it as an Irish word, but it is English and Scots dialect as well.

C41:1, pe40:38, P284:16 **boatbearer** In the rite of blessing the incense during the Mass (or, as in this case, during Benediction of the Blessed Sacrament), the boatbearer carries the boat or container in which the inert incense is held; another server carries the censer (or thurible) in which the incense is burned. The celebrant takes the incense from the boat and puts it in the censer.

C41:2, pe40:38–41:1, P284:17 **the little altar in the wood** The wood at Clongowes is a park or pleasure ground adjoining the college. Processions to the altar in the midst of the park and Benediction of the Blessed Sacrament there were regular features of the annual calendar at the college. During the ceremony of Benediction, the Blessed Sacrament is exposed for worship to the accompaniment of hymns, and the celebrant makes the sign of the cross over the participants with the monstrance after the Host has been placed in it.

C41:13, pe41:12, P284:30 **a sprinter** A bicycle racer, trained for high speeds over short distances.

C41:22, pe41:22, P285:4   **the prof**   Schoolboy slang for captain of the cricket team.

C41:23, pe41:23, P285:6   **rounders**   An English game similar to baseball.

C41:23-24, pe41:24, P285:6   **bowling twisters and lobs**   Bowling in cricket is comparable to pitching in baseball, except that the ball is bounced in front of the batsman. A twister is a curve, much sharper than in baseball since the ball's spin can cause it to bounce at an abrupt angle; a lob is a high arched pitch, difficult for the batsman to judge.

C42:10, pe42:10, P285:31   **the square**   The school urinal.

C42:15, pe42:15, P286:1   **smugging**   Obsolete: to toy amorously in secret (Joseph Wright, *English Dialect Dictionary* [London, 1898–1905], Vol. 5, p. 5622); in context, it means the practice of schoolboy homosexuality.

C42:24, pe42:24-25, P286:12   **the football fifteen**   The college team for Irish football; see *Por* C8:19n.

C42:27, pe42:27, P286:14   **the Bective Rangers**   An Irish football team named for the ancient parish of Bective Abbey (now in ruins), fifteen miles northwest of Dublin. Clongowes Wood College played games against various local or club teams (comparable to semi-professional teams in the United States). The Bective Rangers was regarded as one of the leading football clubs in Ireland.

C42:35, pe42:36, P286:24   *Tower of Ivory*   See *Por* C35:30-31n.

C43:1, pe42:38, P286:26   **the hotel grounds**   The Marine Station Hotel, not far from Stephen's and Eileen's homes, at the corner of Martello Terrace and the Strand in Bray.

C43:8-9, pe43:7-8, P286:35-287:1   *Tower of Ivory. House of Gold*   See *Por* C35:30-31n.

C43:18, pe43:17, P287:10   *Balbus was building a wall*   During the politically troubled year of 47 B.C. Cicero (106–43 B.C.) mocked his fellow Romans for diverting themselves instead of attending to the business of state. In *Letters to Atticus* XII:2 he singles out one Balbus as an example: he "is building [new villas for himself], for what does he care?" The Balbus referred to may have been Lucius Cornelius Major, chosen to protect Julius Caesar's interests and property in Rome during Caesar's campaigns in Gaul.

C43:23, pe43:22, P287:15   *Julius Caesar wrote The Calico Belly*   A schoolboy pun on Caesar's *Commentarii de Bello Gallico* (Commentaries on the Gallic Wars); see *Dub* C20:17-18n.

C43:33-34, pe43:34, P287:27   **six and eight**   The number of strokes (*ferulae*) given as punishment (on the palm of the hand): three on each hand, followed by four on each hand; see *Dub* C22:32-33n.

C43:35–36, pe43:36, P287:29   **twisting the note**   So that the culprit could not read his sentence en route to the place of punishment; see *Dub* C22:32–33n.

C44:2, pe43:39, P287:32   **the prefect of studies**   In effect, dean of studies; an assistant to the rector, he had charge of the College's curriculum and teaching personnel; see *Por* C9:29n.

C44:10, pe44:8, P288:6   **flogged**   To be whipped on the buttocks with a rod or cane, an unusually harsh punishment for an Irish Jesuit school. When imposed, flogging would usually be done in public as an example and a warning to the whole school.

C44:26, pe44:25, P288:22   **twice nine**   Nine strokes on each hand, the maximum punishment administered on a day-to-day basis. Twice nine also involved nine strokes on the buttocks.

C45:4–5, pe45:3, P289:3   **pandybat**   See *Por* C30:1–2n.

C46:11, pe46:11, P290:16   **a wax**   See *Por* C12:10n.

C46:16, pe46:16, P290:21   **a monstrance**   An open-work vessel of gold or silver in which the consecrated Host is exposed to receive the veneration of the congregation.

C46:20, pe46:20, P290:26   **benediction**   For the ceremony of Benediction of the Blessed Sacrament, see *Por* C41:2n.

C47:9–10, pe47:8–9, P291:18   **Gentlemen, the happiest day of my life was the day on which I made my first holy communion**   The story of this remark seems to have been a staple of First Communion (or pre-Confirmation) classes in Ireland in spite of the fact that Napoleon apparently never said it and, if he had, his irreligious life should have pointed the irony. See Austin Clarke, who recalls the same story in *Twice Round the Black Church* (London, 1962), p. 133. Children were thought to be ready for religious instruction and First Communion at the age of six or seven.

C47:19–21, pe47:18–19, P291:29   **decline the noun** *mare* . . . **stopped at the ablative singular and could not go on with the plural**   *Mare* (Latin: the sea) is mildly tricky to decline; it is one of the few neuter i-stem nouns in the third declension. Strangely, Jack Lawton is not stumped by the difficult case (the ablative singular, *mare*) but by the plural which he should have found relatively easy.

C48:9–11, pe48:8–10, P292:23–26   **minister** . . . **rector** . . . **provincial** . . . **general of the jesuits**   For minister and rector see *Por* C9:29n. The provincial is the highest Jesuit authority in Ireland, and the general (in Rome) is the Order's absolute ruler, responsible only to the constitution of the Order and to the pope. Jesuits do not, however, necessarily confess through the chain of command as Stephen thinks but choose (or are assigned) confessors from among the members of their communities.

C48:16, pe48:15, P292:31 **Mr McGlade and Mr Gleeson** Scholastics, young Jesuits who have completed their first novitiate and have entered the second novitiate, bound by simple vows of poverty, chastity, and obedience. They have yet to be ordained as priests.

C48:22, pe48:21, P293:2 **the prefect of studies** See *Por* C44:2n.

C49:7, pe49:5, P293:26–27 **the pandybat came down** Corporal punishment was rarely administered in this public fashion; see *Dub* C22:32–33n and *Por* C44:10n.

C49:26, pe49:26, P294:13 **Tomorrow and tomorrow and tomorrow** A line from Macbeth's soliloquy after he receives the news of the death of his wife, V:v:19ff. Macbeth continues, ". . . creeps in this petty pace from day to day, / To the last syllable of recorded time, / And all our yesterdays have lighted fools / The way to dusty death." In context, Father Dolan's words are not allusion but cliché.

C53:10, pe53:9, P298:17 **The senate and the Roman people declared** An approximation of the opening phrase of a Roman senatorial decree: "Senatus populas que Romanus . . . ."

C53:23–24, pe53:22–23, P298:30–31 **A thing like that had been done before by somebody in history** Reference unknown.

C53:29, pe53:29–30, P299:2 **Richmal Magnall's Questions** Not Magnall but Mangnall (1769–1820), an English schoolmistress whose *Historical and Miscellaneous Questions for the Use of Young People* (1800) was popular throughout the nineteenth century as a text for elementary factual instruction in history and geography. The author's surname is misspelled in the text.

C53:30–31, pe53:31–32, P299:4 **Peter Parley's Tales about Greece and Rome** *Peter Parley's Tales About Ancient and Modern Greece* (Boston, 1832); *Peter Parley's Tales About Ancient and Modern Rome* (Boston, 1833). Peter Parley was the pseudonym of Samuel Griswold Goodrich (1793–1860), American publisher and editor of and collaborator in an extraordinarily popular series of instructional books for children.

C55:35–56:1, pe55:34–36, P301:20–22 **saint Ignatius Loyola . . . Ad Majorem Dei Gloriam** St. Ignatius of Loyola (1491–1556), the Spanish founder of the Society of Jesus (the Jesuit Order); the pose is traditional in portraits of St. Ignatius; the book and motto are symbolic reminders of his role as founder and writer of the constitution and the *Spiritual Exercises* (1548) of the Order (see headnote to chapter III, p. 177 below). The posthumous portrait by Peter Paul Rubens (1577–

1640) has been frequently imitated and is typical. St. Ignatius was attached to the court of Ferdinand and Isabella of Spain; he began a career as a soldier, but was seriously wounded in 1521. His quasi-
miraculous recovery was followed by an intensified interest in religion
and subsequently by self-dedication to a life of piety. His plan for the
Society of Jesus was approved by the pope in 1540; he was elected as
the first general of the Order in 1541. His leadership was militant,
rooted in the demand for complete and unquestioning obedience, for
rigorous piety and penance. See *Por* C107:29n. *Ad Majorem Dei
Gloriam* (Latin: For the Greater Glory of God) is the motto of the
Jesuits.

C56:1, pe55:36–37, P301:22–23   **saint Francis Xavier pointing to his
chest**   St. Francis (1506–52), one of the first of St. Ignatius of Loyola's disciples. He went as a Jesuit missionary to India and the Far
East and became known as the "Apostle of the Indies." St. Francis is
traditionally portrayed as "pointing to his chest," or rather to the crucifix on his chest, because the central emphasis of his missionary sermons is reported to have been the cross. See *Por*, notes to C106:
10–C108:3–5, inclusive.

C56:2, pe55:37, P301:23   **Lorenzo Ricci with his beretta**   Ricci
(1703–75) was elected general of the Jesuit Order in 1758, hence the
beretta as emblem of office. While he was general, though not as a result of his policies, the Jesuits were expelled from one European country after another, and the Order was finally (temporarily) suppressed by
Pope Clement XIII; see *Dub* C163:22n.

C56:3, pe55:38, P301:24   **prefects of the lines**   I.e., the house masters of the college's age and class groups wear similar berettas.

C56:3–5, pe55:38–56:2, P301:24–26   **the three patrons of holy
youth . . . John Berchmans**   The three young saints of the Jesuit
Order and thus patrons of Jesuit schools for boys: St. Stanislaus Kostka
(1550–68), a Jesuit novice, walked 350 miles from Vienna to Rome to
join the Order; St. Aloysius Gonzaga (1568–91), the patron saint of
Clongowes Wood College, died at the age of 23 from attending plague
victims; John Berchmans (1599–1621) was beatified in 1865 and canonized in 1888. Stephen calls him "blessed" because he does not realize
that Berchmans has just been canonized and should be called "saint."
The arrangement of these pictures of Jesuit saints and heroes is intended to reflect a continuous tradition from St. Ignatius into the nineteenth century.

C56:6, pe56:3–4, P301:28   **Father Peter Kenny**   The Jesuit priest
who founded Clongowes Wood College; see *Por* C9:21n and C14:4n.

C56:9, pe56:6, P301:31–32   **Hamilton Rowan**   See *Por* C10:11n.
C56:11, pe56:8, P301:34   **the ghost**   See *Por* C19:18n.
C56:24, pe56:21, P302:12   **a skull on the desk**   A memento mori; traditionally, a reminder that one should be always preoccupied with spiritual preparation for death.
C59:9, pe59:5, P305:10   **obedient**   Obedience was the cardinal virtue in the Jesuit vow from St. Ignatius's point of view. He wrote to the Jesuit scholastics at Coimbra:

> Above all, I desire that you be most outstanding in the virtue of obedience. . . . Let other religious orders surpass us in fasts and vigils and in all things else that, according to their own rule and discipline, they piously undertake; but in true and perfect obedience, and in the abdication of your own will and judgment, I especially desire that you who serve God Our Lord in this Society, be outstanding. [Quoted in Sullivan, *Joyce Among the Jesuits*, p. 119]

C59:15–16, pe59:11, P305:17   **Major Barton's**   Bertram F. Barton, Straffan House, Straffan Station, County Kildare. Barton's estate was two and one quarter miles east of Clongowes. He was a local dignitary, deputy lieutenant of the County, a magistrate (see *Por* C9:9n), and high sheriff (1903–4).
C59:17, pe59:12, P305:18   **gallnuts**   A nutlike gall, especially on oaks.
C59:18, pe59:13, P305:19   **long shies**   In cricket, similar to the long flies hit in baseball practice.

Chapter II: Section A

C60:1, pe60:2, P305:25   **black twist**   A strong, long-leafed tobacco twisted into a thick cord.
C60:20, pe60:21–22, P306:15   ***O, twine me a bower***   A ballad by Thomas Crofton Croker (1798–1854), Irish antiquarian; music by Alexander Roche.

> O twine me a bow'r all of woodbine and roses,
> Far, far from the path of your commonplace joys,
> Where the gem of contentment in silence reposes,
> Unsullied by tears and unshaken by noise,

Yes there would I dwell, in my own flow'ry cell,
Not the dream of ambition, of honor or power,
Should tempt me to part from my own happy tower,
Should tempt me to part from my own happy tower.

True friendship should light up his torch at my dwelling
To cheer me when youth and its pleasures were past;
Without friends where on earth are the joys worth telling,
For friendship thro' years and thro' sorrows will last.

C60:20–21, pe60:22, P306:16   **Blue eyes and golden hair**   Matthew
J. C. Hodgart and Mabel P. Worthington, *Song in the Works of James
Joyce* (New York, 1959) list this as a song by the Irish composer, James
L. Molloy (1837–1909). He did write a song entitled "Blue Eyes," but
the golden hair seems to be missing:

Blue eyes are full of danger,
Beware their tender glow;
They'll make your heart a stranger
To peaceful hours below.
I warn you, men,
Take earnest heed,
Let not bright eyes your sight mislead,
Let not bright eyes your sight mislead.
And when blue eyes your glances win, look not too deep therein.

Blue eyes with soul are beaming;
They look thee through and through;
With light of love they're streaming,
So mild, so warm, so true!
And when my heart is sore distressed,
And sorrow fills my lonely breast,
And sorrow fills my lonely breast,
Then let blue eyes my glances win.
What joy, what bliss I see therein;
What joy, what bliss I see therein!

C60:21, pe60:22–23, P306:16   **The Groves of Blarney**   By Richard
Alfred Milliken (1767–1815), Irish song writer. Chorus:

The groves of Blarney, they look so charming,
Down by the purlings of sweet silent brooks,
All grac'd by posies that spontaneous grow there,
And planted in order in the rocky nooks;
'Tis there the daisy and sweet carnation,
The blooming pink and the rose so fair,
The daffy-down-dilly, besides the lily,
Flow'rs that scent the sweet open air.

C60:23, pe61:1, P306:19 **Blackrock** Stephen's family has moved from Bray, twelve miles south-southeast of Dublin, to Blackrock, a suburban village five and one half miles southeast of Dublin on Dublin Bay, a respectable but slightly less fashionable address. See map for *A Portrait*, chapter I, on p. 132 above.

C60:27–28, pe61:5–6, P306:23–24 **the house in Carysfort . . . main street of the town** In 1892 the Joyces lived for a time at 23 Carysfort Avenue in Blackrock; the house was a scant two hundred yards southwest of Main Street, Blackrock.

C61:11, pe61:18, P307:2 **the park** Blackrock Park, on the shore of Dublin Bay, three hundred yards northwest of Main Street, Blackrock.

C61:14, pe61:21–22, P307:5–6 **the gate near the railway station** The railway tracks are between the park and the beach; the station was on the shore just southeast of the park.

C61:23, pe61:31, P307:16 **athletics and politics** Athletics was a political subject in late nineteenth-century Ireland. One phase of the revival of Irish language, culture, and custom was the founding in 1884 of the Gaelic Athletic Association, dedicated to the revival of Irish sports such as hurling (see *Por* C182:4–5n.), Irish football (see *Por* C8:19n), and handball (see *Por* C196:11n), and to recruiting and developing Irish athletes. The early years of the Association were marked by considerable political contentiousness—including protests in Parliament that English games such as polo (an Oriental game?) were allowed in Phoenix Park while Irish games were not. For a notable instance of this contentiousness see the Cyclops episode of *Ulysses*.

C61:34, pe62:3, P307:27 **the chapel** The Roman Catholic Church of St. John the Baptist at 35 Newtown Avenue, just southeast of the intersection of Main Street and Carysfort Avenue in Blackrock. In Irish usage a "chapel" is a Catholic Church, a "church" is Church of Ireland.

C61:34, pe62:3, P307:28 **the font** A large (and usually ornamented) basin at the church entrance. It contains holy water, with which the worshiper traditionally moistens his fingers and touches his brow or crosses himself in blessing.

C62:2, pe62:8, P307:23 **prayerbook** A book of devotions for Catholic laymen, usually containing prayers, hymns, and explanations of and selections from the more important masses of the Liturgical Year.

C62:6, pe62:12, P308:2 **prayed for the souls in purgatory** Catholic doctrine holds that the dead "who die in venial sin" or those "who die indebted to God's justice on account of mortal sin" go to Purgatory, where they do further penance before gaining entrance to heaven. The souls in Purgatory can be "relieved by our prayers and other good works: for the Scripture says, *It is a holy and wholesome thought to pray* *for the dead, that they may be loosed from their sins* (2 Mach. xii. 46)" (*Maynooth Catechism*, p. 27).

C62:6–7, pe62:12, P308:3   **the grace of a happy death**   The supernatural gift (grace) bestowed by God that would enable him to die with benefit of Extreme Unction, and with all his sins, both mortal and venial, forgiven so that he might enter immediately into heaven. From the Donlevy *Catechism*, p. 323: "Q. What is it we ought oftenest to beg of God? A. The fear and love of God during the whole course of our life, and at length a good end, or happy death."

C62:12, pe62:18, P308:10   **Stillorgan**   An inland village and parish five miles southeast of the center of Dublin and one and one quarter miles west-southwest of Blackrock.

C62:13–14, pe62:19–20, P308:11   **left toward the Dublin mountains**   I.e., south or southwest. The nearest foothills of the Dublin (or Wicklow) Mountains are some two miles from Stillorgan.

C62:14, pe62:20–21, P308:12   **Goatstown road**   Goatstown is a village one and one half miles west of Stillorgan. The road Stephen and his elders take (and apparently call "Goatstown Road" because it leads there) is Kilmacud Road Lower, which leads from Stillorgan to Goatstown. Kilmacud Road Upper would have taken them directly from Stillorgan to Dundrum. Goatstown Road proper leads north from Goatstown toward Dublin.

C62:15, pe62:21, P308:12   **Dundrum**   A village at the foot of the Dublin (or Wicklow) Mountains, four miles south of the center of Dublin and three and three quarter miles west-southwest of Blackrock.

C62:15, pe62:21–22, P308:13   **Sandyford**   A village two miles south-southeast of Dundrum and three miles southwest of Blackrock.

C62:18, pe62:24, P308:16   **Munster**   The southern of the four ancient provinces of Ireland (the poor old woman's "four green fields"), together with Leinster (east), Connacht (west and northwest), and Ulster (northeast). Munster contains the Dedalus's home county of Cork. The inhabitants of the province had a long history of vigorous resistance to British dominion and were well-storied with accounts of reprisal and repression.

C62:27, pe62:35, P308:27   ***The Count of Monte Cristo***   A novel (1844) by Alexandre Dumas *père* (1802–70). The story opens in 1815 when its young Byronic hero, Edmond Dantes, sails his ship into the harbor of Marseilles. He is unaware of the enemies on shore who are plotting his destruction. Among them are a man who wishes to replace Dantes as captain of the ship and another who loves Dantes's fiancée, Mercedes, and wishes to replace Dantes as husband-to-be. The two conspire to have him arrested as a courier for the outlawed Bonapartists just as the Dantes-Mercedes wedding party is ending. Dantes is imprisoned secretly in a dungeon of the Château d'If, where he remains, legally forgotten, for fourteen years, while his enemies prosper. Mercedes remains faithful in her heart to Dantes, but, assured that he is dead, she innocently marries the suitor-conspirator.

Dantes finally escapes from the Château d'If by changing places with a dead prisoner who is to be buried in the sea. Just before his death, this fellow-prisoner had revealed to Dantes the presence of an immense fortune in a cave on the island of Monte Cristo. The escaped Dantes makes his way to the island, discovers the treasure, and then travels to Paris to avenge his wrongs. As the Count of Monte Cristo, he readily gains entrance to the circles in which his old enemies now move, and, one by one, destroys them. By exposing certain treacheries of the man who had married Mercedes, he brings him to disgrace and ruin. Unfortunately, this man and Mercedes have a son, who challenges Monte Cristo to a duel. Mercedes comes to Dantes, reveals that she has known him from the time of his return, and pleads with him to spare her son's life. Dantes agrees, in memory of their former love, to spare the son; however, as a man of honor, he cannot decline the duel, so he must accept death. Overwhelmed by the merciless logic of honor, Mercedes reveals the whole story to her son, who, at the time appointed for the duel, acknowledges the justice of his father's ruin and refuses to kill Dantes.

Mercedes subsequently meets Dantes in a garden, lavishly praises his magnanimity, berates herself for her unworthiness, and receives his pardon. He has come to realize, he tells her, that he is merely an instrument of the Lord, and from this perspective he can now look upon his own misfortunes with equanimity. When Mercedes's ruined husband commits suicide, Dantes does not renew the old romance; he sets Mercedes up in a cottage in Marseilles and then leaves France forever in the company of a beautiful Greek princess whom he had purchased in a Constantinople slave market during his travels.

C62:27–28, pe62:36, P308:28   **that dark avenger**   After he escapes from prison, Dantes is repeatedly described as strikingly pale with dark eyes and jet black hair. He is also "dark" because the Byzantine plots of his revenges work in mysterious ways and because, in his single-minded intensity, Dantes comes close to losing his moral perspective and to overdoing his revenge.

C62:30–31, pe62:39, P308:31   **the wonderful island cave**   After Dantes discovers the treasure cave on the island of Monte Cristo, he buys the island and transforms the cave into a romantic hideout, an oriental fantasy straight out of the *Arabian Nights* (see *Dub* C14:1n and C29:1n).

C62:35, pe63:4, P309:1   **Marseilles, of sunny trellisses**   At the beginning of *The Count of Monte Cristo* the "arbour" of the Café la Reserve is described as bordered by "sunny trellisses." In that arbor, Dantes's enemies plot to betray him, and, on the following day, Dantes is arrested at the Café just as the "wedding-feast" is concluding. At the end of the novel, after Mercedes has left her traitor-husband and committed herself to a life of poverty and penance, Dantes gives her his father's little house in Marseilles, and it is in the garden of that house, "under an arbour of Virginian jessamine," that the final interview between Dantes and Mercedes takes place.

C62:35, pe63:5, P309:2   **Mercedes**   Her name means "mercies," and "Mary of the Mercies" is an appellation of the Blessed Virgin Mary.

C62:36, pe63:5–6, P309:2–3   **the road that led to the mountains**   I.e., to the Dublin or Wicklow Mountains, one of the roads traversed on the Sunday walks; see *Por* C62:13–14n.

C63:1, pe63:6–7, P309:3   **a small whitewashed house**   Mercedes's original home in Marseilles (when she is a poor orphan betrothed to Dantes) is a "poor fisherman's hut," the inside of which is painted with "limewash," i.e., whitewash.

C63:5, pe63:11, P309:8   **a long train of adventures**   The central plot of Dumas's novel does trace the flamboyant career of Edmond Dantes, but that plot is enriched by an elaborate array of subplots and interpolated adventure stories that comprise a catalogue of popular nineteenth-century fictions.

C63:11, pe63:17, P309:14   **Madam, I never eat muscatel grapes**   When the Count of Monte Cristo is mounting his revenge-plots in Paris, Mercedes notices that he never eats or drinks in her husband's house. She invites him into a greenhouse in the garden and urges fruit upon him. He refuses twice with the quoted line. Later, Mercedes's son explains to her that Monte Cristo is almost an oriental, "and it is customary with [orientals] to retain full liberty of revenge by not eating or drinking in the house of their enemies."

C63:17, pe63:23, P309:20–21   **Napoleon's plain style of dress**   At the outset of his career as general Napoleon did dress in an undecorated uniform in order to emphasize the "democratic" nature of his army and its leadership. Later in his career, the colorful costumes affected by his marshalls contrasted with Napoleon's relatively plain (if affluent) uniforms.

C63:21, pe63:27, P309:25 **the castle** One of the several Martello towers on Dublin Bay stands on the shore at the northen end of Blackrock Park. The towers were named after Cape Martello in Corsica, where in 1794 the British had great trouble capturing their prototype. The towers were built (1803–6) to defend the Irish coast against invasion by the French. The most famous of the Martello Towers is the one at Sandycove (three miles east-southeast) where Joyce lived briefly during 1904 and where he set the action of the opening episode of *Ulysses*.

C63:26, pe63:33, P309:31 **Carrickmines** An inland, country village, three miles south of Blackrock.

C63:30, pe63:38, P310:1 **Stradbrook** An inland area one mile south-southeast of Blackrock.

C64:28, pe64:35, P311:5 **the tramtrack on the Rock Road** Rock Road runs northwest from Blackrock toward Dublin. It is part of the sequence of roads and streets that comprises the main road along Dublin Bay that links Bray in the south to Dalkey, Kingstown (now Dun Laoghaire), Blackrock, and Dublin. A tramtrack (horse-drawn before, electric after 1896) ran in the center of the road from Dublin to Dalkey.

Chapter II: Section B

C65:15, pe65:20, P311:30 **caravans** Covered horse-drawn carriages or carts.

C65:23, pe65:28, P312:6 **the Merrion Road** Part of the main thoroughfare from Blackrock to Dublin; it continues Rock Road (*Por* C64:28n) to the northwest and is visible from the railroad line that links Blackrock to Dublin.

C66:18–19, pe66:23, P313:4 **the neighbouring square** In 1893 the Joyces moved from Blackrock to 14 Fitzgibbon Street in the northeastern quadrant of Dublin. The street extends the north side of Mountjoy Square to the east-northeast. The square, a modest but fashionable residential address in the 1890s, was just entering a long period of decline toward its present dereliction.

C66:21–22, pe66:25–26, P313:7–8 **one of its central lines . . . the customhouse** The west side of Mountjoy Square gives south into Gardiner Street, a main thoroughfare which runs south-southeast to the back of the Custom House on the north bank of the Liffey just east of the center of Dublin. Completed in 1791, the Custom House is an impressive structure surmounted by a dome which is supported by a colonade and capped by a statue of "Hope." The building housed not only custom and excise tax offices but also the Board of Public Works and the Poor Law Commission.

C66:33, pe66:38–39, P313:21   **the sunwarmed trellisses of the wineshops**   See *Por* C62:35n.

C67:17, pe67:20, P314:37   **Mabel Hunter**   The index of the Theatre Collection in The Lincoln Center Library, New York, lists a newspaper clipping about her, but the clipping is missing from the file.

C67:21, pe67:24, P314:13   **pantomime**   Pantomimes were a popular form of entertainment in late nineteenth-century Ireland (as they still are at Christmas time). They consisted of songs, dances, and topical jokes held together by a well-known and rather loose story line (Aladdin and His Lamp, Sinbad the Sailor, etc.). The songs and jokes were usually updated when the pantomimes were revived.

C67:29, pe67:33, P314:23   **his stone of coal**   I.e., a 14-pound bag of coal. The fact that the family purchases coal a bag at a time indicates poverty.

C68:27–28, pe68:30–31, P315:25   **Harold's Cross**   A suburban village two and one quarter miles south-southwest of the center of Dublin.

C68:30, pe68:33, P315:27   **crackers**   Small cardboard tubes covered with crepe paper, decorated for the occasion (Christmas, birthdays, etc.). A tape which protrudes from each end of the tube makes a small explosion when pulled and broken (the "crack"). The tube contains party favors: a paper hat, a symbolic trinket, etc.

C69:9, pe69:13, P316:11   **tram. The lank brown horses**   Trams in Dublin were horse-drawn until the gradual conversion of the street railway system to electricity in the late 1890s and early 1900s.

C69:26, pe69:30–31, P316:30   **long black stockings**   In *The Count of Monte Cristo* Mercedes "tapped the earth with her pliant and well-formed foot, so as to display the pure and full shape of her well-turned leg in its red cotton stocking with grey and blue clocks."

C69:31, pe69:36, P317:1–2   **the hotel grounds**   The Marine Station Hotel in Bray; see *Por* C43:1n.

C70:10, pe70:13, P317:19   **emerald exercise**   In the 1890s pamphlets of blank paper with green covers were sold as patriotic souvenirs of Ireland's aspiration to nationhood.

C70:12, pe70:15, P317:21   **A.M.D.G.**   *Ad Majorem Dei Gloriam* (Latin: For the Greater Glory of God), the motto of the Jesuits. Students in Jesuit schools traditionally put the initials at the top of all exercises to remind themselves of the purpose of learning.

C70:13, pe70:17, P317:23   **To E—— C——**   In chapter III:B of *A Portrait* the young woman's first name is given as Emma. In *Stephen Hero* the same (or a similar) young woman is identified as Emma Clery and is much more fully presented than she is in *A Portrait*; see Introduction, pp. 7–8 above.

C70:15, pe70:18, P317:25   **Lord Byron**   George Gordon, Lord Byron (1788–1824), a leading poet of the Romantic Movement in England. His earliest and somewhat callow verse, most of it written while he was still in his teens, ran heavily to personal love lyrics addressed or dedicated with initials ("To E—— C——"). In the late nineteenth century Byron was regarded with proper Victorian suspicion because he was an ironist, because his attitudes toward established church and state were irreverent (and published), and because his private life was "immoral" (and well-publicized).

C70:21, pe70:24–25, P317:31   **second moiety notices**   Legal notices in bankruptcy proceedings.

C71:4, pe71:5, P318:17   **L.D.S.**   *Laus Deo Semper* (Latin: Praise to God Always), another Jesuit motto, traditionally placed at the end of school exercises.

C71:15, pe71:17, P318:29   **him**   Rev. John Conmee, S.J.; see *Por* C9:29n.

C71:16, pe71:18, P318:30   **at the corner of the square**   Belvedere College, where Father Conmee was prefect of studies in the 1890s, is at 5, 6 Denmark Street Great, two short blocks west along the extension of Mountjoy Square North; see *Por* C66:18–19n.

C71:18, pe71:20, P318:32   **Belvedere**   See *Dub* C20:25n.

C71:20, pe71:22, P318:34   **provincial of the order**   In autobiographical time Father Conmee's promotion came somewhat later; see *Por* C9:29n.

C71:21–22, pe71:23–24, P319:1–2   **christian brothers**   See *Dub* C29:3n.

C71:36, pe71:38, P319:17   **Maurice**   Stephen's brother, mentioned only in this scene (and in passing) in *A Portrait*, is much more fully treated in *Stephen Hero*. Stephen recalls him once in *Ulysses*, on p. 211.

C72:16, pe72:17, P320:2   **the corporation**   See *Dub* C121:20n.

C72:27, pe72:29, P320:13   *twice nine*   See *Por* C44:26n.

C73:1, pe73:1, P320:23 **Whitsuntide play** Whitsuntide is the week
beginning with Whitsunday or Pentecost, the seventh Sunday after
Easter, which commemorates the descent of the Holy Spirit upon the
Apostles fifty days after the Resurrection (Acts 2:1–6). The presentation of a play at this time of the Liturgical Year appears to be a local
custom since there is no continuous dramatic or ecclesiastical tradition
linking drama to this season; see *Dub* C100:11n.

C73:2–3, pe73:3, P320:25 **the small grassplot** In the rather cramped
quadrangle which the growth of the college and the attendant building
programs had created behind Belvedere House. In the 1890s the quadrangle was open to the east, but it is now closed, and the grass plot has
given way to pavement.

C73:4–5, pe73:4–5, P320:27 **down the steps from the house** Belvedere House was the main building of the college; access to the quadrangle behind it (and to the buildings opening on the quadrangle) was
through the main entrance hall of the house.

C73:5, pe73:5, P320:28 **Stewards** Persons appointed to maintain
order and to function as ushers during the evening's program.

C73:10, pe73:10, P320:33 **The Blessed Sacrament had been removed from the tabernacle** Thereby assuring that there would be no
desecration of the Host while the college chapel was temporarily in use
as dressing room, property room, and green room.

C73:11, pe73:11, P321:1 **driven** Unfastened (so that they could be
removed).

C73:25–26, pe73:25–26, P321:17–18 **the chief part, that of a farcical pedagogue** Ellmann has identified the play as "F. Anstey's *Vice
Versa*" (p. 57), but this needs clarification. Thomas Anstey Guthrie
(1856–1934; pseudonym, F. Anstey) did publish a novel, *Vice Versa: or
A Lesson to Fathers* (London, 1882). In the following year the actor and
playwright Edward Rose published a dramatized version and starred in
that version in a run that began at the Gaiety Theatre in London on 9
April 1883. The play, a short twenty-eight pages (London, 1883),
proved enormously popular with schools and other amateur organizations, so popular that Guthrie himself finally wrote his own dramatized
version of his novel (London, 1910), a longer and more complex (if not
more mature) version than Rose's. The "farcical pedagogue," Dr.
Grimstone, is stuffy rather than farcical in Rose's version (the only one

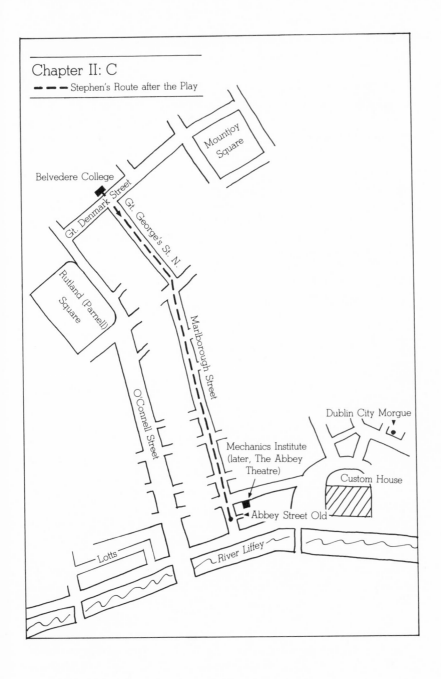

Chapter II: C

▬ ▬ ▬ Stephen's Route after the Play

Mountjoy Square

Belvedere College

Gt. Denmark Street

Gt. George's St. N.

Rutland (Parnell) Square

Marlborough Street

O'Connell Street

Dublin City Morgue

Mechanics Institute
(later, The Abbey
Theatre)

Custom House

◄— Abbey Street Old

Lotts

River Liffey

available in 1898), and Grimstone's is a supporting role, not the "chief part." The chief part in the play is reserved for the boy, Dick Bultitude's "Body," "inhabited" through most of the play by his father's mind, or "Spirit," and tongue, thanks to a magic talisman (the number two role is taken by Mr. Bultitude's Body, "vice versa"). Obviously, Joyce withheld the title and content of the play from *A Portrait* for a reason; apparently he treated the play in fiction as, according to an eyewitness, Eugene Sheehy, he had treated the play in real life:

> Joyce, who was cast for the part of a schoolmaster in the school play, ignored the role allotted to him and impersonated Father Henry [the Rector of Belvedere College]. He carried on, often for five minutes at a time, with the pet sayings of the Rector, imitating his gestures and mannerisms. The other members of the cast collapsed with laughter on the stage—completely missing their cues and forgetting their parts—and the schoolboy audience received the performance with hysterical glee.
>
> Father Henry, who was sitting in one of the front rows, again showed what a sportsman he was by laughing loudly at this joke against himself and Joyce received no word of reprimand for his impudence. [*May It Please the Court* (Dublin, 1951), pp. 8–10]

There is no evidence in *A Portrait* that Stephen has performed in fiction the takeoff Joyce performed in fact.

C73:28, pe73:29, P321:20　**number two**　I.e., Stephen is in the room assigned to those in the "middle grade" at Belvedere, the second to the last year of his studies at the college and the second to the last of the four top grades: senior, middle, junior, preparatory. The senior grade was, of course, housed in room number one.

C74:8–9, pe74:7–8, P322:4–5　**the gospel side of the altar**　The left side of the altar as the congregation faces it—where the Gospels are read, as opposed to the epistle side, on the right, where the Epistles are read.

C75:32–33, pe75:33–34, P323:34–35　**took off the rector in the part of the schoolmaster**　What Joyce did in the "real world" of autobiographical time; see *Por* C73:25–26n.

C76:2–3, pe76:1–2, P324:5–6　*He that will not hear . . . and the publicana*　Jesus, teaching his disciples (Matthew 18:16–17): "But if he will not hear thee, then take with thee one or two more, that in the mouth of two or three witnesses every word may be established. And if he neglect to hear them, tell *it* unto the church: but if he neglect to hear the church, let him be unto thee as an heathen man and a publican."

C76:22, pe76:22, P324:28　**after beads**　The prayer of the Rosary was a regular feature of the college's daily program; see *Por* C148:12n.

C76:22–23, pe76:23, P324:29   **number one**   See *Por* C73:28n.

C76:25, pe76:26, P324:32   **to ask for a free day**   Informal holidays were used by school administrators to improve student morale, to reward a class or a school for outstanding academic achievement or good behavior.

C76:36, pe76:37, P325:7   **butter wouldn't melt in your mouth**   John Heywood, *Proverbs* (London, 1598): "She looketh as butter would not melt in her mouth"; i.e., she looks so innocent that one cannot believe that she is even warm, let alone capable of passion.

C77:31, pe77:33, P326:7   **one sure five**   See *Dub* C169:18n.

C78:9, pe78:12, P326:25   **the *Confiteor***   The prayer which is used in preparation for Confession:

> I confess to Almighty God, to blessed Mary ever Virgin, to blessed Michael the Archangel, to blessed John the Baptist, to the Holy Apostles, Peter and Paul, and to all the Saints, that I have sinned exceedingly in thought, word, and deed, through my fault, through my fault, through my most grievous fault. Therefore I beseech the blessed Mary ever Virgin, the blessed Michael the Archangel, the blessed John the Baptist, the holy Apostles, Peter and Paul, and all the Saints, to pray to the Lord our God for me.
>
> May the almighty God have mercy on me, forgive me my sins, and bring me to life everlasting. Amen.
>
> May the Almighty and merciful Lord grant me pardon, absolution, and remission of all my sins. Amen. [*Maynooth Catechism*, p. 3]

C78:20, pe78:23, P327:2   **number six**   The room numbers at Belvedere indicated the number of years to graduation; see *Por* C73:28n.

C79:5, pe79:6, P327:25   **Mr Tate**   Called mister because he was a lay-teacher, not a member of the Jesuit Order.

C79:21–22, pe79:24–25, P328:8–9   *without a possibility of ever approaching nearer*   I.e., Stephen's essay has argued that the soul yearns for the blessed state of communion with its Creator. The orthodox position is that each soul is granted "sufficient grace" to approach that communion. Stephen's heresy resides in his implication that the soul has not been granted sufficient grace, or that the soul (romantically) yearns for more than its Creator has deemed sufficient.

C79:24, pe79:27, P328:11   *without a possibility of ever reaching*   Stephen "corrects" his heresy by implying that the soul can approach "nearer" to its Creator, but that the soul will never reach oneness with its Creator (because that would mean loss of its identity).

C79:32, pe79:35, P328:19   **Drumcondra Road**   Just north of the Royal Canal; it is a section of one of the main highways from Dublin toward the north; more immediately, it is the main road from Dublin to the suburban village of Drumcondra, two and one half miles north of the center of Dublin.

C80:5, pe80:7, P328:30 **Clonliffe Road** At a right angle off Drumcondra Road Lower, it runs east and slightly south toward Dublin Bay.

C80:11, pe80:13–14, P329:2 **Captain Marryat** Frederick Marryat (1792–1848), an English officer in the Royal Navy, wrote a number of novels of sea life and adventure, many of them for boys.

C80:18, pe80:20, P329:10 **Newman** John Henry Cardinal Newman (1801–90), a safe choice because he was both Catholic and a thoroughly respectable Englishman. Initially a clergyman in the Church of England, he was prominent in the Oxford Movement's attempt to elevate the Church of England's status and nature. His convictions led him to transfer his allegiance to the Roman Catholic Church, in which he rose to the rank of cardinal. His writings on behalf of his principles were regarded by late nineteenth-century critics as distinguished for dignity and eloquence. See *Dub* C188:19n.

C80:28, pe80:30, P329:20 **Lord Tennyson** Alfred, Lord Tennyson (1809–92), the official "great poet" of the Victorian Age, who succeeded Wordsworth as poet laureate in 1850. A critical reaction to the disparity between the elaborate techniques of his prosody and his often rather flimsy and conformist subject matter brought about a rapid decline of his reputation in his last years, and his stature as an important poet did not begin to be reestablished until recent times.

C81:1, pe81:1, P329:30 **Byron** Regarded as both immoral and a heretic. Because he was raised as a Presbyterian, Byron would necessarily have been judged heretical by Catholics, not to speak of the irreligious views of his mature years; see *Por* C70:15n.

C81:9, pe81:10, P330:4 **the slates in the yard** I.e., on the wall of the school's public urinal.

C81:9, pe81:11, P330:5 **sent to the loft** At Belvedere the place appointed for punishment was called "the loft"; see *Dub* C22:32–33n.

C81:14–15, pe81:15–16, P330:9 *As Tyson was riding . . . Alec Kafoozelum* After an anonymous ballad, "The Daughter of Jerusalem," which has several variants, not all of them genteel. The genteel version tells the story of "a perfect lamb" named Sam who tries to run away with a Turkish barber's daughter, Kafoozalem. They are caught, throttled, and thrown into the brook Kedrom near Jerusalem, where their ghosts are seen kissing at the height of the full moon. One parlor version of the ballad begins:

In Ancient days there liv'd a Turk,
A horrid beast, e'en in the East,

Who did the Prophet's holy work,
As barber of Jerusalem.
He had a daughter fair and smirk,
Complexion fair, And light brown hair,
With naught about her like a Turk,
Except her name, Kafoozalem!
My own Kafoozalem, Kafoozalem,
My own Kafoozalem,
The daughter of Jerusalem.

The not-so-genteel versions label Kafoozalem the harlot rather than daughter of Jerusalem, with appropriate emendation of the verses.

C81:23, pe81:24, P330:20 **a trans** A translation, a trot, pony, or crib.

C82:13, pe82:13, P331:13 **Jones's Road** Leads south from Clonliffe Road back toward the Royal Canal and metropolitan Dublin.

C83:9, pe83:7, P332:12 **in a great bake** I.e., angry or anxious, similar to "hot and bothered."

C83:26, pe83:24, P332:29 **obedience** See *Por* C59:9n.

C83:35–36, pe83:34–35, P333:4–5 **When the gymnasium had been opened** See *Por* C61:23n.

C84:1–2, pe83:36–37, P333:7 **the movement towards national revival** See *Dub* C137:25n.

C85:4, pe85:1, P334:15 **The Lily of Killarney** I.e., the overture to the "Irish" opera of that name (1862), composed by the German-born English musician, Sir Julius Benedict (1804–85).

C85:13–14, pe85:11–12, P334:26–27 **For one rare moment he seemed to be clothed in the real apparel of boyhood** I.e., Stephen has been until now an adult in a boy's body; as for the "moment" of the play, *Vice Versa*, Mr. Bultitude's "Spirit" is able through magic to inhabit a boy's body; see *Por* C73:25–26n. But in the play Mr. Bultitude's experience in the "real apparel" of his son's body is a comic nightmare which (as *A Lesson to Fathers*) teaches him that the reverse of the sentimental dictum, "the days of boyhood are the happiest days of your life," is often true.

C85:36, pe85:34–35, P335:16 **the steps from the garden** Led from the quadrangle into the central hall of Belvedere House (and thence to the street).

C86:10, pe86:8, P335:28 **George's Street** Great George's Street North begins across Denmark Street Great from Belvedere College and leads southeast; it gives into Marlborough Street, which continues south to the Liffey in central Dublin.

C86:24, pe86:23, P336:10 **the morgue** Stephen has apparently walked south through Great George's Street North and through Marl-borough Street. But there is potential for geographical confusion here because the Dublin City Morgue in the late 1890s was at 3 Store Street, 400 yards east of Marlborough Street, while Lotts, the "laneway" Ste-phen sees, was 200 yards west of Marlborough Street. Apparently what Stephen is looking at is the "porch" of the Dublin Mechanic's Institute at 27 Abbey Street Lower, on the corner of Marlborough Street (where the new Abbey Theatre building now stands). The building which housed the Mechanic's Institute had formerly housed the City Morgue and was, beginning in December 1904 to house the Abbey Theatre. So, "the dark cobbled laneway at its side" would have been Abbey Street Old, not Lotts.

C86:25, pe86:25, P336:11   *Lotts*   A lane, east of O'Connell Street Lower, parallel to and just north of the Liffey in central Dublin.

Chapter II: Section D

C86:31, pe86:31, P336:17   **Kingsbridge**   Now Séan Heuston Station; see *Dub* C117:22n.

C87:2–3, pe86:36–87:1, P336:23–24   **telegraphpoles . . . every four seconds**   The standard distance between telegraph poles along rail-roads in Great Britain and Ireland in the late nineteenth century was sixty yards: therefore a telegraph pole every four seconds meant a speed of roughly thirty miles per hour. The nightmail train from Dublin to Cork (164 miles) took a little over seven hours in the 1890s.

C87:18, pe87:16, P337:7   **Maryborough**   50 miles from Dublin; 114 miles from Cork.

C87:19, pe87:17, P337:8   **Mallow**   19 miles from Cork; 145 miles from Dublin.

C87:35, pe87:34, P337:26   **a jingle**   A two-wheeled, covered, horse-drawn car which seated three in the front seat and two in the back (with their backs to the front); see *Por* C20:2n.

C88:1, pe87:36, P337:28   **Victoria Hotel**   In St. Patrick's Street, then the main and most fashionable shopping thoroughfare in central Cork. In the 1870s and 80s, the Victoria was *the* hotel in Cork. St. Patrick's Street still prospers at the heart of Cork's downtown shopping district, but the Victoria has closed its doors.

C88:8–23, pe88:5–20, P338:1–16 *'Tis youth and folly . . . The mountain dew* Hodgart and Worthington list this song as a variant of an English and Scots folk song, "Waly Waly," but the meter and content of Mr. Dedalus's song are so markedly different from English and Scots versions of "Waly Waly" which I have examined that I hesitate to include Mr. Dedalus's song in the family. Zack Bowen reprints the song from *A Portrait* but does not identify a source for the text Joyce uses (*Musical Allusions in the Works of James Joyce*, pp. 37–38).

C88:29–30, pe88:27–28, P338:23–24 *come-all-yous* Popular street ballads; see *Por* C35:12–13n.

C89:4, pe88:36, P338:33 **drisheens**

> Drisheen is now used in Cork as an English word to denote a sort of pudding made of the narrow intestines of a sheep, filled with blood that has been cleared of the red colouring matter and mixed with meal and other ingredients. So far as I know, this viand and its name are peculiar to Cork, where *Drisheen* is considered suitable for persons of weak or delicate digestion. . . . [P. W. Joyce, p. 251]

C89:9, pe89:6, P339:5–6 **Queen's College** Opened under the aegis of Queen Victoria in 1849. It was one of three Queen's Colleges established in 1845 (at Belfast, Galway, and Cork) as a compromise solution to the lack of higher education for Catholics in Ireland; Dublin refused the offer; see *Dub* C188:27–28n. Queen's College, Cork, is now University College, Cork.

C89:12, pe89:9, P339:8 **the Mardyke** A once-fashionable Cork promenade that leads west from the island-center of the city. It had declined to commercial use by the late nineteenth century and is now little more than a laneway.

C89:13, pe89:10, P339:9 **the grounds of the college** University College, Cork, is in College Road, south of the River Lee and not quite a mile west-southwest of the Victoria Hotel, which is in the center of Cork.

C90:23, pe90:20, P340:24 **the Groceries** "Groceries" in late nineteenth-century Ireland meant household needs and foodstuffs exclusive of perishables (vegetables, fish, meats, and dairy products), and most grocers were licensed as "grocers, tea, wine, and spirit merchants." Many, so licensed, ran pubs with barely a facade of groceries and tea. Others (and a few still exist in provincial corners of Ireland) were grocery shops with a small stand-up bar appended in a side or back room.

C90:26, pe90:23, P340:27 **when our names had been marked** I.e., when they had been recorded as having met the attendance requirement at a meal which they did not intend to eat.

C90:30, pe90:27–28, P340:32 **the Tantiles** To tantle or tantile is provincial English for to loiter.

C90:36, pe90:35, P341:4 **street arabs** Children of the poor or gypsy children who drift the streets in the hope of finding or begging or stealing some form of sustenance.

C91:10, pe91:7, P341:15 **a free boy** I.e., on full scholarship.

C92:2, pe91:36, P342:10–11 **the South Terrace** Then a fashionable middle-class residential street in the southeastern section of the city of Cork.

C92:2, pe91:37, P342:12 **maneens** Irish dialect: little men, a mildly contemptuous expression.

C92:12, pe92:8–9, P342:23 *Queenstown* Now Cobh, the port city for Cork, eight miles to the southeast (down the River Lee and across Lough Mahon).

C93:5–6, pe93:3, P343:21 **made his first communion** I.e., Stephen received the Sacrament of Confirmation presumably at age seven when, as his catechism put it, he would have "reached the use of reason" and would have been "sufficiently instructed in Christian doctrine" to know what sin was and to become "a soldier of Christ" (*Maynooth Catechism*, pp. 51–52).

C93:6, pe93:3, P343:2 **slim jim** Joyce (*Letters* 3:129): "This is a kind of sweet meat made of soft marshmellow jelly which is coated first with pink sugar and then powdered, so far as I remember with coconut chips. It is called 'Slim Jim' because it is sold in strips about a foot or a foot and a half in length and an inch in breadth."

C93:25, pe93:24, P344:9 **a lob** "A quantity, especially of money or of any valuable commodity" (P. W. Joyce, p. 287). In Cork slang: a penny.

C93:28, pe93:26–27, P344:12 **Peter Pickackafax** Source unknown.

C93:29, pe93:28, P344:13 **a Dublin jackeen** "A nickname for a conceited Dublin citizen of the lower class" (P. W. Joyce, p. 278).

C93:30–31, pe93:29–30, P344:14–15 **Newcombe's coffeehouse** Once a fashionable place to take morning coffee and afternoon tea in St. Patrick's Street, Cork; see *Por* C88:1n.

C94:5, pe94:3, P344:26 **the Lee** The river on which Cork is located. It rises in southwestern Ireland and flows through Cork into Lough Mahon, which provides a waterway between Cork and Cobh (formerly Queenstown) on Cork Harbor.

C94:7, pe94:5, P344:29 **Dilectus** A phrase book of Latin quotations chosen as suitable "learned comments" for a wide variety of situations, on the order of *Bartlett's Familiar Quotations*.

C94:8–9, pe94:6–8, P344:30–32 *Tempora . . . or . . . in illis* The second form is metrically correct, but the two sentences also have different meanings, the first: "Circumstances change us and we change in them"; the second: "Circumstances change and we change with them." The second line is the title (in Latin) of a poem by Robert Greene (1560–92):

Aspyring thoughts led Phaeton amisse,
Proud Icarus did fall he soard so hie:
Seek not to clymbe with fond Semyramis,
Least Sonne revenge the Fathers iniurre.
Take heede, Ambition is a sugred ill
That fortune layes, presumptuous mynds to spill.

The bitter griefe that frets the quiet minde;
The sting that prieks the forward man to woe
Is Envie, which in honor seld we finde,
& yet to honor sworne a secret foe,
Learne this of me, envie not others state,
The fruits of envie is envie and hate, . . .

These blasing comments do foreshew mishap,
Let not their flaming lights offend thyne eye.
Look ere thou leape, prevent an after clap:
These three forewarnd well mayst thou flye.
If now by choyce thou aymst at happie health,
Eschew self love, choose for the Commonwealth.

C94:25, pe94:25, P345:15 **Yerra** See *Dub* C127:16n.
C94:30, pe94:31, P345:21 **Sunday's Well** A fashionable suburb just west of the city of Cork.
C95:17, pe95:17, P346:11 **a fivebarred gate** At least six feet high, a formidable obstacle.
C95:19, pe95:19, P346:13–14 **the Kerry Boy** From County Kerry in the southwestern tip of Ireland. One Kerry Boy was made famous by Finley Peter Dunne in *Mr. Dooley in Peace and War* (Boston, 1898), pp. 124–29, as "the curly-haired angel" who turns out to be a criminal.
C96:7–9, pe96:7–9, P347:4–6 *Art thou pale . . . companionless* The opening lines of an unfinished poem, "To the Moon" (1820, 1824), by Percy Bysshe Shelley (1792–1822). The fragment continues:

Among the stars that have a different birth,—
And ever changing like a joyless eye
That finds no object worth its constancy?

Thou chosen sister of the Spirit
That gazes on thee till in thee it pities . . .

Chapter II: Section E

C96:15, pe96:15, P347:12 **Foster Place** Off College Green, is a dead-end street behind the Bank of Ireland in central Dublin just south of the Liffey.

C96:19–20, pe96:20, P347:17–18 **thirty and three pounds** I.e., a prize of thirty pounds for the exhibition and three pounds for the essay (Ellmann, p. 52); see Introduction, pp. 14–15.

C96:20, pe96:21, P347:18 **exhibition** Distinguished performance in the annual competitive examinations set by the Intermediate Education Board for all the secondary schools in Ireland (the Board used the examinations in effect to dictate the curricula of secondary schools in Ireland; cf. *Dub* C187:1n).

C96:32–33, pe96:33, P347:31–32 **the house of commons of the old Irish parliament** The Act of Union (1800) abolished the independent parliament in Dublin, and the building was sold in 1802 to the Bank of Ireland. It was privately stipulated at the time of the sale that the purchasers would so partition and redecorate the chambers in which the two Irish legislative bodies had met as to make them unusable for public meetings; the object was also to suppress all visual allusion to the building's parliamentary past.

C97:2, pe96:35, P348:2 **Hely Hutchinson** John Hely-Hutchinson (1724–94), an Irish statesman and economist. At various times he held the posts of secretary of state, prime sergeant, and (non-politically) provost of Trinity College. He supported free trade, Catholic Emancipation, and political reform. He was noted for his satirical power as a speaker.

C97:2, pe96:35, P348:2 **Flood** Henry Flood (1732–91), Irish statesman and orator, played a prominent part in Irish political opposition to English dominion. Flood was, for a time, an ally of Grattan, but eventually quarreled with him.

C97:2–3, pe97:1, P348:3 **Henry Grattan** (1746–1820), Irish statesman and orator, a leader in Ireland's struggle for increased legislative independence, author of the so-called Grattan Constitution of 1782—and likewise a leader of the opposition to the British policy of Union. He was also a leader of the movement for Catholic Emancipation (which was not accomplished until nine years after his death).

C97:3, pe97:1, P348:3 **Charles Kendal Bushe** Irish judge and orator (1767–1843), an ally of Grattan against the British policy of Union. He is reputed to have been the most eloquent orator of his day.

C97:6-8, pe97:5-6, P348:7-9 **As I roved out . . . month of sweet July** After an Irish street ballad, "The Bonny Labouring Boy":

> As I roved out one fine May morning,
> All in the blooming spring,
> I overheard a damsel fair,
> Most grievously did sing,
> Saying 'Cruel were my parents
> Who me did sore annoy;
> They would not let me tarry
> With my bonny Irish boy.'

Cf. P. W. Joyce (p. 113): " 'Oh that's all *as I roved out*': to express unbelief in what someone says as quite unworthy of credit. In allusion to songs beginning 'As I roved out,' which are generally fictitious."

C97:9, pe97:7, P348:10 **October** If the novel's time coincides with biographical time, it would be October 1897.

C97:13-14, pe97:11-12, P348:14-15 **a mantle priced at twenty guineas in the windows of Barnardo's** An expensive fur. J. M. Barnardo & Son, court furriers and foreign skin importers and mantle manufacturers, at 108 Grafton Street, a street of fashionable shops that runs south from the Bank of Ireland.

C97:20, pe97:18, P348:21 **Underdone's** Identified by Ellmann (p. 40n) as "probably" the Joyce family nickname for Jammet's, "The Burlington Hotel and Restaurant, Jammet Brothers, proprietors, high class French restaurant" (*Thom's* 1904, p. 1413), at 26 and 27 St. Andrew's Street, about fifty yards south of Foster Place and the Bank of Ireland.

C97:33, pe97:32, P348:35 *Ingomar* *Ingomar the Barbarian* (1851), a play by Maria Anne Lovell, adapted from the German *Der Sohn der Wildnis* (The Son of the Wilderness, 1843) by Frederich Halm, pseudonym of the Austrian dramatist E. F. J. Baron von Münch-Bellinghausen (1806-71). The hero, Ingomar, falls in love with a wandering Greek maiden, Parthenia, a model of filial piety. She "tames and subdues his savage spirit," but filial piety being stronger than love, she determines to leave him and return home. He agonizes and then resolves to accompany and protect her. Faced once more with a "parting" when they reach Greece, he again agonizes and resolves, this time, to become a Greek. He gives up the sword for the plough and refuses to sell his countrymen out to the Greeks but instead makes peace. "*Ingomar*: To love I owe this blessing. *Parthenia*: To love and honor. (Then are they forever joined— / Two souls, with but a single thought— / Two hearts, that beat as one.)"

C97:33–34, pe97:32, P348:35   *The Lady of Lyons*   A romantic comedy by Edward Bulwer-Lytton (1838). Its hero, Claude Melnotte, the son of a gardener, loves Pauline Deschapelles, a much sought-after beauty who scorns alliance with any of her wealthy and titled suitors. A legacy from his father enables Melnotte to go to Paris to obtain an education in the liberal arts and the social graces. Upon his return to Lyons, he courts Pauline anonymously, sending her flowers and verses of his own composition without revealing himself because of his awareness of the social gulf that separates them. Meanwhile, the rejected suitors plot to humble her pride by encouraging a romance between Pauline and someone socially inferior to her. When Pauline rejects Melnotte's poetry, he lends himself to the suitors' plot, openly woos her without revealing his true social station, and succeeds in winning her heart. Melnotte's real love for Pauline makes him ashamed of his fraud, and finally, tormented by his conscience, he goes off to the wars to expiate his deceitfulness. Upon his return several years later, having won great riches, he finds Pauline about to marry one of the detested suitors in order to save her father from bankruptcy. Melnotte rescues Pauline by paying her father's debt. He punishes the suitors and is reconciled with his love.

C98:34, pe98:33, P350:6   **he was in mortal sin**   I.e., guilty of the sin of "impurity" (or lust), which the *Maynooth Catechism* defined as "all unchaste freedom with another's wife or husband" and as "all immodest actions, looks, or words, all immodest songs, novels, and plays, and everything that is contrary to chastity" (pp. 38–39). To be in mortal sin is to have lost "sanctifying grace" (see *Por* C103:32–35n) and to be spiritually dead.

C99:17, pe99:15, P350:27   **Mercedes**   See *Por* C62:27n.

C99:23, pe99:21, P350:34   **Claude Melnotte**   See *Por* C97:33–34n.

C100:19, pe100:18, P351:35   **the quarter of the jews**   Stephen has, of course, wandered into the red light district in east-central Dublin north of the Liffey. To the extent that there was a "jewish quarter" in late nineteenth-century Dublin, it was in the south-central part of the city off Clanbrassil Street.

Chapter III

The retreat at Belvedere College which provides the narrative structure of this chapter is organized on the model of *The Spiritual Exercises* (1548) of St. Ignatius of Loyola (see *Por* C55:35–56:1n). *The Exercises* suggest four weeks of meditation on: (1) sin and its consequences (Hell); (2) Christ's life on earth; (3) Christ's Passion; and (4) His risen life. The fictional Father Arnall's sermons concentrate heavily on week (1), with some attention to week (2). St. Ignatius in part provides for this in paragraph 4 of the *Exercises*:

> Although four weeks are assigned . . . nevertheless this is not to be understood, as if each week necessarily contained seven or eight days. For since it happens that in the First Week some are slower than others in finding what they desire, namely, contrition, grief and tears for their sins; and likewise some are more diligent than others, and more agitated or tried by different spirits, it is sometimes necessary to shorten the Week, at other times to lengthen it . . .

The exercises of the first week:

1. A meditation upon the first, the second, and third sin, with the three powers of the soul . . .
2. A meditation upon sins . . .
3. A repetition of the first and second exercises . . .
4. Made by resuming the third . . .
5. A meditation on Hell: it contains, after the preparatory prayer and two preludes, five points and one colloquy. *Preparatory Prayer*: Let the preparatory prayer be the usual one. *First Prelude*: The first prelude is a composition of place, which is here to see with the eyes of the imagination the length, breadth, and depth of hell. *Second Prelude*: To ask for that which I desire. It will be here to ask for an interior sense of the pain which the lost suffer, in order that if through my faults I should forget the love of the eternal Lord, at least the fear of punishment may help me not to fall into sin. *First Point*: To see with the eyes of the imagination those great fires, and the souls as it were in bodies of fire. *Second Point*: To hear with the ears the wailings, the groans, the cries, the blasphemies against Christ our Lord, and against all His Saints. *Third Point*: To smell with the sense of smell the smoke, the brimstone, the filth, and the corruption. *Fourth Point*: To taste with the sense of taste, bitter things, such as tears, sadness, and the worm of conscience. *Fifth Point*: To feel with the sense of touch how those fires touch and burn the souls.

But while *The Spiritual Exercises* underpin the narrative structure, the specific patterns of Father Arnall's sermons, together with their language, are derived from a devotional text, *Hell Opened to Christians, To Caution Them from Entering into It*, written in 1688 by the Italian Jesuit, Giovanni Pietro Pinamonti (1632–1703), translated anonymously (Dublin, 1868). Joyce borrowed extensively from Pinamonti, rewriting and tailoring his text to the dramatic situation of the novel. James R. Thrane has extensively demonstrated the nature and scope of Joyce's use of Pinamonti.[1] The following notes to chapter III make no attempt at a thorough coverage of Joyce's use of this source since such coverage, while it would provide an interesting case study of Joyce's methods of composition, would not contribute directly to a reader's understanding of Father Arnall's sermons within the larger patterns of the novel. It should be noted, however, as Thrane has pointed out, that there was an intense controversy on the subject of eternal damnation in the late nineteenth century, particularly among Protestant theologians, many of whom condemned as unthinkable cruelty the doctrine of eternal punishment without hope. The Catholic response to this controversy was guarded but also divided between "liberals" and "dogmatists" or "rigorists." Joyce's sermonological versions of Pinamonti's meditations (and their impact on Stephen) are clearly intended as a dramatic instance of the psychic impact of the dogmatist or rigorist point of view. One commentator, Father Noon, acknowledges the sermons' "dramatic effectiveness in context" but at the same time objects: "The purely negative and harrowing sermon of the *Portrait* is neither Catholic nor Ignatian."[2] The objection is instructive since it suggests that Joyce's purpose was not necessarily to be Catholic and representative but to outline one of the opposing points of view in a public controversy and to dramatize its impact on an impressionable mind.

Pinamonti's meditations are divided into two groups: I. on *poena sensus* (the sensory pain suffered by the damned), A. The Prison of Hell, B. The Fire, C. The Company of the Damned; and II. on *poena damni* (the pain that stems from the eternal loss of the beatific vision), A. The Pain of Loss, B. Remorse of Conscience, C. The Pain of Extension, D. Eternity. Father Arnall's sermons follow this general pattern.

1. In "Joyce's Sermon on Hell: Its Sources and Its Backgrounds," *A James Joyce Miscellany: Third Series*, ed. Marvin Magalaner (Carbondale, Ill., 1962), pp. 33–78.

2. William T. Noon, S. J., "Joyce and Catholicism," *The James Joyce Review* 1, no. 4 (December 1957): 13.

Chapter III: Section A

C102:1, pe102:1, P353:13   **December**   If the novel were to conform to autobiographical time, the date would be 30 November 1896, except that 1896 would not fit because St. Francis Xavier's Feast Day, 3 December, would fall on a Thursday rather than on a Saturday as it does in the novel.

C102:6–7, pe102:7–8, P353:19–20   **Stuff it into you, his belly counselled him**   Catholic doctrine holds that to commit one of the seven deadly sins (in Stephen's case, impurity or lust) is in effect to be guilty not just of that one but of all seven, including gluttony, which is obvious here; see *Por* C98:34n, C103:28n, and C106:5–6n.

C103:1, pe103:6–7, P354:13–14 **a widening tail . . . like a peacock's** The peacock displaying its tail is a traditional symbol of vaingloriousness, of vanity and pride.

C103:10, pe103:15, P354:23 **Shelley's fragment** See *Por* C96:7–9n.

C103:17, pe103:23, P354:31 **balefire** A great or blazing fire in the open air, sometimes associated with *bale*, evil. Balefire is also obsolete for a funeral pyre.

C103:22, pe103:29–30, P355:2–3 **to find his body or his soul maimed by the excess** Stephen would have been taught that mortal sin deforms the sinner both mentally and physically.

C103:28, pe103:35, P355:9 **sinned mortally** I.e., has been guilty of one or more of the seven deadly sins (lust, gluttony, covetousness, envy, pride, sloth, wrath). To sin mortally the sinner must commit the wrong in thought, word, or deed; be aware that the wrong is serious; and fully consent to it. Since he is "in sin," nothing Stephen can do for himself (thought, prayer, devotion, charity, etc.) will be of any avail—his sinfulness will pervert whatever he does, compounding his sin, until he confesses, receives absolution, and does penance.

C103:32–35, pe104:1–4, P355:14–17 **sanctifying grace . . . actual grace** Grace is the supernatural gift of God's beneficence, bestowed upon man, through the merits of Jesus Christ, for the ultimate purpose of fitting man for eternal life. Sanctifying grace "confers on the souls of men a new life"—it is also called habitual grace because man possesses this divine grace as a habit of soul. It can be lost only through mortal sin. Actual grace is not "habitual" or "permanent," but a "divine impulse," "the supernatural help of God which enlightens the mind and strengthens the will to do good and to avoid evil." See *Dub* C150:1n.

C104:16–17, pe104:21–22, P356:1–2 **morally present . . . neither see nor hear** The worshippers are assumed to be in the presence of the Blessed Eucharist and to be fulfilling the purpose of attending Mass, "to adore God, to thank Him for his benefits, to make satisfaction for our sins, and to obtain from Him other graces and blessings" (*Maynooth Catechism*, p. 55).

C104:23–24, pe104:29–30, P356:8–9 **his prefecture . . . Blessed Virgin Mary** Stephen's apparent piety has brought him the award of a considerable distinction at Belvedere. He has been appointed student prefect of the Congregation of the Blessed Virgin Mary, one of the college's two sodalities.

C104:25, pe104:31, P356:11 **the little office** The sodality celebrates terce (see *Por* C200:11n) on Saturday mornings by reciting a (circa) eighth-century collection of Biblical passages designed for daily prayer in honor of the Blessed Virgin Mary. The Little Office was included in the manual that the sodality at Belvedere used, *The Sodality Manual; or a Collection of Prayers and Spiritual Exercises for Members of the Sodality of the Blessed Virgin Mary* (Dublin, 1886).

C104:27–28, pe104:34, P356:13–14   **the falsehood of his position** I.e., as a leading participant in a religious ceremony when he is "in mortal sin." Actually Stephen is compounding his sin with the sin of sacrilege; see *Por* C110:19–20n.

C104:31, pe104:38, P356:18   **psalms of prophecy** In the Vulgate (Douay) numbering: Psalms 8, 18, 23, 44, 45, 86, 95–97. In the King James they are: 8, 19, 24, 45, 46, 87, 96–98. The imagery alluded to is to be found primarily in Vulgate Psalm 44:9–10: "Myrrh and stacte and cassea perfume thy garments, from the ivory houses. The Queen stood on Thy right hand, in golden clothing; surrounded with variety" (King James Bible, Psalm 45:8–9).

C104:32, pe104:39, P356:19   **the glories of Mary** The title of a devotional work by St. Alphonsus Liguori (see *Por* C152:9–10n) and part of the title of sermon 17, "The Glories of Mary for the Sake of Her Son," in *Discourses to Mixed Congregations* (1849) by John Henry Cardinal Newman; see *Por* C138:31–139:8n.

C104:33, pe105:1–2, P356:20–21   **the preciousness of God's gifts to her soul** Donlevy *Catechism* (p. 341): the Blessed Virgin Mary

> received greater gifts and favours from God, than any *angel or saint whatsoever*. . . . Because God preserved her from *all sin*; and that she was both *a Mother and a Virgin* at the same time, without losing her *Virginity in any wise*, before or after child-birth; a favour which God never did, nor ever will grant to any woman whatsoever.

C104:34, pe105:2–3, P356:22   **her royal lineage** A reference to the tradition that the Blessed Virgin Mary is descended from King David (as she is called "Tower of David" in The Litany of Our Lady; see *Por* C35:30–31n).

C104:34–35, pe105:3–4, P356:22–23   **her emblems, the lateflowering plant and lateblossoming tree** Symbolic of her patience in awaiting "the growth of her cultus among men" and in awaiting the sinner's impulse to repent, to turn to her as "Refuge of sinners"; see *Por* C35:30–31n.

C105:3–8, pe105:8–13, P356:28–34   ***Quasi cedrus . . . suavitatem odoris*** From Ecclesiasticus 24:17–20:

I was exalted like a cedar of Lebanon and as a cypress tree on Mount Sion. I was exalted like a palm tree in Gades, and as a rose plant in Jericho. As a fair olive tree in the plains, and as a plane tree by the water in the streets was I exalted. I gave a sweet smell like cinnamon and aromatical balm! I yielded a sweet odor like the best myrrh.

This passage is included at the end of the Fourth Lesson for Common Feasts of the Blessed Virgin Mary in the Divine Office, and is the Third Lesson in The Little Office.

C105:10, pe105:15, P357:2   **the refuge of sinners**   From The Litany of Our Lady; see *Por* C35:30–31n.

C105:15, pe105:20, P357:7   **her knight**   A reference to the chivalric and courtly overtones of medieval cults of the Virgin.

C105:17, pe105:22–23, P357:10   **her whose emblem is the morning star**   The Blessed Virgin Mary is called "morning star" in The Litany of Our Lady (see *Por* C35:30–31n) because her appearance announces the coming of the day of Redemption; see *Por* C138:31–139:8, pe138:32–139:7, P396:19–33.

C105:17–18, pe105:23–24, P357:10–11   *bright and musical, telling of heaven and infusing grace*   From Cardinal Newman; see *Por* C138:31–139:8.

C105:23, pe105:29–30, P357:18   **sums and cuts**   "Schoolboy's abbreviation for problems set by a master to his class on the model of some theorem or problem in whatever book of Euclid's Geometry they are reading" (Joyce, *Letters* 3:129).

C105:26, pe105:32, P357:21   *My excellent friend Bombados*   On 2 November 1915 Joyce wrote to his wife's uncle in Dublin to thank him "for having verified the quotation about our excellent friend Bombados." Joyce remarked that he would "correct it on the proof" (*Letters*, ed. Stuart Gilbert 1:86). This would suggest that the line is from a Dublin pantomime (the files of the Lincoln Center Theatre Collection list a pantomime entitled "Bombados"), but the slant and context of the quotation must be listed as unknown.

C105:27, pe105:33, P357:22   **the yard**   See *Por* C81:9n.

C105:30, pe105:36, P357:27   **game ball**   A stroke of good luck, after the winning point in a game of handball.

C105:30, pe105:36, P357:27   **scut**   See *Por* C40:16n.

C105:31–32, pe105:38, P357:29   **questions on the catechism**   I.e, during the daily class in religious instruction; for the purposes of this annotation I have assumed that the catechetical texts used in those classes at Belvedere were the same as at Clongowes, the *Maynooth Catechism* and the De Harbe *Catechism*; see Introduction, p. 11.

C106:5-6, pe106:9, P358:4   **The sentence of saint James**   Epistle of James 2:10: "Whoever keeps the whole law but offends in one part has become guilty in all." The "sentence" is read as asserting that to be guilty of one mortal sin is to be guilty of all. See *Por* C103:28n.

C106:9, pe106:13, P358:8-9   **all other deadly sins**   See *Por* C106: 5-6n.

C106:18-19, pe106:23, P358:19   **the curious questions**   Stephen's religious instructors would have repeatedly warned him that it is not "permitted to pry into the mysteries of faith" (Donlevy *Catechism*, p. 83). The De Harbe *Catechism* cites "pride and subtile reasoning on the mysteries of our religion" as more important than "worldliness and a wicked life" in leading people "to fall away from their faith" (p. 80).

C106:19-23, pe106:23-28, P358:19-24   **If a man had stolen . . . all his huge fortune?**   As posed, the question invites a simoniacal answer because it implies that one could achieve absolution for a mortal sin by payment of a certain quantity of money; see *Dub* C9:13n. The De Harbe *Catechism*, discussing the Seventh Commandment, "Thou shalt not steal," puts the question: "How much must be restored?" and answers:

> If one has *knowingly* and *unjustly* taken or detained his neighbor's goods, he must fully indemnify him. . . . Full restitution must be made not only of the things stolen . . . but also of that which in the meantime, they have produced; those expenses, however, being deducted which even the owner would not have been able to avoid. And, in general, the owner must be compensated for all the profits which he has been deprived of, and for all the losses he has suffered. [P. 201]

C106:23-25, pe106:28-30, P358:24-26   **If a layman . . . mineral water valid?**

> Q. Can every body confer the Sacrament of Baptism?
> A. Yes, in time of need only, and when a priest cannot be had . . .
> Q. What is requisite for the conferring of Baptism?
> A. It is necessary that one should have the intention of conferring it in earnest, and that he should sprinkle natural water on the head (if possible) of the person to be baptized, pronouncing these words: "I baptize thee in the name of the Father, and of the Son, and of the Holy Ghost. Amen." [Donlevy *Catechism*, pp. 211-13]

As for the water: "Any natural water will do for the validity of Baptism. However, when possible, baptismal water, or water blessed for that purpose, should be used" (De Harbe *Catechism*, p. 250).

C106:26-27, pe106:30-33, P358:27-29   **the first beatitude . . . the second beatitude**   Jesus in the Sermon on the Mount, Matthew

5:3-4 (Douay): "Blessed are the poor in spirit: for theirs is the kingdom of heaven. Blessed are the meek: for they shall possess the land." In the King James Bible these are the first and third beatitudes, Matthew 5:3,5. Stephen's question is: why reward one with heaven and the other with earth in the light of Jesus's assertion: "My kingdom is not of this world" (John 18:36)?

C106:28-31, pe106:33-36, P358:30-33 **Why was the sacrament of the eucharist . . . in the wine alone?** De Harbe *Catechism* (pp. 268-69):

> *On Holy Communion* . . . Holy Communion is truly receiving of the real Body and Blood of Jesus Christ for the nourishment of our souls. . . .
>
> 43. Must we also drink the chalice, in order to receive the Blood of Christ? No; for under the appearance of bread we receive also His Blood, since we receive Him whole and entire, His Humanity and His Divinity.
>
> 44. But why, then, did Christ institute the Holy Eucharist in both kinds? Because He instituted it, not only as a Sacrament, but also as a Sacrifice, for which both kinds are required.

C106:31-33, pe106:36-39, P358:34-359:1 **Does a tiny particle . . . the body and blood?** De Harbe *Catechism* (p. 260), "When the Priest breaks or divides the Sacred Host . . . he breaks or divides the appearances only: the Body of Christ itself is present in each part entire and living in a true though mysterious manner."

C106:33-36, pe106:39-107:3, P359:1-4 **If the wine change into vinegar . . . as God and as man?** De Harbe *Catechism* (p. 260), "How long does Christ remain present with His Sacred Flesh and Blood? As long as the appearance of bread and wine continue to exist."

C107:9, pe107:12, P359:14 **the retreat** See *Dub* C32:3-4n.

C107:10, pe107:13, P359:15 **saint Francis Xavier whose feast day is Saturday** For Saint Francis, see *Por* C56:1n. His feast day is 3 December; since the chapter is set in the late 1890s, the day implied would be Saturday, 3 December 1898; cf. *Por* C102:1n.

C107:12, pe107:16, P359:18 **beads** See *Por* C76:22n.

C107:27, pe107:31, P359:35-360:1 **an old and illustrious Spanish family** St. Francis was the youngest son of one of the most distinguished families in the kingdom of Navarre in northern Spain. His father, Juan de Jasso, was privy councilor to the king of Navarre, and his mother, Maria de Azpicueta y Xavier, was the only surviving heiress of two aristocratic Navaresse families. St. Francis was born at his mother's castle of Xavier near Pamplona.

C107:28, pe107:32-33, P360:2 **saint Ignatius** Of Loyola, the founder of the Jesuit Order; see *Por* C55:35-56:1n.

C107:29, pe107:33–34, P360:2–4   **they met in Paris . . . at the university**   St. Francis Xavier was so outstanding as a student of philosophy that in 1528, at the age of 22, he became a lecturer in Aristotelian philosophy at Collège Beauvais in the University of Paris. There in 1529 he met St. Ignatius, who at the age of 38 had come to the university to prepare himself for a career as a religious teacher. They became close friends and joined a pious confraternity which subsequently under St. Ignatius's leadership was to become the core of the Jesuit Order (15 August 1534).

C107:32–33, pe107:37–38, P360:6–8   **he, at his own desire, was sent by saint Ignatius to preach to the Indians**   Something of an oversimplification. In 1540 King John III of Portugal formally requested missionaries for India and asked the pope especially for members of the new order. St. Ignatius chose Bobadilla for the mission, but he was taken ill, and at the last moment St. Francis Xavier was substituted. Once appointed, he undertook his mission with exemplary zeal.

C107:35–36, pe108:1, P360:10   **from Africa to India, from India to Japan**   St. Francis Xavier left Lisbon in April 1541, wintered in Mozambique, and arrived in Goa (Portuguese India) in May 1542. In India he first undertook to reform the European community before he began his missionary work among the natives. In 1548–49 he organized what turned out to be a successful mission to the Japanese Empire.

C107:36–108:1, pe108:2–3, P360:11–12   **baptised as many as ten thousand idolators in a month**   Reported of his visit to the Indian Kingdom of Travancore in 1544 ([Alban] *Butler's Lives of the Saints*, ed. Herbert Thurston, S.J., and Donald Attwater [London, 1956] 4:476).

C108:1–3, pe108:3–5, P360:12–14   **his right arm had grown powerless . . . whom he baptised**   "So great were the multitudes he baptized that sometimes by the bare fatigue of administering the sacrament he was scarcely able to move his arms according to the account he gave to his brethren in Europe [in a letter of 15 January 1544]" (*Butler's*, 4:476).

C108:3–5, pe108:5–7, P360:14–16   **He wished then to go to China . . . island of Sancian**   St. Francis Xavier's desire to found a mission in China was frustrated by the Portuguese authorities and their fear of Chinese law, which excluded foreign visitors from the mainland. Sancian, which Xavier reached in 1552, is an island off the Chinese coast near the port of Macao; it was the Portuguese-Chinese trading post. There St. Francis, whose constitution had been weakened by the intensity of his career and the privations which he had endured, died of an undiagnosed fever.

C108:6, pe108:8, P360:17–18 **A great soldier of God** Stephen would have been taught that "strong and perfect Christians" in this life are "soldiers of Jesus Christ" (*Maynooth Catechism*, pp. 51–52).

C108:9, pe108:11, P360:21 **the faith in him that moves mountains** After I Corinthians 13:2, "and though I have all faith, so that I could remove mountains, and have not charity, I am nothing."

C108:11–12, pe108:13–14, P360:24 *ad majorem Dei gloriam* Latin: to the greater glory of God, the motto of the Jesuit Order.

C108:13, pe108:15, P360:25 **power to intercede** Catholic doctrine holds that prayers to the saint would be answered by the saint's intercession, his supplication in heaven for God's favor to the worshiper.

C108:13, pe108:15, P360:29 **A great fisher of souls!** The source of this metaphor is in Jesus's words to Peter and Andrew in Matthew 4:19, "Come ye after me, and I will make you to be fishers of men" (Douay Bible).

Chapter III: Section B

C108:23–24, pe108:26–27, P361:3–4 *Remember only thy last things . . . not sin forever* The citation is not Ecclesiastes but Ecclesiasticus 7:40, which reads, "In all thy work remember thy last end, and thou shalt never sin" (Douay). Ecclesiasticus is included in the Protestant Apocrypha. The four "last things" are defined in Catholic doctrine as death, judgment, heaven, and hell.

C109:20, pe109:21, P362:4 **their stewardship** The allusion is to Jesus's parable of the unjust steward, Luke 16:1–8, particularly to 16:2, ". . . give an account of thy stewardship: for now thou canst be steward no longer" (Douay). See *Dub* C173:21–24n.

C109:35–36, pe109:37, P362:22 **the four last things** See *Por* C108:23–24n.

C110:7–9, pe110:7–8, P362:31–32 **What doth it profit . . . immortal soul?** A version of Matthew 16:26: "For what doth it profit a man, if he gaineth the whole world, and suffer the loss of his own soul?" (Douay).

C110:19–20, pe110:20–21, P363:9–11 **the sodality of Our Blessed . . . a good example** *The Sodality Manual*, which guided the two sodalities at Belvedere College, made the importance of personal example clear:

> As the [student] Prefect takes precedence in rank and office, and claims the first place after the Director [a priest], so should he excel the other members of the Sodality in virtue. Wherefore he should observe with the greatest diligence not only the rules of his own office but also the common rules, those especially that relate to the frequentation of the sacraments, confessing his sins, and receiving the Blessed Eucharist more frequently than the others; and he should take care to advance the Sodality in the way of virtue and Christian perfection, more by example even than by words. [*The Sodality Manual*, ed. J. A. Cullen, S.J. (Dublin 1896), p. 47]

C110:32–33, pe110:33–34, P363:24–25 **to lose God's holy grace and to fall into grievous sin** The two are not cause and effect but corollary: to lose grace is to fall into sin and to fall into sin is to lose grace; see *Por* C103:28n and C103:32–35n.

C111:9, pe111:9, P364:4 **Ecclesiastes** For Ecclesiasticus; see *Por* C108:23–24n.

C111:36, pe111:37, P364:34 **a bovine god** In Exodus 32:1–20 when Moses is on the top of Mount Sinai, the children of Israel make "a molten calf" and worship it and thus "have corrupted themselves."

C112:1, pe111:38, P364:35 **death and judgment** See *Por* C108:23–24n.

C112:23, pe112:23–24, P365:25–26 **the soul stood terrified before the judgmentseat** Catholic doctrine holds that the individual soul is judged immediately after death in "the particular judgment"; see *Por* C113:6–11n.

C113:6–11, pe113:6–11, P366:12–18 **the particular judgment . . . the general judgment** The judgment of the individual soul immediately after death, and the Last Judgment, when all mankind is to be judged individually and collectively by Christ in his Glory.

> Q. As every one is judged immediately after death, what need is there of a general judgment?
> A. There is need of a general judgment that the providence of God, which often, in this world permits the good to suffer and the wicked to prosper, may appear just before all men. [*Maynooth Catechism*, pp. 64–65]

C113:7–8, pe113:7–8, P366:13–15 **to the abode of bliss . . . howling into hell** Immediately after death, the soul is judged and condemned to Hell (until the Last Judgment, when presumably it will be recondemned for eternity); or the soul is destined for Heaven, either directly ("to the abode of bliss") or, if repentance for sins has been genuine but penance on earth has been incomplete, the soul is committed to Purgatory for further penance before its entry into Heaven.

C113:12–13, pe113:12–13, P366:19–21   **The stars of heaven . . . has shaken**   Revelation ("The Apocalypse of St. John the Apostle" in the Douay Bible), from chapter 6: "What followed upon opening six of the seals." Revelation 6:13: "And the stars from heaven fell upon the earth, as the fig tree casteth its green figs when it is shaken by a great wind."

C113:13–15, pe113:14–15, P366:21–23   **The sun, the great luminary . . . moon was bloodred**   Revelation 6:12: "And I saw, when he opened the sixth seal, and behold there was a great earthquake, and the sun became black as sackcloth of hair: and the whole moon became as blood."

C113:15–16, pe113:15–16, P366:23–24   **The firmament was as a scroll rolled away**   Apocalypse (Revelation) 6:14: "And the heaven departed as a book folded up . . ." (Douay).

C113:16–19, pe113:16–20, P366:24–28   **The archangel Michael . . . death of time**   Revelation 10:1–6 relates the vision of a "mighty angel" with "his right foot upon the sea, and his left foot upon the earth" proclaiming "that time shall be no longer." The Archangel Michael is the angel of the Church Militant, and Catholic doctrine holds that he will announce "the death of time" because he will announce the occasion of the Last Judgment.

C113:20–21, pe113:21–22, P366:29   **Time is, time was, but time shall be no more**   This is (accidentally?) interpolated from *The Honourable History of Friar Bacon and Friar Bungay* (c. 1589–92), a play by the English poet-dramatist-journalist, Robert Greene (1560–92). The main plot of the play is a standard love-triangle; the slapstick subplot involves a series of competitions in magic. In act IV Friar Bacon climaxes seven years of work with the creation of "the brazen head." Properly invoked the head would have uttered great wisdoms and would have created a protective wall of brass around all of England. Unfortunately the head utters its wisdoms ("Time is! . . . Time was! . . . Time is past!") to Bacon's stupid servant Miles, who responds without the proper formulae of invocation, and at the words "Time is past!" a hammer appears and destroys the head.

C113:22, pe113:23, P366:31   **valley of Jehoshaphat**   A valley east of Jerusalem, prophesied in the Old Testament book of Joel as the place where "the Lord shall judge all nations."

C113:27–28, pe113:28–29, P367:1–2   **the supreme judge . . . Lamb of God**   A reference to the dual role attributed to Christ: meek and merciful when he suffered for mankind on earth, austere and uncompromising when he presides at the Last Judgment.

C113:29–33, pe113:30–34, P367:4–8   **He is seen now coming . . . cherubim and seraphim**   After Jesus's description of the Last Judgment, Matthew 25:31: "When the Son of Man shall come in His glory, and all the holy angels with Him." Traditionally, as in Dante, *Paradiso* XXVIII, the angels are divided into a hierarchy of nine choirs, ranging from angels in the ninth or lowest order to seraphim in the first or highest order. Father Arnall interchanges thrones (which should be number three) and dominations (which should be number four).

C114:3–5, pe114:3–5, P367:15–17   *Depart from me, ye cursed . . . and his angels*   Matthew 25:41, in the midst of Jesus's "description of the Last Judgment" (Matthew 25:31–46); see *Por* C119:15–19n.

C114:15, pe114:15–16, P367:28   **hypocrites . . . whited sepulchres**   Jesus speaks against the "bad example" set by the Pharisees, Matthew 23:27: "Woe to you scribes and Pharisees, hypocrites; because you are like to whited sepulchres, which outwardly appear to men beautiful, but within are full of dead men's bones and of all filthiness."

C114:23–24, pe114:23–24, P368:2–3   **the Son of God . . . little expect Him**   After Matthew 25:13: "Watch therefore, for ye know neither the day nor the hour wherein the Son of man cometh."

C114:26–27, pe114:26–27, P368:5–6   **Death and judgment . . . our first parents**   "Because of Adam's sin [original sin], we are born without sanctifying grace, our intellect is darkened, our will is weakened, our passions incline us to evil, and we are subject to suffering and death" (1951 *Catechism*, p. 22).

C115:3–4, pe115:2–4, P368:19–21   **Addison . . . Warwick**   Joseph Addison (1672–1719), English essayist, poet, and statesman, to his stepson, the Earl of Warwick, who was not so much "wicked" as he was young and promising. The evidence for this scene is somewhat circumstantial, though the story is attributed by his contemporaries to Thomas Tickell (1688–1740), Addison's literary executor. Two lines in Tickell's poem, "To the Earl of Warwick on the Death of Mr. Addison" (1721) are cited as an allusion to the deathbed scene: "He taught us how to live, and O too high / The price of knowledge! Taught us how to die." Addison's words were reported to have been: "See in what peace a Christian can die." Addison was, incidentally, a Tory and an apparently staunch supporter of William of Orange (William III of England) and his anti-Catholic, anti-Irish policies; see *Dub* C208:7n.

C115:7–8, pe115:7–8, P368:25–26   *O grave . . . thy sting*   From I Corinthians 15:55, which is followed by the assertion in 15:56: "Now the sting of death is sin." Father Arnall has, however, taken the quotation from the closing lines (17–18) of "The Dying Christian to His Soul" (1712, 1730), a poem by Alexander Pope (1688–1744).

C115:18, pe115:19, P369:4   **jeweleyed harlots**   Cf. Revelation 17:4–5 in which a "woman . . . arrayed in purple and scarlet colour, and decked with gold and precious stones and pearls" is named "MYSTERY, BABYLON THE GREAT, THE MOTHER OF HARLOTS AND THE ABOMINATIONS OF THE EARTH."

C115:21, pe115:22, P369:7   **the square**   I.e., Mountjoy Square; see *Por* C71:16n.

C115:26–28, pe115:28–30, P369:13–15   **the image of Emma . . . from his heart**   When Dante first encounters his ideal, spiritual love Beatrice in *The Purgatorio*: "Mine eyes drooped down to the clear fount; but beholding me therein, I drew them back to the grass, so great a shame weighed down my brow" (XXX:76–78).

C116:14–15, pe116:15–17, P370:4–6   **he stood near Emma . . . elbow of her sleeve**   Emma is imagined as an intercessor for Stephen as Beatrice is for Dante in the "wide land" of the Earthly Paradise at the end of the *Purgatorio* and in the further journey toward "the stars" and the beatific vision of the *Paradiso*. When Dante achieves the vision of the Rose of Paradise (XXX–XXXI) toward which Beatrice has led him, she disappears and her place as intercessor and guide is taken by St. Bernard of Clairvaux, who urges Dante to contemplate the spiritual beauties of the Blessed Virgin Mary.

C116:20–22, pe116:22–24, P370:12–14   **her whose beauty . . .** *bright and musical*   I.e., the Blessed Virgin Mary; see *Por* C138:31–139:8n.

C117:7–8, pe117:8–9, P371:2–3   **Forty days . . . the face of the earth**   A vision of the flood after Genesis 6–8 and particularly after Genesis 7:4 as God prophesies the flood to Noah, ". . . and I will cause it to rain upon the earth forty days and forty nights; and every living substance that I have made will I destroy from off the face of the earth."

C117:10–11, pe117:11–12, P371:5–6   *Hell has enlarged its soul and opened its mouth without any limits*   The verse continues, "and their strong ones, and their people, and their glorious ones shall go down into it" (Isaiah 5:14; Douay), part of Isaiah's prophetic warning to the sinful "inhabitants of Jerusalem."

C117:19–22, pe117:21–25, P371:15–19   **Adam and Eve . . . were created . . . might be filled again**   The De Harbe *Catechism* quotes the Council of Trent (1545–63), "God was not impelled to create by any other cause than a desire to communicate to creatures the riches of His bounty" (p. 92). The *Maynooth Catechism* agrees in somewhat simpler language. Father Arnall's reason for the creation seems to have crept in from another source, perhaps from St. Anselm of Canterbury (c. 1033–1109), who argued this reason in his *Cur Deus Homo* (*Why God Became Man*, c. 1094–c. 1098), chapter XVI. Anselm's premise is that God knew "in what number it was best to create rational beings" so that when the angels fell their place in the perfection of creation had to be filled, but (chapter XVII) could not be filled by substitute angels because then there would be two incompatible classes of angels: those who had "persevered" and witnessed the fall and punishment of Satan and Company and those who had not; therefore only holy men could take the place of the fallen angels. A vigorous proponent of St. Anselm's view (and another possible source for Father Arnall's reasoning) is John Milton, *Paradise Lost*, VIII:150–60.

C117:22–23, pe117:25–26, P371:19–20   **Lucifer, we are told . . . of the morning**   Isaiah 14:12: "How art thou fallen from heaven, O Lucifer, son of the morning!"

C117:24–25, pe177:27, P371:21–22   **there fell with him a third part of the host of heaven**   The source for this does not seem to be Catholic tradition but Milton (*Paradise Lost*, II:689–92), where Death asks Satan, "Art thou that Traitor Angel . . . Who . . . in proud rebellious Arms / Drew after him the third part of Heav'n's Sons?" The Biblical source for this tradition is Revelation 12:3–4:

> And there appeared another wonder in heaven; and behold a great red dragon, having seven heads and ten horns, and seven crowns upon his heads. And his tail drew the third part of the stars of heaven, and did cast them to the earth: and the dragon stood before the woman which was ready to be delivered, for to devour her child as soon as it was born.

C117:26–27, pe117:29–30, P371:23–24   **What his sin . . . the sin of pride**   The Catholic Encyclopedia remarks that "many of the best authorities" regard Satan's sin as "the desire of independence of God and equality with God" (1908; 4:765a). The *Encyclopedia* also cites St. Thomas Aquinas's argument that "the first sin of Satan was the sin of pride" (4:765b), and the *Maynooth Catechism* agrees: "Some of the angels were cast out of heaven because *through pride* they rebelled against God" (p. 13).

C117:28, pe117:31, P371:25   **non serviam**   Latin: I will not serve. The phrase is traditionally assigned to Satan at the moment of his fall, after Jeremiah 2:20, "and thou saidst: I will not serve" (Douay).

C117:33, pe117:36, P371:30   **Eden, in the plain of Damascus**   Curious, because, while there was no agreement about the geographical location of the Biblical Garden of Eden in the late nineteenth century, speculation centered on Genesis 2:10–14, which locates Eden in relation to four rivers. One of them is named the Euphrates, and Biblical scholars assumed it to be identical with the modern Euphrates. The identities of the other three (Pison, Gihon, and Hiddekel) were not so clear, so argument placed the Garden variously near the source of the Euphrates in modern Turkey or near its confluence with the Tigris in modern Iraq. In either case, "the plain of Damascus" is remote. Apparently Father Arnall's rhetorical flourish derives from God's promise to the Israelites through the prophet Amos: "I will break also the bar of Damascus, and cut off the plain of Aven, and him that holdeth the sceptre from the house of Eden: and the people of Syria shall go into captivity unto Kir, saith the Lord" (Amos 1:5). The "house of Eden" is assumed to have been a pleasure palace of the kings of Damascus.

C117:36–118:1, pe118:1, P371:34 **the ills our flesh is heir to** A common misquotation from Hamlet's "To be or not to be" soliloquy:

> To die, to sleep—
> No more, and by a sleep to say we end
> The heartache and the thousand natural shocks
> That flesh is heir to.

                                III:i:60–63

C118:4, pe118:4–5, P372:3–4 **They were not . . . the forbidden tree** "And the Lord God commanded the man, saying, Of every tree of the garden thou mayest freely eat: But of the tree of the knowledge of good and evil, thou shalt not eat of it: for in the day that thou eatest thereof thou shalt surely die" (Genesis 2:16–17).

C118:6, pe118:7, P372:6 **son of the morning** See *Por* C117:22–23n.

C118:7, pe118:7–8, P372:7–8 **a serpent, the subtlest of all the beasts of the field** "Now the serpent was more subtle than any beast of the field which the Lord God had made" (Genesis 3:1).

C118:8–10, pe118:9–12, P372:8–11 **He envied them . . . forfeited for ever** "The devil, envying our first parents their happy state, tempted them to eat the forbidden fruit" (*Maynooth Catechism*, p. 12).

C118:11, pe118:12–13, P372:11–12 **woman, the weaker vessel** After I Peter 3:7, "Likewise, ye husbands, dwell with them according to knowledge, giving honour unto the wife, as unto the weaker vessel."

C118:14, pe118:15–16, P372:15 **they would become as gods, nay as God Himself** Genesis 3:4–5, "And the serpent said unto the woman, Ye shall not surely die: For God doth know that in the day ye eat thereof, then your eyes shall be opened, and ye shall be as gods, knowing good and evil." "As God Himself" is apparently Father Arnall's rhetorical flourish.

C118:16, pe118:18, P372:17–18 **Adam who had not the moral cour-**

age to resist her   Genesis 3:6 says simply, "She took of the fruit thereof, and did eat, and gave also unto her husband with her; and he did eat." The various catechisms cited in this text are similarly neutral. Anti-feminine versions of the fall were much speculated upon in the medieval Church and received Milton's ringing endorsement in *Paradise Lost*: Adam "scrupl'd not to eat / Against his better knowledge, not deceiv'd / But fondly overcome with Female charm" (IX:997–99).

C118:18–19, pe118:20–21, P372:20–21   **the voice of God . . . man to account**   Genesis 3:8–9, "And they heard the voice of the Lord God walking in the garden in the cool of the day: and Adam and his wife hid themselves from the presence of the Lord God amongst the trees of the garden. And the Lord God called unto Adam, and said unto him, Where art thou?"

C118:19–21, pe118:21–24, P372:21–24   **Michael, prince of the heavenly host . . . forth from Eden**   Genesis 3:24, "So [the Lord God] drove out the man; and he placed at the east of the garden of Eden Cherubims, and a flaming sword which turned every way, to keep the way of the tree of life." Michael is not mentioned in Genesis but is identified as "first of the chief princes" in Daniel 10:13. Father Arnall is following Catholic tradition: "According to the Fathers there is often question of St. Michael in Scripture when his name is not mentioned. They say he was the cherub who stood at the gate of paradise 'to keep the way of the tree of life'" (*Catholic Encyclopedia* [1911], 10:276a).

C118:23–24, pe118:25–26, P372:26–27   **to earn their bread in the sweat of their brow**   God curses Adam in Genesis 3:19, "In the sweat of thy face shalt thou eat bread, til thou return unto the ground."

C118:25–31, pe118:27–33, P372:28–34   **He took pity . . . and promised . . . the Eternal Word**   Both the De Harbe *Catechism* (p. 56) and the *Maynooth Catechism* (p. 15) cite Genesis 3:15 as the immediate promise of "a Redeemer," when God says to "the serpent" (Satan), "And I will put enmity between thee and the woman, and between thy seed and her seed; it shall bruise thy head, and thou shalt bruise his heel." The "promise" is not as much Biblical as it is traditional and doctrinal, based in part on the passage in Genesis and in part ("the Eternal Word") on John 1:1, "In the beginning was the Word, and the Word was with God, and the Word was God."

C118:33, pe118:35, P373:1–2   **He was born in a poor cowhouse in Judea**   Bethlehem, Jesus's birthplace, was in Judea; "And she brought forth her firstborn son, and wrapped him in swaddling clothes, and laid him in a manger; because there was no room for them in the inn" (Luke 2:7).

C118:33–34, pe118:36, P373:2   **lived as a humble carpenter for thirty years**   Catholic tradition holds that Jesus's mission (preaching to the people, teaching his disciples, healing the sick, and raising the dead) was accomplished between the ages of 30 and 33. Prior to that time he is said to have labored as a simple carpenter and to have lived quietly and humbly with his parents.

C118:36, pe118:38–39, P373:5   **the new gospel**   As prophesied in John 1:17, "For the law was given by Moses, but grace and truth came by Jesus Christ."

C119:3, pe119:3–4, P373:8–9   **set aside to give place to a public robber**   In each of the Gospels Pilate, the Roman governor, offers to release a prisoner on the occasion of the feast of Passover. The people demand the release of Barabbas and the crucifixion of Jesus. Barabbas is identified in Mark 15:7 and Luke 23:19 as guilty of insurrection and murder. John 18:40 identifies him as "a robber."

C119:3–4, pe119:4, P373:9   **scourged with five thousand lashes**   Two of the Gospels report that Pilate had Jesus "scourged" before He was led away to be crucified (Matthew 27:26 and John 19:1), and it was Roman custom to precede crucifixion with scourging. But I have found no precedent in "pious opinion" for the rhetorical flourish "five thousand lashes" (which would have been a death sentence in itself).

C119:4, pe119:4–5, P373:10   **crowned with a crown of thorns**   Three of the Gospels describe this as one phase of the torture Jesus underwent at the hands of the Roman soldiers, who mocked him as "King of the Jews" (Matthew 27:29ff., Mark 15:16ff., John 19:2ff.).

C119:6, pe119:6, P373:12   **stripped of His garments**   After Matthew 27:28, as the Roman soldiers mock Jesus: "And they stripped him and put on him a scarlet [purple] robe."

C119:6–7, pe119:7, P373:12   **hanged upon a gibbet**   Jesus was, of course, crucified on a cross. To be hanged on a gibbet was to be hung in chains from an arm projecting from the top of an upright post. The executed were so hung as a warning to other malefactors in the Middle Ages.

C119:7–9, pe119:7–9, P373:13–15   **His side was pierced . . . issued continually**   After John 19:33–34, "But when they came to Jesus, and saw that he was dead already, they brake not his legs: But one of the soldiers with a spear pierced his side, and forthwith came there out blood and water."

C119:10–11, pe119:10–11, P373:17   **Our Merciful Redeemer had pity for mankind**   After Luke 23:34, "Then said Jesus, Father, forgive them; for they know not what they do."

C119:11–13, pe119:12–14, P373:18–20   **on the hill of Calvary, He founded the holy catholic church . . . shall not prevail**   Calvary was the site of the crucifixion (Luke 23:33). From a doctrinal point of view, Jesus Christ, through the sacrifice of the crucifixion, "made atonement to God for our sins and merited for us the grace by which from being enemies of God, we can become his adopted children" (1951 *Catechism*, p. 29). The founding of the Church was "promised" (p. 42) in Matthew 16:18–19, "And I say also unto thee, That thou art Peter, and upon this rock I will build my church; and the gates of hell shall not prevail against it. And I will give unto thee the keys of the kingdom of heaven." The "promise" is fulfilled when, after the resurrection, Jesus said to Peter, "Feed my lambs . . . Feed my sheep," John 21:15–17. The occasion of the founding of the Church is, however, the crucifixion when Jesus, "the *Second Adam* becomes the source of eternal life for mankind of which he is the head: from his pierced side there gushes forth, with the blood of sacrifice, the water which carries the gift of the Spirit and the new birth of the *Second Eve*, the Church" (*Layman's Missal*, p. xlv).

C119:14, pe119:14, P373:20–21   **the rock of ages**   "Rock of Ages" is the title of a popular Protestant hymn written by Augustus Toplady (1740–78) in 1776. The hymn is an adaptation of an ancient Hebrew song.

C119:14–15, pe119:14–15, P373:21–22   **endowed it with His grace, with sacraments and sacrifice**   For grace and sacrifice see *Por* C103:32–35n, C106:28–31n, and C119:11–13n. The seven Sacraments are Baptism, Confirmation, Eucharist, Penance, Extreme Unction, Holy Orders, and Matrimony.

C119:15–19, pe119:16–20, P373:22–26   **promised that if men would obey . . . torment: hell**   Matthew 25:31–46 is usually cited as the scriptural basis for this doctrine: "When the Son of man shall come in his glory . . . And he shall set the sheep on his right hand, but the goats on the left. Then shall the King say unto them on his right hand, Come, ye blessed of my Father, inherit the kingdom prepared for you from the foundation of the world; . . . Then shall he say also unto them on the left hand, Depart from me, ye cursed, into everlasting fire, prepared for the devil and his angels."

C119:22, pe119:23, P373:29   **let us try for a moment to realize**   I.e., Father Arnall proposes what St. Ignatius of Loyola prescribed, composition of place; see the headnote to this chapter, p. 177 above.

C119:34, pe119:35–36, P374:7–8   **four thousand miles thick**   After the then widely accepted Catholic opinion "that hell is really within the earth" (which is approximately 8000 miles in diameter). However, *The*

Catholic Encyclopedia goes on to say, "The Church [had] decided nothing on this subject" (1910; 7:207b).

C119:36, pe119:37–38, P374:9–10   **saint Anselm, writes in his book on similitudes**   This passage is after Pinamonti, who had written, "If a blessed saint . . . will be strong enough . . . to move the whole earth: a damned soul will be so weak as not to be able even to remove from the eye a worm that is gnawing it" (quoted by Thrane, p. 38). *De Similitudinibus,* the text which Pinamonti paraphrases, says nothing of the worm "gnawing" but leaves the comparison at the strength of the saint as against the weakness of the damned soul. Also, "*De Similitudinibus* was not written by St. Anselm [of Canterbury; c. 1033–1109], but these are his ideas, his vocabulary and style, his *spirit*" (*Dictionnaire de Théologie Catholique* [Paris, 1909] 1:2:1334b).

C120:3–4, pe120:2–4, P374:13–15   **As, at the command of God . . . but not its light**   One version of the story of the Babylonian furnace is found in the King James Bible, Daniel 3:19–30; another, and much extended version, occurs in the Douay Bible (translated from the Vulgate), Daniel 3:19–100, from which the allusion is taken (verses 49–50).

C120:6–7, pe120:6, P374:17   **a never-ending storm of darkness**   After the description of "the terrible punishment of false teachers" in Jude 13: ". . . the blackness of darkness forever."

C120:9–10, pe120:9–10, P374:20–21   **the plagues with which the land of the Pharaohs was smitten**   The plague of darkness, Exodus 10:21ff., was the ninth of the ten plagues inflicted upon Egypt for its treatment of the Israelites. The plagues are described in Exodus, chapters 7–12.

C120:15–18, pe120:15–18, P374:26–29   **all the filth of the world . . . purged the world**   Quoted with revisions from Pinamonti. This passage is typical of Pinamonti's baroque approach to compilation of the pains of hell. His source seems to have been in part St. Thomas Aquinas, *Summa Theologica* (part III, Query 97, article 1), "Whether in Hell the Damned are Tormented by the Sole Punishment of Fire?" St. Thomas weighs the arguments in favor of "sole punishment of fire" against arguments in favor of "variety" (or piling it on), including St. Basil's (c. 330–79) assertion that "at the final cleansing of the world . . . whatever is ignoble and sordid [will be] cast down for punishment of the damned." In his balanced way St. Thomas concludes that there can be "variety" (filth, "intense heat . . . intense cold") provided that the variety does not provide "respite" for the damned.

C120:20–22, pe120:20–23, P374:32–34   **the bodies of the damned . . . saint Bonaventure . . . whole world**   St. Bonaventure (c. 1221–

74), "the Seraphic Doctor," scholastic philosopher with an emphasis on mysticism; professor of theology at the University of Paris, 1253; general of the Franciscans, 1256; bishop of Albano, 1273; cardinal, 1274. The passage is adapted from Pinamonti, who in turn has paraphrased St. Bonaventure.

C121:2–19, peI21:1–19, P375:17–376:3   **The torment of fire . . . rages forever**   This passage is derived from Pinamonti, who in turn is summarizing St. Thomas Aquinas, *Summa Theologica*, part III, query 97, articles 5 and 6.

C121:23–26, peI21:23–27, P376:7–11   **the devil himself . . . piece of wax**   Pinamonti quotes this story, which is supposed to have had as its source St. Caesarius of Arles (470–543).

C122:30–33, peI22:31–35, P377:21–25   **In olden times . . . to punish the parricide . . . and a serpent**   The Roman *Lex Pompeia de Parricidiis* (B.C. 52) defined parricide as the murder of an ascendant (father, grandfather, etc.) or a son. The punishment: to be sewed up in a leather sack with a live dog, a viper, a cock, and an ape and to be cast into the sea.

C123:15–19, peI23:16–20, P378:10–13   **Catherine of Sienna . . . red coals**   This passage is revised from Pinamonti, who in turn cites St. Catherine of Siena (1347–80).

C123:33–34, peI23:35–36, P378:30–31   **Time is . . . no more!**   See *Por* C113:20–21n.

C124:7, peI24:8, P379:6   **your religious duties**   See *Dub* C66:12n.

C124:13, peI24:14–15, P379:13   **a rebellion of the intellect**   See *Por* C117:26–27n and 28n.

C124:16, peI24:18, P379:17   **temple of the Holy Ghost**   I Corinthians 6:19: "What? know ye not that your body is the temple of the Holy Ghost which is in you, which ye have of God, and ye are not your own?"

C124:20, peI24:22, P379:21   **the last day of terrible reckoning**   See *Por* C113:6–11n.

C124:25–26, peI24:27–29, P379:27–28   *Depart from me . . . and his angels!*   Matthew 25:41; see *Por* C119:15–19n.

C124:34, peI24:37–38, P380:2   **he was plunging headlong through space**   Like Lucifer or Satan; compare Milton, "Him the Almighty Power / Hurl'd headlong flaming from th' Ethereal Sky / With hideous ruin and combustion down / To bottomless perdition" (*Paradise Lost*, I:44–47).

C125:16, peI25:17, P380:21   **a blue funk**   Slang: a state of deep depression.

C125:25, peI25:26, P380:30   **Malahide**   A fishing village and seaside resort, nine miles north of Dublin on the Irish Sea coast.

C125:32–33, peI25:34–36, P381:4–6   **O Mary . . . the gulf of death**   See *Por* C35:30–31n.

C126:1–2, peI26:1–2, P381:10–11   **What did it profit . . . lost his soul?**   See *Por* C110:7–9n.

C126:25, peI26:27, P382:4   **Father, I . . .**   When the penitent enters the confessional, he kneels and says: "Bless me, Father, for I have sinned."

C127:4, peI27:5, P382:21   *I am cast away from the sight of Thine eyes*   In the Douay Bible, Psalm 30:23 (King James 31:22): "But I said in the excess of my mind: I am cast away from before thy eyes"; however, the psalm continues, "But thou dost hear my supplications, when I cried to thee for help" and concludes, "Be strong, and let your heart take courage, all you who wait for the Lord!"

C127:12–13, peI27:14–15, P382:31–32   **what our holy founder . . . the composition of place**   St. Ignatius of Loyola, *The Spiritual Exercises* (1548):

> "The First Exercise," Item 47: "*First Prelude*: The first prelude is a composition, seeing the place. Here it is to be observed that in the contemplation or meditation of a visible object as in contemplating Christ our Lord, Who is visible, the composition will be to see with the eye of the imagination the corporeal place where the object I wish to contemplate is found. I say the corporeal place, such as the Temple or the mountain where Jesus Christ is to be found, or our Lady, according to that which I desire to contemplate. In a meditation on sins, the composition will be to see with the eyes of the imagination and to consider that my soul is imprisoned in this corruptible body, and my whole compound self in this vale (of misery) as in exile amongst brute beasts; I say, my whole self, composed of body and soul.

C127:19–23, peI27:21–26, P383:4–9   **Sin, remember . . . Holy God Himself**   An orthodox definition of mortal sin. Sin involves two levels of malice: the simple malice of seeking forbidden sensual or spiritual gratification (punished by the *poena sensus*, pain of the senses, notably fire) and the compound malice of turning away from God and refusing His gift of Grace (punished by *poena damni*, the pain of loss, i.e., suffering with full awareness that there is no possibility of penance and forgiveness because the gift of Grace has been lost for eternity).

C127:28–32, peI27:30–35, P383:14–19   **Saint Thomas . . . the goodness of God**   St. Thomas Aquinas (1225–74), the "Angelic Doctor"; a Dominican, and a leading scholastic philosopher and theologian, whose writings were made the basic texts for Catholic seminaries in 1879. The goal of his work was to summarize all learning and to demonstrate the compatibility of the revealed truths of Christianity with those of Aristotelian rational thought. The passage attributed to St. Thomas is paraphrased from Pinamonti, who has in turn summarized from the *Summa Theologica*, part III, query 98, "Of the Will and Intellect of the Damned."

C127:35–128:2, peI27:38–128:3, P383:23–26   **the damned in hell . . . lost it for ever**   This is revised from Pinamonti, who in turn is simplifying St. Thomas's argument in *Summa Theologica*, part III, query 98, particularly article 8, in which St. Thomas argues that the damned will "think of God" negatively rather than positively; they will have "remorse of conscience," but they "cannot think of the goodness of God but only of Him as punishing and forbidding."

C128:4–5, peI28:5–6, P383:28–29   **The soul tends towards God as towards the centre of her existence**   A paraphrase and summary of St. Thomas, *Summa Theologica*, part II, query 1, article 8, in which St. Thomas argues that "man's last end is happiness," that happiness is in God "since God is the last end of man," and finally, that "men and other rational creatures attain to their last end by knowing and loving God." See *Por* C79:21–22n and 24n.

C128:22, peI28:24, P384:13   *poena damni*   Latin: the pain of loss, the ultimate punishment of the damned, the loss of any possibility of ever "knowing and loving God." See *Por* C127:19–23n.

C128:27–28, peI28:30–31, P384:20–21   **the worm . . . of the triple sting**   Paraphrased from Pinamonti, who quotes Innocent III (b. 1161, pope 1198–1216) on the worm of conscience, "in his book of the Contempt of the World: 'The Memory will afflict, late repentance will trouble, and want of time will torment.'"

C129:15–18, peI29:17–20, P385:13–16   **as saint Augustine . . . eyes of God Himself**   Revised from Pinamonti, who really seems to be not so much paraphrasing as improving upon St. Augustine of Hippo (354–430), "Doctor of the Church." In *De Civitas Dei* (*The City of God*) Augustine does imply that the "rebel angels" remain aware (book XIII, chapter 26), but he tends to remain aloof about *poena damni*; "the reason for making no mention in Scripture of the anguish of the soul is that it is implied, though not made explicit. When the body is in pain, the soul must be tortured by fruitless repentance" (book XXI, chapter 9). Augustine's emphasis is on the *ignorance* of the damned as against the *knowledge* of the saints; i.e., from Augustine's point of view, it is the saints rather than the sinners who know the "hideous malice" of sin.

C129:24–25, pe129:26–27, P385:23–24   **the sacraments and graces and indulgences**   For Sacraments see *Por* C119:14–15n; for grace see *Por* C103:32–35n. An indulgence is "the remission through the power of the Church of the temporal punishment due to sin, which sometimes remains after the sin itself is forgiven" (*Maynooth Catechism*, p. 60).

C131:20–22, pe131:21–24, P387:34–388:3   **this is what the blood . . . vile, insists upon**   See *Por* C113:27–28n.

C132:29–30, pe132:30–31, P389:16–17   **A holy saint . . . vision of hell**   Not cited by Pinamonti; source unknown.

C132:35, pe132:38, P389:24   **the beatific vision**   The immediate sight of God in the glory of heaven as enjoyed by the blessed dead.

C133:26, pe133:27–28, P390:19   **the hideous malice of mortal sin**   Mortal sin is not only "any wilful thought, word, deed or omission contrary to the law of God," it is also regarded as an act of malicious aggression "because it kills the soul by depriving it of its true life, which is sanctifying grace, and because it brings everlasting death and damnation to the soul" (*Maynooth Catechism*, p. 24). See *Por* C127:19–23n.

C133:28, pe133:29, P390:20   **venial sin**   "Does not deprive the soul of sanctifying grace, or deserve everlasting punishment, but it hurts the soul by lessening its love for God, and disposing it to mortal sin" (*Maynooth Catechism*, p. 24).

C133:36–134:2, pe133:39–134:2, P390:31–33   **A sin, an instant . . . from their glory**   See notes to *Por* C117:19ff., and compare Milton, *Paradise Lost*, "and with lies / [Satan] drew after him the third part of Heaven's Host" (V:709–10).

C134:6–7, pe134:7, P391:3–4   **hanging for three hours on the cross**   According to Matthew 27:45 and Luke 23:44.

C134:11, pe134:11, P391:8   **spit upon that face**   The Roman soldiers do when they mock Jesus as "King of the Jews," Matthew 27:30 and Mark 15:19.

C134:14, pe134:14, P391:11–12   **the awful winepress of sorrow**   An allusion to a passage in Isaiah that is regarded as a prediction of the coming of Christ, 63:3: "I have trodden the winepress alone; and of the people there was none with me: for I will tread them in my anger and trample them in my fury." The passage is echoed in Revelation (Apocalypse) 19:15.

C134:14–15, pe134:15, P391:12–13   **a wound in His tender side**   See *Por* C119:7–9n.

C134:15, pe134:15–16, P391:13–14   **a thorn piercing His head**   See *Por* C119:4n.

C134:20, pe134:20–21, P391:18–19   **which crucifies again the Son of**

God   "Another motive to excite sorrow for our sins is to consider that the Son of God died for our sins and that *we crucify Him again* as often as we offend Him" (*Maynooth Catechism*, p. 59).

C134:23, pe134:24–25, P391:21–22   **those who are in a state of grace**   I.e., those who are not guilty of an unrepented and unconfessed mortal sin.

C134:24, pe134:25, P391:22   **the wavering**   I.e., those guilty of venial sin; see *Por* C133:28n.

C134:28, pe134:29, P391:26–27   **the act of contrition**   The prayer the students and priest repeat in the following passage is a traditional "Act of Contrition"; according to the *Maynooth Catechism* (p. 4) they omit one phrase (italics): "because they displease thee, my God, *Who for thy infinite goodness* art so deserving." As the *Confiteor* (see *Por* C78:9n) is prelude to confession, so the penitent, when he is being absolved, is counseled to contemplate Jesus dying on the cross for his sins and for the sins of all mankind, and to assert his sorrow in the Act of Contrition.

C134:29, pe134:30–31, P391:28   **He is there in the tabernacle**   I.e., the tabernacle contains the consecrated elements, the body and blood of Christ.

Chapter III: Section C

C137:5–7, pe137:5–7, P394:17–19   **He had sinned . . . called God's child**   In Jesus's parable of the prodigal son, the son repents, "I will arise and go to my father, and will say unto him, Father, I have sinned against heaven and before thee, And am no more worthy to be called thy son" (Luke 15:18–19).

C137:11–13, pe137:11–13, P394:23–25   **he had dared . . . mass of corruption**   See *Por* C104:27–28n and C110:19–20n.

C138:31–139:8, pe138:32–139:7, P396:19–33   **He once had meant . . . guide us home**   From John Henry Cardinal Newman, "The Glories of Mary for the Sake of Her Son," discourse XVII in *Discourses to Mixed Congregations* (1849). Stephen quotes the closing lines of the discourse, except that he inverts the phrases which should read, "with a shrouded radiance and a bedimmed Majesty."

C139:29–30, pe139:29–30, P397:24–25   **But does that part . . . or**

what? The question Stephen raises is whether the inadvertent and in-
stinctive act of a part of the body (the penis in this case) constitutes the
"clear knowledge and full consent" to the wrong which makes the sin
mortal (1951 *Catechism*, p. 23). See *Por* C103:28n.

C139:30–31, pe139:30, P397:26 **The serpent . . . beast of the field**
See *Por* C118:7n.

C140:8, pe140:5, P398:5–6 **Who could think such a thought?**   I.e.,
the heretical thought that God had made man's body to be inevitably
sinful whether man knows it or wills it or not. The orthodox position is
that, "Our whole nature was corrupted by the sin of our first parents—
it darkened our understanding, weakened our will, and left in us a
strong inclination to evil." But even though "this corruption of nature"
remains "after original sin has been forgiven," it remains not as an inevitability but as a "trial and an occasion of merit" (*Maynooth Catechism*, p. 14).

C140:9, pe140:7, P398:7 **his angel guardian** Catholic doctrine holds
that each individual has a special guardian angel to whom he is encour-
aged to pray each morning and evening and to whom he should turn in
time of temptation or stress; the angel will help him by praying for him,
by protecting him from harm, and by inspiring him to do good.

C140:12–14, pe140:9–11, P398:9–11 **his own soul had . . . through
his own body** Stephen resolves his questioning with a catechetical
and orthodox definition of "actual sin": the sin which we ourselves
commit by "any wilfull thought, word, deed or omission contrary to
the law of God" (*Maynooth Catechism*, p. 24).

C141:12, pe141:8, P399:15 **Church Street chapel** I.e., in the Franciscan Capuchin Friary, 138–142 [Old] Church Street, just north of the
Liffey in west-central Dublin. The Capuchins (after the Italian *cappuc-
cio*, cowl, of their habit) were founded in 1525 as a branch of the Franciscan Order. The Capuchins in Dublin were noted for the strictness
and integrity of their priestly lives and views; they were regarded as
"ideal confessors," uncompromising and yet kindly in their treatment
of penitents.

C142:2–3, pe141:36–37, P400:9–10 **those whom Jesus . . . had
called first to His side** I.e., the disciples were drawn from among the
common people; they were not from the educated or patrician classes.

C142:9, pe142:3, P400:16–17 **the brown habit of a capuchin** A
brown robe belted with white rope, a cowl, a skull cap, and sandals.

C142:13–14, pe142:9, P400:22 **like a sinful city** I.e., like Sodom
and Gomorrah destroyed, for their "iniquities," by a rain of fire and
brimstone, Genesis 19:24.

C143:7, pe142:39, P401:19–20 **God's yoke was sweet and light**

Jesus speaks, Matthew 11:29–30, "Take my yoke upon you, and learn of me; for I am meek and lowly in heart: and ye shall find rest unto your souls. For my yoke is easy, and my burden is light."

C143:9–10, pe143:2–3, P401:22 **suffered them to come to Him** In Mark 10:14 and Luke 18:16, Jesus is "displeased" with his disciples for preventing children from being brought to him and says: "Suffer the little children to come unto me, and forbid them not: for of such is the kingdom of God" (Mark).

C143:30, pe143:24, P402:9 **prayed of the priest to bless him** Upon entering the confessional, the penitent crosses himself and says: "Bless me, Father, for I have sinned."

C143:31, pe143:25, P402:11 **the *Confiteor*** Instructions for the Sacrament of Penance advise the individual to prepare himself by repeating the *Confiteor* before entering the confessional; see *Por* C78:9n.

C143:33, pe143:28, P402:13 **your last confession** Church law stipulates that Catholics must confess their sins at least once a year. To be in mortal sin for more than a year without confessing is to commit yet another mortal sin. The requirement to confess is particularly telling in Stephen's case because, as prefect of his sodality, he should be exemplary in his behavior and he should certainly guard against the sin of sacrilege; see *Por* C104:27–28n and C110:19–20n.

C144:16, pe144:8, P402:33 **sins of impurity** I.e., lust or carnality; see *Por* C103:28n and C98:34n. Cf. De Harbe *Catechism* (p. 197): "Why must we most carefully guard against impurity? Because no sin is more shameful; and because none is attended with such dreadful consequences." Cf. *Por* C106:18–19n.

C144:30, pe144:22, P403:12 **sixteen** This would make the year 1898 in autobiographical time, and Saint Francis Xavier's Feast Day would fall on Saturday; cf. *Por* C102:1n.

C145:10, pe145:1, P403:30 **that by His holy grace** I.e., the individual cannot hope to keep himself from sin "by his own effort," and if he does so hope he is guilty of the sins of presumption and pride.

C145:21, pe145:13–14, P404:7–8 **the grave words of absolution** The priest who, in his office as confessor, "represents Jesus Christ" would have given absolution in Latin: "*Absolvo te in nominis Patris et Filii et Spiritus Sancti, Amen*" (I absolve you in the name of the Father and of the Son and of the Holy Spirit, Amen).

C145:25, pe145:17, P404:11 **to say his penance** Presumably the priest has instructed Stephen to repeat certain prayers a certain number of times over a period of days—to make "amends" for his past sins and to train and strengthen himself "against future temptation."

C146:7, pe145:35, P404:29–30 **after communion in the college cha-**

pel The retreat at Belvedere was to end with the celebration of a Mass in honor of St. Francis Xavier, at which the students were to take communion. (Had Stephen not confessed and been absolved, he would have further compounded his already sinful state with the sin of sacrilege.)

C146:9, peI45:37–38, P404:32 **And life lay all before him** At the end of Milton's *Paradise Lost*, as Adam and Eve are expelled from the Garden of Eden, "Some natural tears they dropp'd, but wip'd them soon; / The World was all before them, where to choose / Thir place of rest, and Providence thir guide" (XII:645–47). Cf. *Por* C170:3–5n.

C146:21, peI46:12, P405:9 **the ciborium** The cup in which the consecrated bread is carried during communion.

C146:22–26, peI46:14–18, P405:11–15 *Corpus Domini nostri . . . In vitam eternam. Amen* Latin: the Body of our Lord / to everlasting life. Amen. These are the first three and the last three words of the formula of administration, spoken by the priest as each participant in the communion receives the Lord's Body. The full formula: "May the Body of our Lord Jesus Christ keep your soul and bring it to everlasting life. Amen."

Chapter IV: Section A

C147:1–5, peI47:1–6, P405:21–25 **Sunday was dedicated . . . Blessed Virgin Mary** Adapted from *The Sodality Manual; or a Collection of Prayers and Spiritual Exercises for Members of the Sodality of the Blessed Virgin Mary* (Dublin, 1896), from the section entitled "Devotions for Every Day of the Week" (pp. 301–13). Many of Stephen's devotional exercises in the opening section of this chapter are drawn from *The Sodality Manual*; see Kevin Sullivan, *Joyce Among the Jesuits*.

C147:8–9, peI47:10, P405:29 **for the intentions of the sovereign pontiff** Devout Catholics traditionally pray daily for the pope, the Church, and "all other bishops, prelates, and pastors of the Church." For example: "We pray thee, O almighty and eternal God, Who alone art good and holy, to endow with heavenly knowledge, sincere zeal, and sanctity of life, our chief bishop, [the pope's name], the vicar of our Lord Jesus Christ."

C147:11, peI47:12–13, P406:1 **at the sidealtar** A sparsely attended

Mass would usually be celebrated not at the high altar but at a side altar or in a small chapel off the body or off the choir of the church.

C147:12, pe147:13, P406:1-2 **interleaved prayerbook** I.e., a prayerbook with various devotional cards between its pages. The cards would be reminders of the dates when relatives or friends had died, had taken religious orders, etc., and these in turn would serve as reminders of occasion for prayers; see *Por* C62:2n.

C147:14-15, pe147:15-16, P406:4-5 **the two candles which were the old and the new testaments** I.e., the two candles which flank the crucifix on the altar; see *Dub* C9:7n.

C147:15-16, pe147:17, P406:6 **at mass in the catacombs** Stephen imagines the early days of Christianity in Rome when Christians were still being persecuted and therefore worshiped secretly in the catacombs beneath the city.

C147:18, pe147:19, P406:8 **ejaculations** Short exclamatory prayers.

C147:18-20, pe147:20-21, P406:9-10 **for the souls in purgatory . . . quarantines and years** According to Catholic doctrine Stephen's devotional activities would help to foreshorten the time of cleansing punishment suffered by the souls in Purgatory. A quarantine is a rigorous fast of forty days. The indulgence (see *Por* C129:24-25n) of quarantines means the remission of as much temporal punishment due to sin as would equal forty days of rigorous penance. Canonical penances involve contrition (the detestation of sin itself) and acts of self-denial. These penances and acts are performed in atonement for the temporal punishment due to sins already forgiven, especially those acts of self-denial imposed by the priest and accepted by the penitent in the confessional.

C147:25-26, pe148:2-3, P406:16-17 **the purgatorial fire . . . not everlasting** *The Catholic Encyclopedia* presents, as the consensus of Church authorities, the opinion that purgatorial fire is "real" and that "the pain will be more intolerable than anyone can suffer in this life"— though with the proviso that the punishment is only temporary. The *Encyclopedia* does not liken the fire of Purgatory to that of Hell but implies the two fires are different, since the fire of Purgatory cleanses while the fire of Hell does not (1911; 12:578b).

C147:28, pe148:5-6, P406:20 **supererogation** Doing more than duty requires to form a reserve of merit that can be drawn on in favor of sinners.

C148:12, pe148:18, P406:33 **The rosaries** A rosary is a form of prayer in which fifteen decades of Aves (a prayer to the Blessed Virgin Mary: "Hail Mary, full of Grace . . ."; see *Dub* 98:23n), each decade being preceded by a Pater Noster (the Lord's Prayer) and followed by a Gloria (Glory to God in the highest . . .), are recited on beads. One of the fifteen mysteries of the Blessed Virgin Mary is contemplated during the recital of each decade, and the rosary is divided into three parts, each consisting of five decades and known as a corona or chaplet. In the first chaplet the five joyful mysteries are the subject: the Annunciation, Visitation, Birth of the Lord, Christ's Presentation at the Temple, His being found after three days' loss. The sorrowful mysteries contemplated in the second chaplet are the Agony in the Garden, the Scourging, the Crowning with Thorns, the Carrying of the Cross, the Crucifixion. The glorious mysteries which are allotted to the third chaplet are the Resurrection, the Ascension, the Descent of the Holy Ghost, the Assumption, and the Coronation of the Blessed Virgin.

C148:17, pe148:24, P407:4 **chaplets** A third of a rosary, 55 (sometimes 59) beads or the prayers recited on the beads; see preceding note.

C148:18, pe148:25, P407:5 **the three theological virtues** Or, the three divine virtues: faith, hope, and charity, after I Corinthians 13:13.

C148:22-23, pe148:29-30, P407:9-10 **through Mary in the name . . . glorious mysteries** See *Por* C148:12n.

C148:25, pe148:32, P407:12 **the seven gifts of the Holy Ghost** Wisdom, understanding, counsel, fortitude, knowledge, piety, fear of the Lord; after Isaiah 11:2: "And the spirit of the Lord shall rest upon him, the spirit of wisdom and understanding, the spirit of counsel and might, the spirit of knowledge and of the fear of the Lord."

C148:26-27, pe148:34, P407:14 **the seven deadly sins** See *Por* C103:28n.

C149:1-2, pe149:6, P407:26-27 **Paraclete, Whose symbols were a dove and a mighty wind** Paraclete (comforter) is an appellation of the Holy Ghost. The mission of the Paraclete is to abide with the disciples after Jesus has withdrawn His visible presence from them, to bring home to them inwardly the teaching given by Christ. The soul, inwardly renovated by habitual grace, becomes the habitation of the Three Persons of the Trinity, yet that indwelling is rightly appropriated to the Third Person (the Holy Ghost). As to the mode of the Holy Ghost's habitation in the souls of the just, *The Catholic Encyclopedia* (1910; 7:410ff.) remarks that Catholic theologians are not agreed. Indeed, St. Bernard of Clairvaux, in the twelfth-century trial of Peter Abelard, declared that even to speculate about the indwelling of the Holy Ghost was to be in heresy.

The Holy Ghost is symbolized as a dove in Matthew 3:16: "And Jesus being baptized, forthwith came out of the water: and lo the heavens were opened to Him: and He saw the Spirit of God descending as a dove, and coming upon Him"; similarly in Mark 1:10, Luke 3:22, and John 1:32. The symbol of the mighty wind is most clearly stated in Acts 2:2, when the descent of the Holy Ghost upon the Apostles at Pentecost is preceded by "a sound from heaven as of a rushing mighty wind."

C149:2-3, pe149:7-8, P407:27-28 **to sin against Whom was a sin beyond forgiveness** The De Harbe *Catechism* lists "Six Sins against the Holy Ghost . . . 1. Presumption of God's mercy; 2. Despair; 3. Resisting the known Christian truth; 4. Envy at another's spiritual good; 5. Obstinacy in sin; and 6. Final impenitence" (p. 226). On p. 150 the De Harbe *Catechism* holds that, "All sins without exception can be forgiven in the Catholic Church" though the "without exception" is qualified on p. 276: "Not all sins can be forgiven by *every* Priest"; i.e., some sins would require the special attention of a bishop or the pope. From the Donlevy *Catechism*: "Q. Why is it said that the sins against the Holy Ghost shall never be forgiven. . . ? A. Because it is very difficult to obtain the forgiveness of them; for men very seldom do true penance for them." The Donlevy *Catechism* concludes, however, that all can be forgiven "except Final Impenitence" (p. 171).

C149:4-5, pe149:9-10, P407:29-31 **mass once a year, robed in the scarlet tongues of fire** I.e., the Mass for Pentecost (or Whitsunday, the seventh Sunday after Easter), commemorating the day when the Holy Ghost in the form of "cloven tongues like as of fire" (Acts 2:3) descended upon the Apostles. Red is the appropriate color of the vestments for this Mass; see *Dub* C13:6n.

C149:8, pe149:13, P407:34 **the books of devotion which he read** The books apparently present an orthodox summation of scholastic doctrine about the Trinity, doctrine that is either in agreement with or derived from St. Thomas Aquinas.

C149:13-14, pe149:19, P408:5-6 **the simple fact that God had loved his soul from all eternity** In the general sense that God has loved all souls "from all eternity" but not in the sense that each individual soul has existed "from all eternity." "Many modern theologians . . . maintain that a fully rational soul is infused into the embryo at the first moment of its existence" (*Catholic Encyclopedia* [1912], 14:156a).

C150:20-21, pe150:25-26, P409:18-19 **the dangers of spiritual exaltation** The exalted individual is regarded as in danger of losing himself in pleasurable visions and thus of being unprepared to face the inevitable periods of spiritual aridity and depression. He is in danger of the sins of presumption on the one hand and despair on the other; see *Por* C149:2-3n. He is also in danger of wandering from orthodoxy, and is therefore counseled to conform to the conventional patterns of daily devotion.

C150:36, pe151:3, P410:1 **twigging** Brushing with a stiff short broom.

C151:10, pe151:14, P410:13 **all the fasts of the church** I.e., every day of Lent (the forty days exclusive of Sundays), abstinence on Ash Wednesday and every Friday, on the vigils of important Holy Days such as Christmas, and on Ember Days (the Tuesday, Wednesday, and Saturday of each of four weeks during the year in conjunction with four major phases of the liturgical calendar).

C151:36, pe152:2, P411:6-7 **a sensation of spiritual dryness** See *Por* C150:20-21n.

C152:5-6, pe152:7-8, P411:12 **His actual reception of the eucharist** I.e., to take communion. The *Maynooth Catechism*, p. 56: "It is advisable to go often to communion, as nothing can conduce more to a *holy life. He that eateth this bread*, says Christ, *shall live forever* (John, vi, 59)."

C152:8-9, pe152:10-11, P411:15-16 **visit to the Blessed Sacrament** I.e., a visit to a church for the purpose of solitary contemplation and prayer when a service is not in progress. "The conception is that in the tabernacle Jesus Christ, as it were, holds His court, and is prepared to grant audience to all who draw near to Him" (*Catholic Encyclopedia* [1912], 15:484a).

C152:9-10, pe152:12-13, P411:17 **the book which he used . . . saint Alphonsus Liguori** St. Alphonsus (1696-1787) began his career as a brilliant lawyer and after humiliation in his worldly career and at the promptings of an "interior voice" turned to a career in the Church. He founded a missionary order, The Congregation of the Most Holy Redeemer (the Redemptorists, 1732), led a life of constant labor, practiced severe austerities, and is regarded as one of the three great missionaries of the Church. The book alluded to is apparently *Visits to the Most Blessed Sacrament*, which does interweave quotations from the Canticle of Canticles (The Song of Solomon) with a pattern of prayers; in Christian tradition the song is read as a sustained allegory of the love between Christ and His Church.

C152:11, pe152:13, P411:18 **foxpapered** To fox is to discolor by decay (as book leaves).

C152:14, pe152:16, P411:21 **the canticles** I.e., the Canticle of Canticles in the Douay Bible (The Song of Solomon in the King James).

C152:16, pe152:19, P411:24-25 **bidding her arise as for espousal and come away** Canticle of Canticles (Song of Solomon) 2:13, "Arise, my love, my fair one, and come away."

C152:17, pe152:20, P411:25 **Amana** A mountain in or near Lebanon on which Abana, the overflowing river, has its source. The mountains of the leopards are the hilly ranges of Lebanon. Canticle of Canticles (The Song of Solomon) 4:8: "Come with me from Lebanon, my spouse, with me from Lebanon; look from the top of Amana . . . from the lions' dens, from the mountains of the leopards."

C152:19–20, pe152:23, P411:28 *Inter ubera mea commorabitur* Latin: He shall lie betwixt my breasts; from the Canticle of Canticles (Song of Solomon) 1:13. The standard gloss of this passage is that it articulates the Church's love of Christ.

C152:25, pe152:28–29, P411:34 **a single act of consent**

> Q. How shall one know that he has not consented to the temptation?
> A. If he renounced it quickly; or if he endeavoured without delay, to give attention to something else; if he was troubled or grieved while the evil thought lasted; or if he earnestly begged the assistance of God, or the intercession of saint or angel, it is certain he did not consent to it. [Don-levy *Catechism*, pp. 335–37]

C153:1, pe153:3, P412:13 **grace** See *Por* C103:32–35n.

C153:10–11, pe153:12–13, P412:23–24 **the truth of what he had heard about the trials of the saints** I.e., that the saints had not lived in continuous "spiritual exaltation" (see *Por* C150:20–21n) but had suffered periods of spiritual aridity and temptation. Traditionally, the intensity of the trial is regarded as a measure of the purity of the saint's faith.

C153:17, pe153:19–20, P412:30–31 **bidden by his confessor to name some sin of his past life** Instructions for confession explicitly urge the penitent to "accuse himself of all the sins of [his] past life," since he has not fully done penance until the end of this life (and until the end of his stay in Purgatory if he is so adjudged at the Particular Judgment).

C153:25–26, pe153:27–29, P413:4–6 **Perhaps that first hasty confession . . . not been good?** For the confession to be "good" the penitent must confess with "sincere" or "Perfect Contrition"; otherwise the confession is less than good and must be made over again. "When is Contrition Imperfect? When our Love of God is not Perfect, and when, therefore, our fear of Hell and of the loss of Heaven . . . must unite with it in causing us to detest sin above all other evils, and to resolve to offend God no more" (De Harbe *Catechism*, p. 281).

C153:28–30, pe153:31–33, P413:8–10 **the surest sign . . . amendment of his life** "The surest sign that our confessions were good and that we had sincere sorrow for our sins [perfect contrition] is the amendment of our lives" (*Maynooth Catechism*, pp. 59–60).

C153:32, pe153:36, P413:14   **the director**   I.e., the director of studies at Belvedere College.

C154:24, pe154:27, P414:9   **dominican**   The Order of Friars Preachers, founded by St. Dominic (1170–1221), c. 1205. The avowed purpose of the order was the salvation of souls, especially by means of preaching.

C154:25, pe154:28, P414:10   **franciscan**   The Order of Friars Minor, founded by St. Francis of Assisi (1182?–1226). Dedicated to the rule of poverty, the order became wealthy and powerful and was noted in the nineteenth century for its learning and its cultivation of the sciences.

C154:25–26, pe154:28–29, P414:11   **saint Thomas and saint Bonaventure**   Two great Doctors of the Church: St. Thomas Aquinas, a Dominican (*Por* C127:28n), and St. Bonaventure, a Franciscan (*Por* C120:20–22n). Their teaching careers overlapped at the University of Paris, and they became and remained friends.

C154:26, pe154:29, P414:11–12   **capuchin dress**   See *Por* C142:9n. The Capuchins are a branch of the Franciscan Order instituted by Father Matteo da Bassi in 1525. They aimed at strict observance of the rule of poverty, in contrast to what they regarded as the "secularizing tendency" of the Franciscans.

C154:33, pe154:36, P414:18–19   **the example of the other franciscans**   I.e., why did the Capuchins not reform their dress, wearing dark suits and clerical collars in public and reserving the robes and sandals of their traditional habit for the cloister?

C155:7, pe155:7, P414:29   *Les jupes*   French: the skirts, the petticoats.

C155:22, pe155:24, P415:12   **Stradbrook**   See *Por* C63:30n.

C155:34, pe155:36–37, P415:26   **the craft of jesuits**   In the seventeenth and eighteenth centuries the zeal of the Jesuits in the cause of counter-Reformation earned them the reputation of being devious and guileful, particularly among Protestants and in Protestant countries. The Jesuits also had the reputation of being Machiavellian because they appeared to regard the end (the greater glory of God) as justifying any worldly means that might be employed to approach it, including means outside the bounds of conventional morality.

C156:12, pe156:13, P416:7   **a muff**   Slang for a novice, a foolish, silly person; in athletics, a clumsy person, a failure.

C156:13–14, pe156:14–15, P416:8–9   **his equivocal position in Bel-**

vedere Because unlike the other students he did not have to pay tuition and fees. Scholarship students in the British Isles were often regarded as paid dependents, paid to conform to the institution and its expectations—an "equivocal position," suspect from the point of view of their paying contemporaries.

C156:17, pe156:18, P416:13 **obedience** See *Por* C59:9n.

C156:25–27, pe156:27–29, P416:22–24 **Lord Macaulay . . . never committed . . . a deliberate mortal sin** Thomas Babington Macaulay (1800–59), English historian, essayist, and statesman. There are several ironies in the priest's remarks: Macaulay was able to sustain a reputation as the mirror of Victorian propriety in spite of the fact that his life was not without moral blemish; in Catholic doctrine there is no such thing as a mortal sin that is not "deliberate" (see *Por* C152:25n). As a spokesman for Protestant Victorian England Macaulay went in for a "dignified" anti-Roman Catholicism. Finally, inappropriate as the priest's remark is when applied to Macaulay, it is derived from a remark about St. Aloysius Gonzaga (see *Por* C56:3–5n), "In the opinion of his director, Saint Robert Bellarmine, and three of his other confessors, he never in his life committed a mortal sin" (*Butler's Lives of the Saints*, 2:603).

C156:28, pe156:30–31, P416:25–26 **Victor Hugo** French poet, novelist, and dramatist (1802–85), a leader of French Romanticism and a dominant figure in nineteenth-century French literature. His mother had royalist and Catholic sympathies, which she attempted to encourage in her son but with limited success. Hugo's first important volume of poetry (1822) is characterized by an outspoken royalism and a rather perfunctory religiosity. Both royalism and religion soon gave way before Hugo's energy. The priest's evaluation in effect rejects all the work of Hugo's flamboyant maturity in favor of the work of his literary apprenticeship.

C156:35, pe156:37–38, P416:32–33 **Louis Veuillot** French journalist (1813–83), a strident propagandist for the Ultramontane Party in France (the party opposed nineteenth-century political efforts to curtail the secular powers of the Roman Catholic Church in France). He also wrote edifying romances and saintly stories.

C157:7, pe157:8, P417:7 **slim jim** See *Por* C93:6n.

C157:17, pe157:18, P417:18 **a vocation** The director asks whether Stephen has felt himself spiritually qualified for, drawn to, or inspired to strive for a position in the priesthood. Cf. *Dub* C19:19n.

C157:32, pe157:29–30, P417:35 **prefect of Our Blessed Lady's sodality** See *Por* C104:23–24n.

C158:4–10, pe158:3–10, P418:8–16 **No angel or archangel . . . the**

form of bread and wine   Two of the "powers" the director of studies enumerates are sacramental (the Sacrament of Penance and the Sacrament of the Holy Eucharist); those powers are regarded as specifically and exclusively conferred on the priesthood by Jesus Christ. The power to exorcise evil spirits is not as unambiguously conferred exclusively on the priesthood, although some phases of it are: the power to exorcise evil spirits from persons, places, or things has traditionally been regarded as so special that a priest is allowed to use it only with the express permission of his bishop. On the other hand, many Catholic theologians have argued that the Sacrament of Baptism involves a kind of exorcism, and baptism can, when necessary, be administered by a layman.

C158:6, pe158:5, P418:10–11   **the power of the keys**   The power to hear confession and forgive sins in the Sacrament of Penance; from Matthew 16:18–19: "And I say to thee, thou art Peter, and upon this rock I will build my church . . . . And I will give thee the keys of the kingdom of heaven, and whatever thou shalt loose on earth shall be loosed in heaven."

C158:7, pe158:6, P418:12   **the power of exorcism**   From Matthew 10:1: "Then having summoned his twelve disciples, Jesus gave them power over unclean spirits, to cast them out" (Douay).

C158:9–10, pe158:8–10, P418:14–16   **to make the great God . . . bread and wine**   *Maynooth Catechism*: "Christ gave power to the priests of His Church to change bread and wine into His body and blood, when He said unto His Apostles at His last supper, *Do this for a commemoration of me* (Luke, xxii. 19)" (p. 54). The rhetoric the director uses comes close to an assertion that the priesthood has "the power to order God around" and thus shows either an inadvertent or intentional want of humility?

C158:15–16, pe158:15–16, P418:22   **of which angels and saints stood in reverence**   I.e., the priestly powers which can be exercised only by priests and not even by "saints and angels"; see *Por* C158:4–10n and *Dub* C13:13–14n.

C158:25, pe158:26, P418:32   **thurible**   The censer or container in which incense is burned.

C158:25, pe158:26, P418:33   **chasuble**   A long sleeveless vestment worn over the alb by the celebrant at Mass. The alb is a long white linen robe with tapered sleeves. The chasuble opens down the side.

C158:28, pe158:29, P419:1   **the second place**   The office of deacon, the priest (or deacon) who assists the celebrant at Mass.

C158:32–33, pe158:34, P419:6   **the minor sacred offices**   The De Harbe *Catechism* defines these as "the Order of *Sub-deacon*, who has to assist the Deacon when serving at the altar; and the Order of *Deacon*, who immediately assists the Priest at the altar, and helps him also in baptizing, preaching, and giving Holy Communion" (p. 300). These "offices" are almost always filled by ordained priests in the modern Church.

C158:33, pe158:34–35, P419:7   **the tunicle of subdeacon**   The subdeacon prepares the sacred vessels and reads the epistle. The tunicle is the short vestment worn over the alb by a subdeacon.

C158:35, pe158:37, P419:9   **a humeral veil**   A silk veil which covers the shoulders of the subdeacon at High Mass. It is folded over the hands when they are holding the sacred vessels.

C158:35, pe158:37, P419:10   **the paten**   A plate used to hold the Eucharistic bread.

C159:1, pe158:38–159:1, P419:11–12   **as deacon in a dalmatic of cloth of gold**   The dalmatic is the widesleeved vestment the deacon wears over the alb at High Mass.

C159:3, pe159:3, P419:14   *Ite, missa est*   The Dismissal, what the celebrant or deacon says at the conclusion of the Mass: variously translated as, "Go, you are dismissed," or, "Go, the Mass is ended."

C159:4–5, pe159:4–5, P419:16   **his child's massbook**   I.e., an illustrated missal, adapted for children. It would contain the prayers said by the priest at the altar and what is read or sung in the principal Masses in the course of the Liturgical Year.

C159:6, pe159:6, P419:17   **the angel of the sacrifice**   Not a theological concept but a visual image from "his child's massbook," the image of an angelic presence (often with sword in hand) hovering over the altar as the bread and wine are being changed into the body and blood of Christ.

C159:16–17, pe159:17–18, P419:29   **the sin of Simon Magus**   See Acts 8:9–25. Simon Magus was a magician who "bewitched the people of Samaria, giving out that himself was some great one." He was eventually baptized, and when Peter and John came to Samaria, "Simon saw that through the laying on of the apostles' hands, the Holy Ghost was given; he offered them money saying, 'Give me this power, that on whomsoever I lay hands, he may receive the Holy Ghost.'" Peter and John of course severely rejected this request. It is from this story, however, by way of metaphysical elaboration, that the mysteries of the sin of Simon Magus (who gave his name to simony) are developed, and Simon Magus achieves distinction as "Father of Heresies." See *Dub* C9:13n.

C159:17, pe159:18, P419:30   **the sin against the Holy Ghost**   See *Por* C149:2–3n; the catechisms quoted in that note sought to demystify the sin against the Holy Ghost, but the mysterious nature of "Blasphemy against the Holy Spirit" retains its grip on the imagination. The *Catholic Encyclopedia* (1910; 7:414b–415a) says in effect that there is no real consensus among the Fathers of the Church and therefore that the "unforgiveable" nature of the "Blasphemy" cannot be explained. The *Encyclopedia* cites Matthew 12:22–32, in which Jesus heals a man "possessed with a devil, blind and dumb"; the Pharisees complain: "this man casteth not out devils but by Beelzebub the prince of devils." Jesus answers that it is by "the Spirit of God" that He casts out devils, and then says:

> Therefore, I say to you: Every sin and blasphemy shall be forgiven men, but the blasphemy of the spirit shall not be forgiven. And whosoever shall speak a word against the Son of man, it shall be forgiven him: but he that shall speak against the Holy Ghost, it shall not be forgiven him, neither in this world, nor in the world to come.

C159:20, peI59:21, P419:33   **children of wrath**   Ephesians 2:3: "Among whom also we all had our conversation in times past in the lusts of our flesh, fulfilling the desires of the flesh and of the mind; and were by nature the children of wrath, even as others."

C159:24–25, peI59:26, P420:3   **ordination by the imposition of hands**   The Holy Ghost was conferred "through the laying on of the apostles' hands," as Jesus had laid his hands upon Peter (and through Peter and the Apostles upon the priesthood). Thus one generation of the priesthood confers its "powers" upon the next by "imposition of hands." Cf. *Por* C159:16–17n.

C159:26, peI59:28, P420:5   **No touch of sin would linger upon the hands**   Catholic doctrine holds that the Sacrament of Holy Orders, administered by a bishop "gives power and grace to clergymen to offer holily the sacrifice of the Mass" (Donlevy *Catechism*, p. 293).

C159:28–29, peI59:30–31, P420:8–9   **eat and drink damnation to himself, not discerning the body of the Lord**   I Corinthians 11:27, 29: "Wherefore whosoever shall eat this bread and drink this cup of the Lord, unworthily, shall be guilty of the body and blood of the Lord . . . . For he that eateth and drinketh unworthily, eateth and drinketh damnation to himself, not discerning the Lord's body."

C159:32, peI59:34, P420:12   **the order of Melchisedec**   In Hebrews 5:6–7, Jesus is spoken of as "a priest after the order of Melchisedec" (King of Righteousness, Genesis 14:18–20). Since the priesthood of the Catholic Church regards its spiritual descent as being from St. Peter, who in turn received his ordination at the hands of Jesus, the modern priest is a "priest after the order of Melchisedec." Melchisedec is also mentioned in Psalms 110:4 (Vulgate, 109:4), where it is asserted that the Messiah will be a "priest after the order of Melchisedec." The passage in Hebrews quotes the Psalm and thus involves the assertion that Jesus is the Messiah.

C159:33, pe159:35, P420:13   **offer up my mass**   I.e., the priest will offer the "sacrifice" of the Mass to God so that God will reveal to Stephen whether he has a vocation in the priesthood.

C159:35, pe159:37, P420:15   **a novena**   A nine days' devotion for a religious object.

C159:35-36, pe159:37-38, P420:16   **your holy patron saint**   St. Stephen Protomartyr; see *Por* C8:33n.

C160:3, pe160:4, P420:20   **Once a priest always a priest**   "As the priestly character, like that imparted by baptism and confirmation, is indelible, ordination can never be repeated, and a return to the lay state is absolutely impossible" (*Catholic Encyclopedia* [1911], 12:417a). If, however, a priest proves "unworthy," his bishop can deprive him of "jurisdiction," i.e., of the right to celebrate mass, to hear confession, etc., but the bishop cannot deprive the unworthy priest of the "indelible mark" of his "sacramental character" (1908; 3:587a); even excommunication cannot remove that "mark."

C160:4-7, pe160:4-8, P420:21-24   **Your catechism tells . . . never be effaced**   "All the sacraments can be received more than once, except baptism, confirmation, and holy orders, which imprint on the soul a character or spiritual mark that can never be effaced" (*Maynooth Catechism*, pp. 63-64).

C160:14, pe160:16, P420:32   **Findlater's church**   Abbey Church: "A handsome Presbyterian Church has been built in Rutland [now Parnell] Square North at the sole expense of the late Alexander Findlater, esq., J. P., at a cost of upwards of £16,000" (*Thom's* 1904, p. 1335).

C160:31, pe160:34, P421:15   **the novitiate**   A time of probation during which the candidate who has already been admitted to the religious order is prepared for ordination and full entry into the priesthood. The novitiate is also "the house lawfully set apart for the purpose" of housing the novices (*Catholic Encyclopedia* [1911], 11:146b). The Jesuit Novitiate in Ireland was at Tullabeg; see *Por* C14:4n.

C161:19, pe161:20, P422:6   **S. J.**   Society of Jesus (the Jesuit Order).

C161:28-29, pe161:29-30, P422:16-17   **Lantern Jaws . . . Foxy Campbell**   Nicknames of one of the "real-life" teachers at Belvedere College, Father Richard Campbell, S.J.

C161:30-31, pe161:31-32, P422:18-19   **the jesuit house in Gardiner Street**   The Presbytery House attached to the Jesuit Church of St.

Francis Xavier in Gardiner Street Upper, just northeast of the center of Dublin.

C162:18, pe162:19, P423:10   **the bridge over . . . the Tolka**   Bally-bough Bridge. The Tolka is a small river which skirted the then northern boundary of metropolitan Dublin. Stephen has walked almost a mile north-northeast since he passed "the jesuit house in Gardiner Street." See map for *A Portrait*, chapter V: A, on p. 224 below.

C162:19–21, pe162:20–23, P423:12–14   **faded blue shrine . . . poor cottages**   I.e., a statue on a pedestal. The expanse of the blue cape makes the figure look like a bird balanced on a pole (blue and white are the Blessed Virgin Mary's colors). "Tolka Cottages" were really hovels with walls built of mud and straw; they have since been demolished. For a photograph of the statue see Patricia Hutchins, *James Joyce's Dublin* (London, 1950), p. 39.

C163:1, pe163:1, P423:31   **his brothers and sisters**   In *Ulysses* several of Stephen's sisters appear as characters in sections of The Wandering Rocks episode, and some of them are glimpsed or mentioned elsewhere in the novel.

C163:18, pe163:19, P424:17   **Fallon**   William Fallon, who, in autobiographical time, did ask the ill-mannered question about the Joyce family economy, is here paid off for his lack of consideration; see Ellmann, p. 71, and Sheehy, *May It Please the Court*, p. 22.

C163:28, pe163:29, P424:29–30   ***Oft in the Stilly Night***   A poem by Thomas Moore,

> Oft, in the stilly night,
> Ere slumber's chain has bound me,
> Fond memory brings the light
> Of other days around me;
> The smiles, the tears,
> Of boyhood years,
> The words of love then spoken,
> The eyes that shone,
> Now dimmed and gone . . . .

C164:7–11, pe164:7–11, P425:10–15   **And he remembered that Newman . . .** *her children in every time*   John Henry Cardinal Newman, *An Essay in Aid of a Grammar of Assent* (London, 1881), pp. 78–79. Newman is discussing under the heading of "Real Assents" the ways in which passages from classical authors appear to be "but rhetorical commonplaces" to a schoolboy and yet impress the mature

> with their sad earnestness and vivid exactness . . . . Perhaps this is the reason of the medieval opinion about Virgil, as if a prophet or magician; his

single words and phrases, his pathetic half-lines, giving utterance, as the voice of Nature herself, to that pain and weariness, yet hope of better things, which is the experience of her children in every time.

Chapter IV: Section C

C164:13, pe164:13, P425:17 **Byron's publichouse** Apparently fictional, though there was a public house (Patrick Powell, grocer and wine merchant) near the Chapel in what is now Clontarf Road.

C164:13–14, pe164:14, P425:18 **Clontarf Chapel** Clontarf Roman Catholic Church of St. John the Baptist, in what was then called Clontarf-sheds, now Clontarf Road in Clontarf (Irish: Bull's Meadow), an area on Dublin Bay three miles east-northeast of the center of Dublin.

C164:19–20, pe164:20, P425:24–25 **Dan Crosby, the tutor** Apparently fictional.

C164:21, pe164:21, P425:26 **the university** I.e., University College, Dublin; see *Dub* C188:19n.

C164:23, pe164:25, P425:28 **the Bull** A seawall that extends southeast into Dublin Bay from the shore in Clontarf; the wall begins a bit over half a mile east of the footpath Stephen has been pacing. Bull Wall is the northern boundary of Dublin's harbor; it terminates in North Bull Lighthouse, one and one half miles from the Clontarf shore. That light, together with Poolbeg lighthouse to the south, marks the harbor entrance. North Bull Island extends northeast along the coast from the inshore half of the wall.

C164:25, pe164:27, P425:30–31 **the police barrack** Stood approximately 250 yards east of Clontarf Chapel.

C165:8, pe165:7–8, P426:15 **to escape by an unseen path** As Dante and Virgil escape from the heart of the *Inferno*, where they have confronted Satan, who is buried up to his waist in the ice of Lake Cocytus at the exact center of the earth. Dante and his guide turn upside down and climb up Satan's leg (toward his foot) through "a space, not known by sight but by the sound of a rivulet descending in it" (XXXIV: 129–31). The "hidden road" (XXXIV:133) leads to the surface of the earth opposite Italy and to the foot of the Mount of Purgatory. At the top of the Mount in the Garden of the Earthly Paradise Dante is to encounter his ideal love (intercessor and guide), Beatrice.

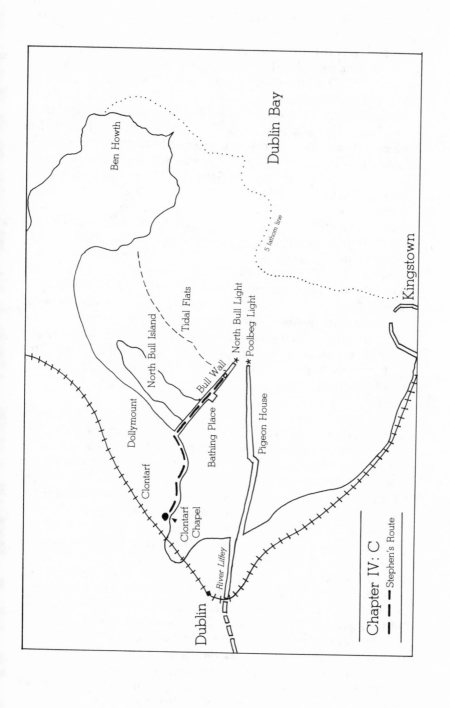

Ben Howth

Dublin Bay

5 fathom line

North Bull Island

Tidal Flats

* North Bull Light

★ Poolbeg Light

Bull Wall

Dollymount

Bathing Place

Clontarf

Pigeon House

Clontarf
Chapel

River Liffey

Dublin

Kingstown

Chapter IV: C

— — Stephen's Route

C165:11–14, pe165:10–14, P426:18–22   **fitful music leaping upwards . . . an elfin prelude**   The source of the melodic fragment Stephen "hears" (C–D–A-sharp–B-sharp[C]–A-flat) has not been identified, but it is a fragment of whole-tone-scale melody, and that suggests the music of Claude Debussy (1862–1918). Debussy, while not the inventor of the whole tone scale, made such systematic use of it in the late nineteenth century that it is often referred to as "his." Debussy was closely associated with literary Paris, with Stéphane Mallarmé (1842–98) and the other poets of the Symbolist Movement, whose works Arthur Symons had called to the attention of the English speaking world in the 1890s, beginning with his essay, "The Decadent Movement in Literature," *Harper's New Monthly Magazine* (November, 1893). Stephen's phrase "elfin prelude" may also be an allusion to Debussy, to his "*Prélude à l'après-midi d'un faune*" ("Prelude to the Afternoon of a Faun," 1892) which Debussy said was "according to Mallarmé," i.e., suggested by Mallarmé's poem, "*L'Après-midi d'un faune*." In other words, the "fitful music" Stephen hears is an echo of the avant-garde aesthetic climate of the 1890s, the climate in which Stephen seems so thoroughly immersed as he composes his "villanelle" in V:B; see headnote to that episode, pp. 257–261 below. The "triplebranching flames" may owe a debt of vision to the "fitful flames" that light the Harz Mountains for the *Walpurgisnacht* in Goethe's *Faust*, I:xxi.

C165:21–22, pe165:22–23, P426:29–31   **a proud cadence from Newman . . . *everlasting arms***   From John Henry Cardinal Newman, *The Idea of a University Defined and Illustrated* (1852). The phrases occur in discourse I, "Introductory." Newman, reviewing the "success" of the Church through the course of history, reaches a climax in a series of rhetorical questions of which this is the last: "What gray hairs are in the head of Judah, whose youth is renewed like the eagle's, whose feet are like the feet of harts, and underneath the Everlasting arms?" Judah was the son of Jacob (Genesis) and ancestor of the clan from which King David of Israel was to emerge.

C165:28–29, pe165:29–30, P427:3–4   **the oils of ordination would never anoint his body**   Priests are ordained in the Sacrament of Holy Orders under the ministry of a bishop. Stephen contemplates one phase of the Sacrament when the priest-to-be is anointed with chrism "of oil of olives and balsam" (De Harbe *Catechism*, p. 255).

C165:30, pe165:31, P427:5   **seaward from the road at Dollymount**   Stephen has been walking east-northeast along Clontarf Road. The Bull Wall is reached by a short span of footbridge which intersects Clontarf Road where the areas of Clontarf and Dollymount (to the north) meet.

C165:32–33, pe165:34, P427:8   **christian brothers**   See *Dub* C29:3n.

C166:8–11, pe166:8–11, P427:21–24   **Brother Hickey . . . Quaid
. . . MacArdle . . . Keogh**   "Brother Hickey" is present and spoken
to; the other names are chosen as connoting lower class backgrounds.

C166:21–24, pe166:22–25, P428:1–4   **the commandment of love . . .
same kind of love**   The distinction between "kind" and "intensity" of
love is traditional in scholastic discussions of the New Law: "The ten
commandments may be reduced to these two principal commandments, which are the two great precepts of Charity: *Thou shalt love the
Lord thy God with all thy heart, and with thy whole soul, and with all thy
mind, and thy neighbor as thyself. This do, and thou shalt live* (Luke X.
27)" (*Maynooth Catechism*, p. 41).

C166:27, pe166:28, P428:7   **A day of dappled seaborne clouds**
From Hugh Miller (1805–56), *The Testimony of the Rocks; or, Geology in
Its Bearings on the Two Theologies, Natural and Revealed* (Boston, 1857).
Miller's book is an elaborate and poetic attempt to rationalize an accord
between Biblical and (the new) geological accounts of the Creation. The
phrase Stephen misquotes is from a passage in which Miller describes
Satan ("that acute intelligence") contemplating but unable to compre-
hend the divine Creation, p. 277:

> And how, as generation after generation passed away, and ever and anon the
> ocean rolled where the land had been, or the land rose to possess the ancient
> seats of the ocean,—how, when looking back upon myriads of ages, and
> when calling up in memory what once had been, the features of the earth
> seemed scarce more fixed to his view than the features of the sky in *a day of
> dappled, breeze-borne clouds,*—how must he have felt, as he became con-
> scious that the earth was fast ripening, and that, as its foundations became
> stable on the abyss, it was made by the Creator a home of higher and yet
> higher forms of existence,—how must he have felt, if, like some old augur
> looking into the inner mysteries of animal life, with their strange proph-
> ecies, the truth had at length burst upon him, that reasoning, accountable
> man was fast coming to the birth,—man, the moral agent,—man, the ulti-
> mate work and end of creation,—man, a creature in whom, as in the inferior
> animals, vitality was to be united to matter, but in whom also, as in no in-
> ferior animal, responsibility was to be united to vitality!

Several pages earlier (pp. 272–73) Miller, discussing the fallen state of
man, cites the persecuted Irish as a case in point, as

> having been exposed to the worst effects of hunger and ignorance, the two
> great brutalities of the human race . . . these spectres of a people that were
> once well-grown, able-bodied, and comely, stalk abroad into the daylight of
> civilization, the animal apparition of Irish ugliness and Irish want.

C167:12, pe167:12–13, P428:30:31 **along the spine . . . river's mouth** I.e., Stephen did not turn north to walk on North Bull Island but continued southeast along the seawall, which not only protects the harbor but also confines the mouth of the Liffey.

C167:15, pe167:16, P428:34 **the slowflowing Liffey** Where it flows through Dublin the Liffey is an estuary, ebbing and flowing with the tide.

C167:18, pe167:19–20, P429:3 **the seventh city of christendom** In the Viking Critical Library edition of *A Portrait* (New York, 1968), p. 519, Chester G. Anderson identifies this phrase as "a name given to Dublin during the Middle Ages," but I have been unable to confirm this identification. Sean O'Faolain applies the term to Dublin's "heyday" (1660–1800) in an article, "Fair Dublin," in *Holiday* 33, no. 4 (April 1963):73. Medieval Dublin was a Danish stronghold and then an English outpost, plagued by raids, sieges, skirmishes, and anarchic politics. Dublin did not come into its own as a city of style and distinction until the period after the Restoration and before the Act of Union. This accounts for O'Faolain's use of what I suspect is Joyce's phrase. I wonder whether the "point" of the phrase in *A Portrait* hinges on the fact that the number seven (as the number three) is traditionally associated with things mystical and sacred (in this case, with the city's "weariness")?

C167:20, pe167:22, P429:6 **the thingmote** The place of the Scandinavian council of law; in this context, the council in Dublin when Dublin was ruled by Scandinavians (Danes) from c. 852 until their power was broken at the Battle of Clontarf (1014). The Dublin thingmote was a huge mound which stood where St. Andrew's Church now stands (at the intersection of St. Andrew's and Suffolk Streets), about 100 yards south of the Bank of Ireland.

C167:22, pe167:24, P429:8 **clouds, dappled and seaborne** See *Por* C166:27n.

C167:35, pe167:38, P429:22 **Stephanos** Greek: crown or garland.

C168:2, pe168:3, P429:25 **a stuff in the kisser** Low slang: a blow in the face.

C168:4–5, pe168:5–6, P429:27–28 **Bous Stephanoumenos! Bous Stephaneforos!** *Bous* is Greek for ox; *bous stephaneforos* means the ox as garland-bearer for sacrifice. "Bous Stephanoumenos" is schoolboy Greek for the ox-soul or bull-soul of Stephen. It is notable in this connection that the young St. Thomas Aquinas (because he remained silent) was mocked as "dumb-ox" by his fellow students when he was at the University of Cologne.

C168:23, pe168:24, P430:12 **Norfolk coat** A loosefitting herring-bone sport-jacket with a loose belt.

C168:35–36, pe168:38, P430:27 **the ancient kingdom of the Danes** See *Por* C167:20n.

C169:1–2, pe169:1, P430:29–30 **the fabulous artificer** Daedalus; see *Por* C5:2n.

C169:26–27, pe169:26–27, P431:22 **the cry of a hawk or eagle** The birdcries here are reminders that Stephen is seeking an augury (see *Por* C224:10–17n ff.) and that he is thinking of his namesake Daedalus. Since Stephen refers consistently to Daedalus as "father," Stephen unconsciously associates himself with the son, Icarus, who flew so near the sun that the wax melted, his wings disintegrated, and he dropped into the sea.

C170:3–5, pe169:39–170:2, P431:35–432:3 **His soul had risen . . . and power of his soul** In Gabriele D'Annunzio's novel *Il Fuoco* (*The Flame of Life*) at the end of part I, "The Epiphany of Flame," the poet-hero has just left the heroine's bed after a night of intense beauty and love-pleasure. He feels himself "being born anew" (p. 145), boards his sailboat and sails out into the morning as "the first rays of the sun . . . flashed on the angels above the towers of San Marco and of San Giorgio Maggiore" (churches in Venice; p. 153); and he responds:

> "Glory to the miracle!" A superhuman feeling of power and freedom swelled the heart of the young man as the wind swelled the sail that was being transfigured for him. He stood in the crimson splendour of that sail as in the splendour of his own blood. It seemed to him that the mystery of so much beauty demanded of him the triumphal act. The consciousness came to him that he was ready for its accomplishment. "To create with joy!"
> And the world was his! [Translated by Kassandra Vivaria (New York, 1900), pp. 153–54]

C170:8, pe170:5, P432:6 **the stoneblock** A bathing place where the water was deep enough for diving on the southwest side of Bull Wall, southeast of North Bull Island.

C170:16, pe170:13, P432:15 **Howth** The Hill of Howth (or Ben Howth) is the northeast headland of Dublin Bay (three and a half miles northeast of where Stephen is walking).

C171:12, pe171:9, P433:17 **A girl stood before him in midstream** In Ibsen's *Brand* (II:ii) the youthful idealist Brand temporarily refuses to become a parson: "I have a greater duty laid on me" (p. 67). Almost immediately he encounters a young woman (Agnes, his wife to be), apparently entranced by "the fjord's meandering channel" (p. 69). Actually Agnes is entranced by a prophetic vision of "the dawn of a new day," and she tells Brand: "Now is the hour / When thou must be created and create" (p. 70). Brand recognizes "the call" and determines on the future uncompromising course of his ministry; see pp. 129–131 above.

C171:17–18, pe171:14–15, P433:22–24 **Her thighs . . . were bared almost to the hips** In Ireland in the 1890s "mixed bathing" was frowned on to the point of being almost unheard of. Women's bathing costumes did not bare the legs but included skirts to mid-calf and black or opaque stockings. In a city where the glimpse of an ankle was an event, this young woman's contemporaries might easily have found her behavior "shocking." For "ivory," see "tower of ivory," *Por* C35:30–31n.

C171:19, pe171:17, P433:25 **slateblue** Blue is a color attribute of the Blessed Virgin Mary.

C172:10, pe172:6, P434:19–20 **the angel of mortal youth and beauty** This and the passage that follows echo in various ways Dante's description of and relation to the ideal spiritual beauty of Beatrice. The description of a meeting with that ideal beauty in *La Vita Nuova*:

> The miraculous lady appeared to me dressed in pure white . . . . While walking down the street, she turned her eyes to where I was standing faint-hearted, and because of her indescribable graciousness . . . she greeted me so miraculously that I felt I was experiencing the very summit of bliss. It was precisely the ninth hour of that day, three o'clock in the afternoon, when her greeting reached me. And since that was the first time her words had ever entered my ears, I was so overcome with ecstasy that I departed from everyone as if intoxicated. I returned to the loneliness of my room and began thinking of this most gracious lady. In my reverie a sweet sleep seized me, and a marvelous vision appeared to me.

In *The Divine Comedy* at the end of the *Purgatorio* Beatrice takes over from Virgil and guides Dante toward the beatific vision; see *Por* C115:26–28n, C116:14–15n, and C165:8n, and see C172:31–37n, below.

C172:31–37, pe172:30–35, P435:9–15 **Glimmering and trembling . . . deeper than other** Reminiscent of the vision of the multifoliate rose of light that Dante achieves in the final cantos of the *Paradiso* (XXXIII:115–20):

> In the profound and shining being of the deep light appeared to me of three circles, of three colours and one magnitude; one by the second as Iris by Iris seemed reflected, and the third seemed a fire breathed equally from one and from the other. [Translated by John Arthur Carlyle (London, 1899)]

C174:10, pe174:11, P436:5 **Dale or MacEvoy** Assumed names under which the Dedaluses have "pledged" (pawned) their belongings.

C174:16, pe174:17, P436:11 **lousemarks** Infestation with lice was chronic among Dublin's poor thanks to the appalling lack of adequate sanitation and a general want of cleanliness of body and clothes.

C174:23, pe174:24, P436:19 **The dear knows** A mild Irish oath; see *Por* 225:17n.

C174:28, pe175:5, P436:24 **I'm going for blue** Dublin slang: I'm working as hard as I can.

C175:23–24, pe175:30–31, P437:17–18 **to rue the day you set foot in that place** From his mother's point of view Stephen's religious faith, his reverence for his parents, etc., have been undermined by the intellectual activity of the university, even though the university's orientation is Jesuit and Catholic. See *Por* C106:18–19n. In Ibsen's *Brand* (II:ii) Brand's mother similarly accuses him of taking unnecessary intellectual risks (pp. 72–73).

C175:27, pe175:34, P437:21 **the terrace** After one of the Joyce family's "temporary" homes, at 8 Royal Terrace in Fairview, just north of the River Tolka and near Convent Avenue; see following note.

C175:29–30, pe175:36–37, P437:23–24 **the nuns' madhouse beyond the wall** St. Vincent's Lunatic Asylum (under the care of the Sisters of Charity) at 3 Convent Avenue, Fairview, was flanked by Royal Terrace.

C176:7, pe176:11, P437:34 **the avenue** Philipsburgh Avenue, a tree-lined north-south thoroughfare in Fairview just east of Royal Terrace.

C176:8–9, pe176:13, P438:5 **Gerhart Hauptmann** German dramatist, novelist, poet (1862–1946). He is generally spoken of as a "naturalist," but his works are characterized by a vacillating combination of lyric romanticism and a tragic or pathetic realism, particularly noticeable in his treatment of "girls and women." See *Dub* C108:4n.

C176:11, pe176:15, P438:7–8 **His morning walk** Stephen walks south along Philipsburgh Avenue and then circles east and south over the River Tolka, past "the sloblands of Fairview" and into North Strand Road, which gives south over Royal Canal and continues into Amiens Street. He walks south through Amiens Street, briefly west on Talbot Street, and immediately south-southwest through Talbot Place and Store Street to Beresford Place, along which he would circle the west flank of the Custom House to the Quays and Butt Bridge over the

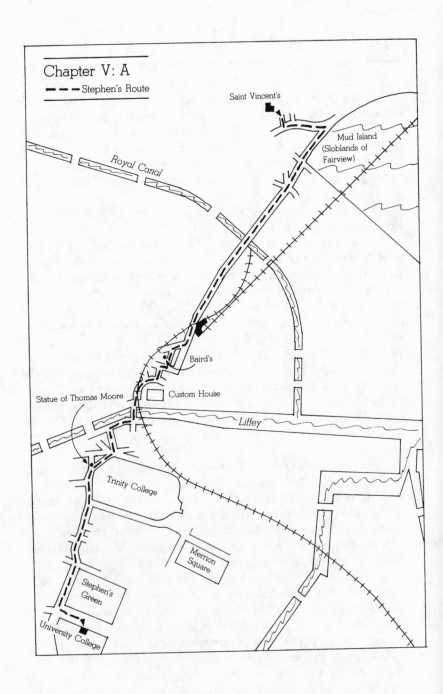

Chapter V: A
– – – Stephen's Route

Saint Vincent's

Mud Island
(Sloblands of
Fairview)

Royal Canal

Baird's

Statue of Thomas Moore

Custom House

Liffey

Trinity College

Merrion
Square

Stephen's
Green

University College

Liffey. On the south bank of the Liffey: west on Burgh Quay past "a grimy marine dealer's shop," then south through Hawkins Street to the north side of Trinity College, which does appear as a "grey block" from that perspective. The statue of Thomas Moore stood (and still stands) above a public urinal on a street island at the intersection of Great Brunswick (now Pearse) Street, College Green and D'Olier Street. As Stephen walked west around Trinity, the grey block on his left would be balanced by Moore on his right, and the visual emphasis would be on Moore's cloak, since Stephen would be approaching the statue from behind. Once past the statue Stephen would curve south around the front of Trinity College and continue south through Grafton Street to the northwest corner of Stephen's Green, across which Stephen would angle toward University College, Dublin, which then stood in Stephen's Green South. He walks a little more than two and a half miles in about an hour.

C176:12, pe176:17, P438:9   **the sloblands of Fairview**   Mud Island, a tidal flat and dumping ground where the River Tolka enters Dublin Bay, since reclaimed as Fairview Park.

C176:13, pe176:17–18, P438:10   **the cloistral silverveined prose of Newman**   Suggested by the rivulets in the tidal flats of Mud Island; silver is traditional for eloquence, as in silver-tongued. See *Por* C138: 31–139:8n, C164:7–11n, C165:21–22n, C188:8–11n.

C176:16, pe176:21, P438:13   **Guido Cavalcanti**   Italian poet (1259–1300) and a friend of Dante's; famous for the "dolce stil nuovo," a late thirteenth-century poetic style derived from troubadour lyrics and intended for the elegant expression of tender and pure feeling. One example of Cavalcanti's "dark humour": some friends find him brooding among the tombs near San Giovanni in Florence. They say: "Let us go plague him" (to ally himself with them). "Guido, you refuse to be of our society; but, when you have found out that there is no god, what good will it have done you?" Guido answers: "Gentlemen, you may use me as you please in your own house." After Guido leaves, his mockers finally understand the nature of his rebuke: "Consider, then, these tombs are the abode of the dead, and he calls them our house to show us that we . . . are, in comparison with him and other men of letters, worse than dead men." The association that links Cavalcanti's "dark humour" with the then numerous (and Irish) "provision shops" in North Strand Road is unknown.

C176:17, pe176:21–22, P438:14–15   **Baird's stonecutting works in Talbot Place**   D. G. Baird and J. Paul Todd, engineers and founders, 20–25 Talbot Place (just behind the Custom House in central Dublin north of the Liffey).

C176:17, pe176:22, P438:15 **Ibsen** Henrik Ibsen (1828–1906), Norwegian dramatist, regarded as the great pioneer of modern drama. He is generally associated with "naturalism" in the theatre and is credited with the origin of the play that treats social problems (the conflict between the individual and social norms and prejudices) in a blunt and outspoken manner. His later work combined realistic dialogue with a monolithic structuring of situation and symbol reminiscent of Greek tragedy. The association of the "spirit of Ibsen" with the "stonecutting works" may pivot on Ibsen's play *When We Dead Awaken* (1899), which Joyce discussed at length in his essay, "Ibsen's New Drama" (1900); Joyce described the sculptor Rubek's estranged (and awakened) wife:

> Her airy freshness is as a breath of keen air. The sense of free, almost flamboyant, life, which is her chief note, counterbalances the austerity of Irene and the dullness of Rubek. [*Critical Writings*, ed. Ellsworth Mason and Richard Ellmann (New York, 1959), p. 65]

C176:19, pe176:24, P438:17 **marinedealer's shop** Ellen Smith, sailor's outfitter, waterproof and flag maker, 9 Burgh Quay (on the south bank of the Liffey) (*Thom's* 1904, p. 1439).

C176:22, pe176:27, P438:19 *I was not wearier where I lay* Ben Jonson (1572–1637), English poet and dramatist; the Epilogue spoken by Aurora in *The Vision of Delight* (1617), lines 237–42:

> I was not wearier where I lay
> By frozen Tython's side tonight,
> Than I am willing now to stay,
> And be a part of your delight;
> But I am urged by the Day,
> Against my will, to bid you come away.

Tython (Tennyson's Tithonus) was a Trojan prince loved by the goddess Aurora (dawn). She married him and asked Zeus to grant him eternal life, but she forgot to ask for the companion gift of eternal youth; hence, he "froze" with age.

C176:29, pe176:34, P438:26 **waistcoateers** Elizabethan: common prostitutes.

C176:30, pe176:35, P438:28 **chambering** Elizabethan: promiscuous lovemaking.

C176:34–35, pe177:2–3, P438:33 **Aristotle's poetics and psychology** *The Poetics* (Aristotle's lecture notes on tragedy, etc.) is his title; "psychology" is not Aristotle's title but probably the title of one of the sections of a college text which collected relevant epigrams and key sentences on the subject from Aristotle, notably from *De Anima* (*Of the Soul*) and *De Sensu* (*Of the Senses*), and presented them as the sum of Aristotle's thought on psychology. See Introduction, pp. 10–11.

C176:35–177:1, pe177:3–4, P438:35–439:1   ***Synopsis Philosophiae Scholasticae ad mentem divi Thomae***   Latin: *A Synopsis of Scholastic Philosophy for the Understanding of St. Thomas* [Aquinas]. This may be an approximation of *Elementa Philosophiae ad mentem D. Thomae Aquinatis*, ed. G. M. Mancini (Rome, 1898), which includes all the passages upon which Stephen draws.

C177:13–14, pe177:17–18, P439:14–15   **the consumptive man with the doll's face and the brimless hat**   A well-known Dublin street eccentric? Unknown.

C177:15, pe177:19, P439:16   **the bridge**   Newcomen Bridge, which carries North Strand Road over the Royal Canal.

C177:23, pe177:28, P439:25–26   **a shooting jacket and breeches**   An eccentric if not comic costume for city wear in 1900. Breeches are knickerbockers or plus fours.

C177:24–25, pe177:29, P439:27   **Hopkins' corner**   Hopkins and Hopkins, manufacturing jewelers, goldsmiths, silversmiths, and watchmakers, at 1 Lower Sackville (now O'Connell) Street on the corner of Eden Quay (*Thom's* 1904, p. 1582).

C177:29, pe177:34, P439:31   **The United States of the Europe of the future**   *The United States of Europe* (London, 1899) was the title of a book by (and the utopian dream urged by) William Thomas Stead (1849–1912), English crusading journalist.

C177:32, pe177:37, P439:34   **Thursday**   It must be a Thursday during Lent because Stephen recalls a pre-Lenten "carnival ball" (*Por* C219:23, pe219:23–24, P488:6); he is quarreling with his mother about his Easter Duty, and he begins his diary (V:D) with an account of the 20 March discussion with Cranly which ends V:C.

C178:1, pe178:3–4, P440:5   **nominal definitions, essential definitions**   From Aristotle, *Posterior Analytics*, book 2, chapter 8. Aristotle uses the distinction to point out that the process of definition moves from descriptions of effect (nominal) to analysis of cause (essential). For example: the nominal definition of an eclipse would be a loss of light in the daytime; the essential definition: an eclipse is a shadow on the earth caused by the interposition of the moon between the earth and the sun.

C178:2–3, pe178:5, P440:7   **a favourable and an unfavourable criticism side by side**   A standard Jesuit method for the pedagogical presentation of philosophers and their philosophies, poets and their works, etc.

C178:6, pe178:9, P440:11 **the green** St. Stephen's Green; University College, Dublin, was then located in Stephen's Green South.

C178:12, pe178:15, P440:17 **Cranly** Derives his name from Thomas Cranly (1337–1417), a monk of the Carmelite Order who succeeded to the archbishopric of Dublin in 1397, but did not arrive in Ireland until October 1398. He was also lord chancellor of Ireland. The combination in one man of Church and State authority implies yet another English betrayal of Ireland. Stephen and Cranly are estranged between the time of *A Portrait* and *Ulysses* (in which Cranly is mentioned on pp. 7, 32, 184–85, 211).

C178:15, pe178:19, P440:21 **a severed head** Stephen envisions Cranly as John the Baptist; see *Por* C248:11–19, pe248:15–23, P520:26–521:2.

C179:15, pe179:17, P441:26 *ivoire, avorio, ebur* "Ivory" in French, Italian, and Latin.

C179:16, pe179:18, P441:27–28 *India mittit ebur* Latin: India exports ivory.

C179:18, pe179:20, P441:29–30 **Metamorphoses of Ovid** See *Por* C5:2n.

C179:21–22, pe179:23–24, P441:33–34 **a ragged book written by a Portuguese priest** The Portuguese Jesuit educator, Emmanuel Alvarez (1526–82), *Prosodia*, a Latin grammar (including rules for versification) which became a standard work in the *Ratio Studiorum* (plan of studies) of the Jesuit Order.

C179:23, pe179:25, P442:1 *Contrahit orator, variant in carmine vates* Latin, from Alvarez's *Prosodia*. Out of context the line can mean: "The orator summarizes; the poet-prophets transform [elaborate] in their verses." In context, the phrases are part of a rule for scansion: "*Si mutam liquidamque simul praeeat brevis una, contrahit orator, variant in carmine vates*"—"If a syllable that is both mute and liquid precedes a short syllable, it is short in prose but long or short in verse."

C179:25, pe179:27–28, P442:3–4 *in tanto discrimine* Latin: in such a great crisis.

C179:27, pe179:29, P442:5–6 *implere ollam denariorum* Latin: to fill the earthenware jar with denarii (originally Roman silver coins, subsequently pennies).

C179:29, pe179:31, P442:8 **Horace** I.e., a text of the poems of Quintus Horatius Flaccus (65–8 B.C.), Roman poet.

C179:32–33, pe179:34–35, P442:11–12 **John Duncan Inverarity . . . William Malcolm Inverarity** Unknown.

C180:8, pe180:8, P442:23 **The grey block of Trinity** See *Dub* C43:23n and *Por* C176:11n.

C180:11, pe180:11–12, P442:27 **the fetters of the reformed con-**

science Trinity College was founded to promote the Reformation in Ireland and thus to broaden English political dominion to include dominion over intellect and conscience.

C180:12, pe180:13, P442:28 **the national poet of Ireland** Thomas Moore (1779–1852). The epithet is an irony, since this was Moore's English reputation but hardly his position from an Irish intellectual's point of view. The fragile eroticism of Moore's early verse and the petty sentimentality of *The Irish Melodies* can be read as "sloth of the body and of the soul." Moore's career appears "servile" because he left Ireland in 1798 and advanced himself by currying favor in the drawing rooms of the influential in London. His laments for "poor old Ireland" were, therefore, not vital Irish rebellion but sentimental complaints acceptable to English ears. All this, together with Moore's willingness to compromise his artistic integrity in the face of criticism and his willingness to abandon his Admiralty post in Bermuda to an embarrassingly dishonest deputy, adds up to Moore's "indignity" and "sloth."

C180:17, pe180:18, P442:33–34 **a Firbolg in the borrowed cloak of a Milesian** The Firbolgs were quasi-legendary inhabitants of prehistoric Ireland, characterized as crude and earthy, a short, dark people, who were displaced by the Tuatha Da Danaan (the legendary race of heroes). Prehistoric Ireland was subsequently invaded by the Milesians, another half-legendary people supposed to have been led by the three sons of Mileadh of Spain. The Milesians were characterized as ideal free spirits, poets, and artists. The statue of Moore depicts him in a classical (Milesian) toga—"the borrowed cloak."

C180:25, pe180:26, P443:8 **formal in speech** Outside the family circle, men of Stephen's class addressed each other by their last names if they were of an age and well-acquainted; otherwise, Mr. and the surname.

C180:26, pe180:27–28, P443:10 **Grantham Street** In south central Dublin just west of University College. In 1900 it was a street of modest, but by no means poor, middle-class houses.

C180:30, pe180:31–32, P443:14 **Firbolg mind** See *Por* C180:17n.

C180:34, pe180:36, P443:19 **Michael Cusack, the Gael** (1847–1907), a founder of the Gaelic Athletic Association; see *Por* C61:23n. Cusack sat for a full-length portrait as the Citizen in the Cyclops episode in *Ulysses*. Ellmann (p. 62n) quotes as his standard greeting: "I'm Citizen Cusack from the Parish of Carron in the Barony of Burren in the County of Clare, you Protestant dog."

C181:1–2, pe181:2, P443:23 **the curfew was still a nightly fear** Curfews were instituted as repressive measures after William III's successful reconquest of Ireland at the end of the seventeenth century. They were imposed in some districts during the Rebellion of 1798 and again during the Great Famine in the late 1840s. They were brutally enforced and were particularly onerous because they not only dictated that the peasants be indoors (variously at dark or at some fixed hour such as eight o'clock), they also dictated that lights be out and therefore gave authorities a much-abused right to claim they saw a light and to enter houses and search.

C181:4, pe181:4, P443:25   **his uncle Mat Davin**   The brothers Davin (Maurice and Pat = Mat) were well-known in late nineteenth-century Ireland for their interest in athletics. Pat was a reputable athlete; Maurice helped Michael Cusack (*Por* C180:34n) to found the Gaelic Athletic Association.

C181:7, pe181:8, P443:29   **fenian**   See *Dub* C125:5n.

C181:12, pe181:12-13, P443:3-4   **the cycles**   The stories of the legendary Irish heroes and heroines: Cuchulain, Finn, Ossian, Fergus, Aengus, Conchubar, Deidre, Maeve, and company. Lady Augusta Gregory (1852–1932), W. B. Yeats, and others were convinced that a reinvigorated Irish culture and literature should be nourished by the "beauty" of these stories.

C181:17, pe181:18-19, P444:5-6   **the foreign legion of France**   A military force based in North Africa and traditionally made up of exiles, expatriates, and non-French nationals under French officers. A recruit signed for five years; and, while the force was noted for the rigors of its service, romantic fiction consistently depicted it as a heroic way to withdraw from the disappointments of civilized life. One example: John Devoy (1842–1928), a radical Fenian leader, who in 1861 "joined both the Irish Republican Brotherhood and the French Foreign Legion, deserting from the latter when the prospects of revolution at home seemed to grow brighter" (Lyons, *Parnell*, p. 72).

C181:20, pe181:21, P444:8-9   **one of the tame geese**   As against the "wild geese." Initially the phrase "wild geese" was applied to those Irish Catholic soldiers who were allowed by the Treaty of Limerick to leave for exile in France after William III's reconquest of Ireland in the 1690s. The phrase was subsequently applied to those who, politically, economically, and culturally disenfranchised in the penal colony that Ireland became in the eighteenth century, went into exile in order to assert themselves as individuals capable of careers and of distinction. See *Por* C243:31–32n.

C181:28-30, pe181:32, P444:18-19   **through the dark narrow streets of the poorer Jews**   In 1900, the area just north of Grantham Street (*Por* C180:26n) in south central Dublin.

C181:33, pe181:35–36, P444:2–3 **disremember** "To forget. Good old English, now out of fashion in England, but common in Ireland" (P. W. Joyce, p. 248).

C182:3–4, pe182:5, P444:30 **Buttevant** A small market town 27 miles northeast of Cork, 137 miles southwest of Dublin.

C182:4–5, pe182:6, P444:31 **a hurling match** An Irish game, something like a cross between field hockey, lacrosse, and rugby; fifteen men are on a side.

C182:5–6, pe182:6–7, P444:31–32 **Croke's Own Boys and the Fearless Thurles** Two teams comparable to semi-pro teams in the United States. Thurles is a town of some importance approximately midway between Dublin and Cork. The Gaelic Athletic Association was founded there in 1884. The Most Reverend William Croke, late nineteenth-century archbishop of Cashel (13 miles south of Thurles), was an ardent supporter of the G. A. A. and a promoter of Irish sports.

C182:7, pe182:8–9, P444:33 **stripped to his buff** "Buff," the skin; to strip to one's buff is to strip naked "except in Munster where it means to strip 'from the waist up'" (P. W. Joyce, p. 227).

C182:7–8, pe182:9, P444:33 **minding cool** "Hurlers and football players always put one of their best players to mind cool or stand cool, i.e., to stand at their own goal or gap, to intercept the ball if the opponents should attempt to drive it through. Irish *cùl* [cool], the back. The man standing cool is often called 'the man in the gap'" (P. W. Joyce, p. 239).

C182:8, pe182:9, P444:35 **the Limericks** Limerick is a town 36 miles west of Thurles.

C182:10, pe182:12, P445:2 **wipe** "In Ulster, a goaly-wipe is a great blow on the ball with the camann" (P. W. Joyce, p. 351).

C182:11, pe182:12, P445:3 **camaun** Or camann, used in hurling; it resembles a short, thick hockey stick.

C182:11, pe182:13, P445:4 **an aim's ace** "A small amount, quantity or distance. Applied in the following way very generally, in Munster: 'He was within an aim's-ace of being drowned (very near).' A survival in Ireland of the old Shakespearian word *ambs-ace*, meaning two aces or two single points in throwing dice, the smallest possible throw" (P. W. Joyce, p. 209).

C182:18, pe182:20, P445:12 **yoke** "Any article or contrivance or apparatus for use in some work" (P. W. Joyce, p. 352).

C182:19, pe182:21–22, P445:14 **a mass meeting** A political rally, often in support of a political cause rather than an individual candidate. Daniel O'Connell developed the technique of using mass or monster meetings as a way of arousing public sentiment and of demonstrating to the English overlords Irish political unanimity on key issues; see *Dub* C214:31n.

C182:20, pe182:22, P445:14   **Castletownroche**   A village five miles east-southeast of Buttevant.

C182:20, pe182:23, P445:15   **the cars**   Horse-drawn wagons or carriages; see *Por* C20:2n.

C182:23–24, pe182:26–27, P445:18–19   **Ballyhoura Hills . . . Kilmalloch**   Davin was walking north; Kilmalloch (Kilmallock) is a small market town approximately fourteen miles north of Buttevant. Davin's route would take him over the western shoulder of the Ballyhoura Hills.

C182:27, pe182:30, P445:23   **to redden my pipe**   "An Irishman hardly ever lights his pipe: he reddens it" (P. W. Joyce, p. 311).

C183:6–7, pe183:7, P446:5   **Queenstown**   Now Cobh, a seaport on Cork Harbor on the southern coast of Ireland, approximately seventy miles south of the "little cottage" where Davin has paused.

C183:12–13, pe183:13, P446:11–12   *there's no one in it but ourselves*   "In it" is a translation of "the Gaelic *Ann* . . . 'in existence'" (P. W. Joyce, p. 25).

C183:19, pe183:20, P446:19   **Clane**   Near Clongowes Wood College; see *Por* C18:6n.

C183:20, pe181:21, P446:21   **a batlike soul**   Cf. "vampire" in the quotation from Walter Pater, pp. 258–59 below.

C183:25, pe183:26, P446:28   **handsel**   Originally a bargain confirmed by shaking hands, subsequently a gift given for good luck at the beginning of a new enterprise or experience or at the new year.

C184:6–7, pe184:7, P447:12   **a student of Trinity**   Figuratively, someone with the advantages of Anglo-Irish wealth and political connections (as against the poorer and relatively powerless Irish of University College, Dublin).

C184:7, pe184:8, P447:12   **Grafton Street**   A street of fashionable and expensive shops; see *Dub* C45:20–21n.

C184:8–10, pe184:8–11, P447:14–16   **In the roadway . . . a slab . . . Wolfe Tone . . . at its laying**   To commemorate the centenary of the Rebellion of 1798 a slab to the memory of Wolfe Tone (1763–98) and the United Irishmen was placed at the northwest corner of Stephen's Green on 15 August 1898, pending completion of the sculpture that was to have been mounted on it. The sculpture was never completed, and the intersecting streets expanded in 1922 to swallow the slab, thanks in part to the pressure of traffic and in part to the new Treaty-born Irish Free State's uneasiness about Tone's secular republicanism.

There is, however, a relatively recent memorial statue of Tone, backed by a semicircular hedge of rough-hewn granite posts, in the northeast corner of Stephen's Green (sculptor: Edward Delaney).

Theobald Wolfe Tone, one of the founders of the United Irishmen, was inspired with republican idealism by the success of the American Revolution and by what then seemed the success of the French Revolution. He was instrumental in attempting to secure French support for revolution in Ireland, though neither of the two French expeditions in which Tone was involved was able to effect a landing. He was captured at sea in 1798 during the second attempted landing, returned to Dublin and condemned to death. He reportedly foiled his captors by committing suicide in prison. Tone's republicanism places him in that Irish revolutionary tradition which envisions a nation with civil and religious liberties for all.

C184:11, peI84:12, P447:17   **scene of tawdry tribute**   The adjective may have something to do with the eye of the beholder. *The Irish Times* for Tuesday, 16 August 1898, gives a thorough and relatively glowing account of the procession (seventy bands strong) that paraded through central Dublin on 15 August and of the slab-laying ceremony at the corner of Stephen's Green. *The Times* describes the crowds as immense and enthusiastic and reports stirring speeches by several of the more important Irish political figures of the day, including John Dillon and John Redmond (and, less political, W. B. Yeats). John O'Leary (1830–1907), the grand old man of the Fenian movement, made the keynote speech, pivoting it on the assertion that "Tone first combined all classes and creeds of his countrymen into one body under the name of United Irishmen." If the "tribute" was "tawdry," perhaps its tawdriness is to be found in the apparent lack of patriotic courage in the "resolutions" to speedily complete the monument instead of speedily to make Ireland free—the latter, however, would have been labeled "seditious conspiracy" and summarily suppressed by the British.

At least one other observer found the ceremony "dispiriting and disappointing" (except for the presence of John O'Leary). From her point of view the ceremony was not sufficiently revolutionary, thanks to the compromising presence of those parliamentarians who still offered what to her seemed "the wilted carrot" of Home Rule "under an English king": the Parnellite Redmond and the anti-Parnellite Dillon (Maud Gonne MacBride, *A Servant of the Queen* [London, 1938], pp. 280–86).

C184:12, peI84:12–13, P447:18   **four French delegates**   Appropriate since Wolfe Tone had been inspired by the republican idealism of the French Revolution and had sought aid from the French. The French gave shelter to Tone's wife after his death, and Tone's son became a French soldier under Napoleon before becoming a United States citizen. *The Irish Times* mentions only one French delegate, a Professeur Meuis du Collège de Chalon-sur-Saône, who spoke briefly in favor of the resolutions (speedy construction of the monument) and who "conveyed to the meeting the true expression of the friendship of Frenchmen for Irishmen in this movement."

C184:14, pe184:15, P447:20 *Vive l'Ireland* French: long live Ireland.

C184:15, pe184:16, P447:21 **Stephen's Green** Stephen would cut through the park from its northwest corner to emerge opposite University College, Dublin, which was then at 85 and 86 Stephen's Green South.

C184:22, pe184:23–24, P447:29 **Buck Egan and Burnchapel Whaley** Two late eighteenth-century "bucks." John ("Bully") Egan (c. 1750–1810) was a politician with an overbearing manner which frequently involved him in duels. He violently opposed the Act of Union (1800) and sacrificed his political career in the process. Richard ("Burnchapel") Whaley combines in Stephen's mind with his son Thomas ("Buck" or "Jerusalem") Whaley. Burnchapel was a staunch Protestant with large property holdings in Ulster. He got his nickname as a result of anti-Catholic arson in the Rebellion of 1798. His son Thomas was a politician and an eccentric and a big spender in eighteenth-century buck style. He took a bribe to vote for the Act of Union and one to vote against it. He also made a bet that he would walk to Jerusalem and play ball against the walls, a bet which he won (sums variously reported between £15,000 and £30,000). He lived in Stephen's Green South in one of the houses subsequently incorporated into University College, Dublin. He was rumored to have performed black masses in the house in company with his crony Egan. (For what it's worth: black masses are traditionally performed on Thursday, and it is Thursday; see *Por* C177:32n.)

C184:28–29, pe184:30–31, P448:1 **was the jesuit house extraterritorial** I.e., since the Jesuits owed strict obedience within their chain of command and since that chain led to the general of the Order in Rome and beyond him to the pope, was their allegiance not to Ireland but "extraterritorial"?

C184:29–30, pe184:32, P448:2–3 **the Ireland of Tone and of Parnell** I.e., the Ireland that aspires to realize itself as a nation and as a republic with religious and civil liberties for all; see *Por* C184:8–10n and *Dub* C118:1–3n.

C185:15, pe185:16, P448:26 **levite** Under Mosaic Law, a subordinate priest appointed for the service of the Tabernacle and of the Temple; cf. *Por* C158:32–33n.

C185:17, pe185:18–19, P448:28 **the canonicals or bellbordered ephod** Canonicals are the vestments prescribed by the canon for officiating ministers on various Church occasions; see *Dub* C13:6n. The ephod as a garment is mentioned several times in the Old Testament. At times it is associated with the high priest, at other times with persons present at religious ceremonies; and in Judges it is associated with idolatrous worship. The ephod was draped with ornaments that symbolized the Urim and Thummim (doctrine and faith), the twelve tribes of Israel, etc. To wear the ephod was to be prepared for communion with God; for example, in I Kings 23:11 (Douay) the disposition of David's enemies is revealed to him through the priest's ephod.

C185:20, pe185:22, P448:31–32 **in waiting upon worldlings** Alludes to the popular suspicion that Jesuits are tolerant of and willing to serve "worldlings" in order to make use of them for "the greater glory of God" when the occasion arises; see *Por* C155:34n.

C185:20–21, pe185:22, P448:32 **in striking swiftly when bidden** I.e., as a "soldier of Christ" and as obedient to one's superiors in the Jesuit chain of command.

C185:24, pe185:26, P449:1 **sweet odour of her sanctity** Odor of sanctity is "a sweet or aromatic odour said to be emitted by the corpses of great saints, either before burial or at exhumation, and regarded as evidence of their sanctity" (*Webster's New International Dictionary* [Springfield, Mass., 1918], p. 1491b).

C185:24–25, pe185:26–28, P449:2–3 **a mortified will . . . obedience** See *Por* C59:9n.

C186:1–2, pe186:1–2, P449:16–17 ***Pulchra sunt quae visa placent*** Latin: beauty is that which gives pleasure to the sight (or to the eye), after St. Thomas Aquinas, *Summa Theologica*, part I, question 5, article 4. The proposition which Stephen misquotes reads: "*pulchra enim dicuntur quae visa placent*"—"we call a thing beautiful when it pleases the eye of the beholder"; see following note.

C186:7, pe186:7–8, P449:22–23 ***Bonum est in quod tendit appetitus*** Latin: the good is comprehended in that which is desired (St. Thomas Aquinas). But Stephen's quotation is again a paraphrase. *Summa Theologica*, part I, question 5, article 4, from which Stephen semi-quotes two propositions, discusses: "What kind of causality is implicit in the notion of goodness?" The paragraph, with Stephen's points in italics:

Hence: 1. A good thing is a beautiful thing, for both epithets have the same basis in reality, namely, the possession of form; and this is why the good is esteemed beautiful. Good and beautiful are not however synonymous. *For good (being what all things desire) has to do properly with desire and so involves the idea of end (since desire is a kind of movement towards something). Beauty on the other hand, has to do with knowledge, and we call a thing beautiful when it pleases the eye of the beholder.* This is why beauty is a matter of right proportion, for the senses delight in rightly proportioned things as similar to themselves, the sense-faculty being a sort of proportion in itself like all other knowing faculties. Now since knowing proceeds by imagining, and images have to do with form, beauty properly involves the notion of form. [From the Dominican Latin text and English translation (London, 1964), 2:73]

C186:17, pe186:17–18, P449:33–34 **Like Ignatius he was lame** For St. Ignatius of Loyola see *Por* C55:35–56:1n. J. F. Byrne describes Father Darlington (the "real" dean of studies at University College, Dublin) as anything but lame: "Quick of movement . . . he definitely gave me the impression of having been an athlete" (*The Silent Years* [New York, 1953], p. 28).

C186:19, pe186:19, P450:1 **the company** The Company of Jesus, another name for the Jesuit Order.

C186:22–23, pe186:22–24, P450:3–5 **he used the shifts and lore . . . Glory of God** See *Por* C155:34n and C185:20n.

C186:25, pe186:26, P450:7 **obedience** See *Por* C59:9n.

C186:27–28, pe186:28–29, P450:10 *Similiter atque senis baculus* Latin: similar to an old man's walking stick (what the good "soldier of Christ" should be in relation to his superiors in the Jesuit Order), from St. Ignatius, *Constitutiones Societatis Jesu dum Declarationibus [Constitution of the Society of Jesus with Explication]* (Antwerp, 1635), pp. 233–34.

C187:4, pe187:3, P450:23–24 **the cliffs of Moher** On the west coast of Ireland south of Galway. The cliffs extend along the coast for almost three miles; they reach a height of 668 feet with a sheer vertical drop to the Atlantic (no beach) at their base.

C187:9–10, pe187:8–9, P450:29–31 **There is no such thing as free thinking . . . its own laws** Part of the standard Roman Catholic refutation of freethinkers or deists (1713ff.), those who form their religious beliefs not on the basis of authority but by the exercise of their own reason; see *Por* C197:12n.

C187:19, pe187:18, P451:6 **Epictetus** Greek Stoic philosopher, born c. 50 A.D. and flourished in the last quarter of the first century. He taught that the highest wisdom is to desire only freedom and contentment. The individual should bear and forbear, recognizing that an unavoidable evil is merely external appearance and that happiness depends on the human will, which Epictetus conceived to be unbreakable.

C187:22–23, pe187:22–23, P451:10–11   **An old gentleman . . . bucketful of water**   Arrian's *Discourses of Epictetus*, III:3:20:

> The soul is something like a bowl of water, while external impressions are something like light shining on the water. When the water is disturbed, it looks as if the ray of light is disturbed too, but it is not.

C187:24–29, pe187:24–29, P451:12–17   **He tells us . . . the iron lamp**   In Arrian's *Discourses of Epictetus*, I:18:15:

> I keep an iron lamp by the side of my household gods, and, on hearing a noise at the window, I ran down. I found that the lamp had been stolen. I reflected that the man who stole it was moved by no unreasonable motive. What then? Tomorrow, I say, you will find one of earthenware. Indeed, a man loses only that which he already has.

C188:7–8, pe188:6–7, P451:33–34   **literary tradition . . . tradition of the marketplace**   In the *Biographia Literaria* (1817) Coleridge makes this distinction:

> Even in real life, the difference is great and evident between words used as the *arbitrary marks* of thought, our smooth market-coin of intercourse, with the image and superscription worn out by currency; and those which convey pictures either borrowed from *one* outward object to enliven and particularize some *other*; or used allegorically to body forth the inward state of the person speaking . . . .

Coleridge remarks that the unexpected occurrence of the latter in everyday conversation can be striking and exciting, "But in the perusal of works of literary *art*, we *prepare* ourselves for such language" (ed. J. Shawcross [Oxford, 1954], 2:98).

C188:8–11, pe188:7–9, P451:34–452:1   **a sentence of Newman's . . . full company of the saints**   In "The Glories of Mary for the Sake of Her Son": "And I *took root* in an honourable people, and in the glorious company of the Saints was I *detained*." The sentence Stephen alludes to is in Newman's translation of Ecclesiasticus 24:16; see *Por* C105:3–8n.

C188:27, pe188:25, P452:18   **tundish**   An English (not an Irish) word, meaning "a wooden dish or shallow vessel with a tube at the bottom fitting into the bunghole of a tun or cask, forming a kind of funnel used in brewing."

C188:32, pe188:30, P452:23   **Lower Drumcondra**   Drumcondra was a suburban village just north of metropolitan Dublin; at the time of chapter V the Dedalus family was living in Lower Drumcondra.

C189:1, pe188:36, P452:29   **the English convert**   Father Joseph Darlington, S. J., who sat for this partial portrait as dean of studies received his M.A. from Brasenose College, Oxford, in 1876 and entered the ministry of the Church of England before he was converted to Roman Catholicism and entered the Jesuit Order.

C189:1–2, pe188:37–38, P452:30–31   **the elder brother . . . on the prodigal**   A reference to Jesus's parable of the prodigal son, Luke 15:11–32. The elder son, who has remained with his father and "served" him "these many years," is "angry" at what appears to be the father's preferential treatment of the younger son, who has not served but has left his father's house and "wasted his substance in riotous living."

C189:3, pe188:38, P452:32   **clamorous conversions**   The Oxford or Tractarian Movement, which began in 1833 as an attempt to reinvigorate the established Church of England and to make it more truly "catholic," aroused strongly Roman Catholic sympathies among many of its followers and climaxed when Newman and a number of other key figures transferred their allegiance to Rome in 1845. This started a mini-stampede of conversions, which were attended by considerable publicity and controversy.

C189:9–10, pe189:6, P453:3   **serious dissenters**   Or nonconformists: English Protestants opposed to the authority and tenets of the established Church of England and committed to the belief that no institution (church) or human agent (priest or minister) can aid the individual to achieve grace and salvation; grace and salvation come exclusively through Jesus Christ.

C189:10, pe189:7–8, P453:4–5   **vain pomps of the establishment**   I.e., the elaborate rituals of the established Church of England (and of the Church of Rome) as seen from the perspective of "serious dissent."

C189:12–13, pe189:10–11, P453:7–8   **six principle men . . . supralapsarian dogmatists**   Four Baptist (or dissenting) sects. "Six principle men" were Six-Principle Baptists, a sect that had its origin in London (1690) and that asserted as its basis the "six principles" set forth in Hebrews 6:1–2 (repentance, faith, baptism, laying on of hands, resurrection of the dead, eternal life). "The peculiar people" (Original Freewill Baptists) had their origin in late eighteenth-century North Carolina. They trusted in Providence to cure their sick of all diseases; they anointed the sick with oil and prayed over them, but gave

no medicine and called in no medical advisors. "Seed and snake baptists" (Two-Seed-in-the-Spirit Baptists) were organized in Tennessee in
the early nineteenth century. They believed that some of Eve's offspring were the seed of God and thus elect to eternal life; the balance of
Eve's offspring (and of mankind) were the seed of Satan (the snake) and
foredoomed to eternal damnation. "Supralapsarian dogmatists" (Old
School, Primitive, or Hard Shell Baptists) date from c. 1835; their
hyper-Calvinist doctrine maintained that man's salvation depends entirely on God's gift of divine grace and not at all on human effort. They
consequently resisted any institutional organization such as Sunday
schools, missionaries, or a paid ministry because such institutions implied that human effort could be effective in the achievement of grace.

C189:15–16, pe189:14, P453:11   **insufflation**   Blowing or breathing
on a person or thing to symbolize the influence of the Holy Ghost (see
Por C149:1–2n) and the expulsion of evil spirits; also, to breathe upon
catechumens or upon the baptismal waters.

C189:16, pe189:14, P453:11   **the imposition of hands**   Symbolizes
the expulsion of evil spirits and the inspiration of a new spiritual life.
Part of the Church's claim that it is "One, Holy, Catholic, and Apostoli-
cal," the only "true Church," is the unbroken succession from Jesus to
St. Peter to the present through "the imposition of hands" (*Maynooth
Catechism*, p. 21). See *Por* C159:24–25n.

C189:16–17, pe189:14–15, P453:12   **the procession of the Holy
Ghost**   The doctrine that the Holy Ghost proceeds from the Father
(God) and the Son (Christ) and is sent by both to dwell in the one "true
Church."

C189:18, pe189:16, P453:13–14   **that disciple**   In Matthew 9:9:
"And as Jesus passed forth from thence, he saw a man, named Mat-
thew, sitting at the receipt of custom: and he saith unto him, follow me.
And he arose, and followed him."

C189:19, pe189:17–18, P453:15   **zincroofed chapel**   In England
churches of dissenting sects (see *Por* C189:9–10n) are called "chapels"
to distinguish them from the "churches" of the established.Church of
England. Similarly Roman Catholic Churches are called chapels in Ireland (see *Por* C61:34n) as Roman Catholics were also once called
dissenters.

C189:30, pe189:29, P453:28   **The language in which we are speaking**   I.e., English; cf. *Por* C195:28n.

C190:14, pe190:13, P454:16   **Mr Moonan**   Stanislaus Joyce in *My
Brother's Keeper* (New York, 1958), p. 188, tells the story of this scene
in James Joyce's life and suggests that the "successful" Mr. Moonan is
"named in the [Aeolus] episode in *Ulysses*." If so, Mr. Moonan could

be "J. J. O'Molloy," whom Bloom regards (p. 125) as "a might have been," once "cleverest fellow at the junior bar" but by 16 June 1904 in "decline poor chap" (thanks to drink and gambling). Bloom also thinks that O'Molloy "does some literary work," and this might in turn suggest that O'Molloy had worked his way through the University and the study of law by practicing a sort of literary journalism.

C190:19, pe190:19, P454:21 *Per aspera ad astra* Latin: along the rough (road) to the stars. An overquoted cliché.

C190:21, pe190:21, P454:23 **the first arts' class** The curriculum of University College, Dublin, was punctuated by four sets of annual examinations (satisfactory passage of which qualified a student for his degree): (1) Matriculation, (2) First University or First Arts, (3) Second University or Second Arts, (4) Bachelor of Arts.

C190:26, pe190:27, P454:29 **the knightly Loyola** See *Por* C55:35n.

C190:27, pe190:27, P454:29–30 **this halfbrother of the clergy** As a Jesuit the dean of studies is technically a member of the clergy. It is not clear whether "halfbrother" is a turn on his not having been born a Catholic but having been converted from the Anglican ministry or whether the turn is on his being a teacher rather than a parish priest.

C190:29, pe190:29, P454:32 **his ghostly father** His confessor.

C190:29–33, pe190:30–34, P454:32–455:2 **he thought how . . . and the prudent** An allusion to frequently voiced criticisms of the Jesuits: that as a religious order they were not sufficiently cloistered and that their missionary zeal meant that they were prone to accept as genuine conversions which were only half-hearted spiritual commitments on the part of their converts.

C190:35, pe190:36, P455:4 **Kentish fire** A prolonged and ordered volley of applause (with hands or feet), a demonstration of impatience or dissent, said to have originated at meetings held in Kent (1823–29) in opposition to the Catholic Relief Bill (Catholic Emancipation, passed in 1829).

C191:14, pe191:13, P455:21 **Leopardstown** A racecourse six miles south-southeast of the center of Dublin.

C191:24, pe191:24–25, P455:32 **In case of necessity any . . . can do it** I.e., administer the Sacrament of Baptism; see *Por* C106:23–25n.

C191:29, pe191:30, P456:3–4 **an atheist freemason** A contradiction of terms since the *Antient Charges* (1723) of British Freemasonry required that all Masons believe in "The Great Architect of the Universe." But the phrase reflected (and still reflects) a firmly established Irish Catholic suspicion of Freemasonry; see *Dub* C32:21n.

C192:3–5, pe192:3–5, P456:15–17 *On a cloth untrue . . . billiard balls* Words by William S. Gilbert (1836–1911) from the comic opera, *The Mikado* (1885), music by Arthur S. Sullivan (1842–1900). The song occurs in the final act when the Mikado asserts that "a more humane Mikado ne'er did in Japan exist" and announces his "endeavor / To make, to some extent, / Each evil liver / A running river / Of harmless merriment." He proceeds to tell what will be done to various "evil livers" and concludes:

> The billiard sharp whom anyone catches,
> His doom's extremely hard,
> He's made to dwell
> In a dungeon cell
> On a spot that's always barred.
> And there he plays extravagant matches
> In fitless finger stalls
> On a cloth untrue,
> With a twisted cue
> And elliptical billiard balls!

C192:14, pe192:15, P456:27–28 **a sabbath of misrule** I.e., like a witches' sabbath, when the established spiritual order is inverted.

C192:15, pe192:16, P456:28 **the community** See *Por* C10:16n.

C192:19, pe192:21, P456:33–34 **mental science** Study of the "general laws" that govern human mental behavior (particularly the behavior of consciousness) as distinct from "moral science," which would consider the rightness or wrongness of the mental choices on which human behavior was assumed to be based.

C192:21, pe192:21–22, P456:34 **a case of conscience** A question of the rightness or wrongness of what a man may do, i.e., a case for moral rather than mental science.

C192:36, pe198:38, P457:18 **F. W. Martino** Dog-Latin for Fernando Wood Martin (b. 1863), an American chemist who developed the alloy platinoid and was the author of several textbooks including *Inorganic Chemistry: A Lecture and Laboratory Syllabus* (Lynchburg, Va., 1906) and *Collegiate Chemistry* (Lynchburg, Va., 1914).

C193:18, pe193:21, P458:4 **Ulster** Once one of the four provinces of Ireland (with Leinster, Munster, and Connacht); in context, the Protestant-dominated, northeastern section of the country.

C193:24, pe193:30, P458:13 **for his pound of flesh** An allusion to Shylock's demand for "due and forfeit" (Shakespeare, *The Merchant of Venice*, I:iii:144–152 and *passim*), but more cliché than allusion.

C193:28, pe193:34–35, P458:18 **wilful unkindness** I.e., he has transformed a minor moment of irritation into a more serious sin through an "act of consent"; see *Por* C152:25n.

C193:30, pe193:36, P458:20 **to Belfast** I.e., to Queen's College, Belfast (established 1849), Protestant, pro-British (and by implication more successfully vocational) in its orientation.

C194:2, pe194:7-8, P458:31 **Epictetus** See *Por* C187:19n, 22-23n, and 24-29n.

C194:11, pe194:17, P459:5 **Closing time, gents!** The formula a bartender uses to announce the legal closing time in a pub.

C194:13, pe194:19, P459:7 **two photographs** Of the tsar and tsarina of Russia, Nicholas II (1868-1918, tsar 1894-1917) and Alexandra Feodorovina (1872-1918, tsarina 1894-1917). In 1898 Nicholas II issued a "Peace Rescript" and solicited petitions from "the peaceloving peoples of the world." Response to his initiative resulted in the Hague Peace Conference in 1899. That conference of national powers did not manage "universal disarmament" or even a plan for curtailment of armaments, though it did manage to set up a tribunal for the arbitration of international laws of war. It is something of an irony that Nicholas II's crusade for peace was a prelude to the Russo-Japanese War of 1904-5. In retrospect the crusade appears to have been motivated (at least in part) by a desire to stall for time so that Russia could build up an armament comparable to that of Germany and the Austro-Hungarian Empire on its western frontier.

C194:26, pe194:32, P459:21 *Ego habeo* Dog-Latin: I have. The conversation that follows is salted with dog-Latin, a schoolboy jargon in imitation of Latin.

C194:28, pe194:34, P459:23 *Quod* Dog-Latin: what?

C194:32, pe194:38, P459:27 *Per pax universalis* Dog-Latin: for universal peace.

C194:33, pe194:39, P458:11 **the Csar's photograph** See *Por* C194:13n.

C195:5-6, pe195:8-10, P460:1-3 *Credo ut vos . . . estis* Dog-Latin: I believe you (are) a bloody liar because your face shows you are in a damned bad humor.

C195:9, pe195:14-15, P460:7-8 **No stimulants and votes for the bitches** Temperance and women's rights were two of the great reform impulses of the Victorian era, linked with agitation for the abolition of slavery at midcentury and associated with campaigns for the abolition of war and the realization of an ideal industrial socialism at the end of the century.

C195:17, pe195:24, P460:17 **A sugar** Echoes the Irish epithet "a sugan," literally a rope made of twisted straw, figuratively, a weak, flabby person. "Sugar" is also Dublin slang for a lower-class grocer.

C195:18, pe195:25, P460:18–19   *Quis est . . . vos*   Dog-Latin: who is in a bad humor, you or me?

C195:28, pe195:35, P460:29–30   **rare phrases of Elizabethan English**   Phrases, along with what have been regarded as Elizabethan intonations, have survived to modern times among the English-speaking populations of some of the more remote rural districts in Ireland.

C195:31, pe195:37–38, P460:33   **the sacred eloquence of Dublin**   As reviewed in the Aeolus episode and elsewhere in *Ulysses*, the eloquence of Swift, of Richard Brinsley Sheridan (1751–1816), Edmund Burke (1729–97), and the great Irish orators: James Whiteside (1804–76), Isaac Butt (1813–79), Thomas O'Hagan (1812–85), Henry Grattan, Henry Flood, John Philpot Curran (1750–1817), and Charles Kendal Bushe (1767–1843).

C195:32, pe195:39, P460:34   **Wicklow**   A small seaport and seaside resort 32 miles south-southeast of Dublin. It is the county town of County Wicklow, which borders County Dublin on the south.

C196:1–2, pe196:6–7, P461:5–6   **the progressive tendency**   I.e., socialism; see *Dub* C110:33n.

C196:11, pe196:17, P461:15   **handball**   In the original Irish version of the game the court or "alley" is 60 by 28 feet with not just an end wall (as in the U.S.A.) but also side walls that extend the length of the court.

C196:28–29, pe196:34, P461:33   **the Csar's rescript**   See *Por* C194:13n.

C196:29, pe196:34, P461:33   **Stead**   William Thomas Stead is credited with having introduced "raucous American journalism" into England, but that is more of a slur on his crusading energy than an accurate moment in the history of journalism. He was more reformer than journalist, and he crusaded with more verve than discretion for a variety of causes; in this context the reference is to his unskeptical response to the tsar's Rescript and to the weekly newspaper, *War Against War*, which he started in 1898 to oppose British conflicts with the Boers (South African settlers of Dutch descent), conflicts which resulted in the Boer War (1899–1902).

C196:29–30, pe196:34–35, P461:33–34   **arbitration in cases of international disputes**   As a result of the Hague Peace Conference (see *Por* C194:13n) a Permanent Court of Arbitration was established at The Hague in 1900.

C196:31, pe196:36, P461:35–462:1   **the new gospel of life**   What W. T. Stead was (in his own phrase) trying to preach.

C196:33–34, pe196:38–39, P462:2–3   **the greatest possible happiness of the greatest possible number**   Jeremy Bentham's (1748–1832) utilitarian ideal; later, the motto of the social democrats.

CI97:4, peI97:7, P462:11 **Marx** Temple is alluding to Karl Marx's (1818–83) assertion of the inevitability of class warfare and therefore to what can appear to be Marx's rejection of "universal brotherhood."

CI97:5, peI97:8, P462:11 **bloody cod** Cod is slang for joker; bloody, a contraction of the oath "God's Blood," was, for some mysterious reason, profoundly shocking to the Victorian and Edwardian middle-class ear.

CI97:11, peI97:14, P462:17 **Socialism was founded by an Irishman** A splendid oversimplification of a well-clouded and controversial subject. The Irish candidate was James (Bronterre) O'Brien (1803–64), an Irish lawyer and reformer associated with the Chartist movement in England (1836–48). He is credited with the 1838 coinage of the terms "social democrat" and "social democracy."

CI97:12, peI97:16, P462:19 **Collins** Anthony Collins (1676–1729), an English theologian and philosopher, a friend of John Locke's and a controversial advocate of "freethinking" (thought free from the dictates of "Christian revelation"). He was treated as an infidel by many of his contemporaries, including Swift. By reputation he was a subtle disputant as well as a man of integrity and benevolence. His most famous work: *Discourse of Freethinking* (1713). See *Por* CI87:9–10n.

CI97:19–20, peI97:23–24, P462:26–27 *Lottie Collins lost her drawers; / Won't you kindly lend her yours?* Lottie Collins (no relation to Anthony) was an English music-hall star in the 1890s. She earned "a personal notoriety with the verve (as the posters described it) of her dancing" (Iona and Peter Opie, *The Lore and Language of Schoolchildren* [Oxford, 1959], p. 107). The Opies quote the street rhyme on p. 108 and add two lines Monyhan omits: "She is going far away / To sing Ta-ra-ra-boom-de-ay."

CI97:23, peI97:27, P462:30 **five bob each way** As in betting on a horse race: five shillings to win, five shillings to place, and five to show.

CI98:3, peI98:6, P463:16 *Pax . . . globum* Dog-Latin: peace over all this bloody globe.

CI98:20, peI98:24, P464:1 **Do you believe in Jesus? I believe in man.** Temple's question means: do you believe in the Divinity of Jesus? Some liberal (Christian) humanitarians in the nineteenth century refused to affirm a belief in the Divinity of Jesus and sought instead to portray him as an extraordinarily gifted human being, an inspiring teacher whose teachings should not be obscured by theological codification and elaboration.

CI98:31, peI98:35, P464:12 *Nos . . . jocabimus* Dog-Latin: let's go play handball.

CI99:9, peI99:11–12, P464:26–27 **like a celebrant attended by his**

ministers   I.e., Cranly is cast in the role of the priest about to celebrate Mass; see *Dub* C13:5–6n and *Por* C158:32–33n; and cf. *Por*
C232:26n and *Dub* C13:13–14n.

C199:23, pe199:25–26, P465:5–6   **the prefect of the college sodality**   Cf. *Por* C104:23–24n.

C199:27–28, pe199:29–30, P465:10   **the matric men . . . first arts
. . . Second arts**   See *Por* C190:21n.

C200:3, pe200:3, P465:22–23   **take my dying bible**   On the sacred
oath of my last words.

C200:11, pe200:11, P465:31   **reading his office**   I.e., the Divine Office, prayers for the different hours of the day which monks and nuns
celebrate in choir each day and which priests recite daily from the breviary, "praying in the name of the Church and for the whole Church."
There are eight canonical hours: four great hours (Matins, at about
midnight; Lauds, at dawn; Vespers, at sunset; and Compline at bedtime), and four little hours (Prime, the first hour, in the early morning,
6:00 A.M.; Terce, the third hour, in midmorning; Sext, the sixth hour,
at midday; and Nones, the ninth hour, in the early afternoon, 3:00
P.M.).

C200:21–22, pe200:22, P466:8   **Jean Jacques Rousseau**   (1712–78),
French philosopher. "The Father of Romanticism," he speculated that
man was created good, only to be corrupted by the onset of civilization;
similarly, each individual is born innocent and good, only to be corrupted and degraded by induction into civilized life. Thus "salvation"
for man and society lies in liberty achieved by the return to natural,
primitive life and its values. The question of Rousseau's sincerity is, to
say the least, tangled, since his life was anything but modeled on the
simple virtue and liberty which he preached.

C200:28, pe200:28, P466:14   ***super spottum***   Dog-Latin: on the spot.

C201:9–10, pe201:6–7, P466:32–33   **go-by-the-wall**   A creeping,
helpless person.

C201:17, pe201:15, P467:6   **Lynch**   Takes his name from one of the
"Tribes of Galway," hibernicized families of Norman origin like the
Lynches, Joyces, Bodkins, etc. The Lynches of Galway have a special
distinction: in 1493, James Lynch, the chief magistrate of Galway,
hanged his own son Walter for the crime of murder to prevent the sym-
pathetic citizenry of Galway from freeing the murderer; see Joyce,
Critical Writings, pp. 231–32. Lynch appears as a character in The
Wandering Rocks, Oxen of the Sun, and Circe episodes in *Ulysses*.

C201:28, pe201:27, P467:19   **tame goose**   See *Por* C181:20n.

C202:2–3, pe201:38–39, P467:30–31   **Long pace, fianna! . . . salute,
one, two!**   "Fianna" is the rallying cry of the Fenians (the Irish Re-

publican Brotherhood, see *Dub* C125:5n); and Davin's "copybook" is apparently the Fenian manual of arms.

C202:7, pe202:4, P467:35–468:1 **hurley-sticks** For camann or camaun; see *Por* C182:11n.

C202:8, pe202:5, P468:1–2 **the indispensable informer** An ironic reference to the frequency with which Irish patriots and patriotic groups have been betrayed by informers.

C202:12–13, pe202:10, P468:6 **Are you Irish at all?** A question much discussed in the columns of Arthur Griffith's *United Irishman*, 1901 ff. The purists argued that "only Gaels" were truly Irish; the more liberal view was that any "Irish-born man," in Thomas Osborne Davis's (1814–45) phrase, should be affirmed as Irish. Interestingly enough, the purist position would deny the distinction "Irish" to many outstanding Irish-born men, including Grattan and most of the members of his Parliament, Wolfe Tone and most of the United Irishmen, Parnell, Yeats, Synge, and Joyce himself (since the Joyce family was descended from one of the hibernicized Anglo-Norman "Tribes of Galway"; see *Por* C201:17n). A landmark purist document in this controversy is Daniel Corkery's *Synge and Anglo-Irish Literature* (Dublin, 1931). And the controversy has continued to this day; many Irish still ask: "Why do you Americans have such a high regard for Yeats when he's not one of us?"

C202:14, pe202:11, P468:7 **the office of arms** The office of Ulster king-of-arms in Dublin Castle. The Dublin office (together with a branch office in Cork) had charge of coats of arms, heraldic records, and genealogical tables of Irish families.

C202:17, pe202:14, P468:10 **the league class** I.e., a class in the Irish language given by the Gaelic League; see *Dub* C137:25n.

C202:29–30, pe202:27, P468:24 **to address the jesuits as father** I.e., Davin does not distinguish between the ordained priests, who should be called "father," and the "scholastics," Jesuits who are still in training and not yet ordained, but who are serving a sort of internship as teachers. Scholastics dressed as the ordained fathers but were addressed as "mister."

C202:33, pe202:30, P468:28 **Harcourt Street** In south-central Dublin; it runs south from the southwest corner of Stephen's Green and would lie on the route from University College, Dublin, to Davin's lodgings in Grantham Street.

C203:15, pe203:12, P469:15 **from the days of Tone to those of Parnell** I.e., for the last century; see *Por* C184:29–30n, C184:8–10n, and *Dub* C118:1–3n.

C203:27–28, pe203:25–26, P469:28–29   **nationality, language, religion . . . fly by those nets**   Cf. William Blake (1757–1827), *The* [First] *Book of Urizen* (Lambeth, 1794), plate 25, lines 15–22:

> Till a Web dark & cold, throughout all
> The tormented element stretch'd
> From the sorrows of Urizens soul
> And the Web is a Female in embrio.
> None could break the Web, no wings of fire.
>
> So twisted the cords, & so knotted
> The Meshes: twisted like to the human brain
>
> And all calld it, The Net of Religion.

C204:8, pe204:3, P470:12   **Your soul**   For "Damn your soul" (Joyce, *Letters* 3:130)

C204:14ff., pe204:9ff., P470:18ff.   **out through the hall . . .**   Stephen and Lynch walk through the hall which bisects the main building of the then University College, Dublin, complex. They turn east-southeast along Stephen's Green South, then southeast through Leeson Street Lower to Wilton Terrace, the north bank of the Grand Canal, along which they walk east-northeast to Grand Canal Street (and Sir Patrick Dun's Hospital). They then retrace their steps along the canal to Mount Street Lower, through which they walk into Merrion Square North, then southwest along Merrion Square West into "the duke's lawn" in front of Leinster House, then west to the National Library on the other side of Leinster House.

C204:20, pe204:16, P470:25   **This second proof of Lynch's culture**   Joyce, *Letters* 3:130:

> Cranly misuses words. Thus he says "let us eke go" where he means to say "let us e'en go" that is "let us even go," eke meaning also and having no sense in the phrase, whereas even or e'en is a slight adverbial embellishment. By quoting Cranly's misquotation Lynch gives the first proof of his culture. The word yellow . . . is his personal substitution for the more sanguine hued adjective, bloody.

Lynch's swearing in yellow may also owe something to the Irish epithet *Seón Buidhe*: literally, "yellowjohns," figuratively, "filthy John (Bull)" or "filthy British."

C204:26, pe204:22, P470:31   **Aristotle has not defined pity and terror**   Aristotle defines tragedy as the imitation "not only of a complete action but also of events that are fearful and pathetic, and these come about best when they come about contrary to one's expectation yet log-

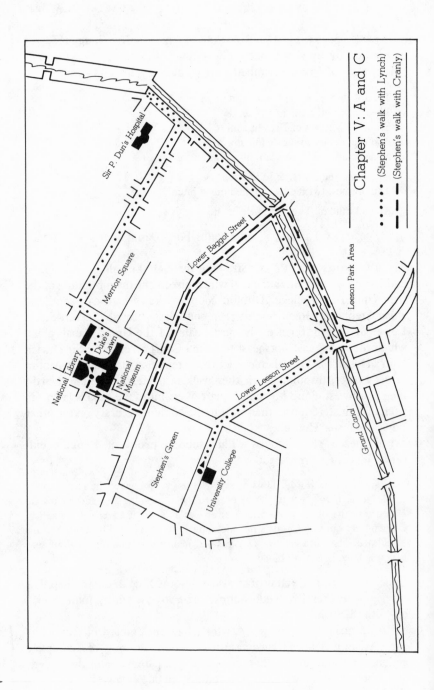

Chapter V: A and C

.... (Stephen's walk with Lynch)

– – – – (Stephen's walk with Cranly)

Sir P. Dun's Hospital

Merrion Square

Lower Baggot Street

Leeson Park Area

National Library

Duke's Lawn

National Museum

Stephen's Green

University College

Lower Leeson Street

Grand Canal

ically," not, he says, "merely at random, by chance." He then goes on to imply that pity and terror are aroused in order that tragedy may achieve its ultimate goal: catharsis (undefined). The text of Aristotle's *Poetics* is the abrupt and elliptical text of his lecture notes; definitions are not always included because his terms must have been familiar coinage to him, but he does at least imply definitions of pity and terror: pity "is directed toward the man who does not deserve his misfortune and the other (fear) towards the one who is like the rest of mankind" (translated by Gerald F. Else [Ann Arbor, Mich., 1967] pp. 34–35 and 38).

C205:24, pe205:20, P471:33   **the Venus of Praxiteles in the Museum**   A plaster cast of the Cnidian Venus (nude) of Praxiteles (Greek sculptor of the fourth century B.C.) stood among the reproductions of classical antiquities in the National Museum in Kildare Street across the quadrangle from the National Library. The reproductions have since been removed in favor of Irish antiquities.

C205:27, pe205:23–24, P472:2   **carmelite**   Roman Catholic Order of Our Lady of Mount Carmel (founded at Mount Carmel in Syria, c. 1156), an order noted for the rigors of its discipline.

C207:6, pe207:1, P473:24   **the canal bridge**   The Grand Canal circles what was then the southern boundary of metropolitan Dublin. Stephen and Lynch have been walking southeast; they turn and walk east-northeast along the tree-lined towpath beside the canal.

C207:15, pe207:11, P473:35   **Wicklow**   See *Por* C195:32n.

C207:32, pe207:31–32, P474:20–21   *Pulchra sunt quae visa placent*   See *Por* C186:1–2n and 7n.

C208:5–6, pe208:5, P474:32   **the Venus of Praxiteles**   See C205:24n.

C208:7–8, pe208:6–7, P474:33–34   **Plato . . . said that beauty is the splendour of truth**   Remarks of this sort occur in both *Phaedrus*, 277–78, on the subject of rhetoric, and in the *Symposium*, 210–11, on the nature of the ultimate object of love, but Stephen's remark is epigrammatic paraphrase rather than quotation. According to Ellmann, Joyce took the quotation not from Plato but from Flaubert's Letter to Mlle. Leroyer de Chantepie, 18 March 1857; see *Por* C215:15–18n.

C208:15–16, pe208:15–16, P475:7–8   **Aristotle's entire system . . . book of psychology**   Strictly speaking there is no "book of psychology"; see *Por* C176:34–35. From Aristotle's point of view his "entire system" rests on the *Metaphysics*; the "psychology" is an integral part of the system, but it is not as central to Aristotle's system as it is to Stephen's subjectivism.

C208:17–19, pe208:17–19, P475:9–11   **the same attribute cannot . . . to the same subject**   Aristotle, *Metaphysics*, book gamma, III, 1005b, 19–20: "[A principle that is the most certain of all] is, that the same attribute cannot belong and not belong to the same subject and in the same respect."

C209:1, pe209:1, P475:31–32 *The Origin of Species* (1859) by Charles Darwin (1809–82). The allusion is to the popular assumption that by natural selection Darwin had meant that the strong seek the strong for mates. Stephen's remark also echoes the orthodox Christian assumption that Darwin's theories, if accepted, would reduce man to total animal.

C209:12, pe209:14, P476:10 sir Patrick Dun's hospital The hospital is between Mount Street Lower and Grand Canal Street and near the canalside where Stephen and Lynch are walking. Built in 1803, the hospital was financed by the estate of Sir Patrick Dun (1642–1713), an influential Scotch-Irish physician and politician.

C210:7, pe210:8, P477:11 *Pange lingua gloriosi* Latin: "*Tell, my tongue* of the victory gained in *glorious* conflict," the first line of St. Thomas Aquinas's hymn in praise of Christ's triumph on the Cross. Maundy Thursday (the day before Good Friday) commemorates Christ's institution of the Sacrament of the Eucharist at the Last Supper. St. Thomas's hymn is sung on that day as the Host (consecrated for the Mass of the Presanctified on Good Friday, in which no consecration takes place) is carried through the church to an altar of repose.

C210:10, pe210:11–12, P477:15 *Vexilla Regis* "Vexilla Regis Prodeunt," Latin: "The Banners of the King Advance," a hymn by Venantius Fortunatus (c. 530–600), bishop of Poitiers and chief Latin poet of his time. The hymn celebrates the Crucifixion. It is repeated daily during Vespers at Passiontide. On Maundy Thursday, after the second Host has been placed on an altar of repose, the procession returns and Vespers (including Fortunatus's hymn) are sung in the choir. Lynch sings the third stanza, which announces the fulfillment of "the prophecies of the crucifixion made by David" in the Psalms: "Fulfilled is all that David told / In true prophetic song of old: / Amidst the nations, God, saith he, / Hath reigned and triumphed from the Tree."

C210:19, pe210:20, P477:24 Lower Mount Street Leads northwest toward the center of Dublin from the banks of the Grand Canal along which Stephen and Lynch have been walking.

C210:23, pe210:24, P477:28 plucked Student slang: flunked.

C210:23, pe210:24–25, P477:29 all through the home civil I.e., they managed to pass the civil service examinations that qualified successful candidates for government employment in Great Britain and Ireland. It is worth noting that then as now civil servants in Ireland were regarded as bureaucratic obstructionists, professional killjoys.

C210:24–25, pe210:25, P477:29 **fifth place in the Indian . . . four-teenth** Fifth place would qualify the candidate for a relatively good position in the British Colonial government in India, and fourteenth place would not have been a poor showing.

C210:25, pe210:26, P477:30–31 **The Irish fellows in Clarke's** It has been suggested (Chester G. Anderson in The Viking Critical Library edition of *A Portrait*, p. 535) that these "fellows" are Irish-speaking patriots who hung out at Thomas J. Clarke's Tobacco and Newsagent shop at 176 Great Britain (now Parnell) Street. If so, there is a small mystery involved. Clarke (1857–1916) was a super-patriot and one of the key figures in the Easter 1916 Rising, but he was in the United States from 1899 until 1907, when he returned to Dublin and took over the shop in question from Hanna Clarke. The Irish-speaking "fellows" could, of course, have hung out at Hanna Clarke's (though that seems less likely). But if "the Irish fellows" were indeed super-patriots, the irony of their entertaining future British civil servants would hold in either case.

C210:36, pe210:37, P478:8 **the field club** Field studies in botany were not part of the University College, Dublin, curriculum in the early twentieth century (though laboratory studies were). The Field Club provided an extracurricular substitute for field studies crossed with a picnic and social group.

C211:8, pe211:9, P478:17 **Glenmalure** A wild valley in the heart of the Wicklow Mountains 27 miles south of Dublin.

C211:15, pe211:16, P478:25 **Goethe** Johann Wolfgang von Goethe (1749–1832), the "giant" of German letters, both in his own time and in retrospect. The emphasis of his aesthetics is a refusal to separate artistic ideals from the realities of artistic practice.

C211:15, pe211:16, P478:25 **Lessing** Gotthold Ephraim Lessing (1729–81), a German critic and dramatist who is regarded as the earliest of the great German *classical* writers.

C211:16, pe211:17–18, P478:26–27 **the classical school and the romantic school** Goethe and Lessing have been regarded as "classical" writers by German literary historians, but Donovan's implication that the two wrote about the two "schools" as though they were institutions is empty-headed generalization, based on the fashionable late nineteenth-century division of all art (artists, artistic creation, aesthetics, and art history) into two opposing tendencies or personalities: "classical" implied a balanced and formal dependence on the arts of the past and the effort to modify and sustain literary and philosophical traditions; "romantic" implied a revolutionary rejection of attempts to imitate the past and a free-spirited, on-the-wings-of-inspiration attempt to achieve the new and the vital. At any rate, the two categories and the distinctions they imply were unknown to Goethe and Lessing.

C211:17, pe211:18, P478:27 **Laocoon** Lessing's book (1766), one third completed, was an attempt to distinguish between poetry and painting and to define the limits of the two arts. Lessing based his discussion on the then-famous Greco-Roman sculpture of Laocoön and his sons being destroyed by snakes. Laocoön was a priest of Troy who tried to prevent the Trojans from accepting the Greek gift of the wooden horse. The gods intervened to silence Laocoön; his two sons were attacked by snakes, and when he went to their rescue all three were destroyed. The German archaeologist Johann Joachim Winckelmann (1717–68) had argued that the sculptural expression of Laocoön's agony indicated a higher order of tragic heroism than the priest's cries as described by Virgil in the *Aeneid* (see *Por* C214:24–25n). Lessing set out to challenge this view and in the process maintained that the limits of the two arts (poetry in time and sculpture in space) made such a comparison and evaluation impossible. Goethe's response to Lessing's *Laocoön*: "That long misunderstood phrase, a painting in words [attributed to Simonides (556–467 B.C.), Greek poet], was set side. The distinction between the speaking and the plastic arts was clear. All the results of this glorious thought were revealed to us by a lightning flash."

C211:18, pe211:19–20, P478:28–29 **idealistic, German, ultraprofound** In philosophy, idealism is the theory that no reality is independent of consciousness. Neither Goethe nor Lessing qualify as philosophical idealists. Lessing's *Laocoön* is the work of a dramatist and critic bent upon examining Winkelmann's generalizations about the visual and verbal arts through the lens of a practical criticism. Lessing's book was written at least a quarter of a century before the heyday of "ultraprofound" German philosophical or transcendental idealism.

C211:32, pe211:34, P479:8 **towards Merrion Square** Stephen and Lynch have been walking northwest through Mount Street Lower; Merrion Square North is a continuation of Mount Street Lower.

C212:1–2, pe212:2–3, P479:14–15 *ad pulcritudinem tria requiruntur, integritas, consonantia, claritas* *Summa Theologica*, part I, question 39, article 8. Again Stephen paraphrases the passage from Aquinas, which in its entirety reads:

> For in respect to beauty three things are essential: first of all, integrity or completeness, since beings deprived of wholeness are on this score ugly; (secondly) a certain required design or patterned structure; and finally, a

certain splendor, inasmuch as things are called beautiful which possess a pleasing color [glossed: a certain blaze of being!].

C212:17–18, pe212:19–20, P479:31–33 **What is audible is presented in time, what is visible is presented in space** In chapter 15 of the *Laocoön* Lessing distinguishes between subjects appropriate to painting and subjects appropriate to poetry: "In the one case the action is visible and progressive, its different parts occurring one after the other in a sequence of time, and in the other the action is visible and stationary, its different parts developing in co-existence in space." Lessing implies that the first is the subject of poetry and asserts that the second is the subject of painting. *Laocoön*, translated by Edward Allen McCormick (Indianapolis, N.Y., 1962), p. 77.

C212:35ff., pe212:38ff., P480:17ff. **The connotation of the word . . . is rather vague** In his discussion of the term *claritas* Stephen distorts Aquinas's meaning. Aquinas defines *claritas*, the radiance (or "certain blaze of being") of the beautiful object, as *resplendentia formae*, the splendor of the *form* of the object itself. Stephen is echoing Aquinas's *resplendentia formae* when he speaks of "the clear radiance of the esthetic *image*," but he has substituted the image-as-apprehended for Aquinas's emphasis on the form of the object itself. In this way the objective and realist view of Aquinas is transformed by Stephen into something very like the subjective, romantic idealism of Shelley.

C213:2, pe213:2, P480:20 **symbolism or idealism** Stephen uses the term "symbolism" here in the sense in which it is used in nineteenth-century transcendental idealism: that all of "nature" is symbol, that "particular natural facts," as Emerson said, "are symbolic of particular spiritual facts," that all apparently physical presences (because they are symbolic to the idealized eye) are really noumenal- or mind-presences.

C213:2–5, pe213:2–5, P480:21–23 **the supreme quality of beauty . . . is but the symbol** This suggests a neoplatonic or Shelleyesque transcendental idealism in which material things become not only "shadows" but also the flawed (or debased) symbols of ideal spiritual reality.

C213:14–15, pe213:15–16, P480:34–35 **the scholastic *quidditas*** In medieval thought: the essence of a thing, that which answers the question, "*Quid est?*" (What is it?) and therefore that which answers the question: where does it belong in the order of God's creation?

C213:17–18, pe213:18–19, P481:3–4 **Shelley likened beautifully to a fading coal** In "A Defence of Poetry" (1821, published 1840):

254 NOTES FOR *A Portrait of the Artist*

Poetry is not like reasoning, a power to be exerted according to the determination of the will. A man cannot say, "I will compose poetry." The greatest poet even cannot say it; for the mind in creation is as a fading coal, which some invisible influence, like an inconstant wind, awakens to transitory brightness; this power arises from within, like the colour of a flower which fades and changes as it is developed, and the conscious portions of our natures are unprophetic either of its approach or its departure.

C213:24, pe213:25, P481:10 **Luigi Galvani** An Italian physicist and physiologist (1737–98) who was an ardent Roman Catholic and who gave up his post at the University of Bologna rather than compromise his religious principles by taking an oath against them. He thus became a hero for eighteenth- and nineteenth-century Catholic educators who were concerned with the conflict between the ontological implications of the natural sciences and of their religion. Galvani used the phrase "enchantment of the heart" to describe the momentary cessation of a frog's heartbeat when a needle is inserted in its spinal cord.

C213:31, pe213:33, P481:18 **In the marketplace** See *Por* C188: 7–8n.

C214:1–7/28–215:14, pe213:39–214:7/29–215:14, P481:25–32/482: 20–483:11 **art necessarily divides itself . . . immediate relation to others. . . . The lyrical form . . . the human imagination** Victor Hugo developed the lyric-epic-dramatic triad at length in "*Préface*" to his drama *Cromwell* in 1827 (passages cited below, translated by the author from the Paris, 1912, edition of Hugo's works). Lyric poetry, Hugo said, was the poetry of

> primitive times, when man awoke in a world which stemmed from nature and poetry awoke with him . . . . His lyre had but three chords, God, the soul and the creation; but that triple mystery contained everything, that triple idea made everything comprehensible. [P. 9]

Epic poetry was the poetry of the society of antiquity, a society which "Homer, in effect, dominated . . . . Poetry was religion, religion was law" (p. 10). Even drama in that age was "grand, pontifical, epic" (p. 10). Eventually, Hugo says, a new religion (Christianity)

> said to man, "You are double, you are composed of two beings, one perishable, the other immortal . . . ." The poetry given birth by Christianity, the poetry of our time is thus the dramatic; characteristic of the dramatic is reality, and reality results from the completely natural combination of the two fundamental types, the sublime and the grotesque, which realize themselves in the drama as they realize themselves in life and in creation. [P. 23]

The dramatic is "complete poetry" (p. 22), the poetry of "Shakespeare, Dante and Milton" (p. 23); it is "romantic poetry" as distinct from "the classical poetry" of "antiquity" (p. 15). Hugo's distinctions are basically historical and cultural. He does not focus on literary genre or on the subjective process of creation but on the "spirit of the age" in which the literature was created.

C214:15, pe214:15, P482:5–6   *the portrait of Mona Lisa*   A portrait (c. 1503–5) of Lisa, the wife of a Florentine, Francesco del Giocondo, by Leonardo da Vinci (1452–1519). The portrait, also called *La Gioconda*, hangs in the Louvre; for a notable nineteenth-century commentary see pp. 258–59 below. For *"good if I desire to see it,"* cf. *Por* C186:7n.

C214:15–16, pe214:16, P482:6–7   *the bust of Sir Philip Crampton*   The bust stood above a public drinking fountain (a cup on a chain) at the intersection of College Street and Great Brunswick (now Pearse) Street, just north of the west front of Trinity College; the bust and fountain have since been removed. Crampton (1777–1858) was a Dublin surgeon whose "fame was almost European."

C214:24–25, pe214:25–26, P482:15–16   **Lessing . . . should not have taken a group of statues**   The point of departure for Lessing's discussion in *Laocoön* was a group of statues thought to be the work of Agesander, Athenodorus, and Polydorus of Rhodes (late second century B.C.); see *Por* C211:17n. In Lessing's time and until late in the nineteenth century the group was regarded and much overquoted as the ultimate depiction of "sublime tragedy" in classical sculpture. Stephen's remark is curious, however, because Lessing wrote about the sculpture in order to challenge Winckelmann's assertion that the group of statues was "more sublimely tragic" than Virgil's handling of the scene in the *Aeneid*. Lessing does not regard one art as superior to the other but evenhandedly argues that the difference between the two media (particularly with respect to the audience's experience of them in time) makes comparisons misleading and inappropriate.

C214:25–27, pe214:26–29, P482:16–19   **the art, being inferior . . . literature, the highest and most spiritual art**   In the nineteenth-century English-speaking world the opinion that sculpture was an inferior art derived in part from a preference for art that was not too "fleshly" but that aspired to "the true, the beautiful, and the intellectual" (in John Ruskin's phrase); the "true" of which the visual arts were capable was expected to be cognate with literary statements of the "true" (hence the popularity of story-telling sculptures like the Laocoön group). The tendency to denigrate sculpture also derived from a crisis in sculpture itself: in practice sculpture was at its best in portraiture but otherwise reduced to mechanical and decorative imitations of Greek, Roman, Medieval, and Renaissance forms.

C215:5, pe215:5, P482:34   **Turpin Hero**   Sometimes called "Dick Turpin." There is at least one extant version of the ballad which has this shift from first- to third-person narration, but the more usual version of the ballad is narrated in the third person with extensive quotation of the dialogue between Dick Turpin and the lawyer he is robbing:

> As Turpin was a-riding throu Hounslow moor,
> He saw an old lawyer just trotting on before.
> So he trots up to the old lawyer:
> "Good morning, Sir," he says,
> "Aren't you afraid of meetin' Dick Turpin,
> O that such mischievous plays?"
> Singing, hero, Turpiny hero.

The lawyer responds that Turpin will never find his money because he has hidden it in his "coatcape." At the top of the hill Turpin demands the coatcape, robs the lawyer, and advises him to say in the next town that he was robbed by Dick Turpin.

C215:11, pe215:11, P483:6   **lambent**   See *Por* C232:35n.

C215:15–18, pe215:16–18, P483:11–14   **The artist, like the God of creation . . . paring his fingernails**   After Gustave Flaubert's (1821–80) letter to Mlle. Leroyer de Chantepie, 18 March 1857:

> It is one of my principles that a writer should not be his own theme. An artist must be in his work like God in creation, invisible and all-powerful; he should be everywhere felt, but nowhere seen.
>
> Furthermore, Art must rise above personal emotions and nervous susceptibilities. It is time to endow it with pitiless method, with the exactness of the physical sciences. Still, for me the capital difficulty remains style, form, that indefinable Beauty, implicit in the conception and representing, as Plato said, the splendor of Truth. [Translated by Francis Steegmuller, *The Selected Letters of Gustave Flaubert* (New York, 1953), p. 195]

C215:21, pe215:22, P483:18–19   **the duke's lawn . . . the national library**   The Duke's Lawn is a small park east of Leinster House (which presently houses the Irish parliament and once housed the dukes of Leinster and at least one lord of Kildare). The National Library is west of Leinster House in Kildare Street but in the same complex of public buildings.

C215:28, pe215:30, P483:26   **the royal Irish academy**   Baffling, because the Academy, "incorporated in 1786 for promoting the study of science, polite literature and antiquities," was located 300 yards to the west at 19 Dawson Street. The complex of public buildings through which Stephen and Lynch move toward the National Library also housed the Royal Dublin Society, the Metropolitan (now National)

School of Art, and the Dublin Museum of Science and Art (which did exhibit some works of art belonging to the Royal Irish Academy). But Joyce's purpose in the misuse (?) of this detail remains obscure.

C216:10, pe216:12, P484:12   **Liverpool**   Notorious for the poverty of its lower classes and for its slums at the beginning of the twentieth century, but nothing to match Dublin's poverty and slums; see the passages from F. S. L. Lyons quoted above, p. 15.

C216:12, pe216:14, P484:14   **Half a crown cases**   I.e., charity cases for which the attending physician would only be paid two shillings and sixpence.

C216:15, pe216:17, P484:18   **stewing**   Student slang: dogged and unimaginative hard work.

C216:20–21, pe216:22–23, P484:23–24   *Ego credo . . . in Liverpoolio*   Dog-Latin: I believe that the life of the poor is simply frightful, simply bloody frightful, in Liverpool.

C216:26, pe216:28, P484:29–30   **the quadrangle**   Off the east side of Kildare Street between the matching arcades of the National Library (north) and the National Museum (south).

C216:33, pe216:36, P485:2   **rosary of hours**   A rosary is a loop of beads on which prayers are counted and the devotional prayers to the Blessed Virgin Mary so counted (see *Por* C148:12n). A rosary is also (in an archaic sense) a garland or garden of roses.

Chapter V: Section B

The suggestiveness of this section depends not so much on a play of direct allusion as on an evocation of the avant-garde aesthetic climate of the 1890s, a climate which Arthur Symons (1865–1945) characterized in (and as) *The Symbolist Movement in Literature* (London, 1899). The symbolist movement was dominated by the aesthetic philosophy of Walter Pater (1839–94), who displaced Matthew Arnold's (1822–88) dictum that "the function of criticism" (1864) was "to see the art object as in itself it really is" in favor of "to know one's impression as it really is, to discriminate it, to realize it distinctly."[1] The corollary role of the artist is then conceived not as "to teach lessons . . . or even to stimulate us to noble ends" but to record the "depth and variety" of the "impressions" to which as artist he is hypersensitive. Yeats qualified Pater's do-

1. Walter Pater, "Conclusion," *The Renaissance* (London, 1873).

minion in *The Autobiography*: "If [Dante Gabriel] Rossetti was a subconscious influence, and perhaps the most powerful of all, we looked consciously to Pater for our philosophy."[2] Characteristic of this aesthetic climate was the poetry of Swinburne (1837–1909) and of the Rhymer's Club (1890s), the drawings of Aubrey Beardsley (1872–98), the writings of W. B. Yeats and Oscar Wilde (1859–1900), and (for at least Arthur Symons and the young Joyce) the novels of the Italian poet, playwright, and novelist, Gabriele D'Annunzio (1863–1938).[3]

Several literary works can be regarded as exemplary of that climate as Joyce images it in *A Portrait*, and some appear to have contributed more or less directly to the mood, textures, and form of chapter V: B. Stephen's villanelle and the atmosphere in which it is composed (exclusive of the "rude" interruptions) are characteristic of the blend of soft-sex, soft-religion, and Pateresque verbal textures that fascinated the Rhymers, notable among them Ernest Dowson (1867–1900) and Arthur Symons, both of whom experimented with the villanelle (compare also Symons's "Rosa Flammae"). Many Swinburne poems, particularly his sensual and erotic ones, suggest kindred resonances; see, for example, "Dolores" (and its provocative apostrophe, "O mystical rose of the mire," line 21) and "Mater Triumphalis." Francis Thompson's (1859–1907) poem "The After Woman" (1896) also invites comparison: in it the speaker urges the "Daughter of the newer Eve" (i.e., the Blessed Virgin Mary) to

> The celestial traitress play,
> And all mankind to bliss betray;
> With sacrosanct cajoleries
> And starry treachery of your eyes,
> Tempt us back to Paradise!
> Make heavenly trespass;—ay, press in
> Where faint the fledge-foot seraphin

For possible echoes from Oscar Wilde's poem "The Sphinx" (1894), see *Por* C217:31n.

Walter Pater: In addition to the general presence of Pater's aesthetic philosophy and the echoes of his poeticized prose, one passage from his essay "Leonardo da Vinci" (1869) seems to have made a specific contribution to the imagery of this section. In the following passage Pater develops his "impressions" of Leonardo's *La Gioconda* (see *Por* C214:15n).

> The presence that thus rose so strangely beside the waters, is expressive of what in the ways of a thousand years men had come to desire. Hers is the head upon which all "the ends of the world are come" [I Corinthians 10:11], and the eyelids are a little weary. It is a beauty wrought out from within upon the flesh, the deposit, little cell by

2. (New York, 1958), p. 201.

3. In the "Introduction" to Georgina Harding's translation of D'Annunzio's *Il Piacere* (1889) as *The Child of Pleasure* (Boston, 1898) Arthur Symons suggests that D'Annunzio "has begun, a little uncertainly to mould a form of his own, taking the hint, not only from some better French models, but also from an Englishman, Pater" (p. x). The "form" Symons had in mind was the poetic novel, free "from the bondage of mere 'truth' (likeness, that is to appearances)" (p. x).

cell, of strange thoughts and fantastic reveries and exquisite passions. Set it for a moment beside one of those white Greek goddesses or beautiful women of antiquity, and how would they be troubled by this beauty, into which the soul with all its maladies has passed! All the thoughts and experience of the world have etched and moulded there, in that which they have of power to refine and make expressive the outward form, the animalism of Greece, the lust of Rome, the reverie of the middle age with its spiritual ambition and the imaginative loves, the return of the Pagan world, the sins of the Borgias [Italian Renaissance family noted for its licentiousness and crime]. She is older than the rocks among which she sits; like the vampire she has been dead many times, and learned the secrets of the grave; and has been a diver in deep seas, and keeps their fallen day about her; and trafficked for strange webs with Eastern merchants; and, as Leda, was the mother of Helen of Troy, and, as Saint Anne, the mother of Mary; and all this has been to her but as the sound of lyres and flutes, and lives only in the delicacy with which it has moulded the changing lineaments, and tinged the eyelids and the hands. The fancy of a perpetual life, sweeping together ten thousand experiences, is an old one; and modern thought has conceived the idea of humanity as wrought upon by, and summing up in itself, all modes of thought and life. Certainly Lady Lisa might stand as the embodiment of the old fancy, the symbol of the modern idea.

W. B. Yeats: Three of his short stories and three of his poems seem to haunt this episode: the stories "Rosa Alchemica" (1897), "The Tables of the Law" (1897), and "The Adoration of the Magi" (1897) and three rose-poems from the volume entitled *The Rose* (1893), "The Rose of the World," "The Rose of Peace," and "The Rose of Battle."[4]

The three stories evoke the world of alchemy and the occult. In each of the stories the speaker seems to vacillate between (and for the reader, to mediate between) the "indefinite world" of mystical "exultation and lamentation" and a more secure (if more drab) world of conventional faith and prudence. The effect is that the occult world remains hidden behind a partially lifted veil, alluring and yet vaguely threatening.

As he composes his villanelle, Stephen seems to be in the psychological state which the narrator describes in "The Tables of the Law": "the incertitude, as of souls trembling between the excitement of the spirit and the excitement of the flesh" (p. 501). See also *Por* C217 : 14–15n and 15–16n and C221 : 14–16.

In Yeats's "The Rose of the World" there is the suggestion that the archangels should "bow down" before the prior existence of the Rose, for whom "He made the world to be a grassy road/Before her wandering feet" (lines 14–15) as the "seraphim" bow down before "the temptress" of Stephen's villanelle. In "The Rose of Peace" the speaker imagines that if the Archangel Michael (*Por* C113 : 16–19n) "looked down on" the Rose (line 3), he would "bow down" (line 9) and "weave out of the stars/A chaplet for [her] head" (lines 7–8). In Stephen's imagination the Archangel Gabriel, promoted to seraph, stands in for Yeats's Archangel Michael, and as Michael would weave a chaplet (a wreath or garland for the head as well as one third of a rosary), so Stephen imagines his temptress's life as "a simple rosary of hours." This is not

4. Yeats, *Early Poems and Stories* (New York, 1925), pp. 109–12, 465–526.

necessarily to say that Joyce expropriated from Yeats but that the aesthetic climate in which Stephen is immersed as he composes his villanelle is rich with the verbal textures and the vocabulary of metaphor that Yeats exploited in the 1890s.

Gabriele D'Annunzio: [5] Two of D'Annunzio's novels, *Il Fuoco* (1900) [6] and *Il Piacere* (1889), [7] seem to have suggested not only atmosphere, vocabulary of metaphor, and incident [8] but also, in the case of *Il Piacere*, structural pattern. At a pivotal point in *Il Piacere* (book II, chapter 1) the poet-hero composes a sonnet sequence in order to test his strength and to prove that dissipation has not sapped his creative vitality; the question that nags at him: "What if my intellect has become decadent?" (p. 101). Stephen, of course, composes his villanelle for quite different reasons (many of them Joyce's reasons more than they are Stephen's), but the specific parallels between *A Portrait* V:B and book II, chapter 1 of *Il Piacere* are impressive. Both episode and chapter trace the course of composition and end by quoting the created poem (in each case a proof of strength) in full.

From *Il Piacere*:

> With the new day, he awoke to new life, one of those awakenings, so fresh and limpid, that are only vouchsafed to adolescence in its triumphant springtide . . . . A sense of nuptial joy and religious grace emanated from the concord between earth and sky . . . sacred music . . . . Some vision, vague but sublime, hovered over him like a rippling veil through which gleamed the splendour of the mysterious treasure of ultimate felicity. [pp. 99–100]

> This poetic agitation caused him inexpressible happiness. [p. 103]

> Then suddenly some obstacle would intercept the flow. . . . [p. 104]

Central to the poet-hero's sequence of four sonnets in *Il Piacere* is the image of the "madonna" (line 51), "a fair / White woman, in the act of worship, [holding] / In her pure hands the sacrificial Host" (lines 26–28). In the fourth and final sonnet the woman proclaims herself "the unnatural Rose . . . the Rose of Beauty" who instills "the drunkenness of [artistic] ecstasy" (lines 43–45).

On a more general level, the doomed poet-hero of *Il Piacere* is hung up between two symbolic women: Elena (after Helen of Troy), the pagan temptress, and Maria (after the Blessed Virgin Mary), the devout and virtuous Christian, the poet-hero's "tower of ivory" (cf. *Por* C35:30–31n). The provocative juxtaposition of sacred love and profane love and a soft fusion of the two are characteristic of the aestheticism of the 1890s. This fusion is present not only in

---

5. I have to thank Mary T. Reynolds for calling my attention to the parallels between D'Annunzio's *Il Piacere* and Joyce's *A Portrait*; see her article, "Joyce's Villanelle and D'Annunzio's Sonnet Sequence," *Journal of Modern Literature* 5, no. 1 (February 1976): 19–45.

6. Translated as *The Flame of Life* by Kassandra Vivaria (New York, 1900).

7. Translated as *The Child of Pleasure*, verses translated by Arthur Symons, who also wrote the "Introduction."

8. See *Por* C170:3–5n, C217:22–23n, C221:24n, and C221:35–222:1n.

Stephen's villanelle but also in his vision of Emma as Dante's Beatrice in chapter III : B and his vision of "the angel of mortal youth and beauty" as a second Beatrice in chapter IV : C.

The use of a religious vocabulary as a sustained metaphor for artistic vision and creation, while by no means original with D'Annunzio, is given an elaborate development (or overdevelopment) in *Il Fuoco*, a later novel in which the doomed poet-hero of *Il Piacere* is reincarnated as the successful poet-superman. The first of the two parts of *Il Fuoco* is entitled "The Epiphany of Flame." That title and the development of its metaphoric potential in D'Annunzio's novel suggest an affinity with Joyce's early interest in "epiphany," but it is notable that the term, central to Stephen's aesthetic theory in *Stephen Hero*, is omitted from that theory in *A Portrait* and that the vocabulary of religious metaphor, except for Flaubert's contribution, "the artist, like the God of creation" (*Por* C215 : 15–18n), is largely absent from Stephen's theoretical presentation in *A Portrait*, chapter V : A. The vocabulary of religious metaphor is concentrated instead in the villanelle and the process of its composition in chapter V : B.

C217 : 2–3, pe217 : 2–3, P485 : 6–7 **pale cool waves of light** Cf. Dante, *Paradiso*, as Dante sees "the things of heaven in symbolic form," XXX : 61–63: "And I saw a light, in river form, glow tawny betwixt banks painted with marvelous spring." See *Por* C172 : 31–37n.

C217 : 8, pe217 : 8, P485 : 13 **the seraphim** The highest of the nine orders of angels; see *Por* C113 : 29–33n. The seraphim are usually portrayed as fiery and purifying ministers of God.

C217 : 13, pe217 : 13, P485 : 18 **An enchantment of the heart** See *Por* C213 : 24n.

C217 : 14–15, pe217 : 14–15, P485 : 20 **the ecstasy of seraphic life** In W. B. Yeats's short story "The Tables of the Law," the mystic Owen Aherne tells the relatively orthodox and timid narrator that "the angels have hearts of the Divine Ecstasy"; Aherne then says: "I have lost my soul because I have looked out of the eyes of the angels" (*Early Poems and Stories* [New York, 1925], p. 514).

C217 : 15–16, pe217 : 15–16, P485 : 20–21 **Was it an instant . . . or . . . years and ages?** In "The Tables of the Law" the narrator accosts Owen Aherne after an absence of ten years: "He turned quite without surprise; and indeed it is possible that to him, whose inner life had soaked up the outer life, a parting of years was a parting from forenoon to afternoon" (p. 511).

C217 : 22–23, pe217 : 22–23, P485 : 28 **In the virgin womb . . . made flesh** Cf. Stelio Effrena, the poet-hero of D'Annunzio's *Il Fuoco*. He makes an impassioned speech about the "creative force" (p. 72) of Italian Renaissance painters. The speech, offered to "their parched lips"

(p. 76) as "a cup of his own wine" (p. 77) climaxes with Stelio's rallying cry: "To create with joy!" (p. 73). In the aftermath, Stelio, "alone," hears "the first notes of the symphony of Benedetto Marcello" (p. 77), which recalls "the virtue of the same principle" (p. 78), and Stelio reacts: "In the pause which followed, Stelio underwent a singular bewilderment, almost a religious stupor, as if he had assisted at an annunciation . . . in that inestimable lyric moment" (p. 78). Benedetto Marcello (1686–1739) was an Italian composer.

C217:23, pe217:23–24, P485:29–30 **Gabriel the seraph had come to the virgin's chamber** Gabriel, the Archangel of the Annunciation, who announced the coming birth of Jesus, the Messiah, to the Blessed Virgin Mary (Luke 1:26–38), has been promoted from the eighth to the first order of angels; see *Por* C113:29–33n. Theologically, the Annunciation signals Mary's conception of the Word-Made-Flesh (John 1:14), and Stephen here uses the Annunciation as a metaphor for the creative act of the artistic imagination, an act that results in the "word" of the villanelle he composes.

C217:28–30, pe217:29–31, P486:2–3 **lured by that ardent . . . were falling from heaven** Some speculative (and heretical) accounts of the fall of the Archangel Lucifer and his companion angels describe them as having been overcome with sexual desire at the sight of Eve in the Garden of Eden.

C217:31, pe217:32, P486:4 *Are you not weary of ardent ways* Oscar Wilde's poem "The Sphinx" (1894) is a sustained reverie about the sphinx as woman-cat-multiform-temptress who wakens in the speaker "each bestial sense" (line 168). The sphinx is seen as a kaleidoscope of sexual roles and attractions before her image begins to pall: "I weary of your sullen ways" (line 149), and the speaker finally turns to his "crucifix" (line 172).

C217:35, pe217:37, P486:9 **a villanelle** A nineteen-line poem divided into five tercets and a final four-line stanza, with only two rhymes in the whole poem: *aba aba aba aba aba abaa*. Line 1 is repeated as lines 6, 12, and 18; line 3 is repeated as lines 9, 15, and 19; so eight of the poem's nineteen lines are refrain. Technically, the villanelle is a very difficult form in English and one that has not been particularly popular with English poets because (apart from its demonstration of *tour de force* skill) it gives the impression of a poetry poised in admiration of its own textures, calling attention to pattern and sound almost to the exclusion of sense and content. Some poets, notably Ernest Dowson and Arthur Symons, attempted to revive the form in the 1890s.

C219:8, pe219:7, P487:23 **the print of the Sacred Heart** See *Dub* C37:13–14n.

C219:9, pe219:7, P487:24   **the untenanted sideboard**   Where the alcoholic beverages would have been set out (as they are in "The Dead") if any were to be served.

C219:14, pe219:13, P487:29–30   **a dainty song of the Elizabethans**   See *Dub* C46:16–17n.

C219:14–15, pe219:14, P487:30   **loth to depart**   "A loth to depart was the common term for a song sung or a tune played on taking leave of friends," William Chappell, *Old English Popular Music* (London, 1961). One sample anonymous lyric:

> Sing with thy mouth,
> Sing with thy heart,
> Like faithful friends
> Sing loath to depart;
> Though friends together
> May not always remain,
> Yet loath to depart
> Sing once again.

C219:15, pe219:14, P487:31   **victory chant of Agincourt**   "The Agincourt Song," a fifteenth-century popular song, is early enough so that part of the refrain is in Latin: "*Deo gratias Anglia! / Redde pro victoria!*" (England, give thanks to God for the victory):

> Our king went forth to Normandy
> With grace and might of chivalry,
> There God for him wrought marvelously,
> Wherefore England may call and cry:
> *Deo gratias Anglia!*
> *Redde pro victoria!*
>
> He set a seige, for sooth to say,
> To Harfleur town with royal array,
> That town he won and made a fray
> That France shall rue till doomësday,
> *Deo gratias Anglia!*
> *Redde pro victoria!*
>
> Almighty God, O keep our king,
> His people and all those well willing,
> And give them grace without ending:
> Then may we call and safely sing
> *Deo gratias Anglia!*
> *Redde pro victoria!*

C219:15–16, pe219:15, P487:31–32   **the happy air of Greensleeves**   "A New Courtly Sonnet, of the Lady Greensleeves" appeared in *A*

Handful of Pleasant Delights (London, 1584), though it was probably composed earlier. First stanza and chorus:

> Alas, my love, ye do me wrong
> To cast me off so discourteously;
> And I have loved you so long,
> Delighting in your company.

> Greensleeves was all my joy,
> Greensleeves was my delight;
> Greensleeves was my heart of gold,
> And who but Lady Greensleeves?

C219:19, pe219:19, P488:1   **called by their christian names**   In Irish (as in English) middle-class society young men and women would have called each other Mr. and Miss (as young men would have addressed each other by their surnames; see *Por* C180:25n). First names were used in the family and with close acquaintances.

C219:23, pe219:23–24, P488:6   **the carnival ball**   In this case a dance given in the season just before the beginning of Lent.

C219:25, pe219:25, P488:7–8   **She danced lightly in the round**   In French *la grande ronde* and *la chaîne* (the chain) were mid-nineteenth-century names for two of the five movements of a quadrille.

C219:27, pe219:28, P488:10   **the chain of hands**   *La chaîne*, as a file of men and a file of women meet in a dance and intertwine as they pass, each person giving alternate hands as he or she advances.

C220:1–2, pe219:39–220:1, P488:23–24   **a heretic franciscan . . . Gherardino da Borgo San Donnino**   A leader (d. 1276) of the "Spirituals," a party within the Franciscan Order whose aim was to recall the Order to its original austerity; see *Por* C154:25n. Gherardino's most important book was condemned as heretical, and he died in prison, deprived of his priestly powers. "She" (via Stephen's imagination) may associate heresy with amorous seduction, but there is nothing in Gherardino's history to connect him with loose living or amorous adventure. For "serve," see *Por* C117:28n.

C220:6, pe220:5–6, P488:29   **her Irish phrasebook**   Probably Father Eugene O'Growney's (1863–99) *Simple Lessons in Irish*, widely used in Gaelic League Classes; see *Por* C202:17n and *Dub* C137:25n.

C220:16, pe220:16, P489:4   **scullerymaid**   The lowest in the hierarchy of domestic servants.

C220:23–24, pe220:23, P489:12   **handsel**   See *Por* C183:25n.

C220:26, pe220:25–26, P489:14–15   ***By Killarney's Lakes and Fells***   See *Dub* C147:10n.

C220:27–28, pe220:27, P489:17   **the footpath near Cork Hill**   Cork

Hill or Castle Street skirts the west side of City Hall in south-central Dublin just west of the Castle.

C220:30, pe220:30, P489:19–20   **Jacob's biscuit factory**   W. and R. Jacob & Co., Ltd., Steam Biscuit Bakery, in Peter's Row, and Bishop Street, a factory and warehouse complex 250 yards west of Stephen's Green West.

C221:4, pe221:3, P489:30   **a batlike soul**   See quotation from Pater's "Leonardo da Vinci," pp. 258–59 above.

C221:8, pe221:6–7, P489:34   **the latticed ear of a priest**   The priest in the confessional hears the penitent through a small windowlike opening which is usually screened with some sort of lattice or grill.

C221:11, pe221:11, P490:3   **a potboy**   A boy who serves pots of ale or beer, a waiter in a public house.

C221:12, pe221:11, P490:4   **Moycullen**   A hamlet seven miles northwest of Galway in County Galway in the west of Ireland.

C221:14–16, pe221:13–15, P490:6–8   **a priest . . . transmuting the daily bread . . . everliving life**   The obvious reference is to the Sacrament of the Eucharist and to the *transubstantiation* (not *transmutation*) of the bread and wine into the body and blood of Christ. The substitution of the alchemical term transmutation for the religious term transubstantiation recalls a passage from Yeats's story "Rosa Alchemica":

> [The alchemists] sought to fashion gold out of common metals merely as part of an universal transmutation of all things into some divine and imperishable substance; and this enabled me to make my little book a fanciful reverie over the transmutation of life into art, and cry of measureless desire for a world made wholly of essences. [*Early Poems and Stories*, p. 466]

C221:24, pe221:23, P490:16   *The chalice flowing to the brim*   In D'Annunzio's *Il Fuoco* the poet-hero describes a woman who has literally but momentarily been blinded by the aesthetic impact of a painting. She has to be led from the museum because what she experienced was "a filling up of the chalice to the brim" (p. 4).

C221:35–222:1, pe221:33–34, P490:27–28   **the great overblown scarlet flowers of the tattered wallpaper**   At the end of D'Annunzio's *Il Piacere*, the decadent poet-hero faces an image of his own disintegration in his dismantled rooms: "Some men were taking down the hangings from the walls, disclosing a paper with great vulgar flowers, torn here and there and hanging in strips" (p. 310).

C222:12–13, pe222:10–11, P491:7   **tram; the lank brown horses**   See *Por* C69:9n.

C222:33–34, pe222:33–34, P491:32   **the strange humiliation of her nature**   I.e., her menstrual period.

C224:3, pe224:2, P493:6 **the library** The National Library in Kildare Street functioned as a meeting place and study hall for students at University College, Dublin (because the facilities of the university were at that time so limited).

C224:4, pe224:2, P493:6 **ashplant** In Celtic tradition the ash is the "cruel" wood from which spear shafts are made; "*Straight at the heart runs he*" (Graves, *The White Goddess* [New York, 1948], p. 22). And it is the tree of seapower; oars and curragh-slats were made of ash (p. 140). The curragh, once hide-covered, is now a canvas-covered Irish rowboat. Cf. hazel, *Dub* C108:28n.

C224:5–6, pe224:4, P493:8 **Molesworth Street** Runs west from Kildare Street, beginning at a point opposite the quadrangle (now parking lot) between the National Library and the National Museum.

C224:10–17, pe224:8–16, P493:12–20 **He watched their flight . . . a temple of air** Roman augurs began the process of divination by marking out a pattern of spaces on the ground (a *templum*) which described a corresponding pattern or "temple of air." The augur then faced south, asked the gods for a sign, and waited for the answer, which was to be read in the behavior of birds within the *templum* of the air. The types of birds, their numbers, cries, and flight patterns were all regarded as significant. Since the augur faced south (as Stephen is facing slightly west of south), the east, the region of light and therefore of good omens, was on his left; the west, the region of darkness and bad omens, was on his right. Stephen observes the birds "flying from left to right"; thus, in Roman terms, the omen would not be propitious. Heinrich Cornelius Agrippa (*Por* C224:31n) also cites this direction of flight as "an evil sign concerning thy business" in *De Occulta Philosophia* (1531), translated as *The Philosophy of Natural Magic* (Chicago, 1913), p. 164.

C224:13–14, pe224:12, P493:16 **odd or even in number** In Pythagorean and medieval numerology odd numbers are masculine (associated with limit and the one); even numbers are feminine (associated with the unlimited and the many).

C224:14, pe224:12, P493:16 **thirteen** Traditionally, an unlucky number, but in the occult lore which Stephen is contemplating in these paragraphs, the number thirteen is associated with water and the mother as well as with death (Agrippa, *Philosophy of Natural Magic*, pp. 246–47).

C224:31, pe224:31–32, P494:4 **A phrase of Cornelius Agrippa** The particular phrase Stephen has in mind is unknown. Heinrich Cornelius Agrippa von Nettesheim (1486–1535) was a German physician, philosopher, and, by reputation, magician. He led a wandering life, not only mentally (Hebrew language studies, alchemy, theology, the medieval Cabala) but also geographically. His works were regarded as occult and were rejected as heretical by most of his contemporaries. Chapters 53 and 54 of *The Philosophy of Natural Magic* (*De Occulta Philosophia*) contain a discussion of divination by augury.

C224:33, pe224:33, P494:6 **Swedenborg** Emanuel Swedenborg (1688–1772), Swedish scientist, philosopher, and visionary, nicknamed *Daedalus Hyperboreus*, the Daedalus of the north. One relevant passage is from *The True Christian Religion* (1771), translated by John C. Ager (New York, 1906), vol. 1, pp. 64–65, number 42:

> It must be further understood that it is not in thought that the perfection of life consists, but in the perception of truth from the light of truth. From this it may be inferred what the differences of life are in men; for there are some who the moment they hear a truth perceive that it is true; and these in the spiritual world are represented by eagles. There are others who have no perception of truth, but reach conclusions by means of confirmations from appearances; and these are represented by singing birds. Others believe a thing to be true because it has been asserted by a man of authority; these are represented by magpies. Finally, there are some who have no desire and no ability to perceive what is true, but only what is false, for the reason that they are in a delusive light, in which falsity appears to be true, and what is true seems either like something overhead concealed in a dense cloud, or like a meteor, or like something false. The thoughts of these are represented by birds of night, and their speech by screech owls.

C225:7, pe225:4, P494:14–15 **the curved stick of an augur** The *lituus*, the crooked staff with which Roman augurs marked out the *templum*; see *Por* C224:10–17n.

C225:9–10, pe225:6–7, P494:17 **the hawklike man whose name he bore** Daedalus; see *Por* C5:2n.

C225:11, pe225:8, P494:18 **Thoth** The ancient Egyptian god of learning, invention, and magic, usually depicted with an ibis head crowned with the horns of the moon. In Egyptian myth he was keeper of the divine archives, patron of history, and the herald, clerk, and scribe of the gods. ("Ra has spoken; Thoth has written.") When the dead are judged before Osiris, Thoth will weigh the heart and find it wanting or not wanting.

C225:17, pe225:15, P494:25 **like an Irish oath** P. W. Joyce has the following entry on "Swearing," p. 69:

The expression *the dear knows* (or correctly *the deer knows*), which is very common, is a translation from Irish . . . . The original expression is *thauss* [Thoth] *ag Dhee* (given here phonetically), meaning *God knows*: but as this is too solemn and profane for most people, they changed it to *thauss ag fee*, i.e., *the deer knows*; and this may be uttered by anyone.

C225:18, pe225:17, P494:27   **the house of prayer and prudence**   I.e., middle-class Catholic Ireland, the realm of those whom Yeats called the paudeens or hucksters.

C225:23, pe225:21, P494:33   **swallows**   Cornelius Agrippa (p. 169): "Swallows, because when they are dying they provide a place of safety for their young, do portend a great patrimony or legacy after the death of friends."

C225:28–31, pe225:26–29, P495:3–6   ***Bend down your faces . . . wander the loud waters***   The opening lines of the death-speech of the Countess in Yeats's play, *The Countess Cathleen* (1892). She has sold her soul to the powers of darkness in exchange for bread for her people, who are suffering from a prolonged famine. Here she bids farewell to Oona, her nurse, and Aleel, a poet and friend. The speech (a fine example of the "Celtic Twilight" mood) continues:

> Do not weep
> Too great a while, for there is many a candle
> On the High Altar though one fall. Aleel,
> Who sang about the dancers of the woods
> That know not the hard burden of the world,
> Having but breath in their kind bodies, farewell!
> And farewell, Oona, you who played with me,
> And bore me in your arms about the house
> When I was but a child and therefore happy,
> Therefore happy, even like those that dance.
> The storm is in my hair and I must go. [*She dies.*]

The "storm" that carries the Countess away, presumably to the hell stipulated in her bargain, actually carries her to heaven, as the Angel sees and explains to Aleel at the play's end: "The Light of Lights / Looks always on the motive, not the deed, / The Shadow of Shadows on the deed alone."

C226:10, pe226:6, P495:20   **Symbol of departure or of loneliness?**   In the context of the play the Countess's lines do reflect the loneliness of her position as "porcelain" in the midst of "so many pitchers of rough clay" (in Oona, her nurse's words), but the lines are also her departure speech.

C226:12–13, pe226:8–9, P495:23   **the night of the opening of the na-**

tional theatre   The first production of *The Countess Cathleen* (8 May 1899) was also the first production of the Irish Literary Theatre, the forerunner of the Irish National Theatre (more generally known as The Abbey Theatre; see *Por* C86:24n). The performance provoked a storm of public protest from Irish Catholics and Nationalists. The following extract from a lead editorial in *The Daily Nation* (see *Por* C228:34n) for 9 May 1899 indicates the temper of the outburst:

> We wish to protest in the name of morality and religion and Irish nationality against the performance . . . . The audience should hoot the impersonators of such grotesque impiety from the Irish stage . . . . Is our ideal of Catholic and Celtic Ireland in its golden or any other age, a famine-stricken island with brutalizing inhabitants outdistancing each other in their eagerness to sell their souls for food without manliness, religion, or morality? Does it offer us anything more than the blasphemous perversion of our people's historical attitude towards the Faith and a hideous caricature of our people's mental and moral character?

C226:21, pe226:18, P495:33   **Made in Germany**   A catch phrase for shoddy or unfairly subsidized industrial products with which Germany was seeking to flood the world market in the late nineteenth century. The phrase was popularized by Ernest Williams in a short, racy, and alarming account of the impact of German industrial expansion on British industry, *Made in Germany* (London, 1896). In context the slogan also alludes to Protestantism, made in Germany (by Martin Luther).

C226:26, pe226:23, P496:3   **budding buddhists**   Echoing Irish prejudice against the interest in theosophy and the occult evinced by Yeats and some of his associates. Theosophists were then an avant-garde group fascinated by the mysticisms of Eastern religions, of various Christian heresies, and of the medieval Cabala. Theosophical doctrine derived in part from Buddhist teachings.

C226:29, pe226:26, P496:6–7   **the pillared hall**   The circular entry hall on the ground floor of the National Library has a ring of pillars beneath its domed ceiling. The reading room is above on the first floor.

C227:2, pe226:35, P496:16   ***The Tablet***   An ultraconservative Roman Catholic weekly, published in England.

C227:6, pe227:1, P496:19   **Pawn to king's fourth**   A conventional opening move in chess.

C227:25, pe227:22, P497:4   **a man of dwarfish stature**   Rumored to be "noble and come of an incestuous love" (C228:18, pe228:14–15, P497:34–35). Unknown, though he may have been a well-known or at least recognizable Dublin eccentric?

C228:8, pe228:4, P497:24   ***The Bride of Lammermoor***   By Sir Walter

Scott (1819), one of the *Tales of My Landlord* series. It is regarded as a masterpiece of Gothic fiction, compounded of doom foretold and fulfilled. The hero-lover, Ravenswood, is rejected by the prejudiced family of his true love (the "bride"). The outcome is a curse that dooms the bride, the groom of her family's choice, and Ravenswood to death. Ravenswood's drowning in quicksand extinguishes an ancient noble family.

C228:15–16, pe228:11–12, P497:31–32 **a genteel accent . . . marred by errors** The "errors" would imply a want of the education appropriate to the accent.

C228:17–18, pe228:13–15, P497:33–35 **was the story true . . . an incestuous love** See *Por* C227:25n.

C228:20, pe228:17–18, P498:1–2 **A game of swans** A game (since 1482) has meant a flock or herd of animals kept for pleasure. The term is now obsolete except for a game of swans.

C228:34, pe228:32, P498:17 **the Bantry gang** Notably Timothy Michael Sullivan (1827–1914) and his nephew-son-in-law, Timothy Michael Healy (1855–1931). Both came from Bantry (near the southwestern tip of Ireland); both were politicians; both were outwardly pro-Parnell during his ascendency but covertly jealous of him and ambitious for his downfall. Sullivan owned *The Daily Nation*, a Dublin newspaper that was anti-Fenian, pro-constitutional; it advocated conservative achievement of Irish independence. Healy was one of Parnell's lieutenants and ultimately earned the reputation among staunch Parnellites of having been Parnell's "betrayer"; see *Dub* C118:1–3n.

C229:16, pe229:15, P449:5 **a touch** Slang for sexual intercourse.

C229:17, pe229:16, P499:6 **riding a hack to spare the hunter** Proverbial: riding a common horse to spare a well-bred and more valuable one.

C229:21, pe229:20, P499:10 **your intellectual soul** Medieval scholastics followed Aristotle in postulating three parts or levels of soul in the human being: the vegetable soul, the animal soul, and the rational or intellectual soul.

C229:25, pe229:24–25, P499:14–15 **Forsters are the kings of Belgium** Genealogical nonsense: Leopold I (b. 1790, king 1831–65) was elected constitutional monarch by a national congress after Belgium had achieved its independence from Holland in 1830. Leopold was not descended from the Forsters or from the House of Flanders but from the ruling family of the duchy of Saxe-Coburg in Germany. His son, Leopold II (b. 1835, king 1865–1909) was the king of record when Temple was speaking.

C229:35–36, pe229:34–35, P499:24–25 **The Forster family . . .**

from Baldwin the First, king of Flanders   Baldwin I (1058–1118) of the House of Flanders was king of Jerusalem (1100–1118), not of Flanders. Another Baldwin I (1171–c. 1206) from the House of Flanders was the first Latin emperor of Constantinople. He is assumed to have died as a captive of the Bulgarians. Baldwin the Forester (early thirteenth century) was a Flemish imposter who claimed (about 1226) to be the escaped emperor, returned to assume his "rightful" role as Baldwin IX, count of Flanders and Hainault. He was exposed as a fraud and executed by the French.

C230:1–2, pe229:38–230:1, P499:27–29   **captain Francis Forster . . . last chieftain of Clanbrassil**   More nonsense genealogy: the Irish clan system was demolished during the Elizabethan phase of the English conquest of Ireland, so Captain Francis would have had to reach Ireland in the early seventeenth century. Or does this all owe something to a free association of Clanbrassil Street in south-central Dublin and "Lt. Col. Francis R. Forster (retired list, late 4th Dragoon Guards), Deputy Ranger of Curragh of Kildare, Dublin Castle" (*Thom's* 1904, p. 1157)?

C230:3, pe230:1, P499:30   **Blake Forsters**   The *Thom's* 1904 "List of the Nobility, Gentry, Merchants . . . etc., in the City of Dublin and Suburbs" has never heard of this branch of the family.

C230:8, pe230:8–9, P500:2–3   **Giraldus Cambrensis**   Geraldus de Barri (c. 1146–1220), Welsh ecclesiastic and chronicler who wrote two books about Ireland, *The Topography of Ireland* and later *The History of the Conquest of Ireland*. The former is an account of a visit to Ireland in the entourage of Prince John (Henry II's youngest son). Giraldus emerges as an outspoken apologist for the Anglo-Norman invasion. He has nothing good whatsoever to say about the native Irish, whom he regards as infected with "abominable guile" and with "the pest of treachery." Even among the Irish clergy he found "very little grain, but much chaff." Needless to say, the Dedalus family is not mentioned in either of these books on Ireland.

C230:14, pe230:14, P500:8   ***Pernobilis et pervetusta familia***   Latin: a very noble and very ancient family. In *The History of the Conquest of Ireland*, Giraldus uses this phrase to compliment the Fitz-Stephen (the sons of Stephen) family for its role in the Anglo-Norman conquest of Ireland. The joke (at Temple's expense) is that Stephen considers himself Irish, not Anglo-Irish.

C230:24, pe230:27, P500:21   ***paulo post futurum***   A Latin phrase "designating, or pertaining to, the future perfect tense (passive) of Greek verbs, in its use to express an act or event as about to happen immediately" (*Webster's New International Dictionary*, 1909).

C230:36, pe231:1, P500:33   **the law of heredity**   Much of the scientific discussion of human physiology and behavior in the late nineteenth century turned on the conflicting claims of those who argued the primacy of "the law of heredity" and of those who argued the primacy of "the law of environment." Claimants for both sides agreed, however, that the biological and social sciences would eventually achieve the discovery of inexorable law and that, as Zola put it, "a like law would be found to govern the stones of the roadway and the brains of men" ("The Experimental Novel," 1880).

C231:5–6, pe231:7, P501:2–3   **the sentence . . . Reproduction is the beginning of death**   Specific source unknown, though the sentiment is not unusual in late nineteenth-century discussions of zoology. For example, in Richard Hertwig, *Zoology* (New York, 1902) reproduction is defined as "the fundamental property of the organic world, essential in repairing losses by death."

C231:26, pe231:28, P501:24   **ballocks**   Testicles; a word which is obsolete, the *Oxford English Dictionary* (New York, 1971) says, "in polite use." Figuratively: a crude, stupid or clumsy person; a hopelessly messed up situation.

C231:35–36, pe231:38–232:1, P501:36   **the only English dual number**   In linguistics a dual number is a special form of the plural to indicate two or a pair. There are only traces of dual numbers in Anglo-Saxon and none in modern English. brace, couple, team

C232:7, pe232:8, P502:8   **an iron crown**   The Iron Crown, symbolic of dominion over Italy, belonged originally to the Lombard kings. It was made of gold encrusted with jewels and contained a circlet of iron said to have been forged from one of the nails used in the crucifixion of Jesus. In the Middle Ages crowns made of iron (and heated) were occasionally used in the punishment of traitors and illegitimate aspirants to thrones.

C232:19, pe232:21, P502:21   **Malahide**   Then a fishing village and summer resort on the coast of the Irish Sea nine miles north of Dublin.

C232:22, pe232:23–24, P502:25   **constabularymen**   See *Dub* C154:16–17n.

C232:24, pe232:26, P502:27   **the last pantomime**   See *Por* C67:21n.

C232:26, pe232:28–29, P502:30–31   **Had Cranly not heard him? Yet he could wait**   Stephen wishes to "confess" to Cranly, and Cranly's manner is reminiscent of the manner of some priests who, when the penitent enters the confessional, appear not to have heard and leave the penitent to kick his heels (and presumably to worry about his sins) in the interim.

C232:34, pe232:37, P503:3   *Darkness falls from the air*   Stephen misquotes line 17 of "A Litany in Time of Plague" (1592) by Thomas Nashe (1567–1601), English pamphleteer, poet, and playwright. The third stanza (lines 15–21 of the poem):

> Beauty is but a flower
> Which wrinkles will devour;
> Brightness falls from the air;
> Queens have died young and fair;
> Dust hath closed Helen's eye.
> I am sick, I must die.
>   Lord, have mercy on us!

In "The Symbolism of Poetry" (1900) Yeats quotes lines 17 through 19 and says that if one begins a "reverie" with these lines the result will be an experience of "symbols . . . the most perfect of all, because the most subtle, outside of pure sound, and through them one can best find out what symbols are" (*Essays* [New York, 1924], p. 192).

C232:35–36, pe232:38–233:1, P503:4–5   **A trembling joy, lambent as a faint light, played like a fairy host around him**   In Virgil's *Aeneid* XII:168, Aeneas's son Ascanius is described as "the second hope of mighty Rome"; in book II:68off., during the fall of Troy, Ascanius (or Iulus) is marked as favored by the gods when "a blaze of gentle light, a lambent flame . . . played over his soft hair and around his temples."

C233:6–7, pe233:8, P503:12   **the age of Dowland and Byrd and Nash**   I.e., the Elizabethan Age. John Dowland (c. 1563–1626) was an English lutanist and composer of books of songs and airs for the lute. William Byrd (1543–1623), "the Atlas of English music," was a composer not only of madrigals ("songs grave and gay for private singing") but also of large-scale church music. For Nashe, see note on *Por* C232:34 above.

C233:10, pe233:11, P503:15   **chambering**   See *Por* C176:30n.

C233:12, pe233:13, P503:17   **a slobbering Stuart**   James I (b. 1566, king of England 1603–25). The mood of his reign is frequently characterized as the dark, pessimistic counterpart of the brightness of the Elizabethan mood. James was described by his contemporaries as crude in manner and as having a tongue so large that it protruded between his lips and caused him to drool.

C233:13, pe233:14, P503:18–19   **ambered wines**   I.e., wines perfumed with ambergris, as in Francis Beaumont and John Fletcher, *The Custom of the Country*, III:ii, "Be sure / The wines be lusty, high, and full of spirit, / Ambered all."

C233:14, pe233:15, P503:19   **the proud pavan**   A grave and stately dance introduced into England from the continent in the opening decades of the sixteenth century.

C233:15, pe233:16, P503:21   **Covent Garden**   The square with the balconies to which Stephen refers (with sensual if not poetic license) was not laid out until 1632, and the neighborhood of Covent Garden did not become fashionable until the latter half of the seventeenth century.

C233:32, pe233:34, P504:5   **A louse**   See *Por* C174:16n.

C233:37–234:1, pe233:39–234:1, P504:10–13   **a curious phrase . . . on the sixth day**   Cornelius a Lapide (1567–1637), Flemish Jesuit and commentator on the Bible. In his book *The Great Commentary on the Bible* he cites Genesis 1:25 ("And God made . . . everything that creepeth upon the earth after his kind") and argues that lice, flies, maggots, etc., were not created directly by God but by spontaneous generation: as lice from sweat, flies from decaying meat, etc.

C234:9, pe234:10, P504:20   ***Brightness falls from the air***   See *Por* C232:34n.

C235:18, pe235:20, P505:35   **the Adelphi**   A hotel at 20 and 21 Anne Street South, not far to the southwest of the National Library.

C235:28, pe235:32, P506:13   **I suffer little children to come unto me**   Jesus to his disciples; see *Por* C143:9–10n.

C236:1–2, pe236:3–4, P506:23–25   **why does the church . . . die unbaptized**   Church doctrine holds that unbaptized children go not to Hell but to Limbo, a region bordering on Hell, where their lot is, in Dante's phrase, "sadness without torment," sadness because they can never achieve the beatific vision but not the torment of "the pain of loss" suffered by the damned. *The Catholic Encyclopedia* says that those "dying without grievous personal guilt, are excluded from the beatific vision on account of original sin alone" (1910; 9:256a).

C236:17–18, pe236:21, P507:5–6   **Saint Augustine . . . to hell**   The concept of Limbo predates St. Augustine, but he argued against the alleviation of the condition of the unbaptized, and held that the taint of original sin was so abhorrent to God that unbaptized infants "fall under condemnation" and are "sentenced to the loss of God," i.e., to hell (chapter VII, *De Correptione et Gratia* [Admonition and Grace]). Augustine's argument has not been widely accepted in the Church.

C236:23, pe236:27, P507:12   **a sugan**   Irish: a rope made of twisted straw; see *Por* C195:17n.

C236:36, pe236:39, P507:24   **grey spouse of Satan**   In Milton's *Paradise Lost*, book II, Satan encounters his daughter-wife Sin and the son of their incest, Death, at the gates of Hell; she is not described as "grey" but as "fair" above and "foul" below.

C237:8, pe237:9, P507:33   **Roscommon**   A market town and the county town of County Roscommon in north-central Ireland, 85 miles west-northwest of Dublin.

C237:29, pe237:31, P508:22   **The birdcall from *Siegfried***   A sequence of passages in Richard Wagner's (1813–83) opera, *Siegfried* (1876), the third of the four operas in *The Ring of the Nibelungs*. At the beginning of act II Siegfried tries to converse with the forest birds but cannot understand them. His attempt at birdsong awakens the dragon Fafner, whom Siegfried then slays. Siegfried removes a drop of dragon-blood from his fingers by putting them in his mouth. Instantly he can understand the birds, who tell him about the hoard of Rhinegold, about the Tarnhelm (which renders its wearer invisible), and about the Ring, which will render its maker the ruler of the world (if he forswears love). The bird then warns Siegfried about the murderous intentions of Mime, the dwarf who has been his foster-father. Siegfried kills Mime, and then the bird tells him about Brünnhilde, his bride-to-be, and leads Siegfried to her. Interest in Wagner marked one as an initiate in the cultural avant-garde of the 1890s.

C237:35, pe237:37, P508:33   **the Adelphi hotel**   See *Por* C235:18n.

C237:36, pe237:38, P508:30   **Kildare Street**   On the west side of the National Library and of the quadrangle (now parking lot) which is south of the library's facade.

C237:36–37, pe237:39, P508:30   **Maple's hotel**   Frederick Maple, proprietor, at 25–28 Kildare Street, on the west side of the street just south of the National Library. The hotel was small, quiet, fashionable, and expensive.

C238:4, pe238:5, P508:35   **the patricians of Ireland**   I.e., the Anglo-Irish landed gentry, many of whom would put up at Maple's because it was only a short walk from the Kildare Street Club; see *Dub* C54:7n.

C238:5, pe238:6, P509:1   **army commissions**   Careers in the British Army were fashionable and traditional among the Irish landed gentry not only for "second sons" as in England but also for first sons, thanks to the tradition of absentee landlordism. Considerable affluence was needed to obtain (i.e., purchase) a commission and to maintain the style thought appropriate to the officer class. The sale of commissions was discontinued in 1871, and army reforms sought to make officers less dependent on private wealth, but the army continued to be a fashionable career for the Anglo-Irish gentleman.

C238:5, pe238:6, P509:1–2   **land agents**   Estate managers who oversaw the work on the large estates. They planned the farm program, supervised the tenant-farmers, collected rents, etc.

C238:8, pe238:8, P509:4   **jarvies**   Hackney coachmen, particularly the drivers of Irish outside cars; see *Dub* C153:5n.

C238:23, pe238:26, P509:21   **They walked southward**   Stephen and Cranly walk south through Kildare Street and turn left (east) along Stephen's Green North and thence into Merrion Row. They continue southeast into Baggot Street Lower and apparently cross the Grand Canal into Baggot Street Upper "towards the township of Pembroke" (to the southeast) before they turn west along the canal (or parallel to it) toward the area where Leeson Streets Upper and Lower meet at another bridge over the Grand Canal; near the bridge is a street called Leeson Park. See map for *A Portrait*, chapter V:A, on p. 248 above.

C239:1–2, pe239:4, P510:5   **easter duty**   The *Maynooth Catechism* cites as one of the "six commandments of the Church": "To receive *worthily* the Blessed Eucharist at Easter, or within the time appointed; that is, from Ash Wednesday to Ascension, or, where it is so permitted, to the Octave Day of SS. Peter and Paul" (pp. 42–43). The emphasis on "worthily" reminds the communicant that it is a mortal sin (sacrilege) to receive communion when not in a state of grace; therefore, by implication, Easter Duty carries with it the obligation to go to confession as well as communion.

C239:6, pe239:8, P510:9   **I will not serve**   See *Por* C117:28n.

C239:18, pe239:20, P510:21   **believe in the eucharist**   I.e., believe that the consecrated elements of bread and wine are "the body and blood, soul and divinity of Jesus Christ" (*Maynooth Catechism*, p. 53).

C239:35, pe239:38, P511:5   **Depart from me . . . everlasting fire**   Jesus, describing the last judgment; see *Por* C119:15–19n.

C240:2, pe240:3, P511:8   **the day of judgment**   See *Por* C113:6–11n.

C240:6–7, pe240:7–8, P511:13–14   **bright, agile, impassible and . . . subtle**   From *The Catholic Encyclopedia* (1912, 12:793b):

> Three characteristics, identity, entirety, and immortality, will be common to the risen bodies of the just and the wicked [after the Resurrection]. But the bodies of the saints shall be distinguished by four transcendent endowments, often called qualities. The first is "impassibility" which shall place them beyond the reach of all pain and inconvenience . . . . The next quality is "brightness" or "glory," by which the bodies of the saints shall shine like the sun. . . . The third quality is that of "agility," by which the body shall be freed from its slowness of motion, and endowed with the capability of moving with the utmost facility and quickness wherever the soul pleases . . . . The fourth quality is "subtility," by which the body becomes subject to the absolute dominion of the soul.

C242:10, pe242:10, P513:29 **Pascal** Blaise Pascal (1623–62), French mathematician, philosopher, and apologist for Jansenism, a puritanical and quasi-heretical movement in seventeenth-century French Roman Catholicism. Pascal reputedly refused to allow his mother to touch him.

C242:13, pe242:13, P513:32 **Aloysius Gonzaga** See *Por* C14:7n.

C242:20ff., pe242:21ff., P514:5ff. **Jesus, too, seems to have treated** The reference is to such passages in the Gospels as Mark 3:31–35 and John 2:1–4, in which Jesus appears to snub or rebuke his mother for asking for his attention. Francisco Suarez (1548–1617), a Spanish Jesuit theologian, argued that Jesus's words: "Woman, what have I to do with Thee?" (John 2:4) were courteous in the original Aramaic.

C242:23–26, pe242:25–27, P514:9–11 **Jesus was not what he pretended to be . . . Jesus himself** Matthew 27:46, when Jesus is hanging on the cross, is frequently cited as evidence of this "self-doubt": "And about the ninth hour Jesus cried with a loud voice, saying, Eli, Eli, lama sabachthani? that is to say, My God, my God, why hast thou forsaken me?"

C242:29, pe242:30–31, P514:15 **a whited sepulchre** See *Por* C114:15n.

C243:7–8, pe243:7–8, P514:30–31 **He is more like a son of God than a son of Mary** See *Por* C248:30–31n.

C243:11–12, pe243:11–12, P514:34–35 **the host too may be . . . not a wafer of bread** See *Por* C239:18n.

C243:24, pe243:26, P515:13 **a sacrilegious communion** I.e., if Stephen, whose rebellion against religion has plunged him into mortal sin, were to act on Cranly's suggestion and hypocritically conform and do his Easter Duty (see *Por* C239:1–2n), he would be guilty of compounding his apostasy with sacrilege. *Maynooth Catechism*, p. 31: "The conversion of apostates is very difficult because by their apostasy they *sin against the Holy Ghost, crucify again the Son of God, and make a mockery of Him* (Heb. 6:6)."

C243:31–32, pe243:34, P515:21 **the penal days** After William III had defeated James II and reconquered Ireland in 1690–91 and after he had freed himself from obligation to the Catholic powers on the Continent (whose deliberate *laissez faire* had made the reconquest possible), he sanctioned a move to discipline Ireland. The Penal Laws originating in 1697 and 1699 and repeatedly modified after William's death (1702) through 1715, were that discipline—an elaborate program for the final suppression of Roman Catholicism in Ireland. The laws ordered the Catholic hierarchy and all Catholic religious orders into exile, thus, presumably, forbidding worship. Catholics were disenfranchised, forbidden to have schools or to teach in them, barred from public office, from membership in Parliament, from careers in law and the judiciary, from the universities, and from commissioned service in the military. Catholics found in violation of the laws were at the least subject to having their property confiscated and awarded to those who informed on them; at the worst the application of the laws was far more Draconian. The result for the Irish Catholic population was life in a penal colony, the constraints of which gradually relaxed in the course of the eighteenth century as the laws proved unenforceable, not only because they were ridiculous but also because the Protestant community in Ireland came to regard them as English rather than Irish laws and effectively avoided enforcing them. The Penal Laws were repealed piecemeal in the late eighteenth century and were finally eliminated completely by the Catholic Emancipation Act of 1829.

C244:4, pe244:5, P515:31–32   **the township of Pembroke**   The township which contains Ballsbridge on the then southeastern outskirts of metropolitan Dublin.

C244:6, pe244:7, P515:33   **the villas**   Detached dwellings in a fairly well-to-do suburban district on the southeast bank of the Grand Canal.

C244:11, pe244:12, P516:3   *Rosie O'Grady*   Words and music by Maud Nugent (Jerome):

> Sweet Rosie O'Grady,
> My dear little rose,
> She's my steady lady
> Most everyone knows,
> And when we are married,
> How happy we'll be,
> I love sweet Rosie O'Grady
> And Rosie O'Grady loves me.

C244:13, pe244:14, P516:5   *Mulier cantat*   Latin: a woman sings. Cranly's Latin phrase reminds Stephen of the ceremonies of Holy Week, the week leading up to Easter Sunday. It is customary during that season of the liturgical year for the Gospel accounts of the Passion to be sung in oratorio, the direct quotations being distributed to solo voices.

C244:19–20, pe244:20–21, P516:12–13   **a whiterobed figure . . . with a falling girdle**   The scene in Stephen's mind's eye, particularly the boy-woman with her "falling girdle" (about the hips instead of the waist), is reminiscent of nineteenth-century British depictions of Biblical scenes, depictions which, with their Pre-Raphaelite affinities, form part of the aesthetic heritage in which Stephen is immersed as he composes his villanelle in chapter V:B; see pp. 257–61 above.

C244:24, pe244:26, P516:17 *Et tu cum Jesu Galilaeo eras* Latin: "Thou also wast with Jesus of Galilee" (Matthew 26:69). These are the first words spoken or sung by a woman in the Passion according to Saint Matthew, which is part of the Palm Sunday service. In Matthew 26:34 Jesus predicts to Peter: "That this night, before the cock crow, thou shalt deny me thrice." The voice of this woman provokes the first of the three denials (Matthew 26:69–75).

C244:27, pe244:29, P516:20 **proparoxyton** A word having the acute accent on the antepenult as, in this case, the third syllable in *Galiláeo*.

C245:29, pe245:32, P517:29 **Harcourt Street station** On the corner of Harcourt Street and Harcourt Road, 600 yards south of the southwest corner of Stephen's Green. At the turn of the century the station was the terminus of the Dublin, Wicklow, and Wexford Railway.

C245:33, pe245:37, P517:33–34 **the shortest way from Sallygap to Larras** Sallygap is in the Wicklow Mountains fifteen miles south of Dublin. The shortest (and most beautiful) route from Sallygap to Larras (or Laragh, eight air miles further south) is an almost direct route over the mountains. The road (whether Cranly/Joyce were aware of it or not) was constructed by the British Army during the Rebellion of 1798 in order to deny rebels in County Wicklow the wilderness sanctuary of the mountains.

C246:15–18, pe246:19–23, P518:18–22 **Juan Mariana de Talavera . . . saddlebow** Juan Mariana (1536–1623), Spanish Jesuit historian and scholar, who argued in his treatise *De Rege et Regis Institutione* (*Of Tyrants and Tyrannical Institutions*, 1599) that it is right for any man to kill or overthrow a tyrant even if the tyrant is not a usurper. His doctrine was frequently cited in attempts to impugn the motives and ethics of the entire Jesuit Order—something of an irony since several of his Protestant contemporaries (and later, John Milton) espoused similar doctrines.

C246:20–21, pe246:25, P518:25 **the chastisement of the secular arm** The verbal formula with which the Inquisition (the Holy Office) turned convicted heretics over to the state for execution. In many cases the Inquisition imposed lighter sentences (pilgrimages, the wearing of a yellow cross, imprisonment) which it could enforce under its own authority, but the death penalty could only be enforced by the state.

C246:37, pe247:2, P519:6–7 **I will not serve** See *Por* C117:28n.

C247:4–5, pe247:6–7, P519:11–12 **the only arms . . . silence, exile, and cunning** These "weapons" Stephen has previously associated with the Jesuits: "bearing tidings secretly" (C185:19–20, pe185:21, P488:31), "the shifts and lore and cunning of the world" (C186:22, pe186:22–23, P450:4), and "among aliens," *in exile* (C184:29, pe184:31–32, P488:2). Ellmann (p. 365) suggests a possible source: early in Honoré de Balzac's (1799–1850) novel, *Splendeurs et misères des courtisanes*, the young hero Lucien de Rubempré announces, "I have put into practice an axiom which assures me a life of tranquility: *Fuge, late, tace*" (*Oeuvres complètes de H. de Balzac* [Paris, 1855] Vol. 11, p. 344 [my translation]). The Latin axiom can be rendered "Flight, subterfuge, silence." The hero's practice of that axiom in Balzac's novel ends ironically in a false charge of complicity in a murder and subsequent suicide in prison.

C247:7, pe247:9, P519:14   **to head back towards Leeson Park**   See *Por* C238:23n. Presumably once they reached the bridge near "Leeson Park" they would turn right and walk toward central Dublin through Leeson Street Lower, which gives into the southeast corner of Stephen's Green.

C247:13, pe247:16, P519:21   **Yes, my child**   The mode of address the priest uses with the penitent in the confessional.

Chapter V: Section D

C248:4–5, pe248:8, P520:17–18   **coursing matches**   Greyhound (or whippet) races, in which the dogs are released in pursuit of live game.

C248:5–6, pe248:9, P520:19   **Father Dwyer of Larras**   Apparently fictional; for Larras or Laragh in County Wicklow see *Por* C245:33n.

C248:13, pe248:16, P520:26   **Elisabeth and Zachary**   Or Zacharias, the parents of John the Baptist (Luke 1:5–25), who was the "precursor" of Jesus, the one who came before to announce the coming of Jesus as the Messiah (Matthew 3). In Luke the parents are described as "well-stricken in years" and Elisabeth is described as "barren." The Archangel Gabriel announces the coming of their child to the father, Zacharias, a priest, and prophesies that the child will "make ready a people prepared for the Lord."

C248:14–15, pe248:18, P520:28   **locusts and wild honey**   John the Baptist's food during his years as hermit in the desert wilderness: "and his meat was locusts and wild honey" (Matthew 3:4).

C248:16–17, pe248:19–21, P520:29–31   **stern severed head . . . ve-ronica. Decollation . . . in the fold**   John the Baptist, because he condemned as incestuous King Herod's marriage with Herodias, was imprisoned at the instigation of Herodias. Her daughter Salome, having "pleased" Herod by dancing before him, requested and received "John Baptist's head in a charger" (Matthew 14:1–12). "Decollation," the "beheading of St. John the Baptist," is celebrated in the Church ("the fold") on 29 August. A veronica is a cloth bearing an image of the face of Jesus, after the story of Veronica, one of the mourners who followed Jesus up Calvary. She wiped his bleeding face with a cloth and afterwards found his image miraculously imprinted on it.

C248:18, pe248:21–22, P520:32   **saint John at the Latin gate**   A Feast celebrated on 6 May which commemorates the divine intervention that released St. John the Evangelist ("the disciple whom Jesus loved") from the hands of his Roman persecutors near the Latin Gate (subsequently the Gate of St. John) in Rome. The Feast also celebrates the dedication of the Basilica of St. John Lateran in Rome. The Basilica is dedicated not only to St. John the Evangelist but also to St. John the Baptist, i.e., to both the "precursor" who goes before and announces and to the Beloved Disciple who follows after and commemorates in the New Testamental writings attributed to him (the Gospel according to John, three Epistles, and the Apocalypse of St. John the Apostle—Revelation).

C248:20–21, pe248:25, P521:4   **Let the dead bury the dead**   Jesus to one who would follow him in Luke 9:59–60: "But he said, Lord, suffer me first to go and bury my father. Jesus said unto him, Let the dead bury their dead: but go thou and preach the kingdom of God."

C248:21, pe248:25, P521:4–5   **And let the dead marry the dead**   In Matthew 22 the Sadducees, "which say that there is no resurrection" (22:23) seek to confute Jesus's assertion of the resurrection by asking: if a woman has had and outlived seven husbands, "in the resurrection whose wife shall she be of the seven?" (22:28). Jesus answers:

> Ye do err, not knowing the scriptures nor the power of God. For in the resurrection they neither marry, nor are given in marriage, but are as the angels of God in heaven.

C248:29, pe248:34, P521:14   **B.V.M.**   Blessed Virgin Mary.

C248:30–31, pe248:35–36, P521:15–16   **relations between Jesus . . . Mary and her son**   I.e., Stephen has argued that the relation between God the Father and Jesus as the Son of God is (or should be) more central to Catholic doctrine than the relation between the Blessed Virgin Mary and her immaculately conceived Son, in spite of the popular preoccupation with the latter (and the preoccupation with Mary as inter-cessor with her Son). In *Ulysses* a more mature Stephen summarizes the argument with a flourish: "[Fatherhood] is a mystical estate, an apos-tolic succession, from only begetter to only begotten. On that mystery and not on the madonna which the cunning Italian intellect flung to the mob of Europe the church is founded" (p. 207).

C249:2, pe249:6, P521:26–27 **Bruno the Nolan** Giordano Bruno of Nola (1548–1600), Italian Dominican, philosopher, metaphysician, and proponent of a religion of universal love. He asserted that there is no form without material embodiment. This doctrine led him to ques-tion (among other things) the doctrine of transubstantiation: he left his order (and Italy) for exile in Geneva, and subsequently prolonged his exile, wandering from city to city throughout Western Europe. When he went "home" to Italy in 1593 he was apprehended by the Inquisition in Venice and subjected to seven years of persecution and imprison-ment in Rome (in the hopes that he would recant). He was finally "punished . . . without bloodshed," i.e., burned at the stake, in 1600.

C249:6, pe249:10, P521:30–31 *risotto alla bergamasca* A rice dish after the manner of the residents of Bergamo, an Italian town thirty miles northeast of Milan.

C249:12–14, pe249:17–20, P522:2–5 **A quartet of them . . . the overcoat of the crucified** A reference to the Roman soldiers who cru-cified Jesus, John 19:23–24:

> Then the soldiers, when they had crucified Jesus, took his garments, and made four parts, to every soldier a part; and also his coat: now the coat was without seam, woven from the top throughout. They said therefore among themselves, Let us not rend it, but cast lots for it, whose it shall be: that the scripture might be fulfilled, which saith, They parted my raiment among them, and for my vesture they did cast lots. These things therefore the sol-diers did.

A regiment is a unit in the British Army; the Roman army was sub-divided into legions, which in turn were made up of several cohorts. According to David Jones (*In Parenthesis* [New York, 1961], p. 210), "The Xth Fretensis is said [in Italian legend] to have furnished the es-cort party at the execution of our Lord." At the time of the Crucifixion there was nothing approaching a major unit like a legion in Palestine, only a procurator's guard of about 600 troops.

In the British Army the 97th Regiment of Foot was the Earl of Uls-ter's Regiment until 1881 when it was merged with the 50th, the Queen's Own Regiment of Foot, to form the Queen's Own Royal West Kent Regiment. The merger was part of a general army reform; it occasioned considerable publicity in northeastern Ireland, where many felt that the elimination of the term Ulster was a slur on that province's historic claim to patriotic belligerence.

C249:15, pe249:21, P522:6 **three reviews** I.e., three "little magazines."

C249:19–20, pe249:25–26, P522:10–11 *I wonder if . . . he is very ill* Lines 3 and 4 of William Blake's poem "William Bond":

> I wonder whether the Girls are mad
> And I wonder whether they mean to kill
> And I wonder if William Bond will die
> For assuredly he is very ill
>
> He went to Church in a May morning
> Attended by Fairies one two & three
> But the Angels of Providence drove them away
> And he returned home in Misery
>
> He went not out to the Field or Fold
> He went not out to the Village nor Town
> But he came home in a black black cloud
> And took to his Bed & there lay down
>
> And an Angel of Providence at his Feet
> And an Angel of Providence at his Head
> And in the midst a Black Black Cloud
> And in the midst the Sick Man on his Bed
>
> And on his Right hand was Mary Green
> And on his Left hand was his Sister Jane
> And their tears fell into the black black Cloud
> To drive away the sick mans pain
>
> O William if thou dost another Love
> Dost another Love better than poor Mary
> Go & take that other to be thy Wife
> And Mary Green shall her Servant be
>
> Yes Mary I do another Love
> Another I Love far better than thee
> And Another I will have for my Wife
> Then what have I to do with thee
>
> For thou art Melancholy Pale
> And on thy Head is the cold Moons shine
> But she is ruddy & bright as day
> And the sun beams dazzle from her eyne
>
> Mary trembled & Mary chilld
> And Mary fell down on the right hand floor

That William Bond & his Sister Jane
Scarce could recover Mary more

When Mary woke & found her Laid
On the Right hand of her William dear
On the Right hand of his loved Bed
And saw her William Bond so near

The Fairies that fled from William Bond
Danced around her Shining Head
They danced over the Pillow white
And the Angels of Providence left the Bed

I thought Love livd in the hot sun shine
But O he lives in the Moony light
I thought to find Love in the heat of day
But sweet Love is the Comforter of Night

Seek Love in the Pity of others Woe
In the gentle relief of anothers care
In the darkness of night & the winters snow
In the naked & outcast Seek Love there

C249:21, pe249:27, P522:12 **Alas, poor William!** After Hamlet's speech (V:i:202–4) on the court jester's skull which has been thrown up by the Clowns, who are digging Ophelia's grave: "Alas, poor Yorick! I knew him, Horatio—a fellow of infinite jest, of most excellent fancy."

C249:22, pe249:28, P522:13 **a diorama** "A mode of scenic presentation invented by Daguerre and Bouton [in the 1820s] in which a painting (partly translucent) is seen from a distance through an opening. By a combination of translucent and reflected light, and by contrivances such as screens and shutters, much diversity of scenic effect is produced" (*Webster's New International Dictionary*, 1909). Typical dioramas took as their subjects geographical or historical travelogues: the Wonders of Ancient Egypt, Decisive Battles, etc.

C249:22, pe249:28, P522:13 **Rotunda** See *Dub* C109:18n.

C249:23, pe249:29–30, P522:14–15 **William Ewart Gladstone** Four times prime minister of England (died 19 May 1898) and something of a hero to the Irish as a result of his qualified support for Home Rule, a support that stopped well short of enthusiasm for Irish national independence.

C249:24, pe249:31, P522:15–16 **O, Willie, we have missed you** By the American song writer Stephen Foster (1826–64):

Oh! Willie, is it you dear,
Safe, safe at home?
They did not tell me true, dear,

They said you would not come;
I heard you at the gate,
And it made my heart rejoice,
For I knew that welcome footstep,
And that dear familiar voice,
Making music on my ear,
In the lonely midnight gloom:
Oh! Willie we have missed you;
Welcome, Welcome home.

C250:5–6, pe250:10–11, P522:33–34 **Still harping on the mother**
As Polonius, in an aside about Hamlet's presumably "mad" behavior
and his crude jokes about Polonius's daughter and "conception": "Still
harping on my daughter. Yet he knew me not at first" (II:ii:188–89).

C250:6–8, pe250:11–13, P522:34–523:3 **A crocodile seized . . . or
not eat it** The mother's answer to this much quoted conundrum
should be: "You are going to eat it." That answer confounds the crocodile because he cannot both eat the child and keep his word (as he could
have done had the mother not been so clever).

C250:9–10, pe250:14–15, P523:4–5 **bred out of your mud by the operation of your sun** In Shakespeare's *Antony and Cleopatra* (II:
vii:29–31) Lepidus, a triumvir with Marc Antony and Octavius Caesar, drunkenly remarks: "Your serpent of Egypt is bred now of your
mud by the operation of your sun. So is your crocodile."

C250:13–14, pe250:19, P523:9 **Johnston, Mooney and O'Brien's**
Biscuit makers who ran a chain of shops and tearooms in Dublin;
which of their ten or so shops is not clear.

C250:17–18, pe250:22–23, P523:13–14 **Shining quietly behind a
bushel of Wicklow bran** In the Sermon on the Mount Jesus says: "Ye
are the light of the world . . . Neither do men light a candle and put it
under a bushel but on a candlestick; and it giveth light unto all that are
in the house" (Matthew 5:14–15). Cranly is from a back-country town
in County Wicklow south of Dublin.

C250:19–20, pe250:24–25, P523:15–16 **the cigar shop opposite
Findlater's church** C. S. M'Garvey, tobacconist, 1 B Frederick
Street North (significance unknown), was across the street from Findla-
ter's Church, which stands on the corner of Rutland (now Parnell)
Square North and Frederick Street North; see *Por* C160:14n.

C250:22, pe250:27, P523:18–19 **shortest way to Tara was *via* Holyhead** Tara, the ancient seat of the half-legendary High Kings of Ireland and symbolic of Ireland's half-legendary golden age. Holyhead, a
seaport on the northwestern coast of Wales, the eastern terminus for
the steam packets that formed Ireland's main "bridge" to England and

the Continent. The sense of Stephen's epigram is that the best way to achieve a second coming of Ireland's golden age is to do it in exile.

C250:27–28, pe250:33–34, P523:25   **how he broke Pennyfeather's heart**   Ellmann (p. 38) remarks that the story is now lost but suggests that it had something to do with property assigned to Joyce's grandfather.

C251:6–8, pe251:9–12, P524:6–9   **Michael Robartes . . . long faded from the world**   After the opening lines of Yeats's poem, "Michael Robartes Remembers Forgotten Beauty" in *The Wind among the Reeds* (1899), subsequently titled "He Remembers Forgotten Beauty" in *The Collected Poems of W. B. Yeats* (New York, 1956), p. 60, lines 1–3: "When my arms wrap you round I press / My heart upon the loveliness / That has long faded from the world."

C251:8–9, pe251:12, P524:9   **Not this. Not at all**   I.e., a rejection of the romantic nostalgia characteristic of the "Celtic Twilight" and the dreamy aesthetic escapism of the late nineteenth century (associated here with Yeats's early poetry).

C251:12, pe251:15–16, P524:13–14   **from dreams to dreamless sleep**   A curious and probably anachronistic coincidence: Yeats, *A Vision* (1926; New York 1956), p. 220:

> Certain Upanishads describe three states of the soul, that of waking, that of dreaming, that of dreamless sleep, and say man passes from waking through dreaming to dreamless sleep every night and when he dies. Dreamless sleep is a state of pure light, or of utter darkness according to our liking, and in dreams "the spirit serves as light for itself." There are no carts, horses, roads, but he makes them for himself.

C251:23, pe251:27, P524:25   **tundish**   See *Por* C188:27n.

C251:28, pe251:32, P524:31   **John   Alphonsus   Mulrennan**   Unknown.

C251:29, pe251:33, P524:32   **the west of Ireland**   See *Dub* C188:32–33n.

C251:29–30, pe251:33–34, P524:32–33   **(European and Asiatic papers please copy.)**   A standard formula in the court news (news of the Royal family's activities), society, and obituary columns in British newspapers. The formula announced that the paper did not regard the published material as protected by its copyright.

C252:1–2, pe252:3–4, P526:6–8   **It is with him I must struggle all through this night till day come**   Cf. Genesis 32:24–30:

> And Jacob was left alone; and there wrestled a man with him until the breaking of the day. And when he saw that he prevailed not against him, he touched the hollow of his thigh; and the hollow of Jacob's thigh was out of

joint, as he wrestled with him. And he said, Let me go, for the day break-eth. And he said, I will not let thee go, except thou bless me. And he said unto him, What is thy name? And he said Jacob. And he said, Thy name shall be called no more Jacob, but Israel: for as a prince hast thou power with God and with men, and hast prevailed. And Jacob asked him, and said, Tell me, I pray thee, thy name. And he said, Wherefore is it that thou dost ask after my name? And he blessed him there. And Jacob called the name of the place Peniel: for I have seen God face to face, and my life is preserved.

But the angel with whom Stephen wrestles is the Irish peasant whom Yeats and others were urging upon young Irish writers as the touch-stone of folk wisdom and vision, the true source of poetic inspiration. What Yeats and others who idealized the peasant tended to overlook was that peasants in actuality could be grasping, superstitious, and vio-lently prejudiced bludgeon-men as well as generous dreamers of folk and mythic truths.

C252:5, pe252:7, P525:11–12 **Grafton Street** See *Dub* C45:20–21n.

C252:11–12, pe252:13–15, P525:18–19 **the spiritual-heroic . . . Dante Alighieri** A reference to Dante's delicately controlled platonic admiration for Beatrice in *La Vita Nuova* (The New Life); see *Por* C172:10n.

C252:26–32, pe252:28–35, P525:33–526:6 **The spell of arms . . . the wings of their . . . youth** The arms/wings imagery of this para-graph echoes Ovid's account of the flight of Daedalus and Icarus; see *Por* C5:2n.

C253:1–2, pe253:3–4, P526:12–13 **to forge in the smithy of my soul the uncreated conscience of my race** In Ibsen's *Brand* the uncom-promising hero asserts himself against "the sickly generation of our time" (p. 44) in favor of "one thing indestructible . . . the uncreated soul of man" (p. 48). His overriding purpose: to "stir the nation's con-science to repent" (p. 81). Stephen's resolve also recalls the blacksmith imagery with which William Blake invests the figure of Los (prophetic inspiration) in *Milton* and other poems. Also compare Yeats in "The Tables of the Law" (p. 301): "Jonathan Swift made a soul for the gen-tlemen of this city by hating his neighbour as himself."

C253:3–4, pe253:5–6, P526:14–15 **Old father, old artificer** The prayer is addressed to Daedalus, "the fabulous artificer," and the form of address is as Icarus might have asked his father's blessing on the eve of their flight from the labyrinth; see *Por* C5:2n.

Appendix

THE SISTERS
by Stephen Daedalus

Three nights in succession I had found myself in Great Britain-street at that hour, as if by Providence. Three nights also I had raised my eyes to that lighted square of window and speculated. I seemed to understand that it would occur at night. But in spite of the Providence that had led my feet, and in spite of the reverent curiosity of my eyes, I had discovered nothing. Each night the square was lighted in the same way, faintly and evenly. It was not the light of candles, so far as I could see. Therefore, it had not yet occurred.

On the fourth night at that hour I was in another part of the city. It may have been the same Providence that led me there—a whimsical kind of Providence to take me at a disadvantage. As I went home I wondered was that square of window lighted as before, or did it reveal the ceremonious candles in whose light the Christian must take his last sleep. I was not surprised, then, when at supper I found myself a prophet. Old Cotter and my uncle were talking at the fire, smoking. Old Cotter is the old distiller who owns the batch of prize setters. He used to be very interesting when I knew him first, talking about "faints" and "worms." Now I find him tedious.

While I was eating my stirabout I heard him saying to my uncle:

"Without a doubt. Upper storey—(he tapped an unnecessary hand at his forehead)—gone."

From *The Irish Homestead* for 13 August 1904, pp. 676–77, under the heading "Our Weekly Story."

"So they said. I never could see much of it. I thought he was sane enough."

"So he was, at times," said old Cotter.

I sniffed the "was" apprehensively, and gulped down some stirabout.

"Is he better, Uncle John?"

"He's dead."

"O . . . he's dead?"

"Died a few hours ago."

"Who told you?"

"Mr. Cotter here brought us the news. He was passing there."

"Yes, I just happened to be passing, and I noticed the window . . . you know."

"Do you think they will bring him to the chapel?" asked my aunt.

"Oh, no, ma'am. I wouldn't say so."

"Very unlikely," my uncle agreed.

So old Cotter had got the better of me for all my vigilance of three nights. It is often annoying the way people will blunder on what you have elaborately planned for. I was sure he would die at night.

The following morning after breakfast I went down to look at the little house in Great Britain-street. It was an unassuming shop registered under the vague name of "Drapery." The drapery was principally children's boots and umbrellas, and on ordinary days there used to be notice hanging in the window, which said "Umbrellas recovered." There was no notice visible now, for the shop blinds were drawn down and a crape bouquet was tied to the knocker with white ribbons. Three women of the people and a telegram boy were reading the card pinned on the crape. I also went over and read: —"July 2nd, 189– The Rev. James Flynn (formerly of St. Ita's Church), aged 65 years. R. I. P."

Only sixty-five! He looked much older than that. I often saw him sitting at the fire in the close dark room behind the shop, nearly smothered in his great coat. He seemed to have almost stupefied himself with heat, and the gesture of his large trembling hand to his nostrils had grown automatic. My aunt, who is what they call good-hearted, never went into the shop without bringing him some High Toast, and he used to take the packet of snuff from her hands, gravely inclining his head for sign of thanks. He used to sit in that stuffy room for the greater part of the day from early morning, while Nannie (who is almost stone deaf) read out the newspaper to him. His other sister, Eliza, used to mind the shop. These two old women used to look after him, feed him, and clothe him. The clothing was not difficult, for his ancient priestly clothes were quite green with age, and his dogskin slippers were everlasting. When he was tired of hearing the news he used to rattle his snuff-box on the arm of his chair to avoid shouting at her, and then he used to make believe to read his Prayer Book. Make believe, because, when Eliza brought him a cup of soup from the kitchen, she had always to waken him.

As I stood looking up at the crape and the card that bore his name I could not realise that he was dead. He seemed like one who could go on living for ever if he only wanted to; his life was so methodical and un-eventful. I think he said more to me than to anyone else. He had an egois-tic contempt for all women-folk, and suffered all their services to him in polite silence. Of course, neither of his sisters were very intelligent. Nan-nie, for instance, had been reading out the newspaper to him every day for years, and could read tolerably well, and yet she always spoke of it as the *Freeman's General*. Perhaps he found me more intelligent, and honoured me with words for that reason. Nothing, practically nothing, ever oc-curred to remind him of his former life (I mean friends or visitors), and still he could remember every detail of it in his own fashion. He had stud-ied at the college in Rome, and he taught me to speak Latin in the Italian way. He often put me through the responses of the Mass, he smiling often and pushing huge pinches of snuff up each nostril alternately. When he smiled he used to uncover his big, discoloured teeth, and let his tongue lie on his lower lip. At first this habit of his used to make me feel uneasy. Then I grew used to it.

That evening my aunt visited the house of mourning and took me with her. It was an oppressive summer evening of faded gold. Nannie received us in the hall, and, as it was no use saying anything to her, my aunt shook hands with her for all. We followed the old woman upstairs and into the dead-room. The room, through the lace end of the blind, was suffused with dusky golden light, amid which the candles looked like pale, thin flames. He had been coffined. Nannie gave the lead, and we three knelt down at the foot of the bed. There was no sound in the room for some minutes except the sound of Nannie's mutterings—for she prays noisily. The fancy came to me that the old priest was smiling as he lay there in his coffin.

But, no. When we rose and went up to the head of the bed I saw that he was not smiling. There he lay solemn and copious in his brown habit, his large hands loosely retaining his rosary. His face was very grey and mas-sive, with distended nostrils and circled with scanty white fur. There was a heavy odour in the room—the flowers.

We sat downstairs in the little room behind the shop, my aunt and I and the two sisters. Nannie sat in a corner and said nothing, but her lips moved from speaker to speaker with a painfully intelligent motion. I said nothing either, being too young, but my aunt spoke a good deal, for she is a bit of a gossip—harmless.

"Ah, well! he's gone!"

"To enjoy his eternal reward, Miss Flynn, I'm sure. He was a good and holy man."

"He was a good man, but, you see . . . he was a disappointed man. . . . You see, his life was, you might say, crossed."

"Ah, yes! I know what you mean."

"Not that he was anyway mad, as you know yourself, but he was always a little queer. Even when we were all growing up together he was queer. One time he didn't speak hardly for a month. You know, he was that kind always."

"Perhaps he read too much, Miss Flynn?"

"O, he read a good deal, but not latterly. But it was his scrupulousness, I think, affected his mind. The duties of the priesthood were too much for him."

"Did he . . . peacefully?"

"O, quite peacefully, ma'am. You couldn't tell when the breath went out of him. He had a beautiful death, God be praised."

"And everything . . . ?"

"Father O'Rourke was in with him yesterday and gave him the Last Sacrament."

"He knew then?"

"Yes: he was quite resigned."

Nannie gave a sleepy nod and looked ashamed.

"Poor Nannie," said her sister, "she's worn out. All the work we had, getting in a woman, and laying him out; and then the coffin and arranging about the funeral. God knows we did all we could, as poor as we are. We wouldn't see him want anything at the last."

"Indeed you were both very kind to him while he lived."

"Ah, poor James; he was no great trouble to us. You wouldn't hear him in the house no more than now. Still I know he's gone and all that . . . I won't be bringing him in his soup any more, nor Nannie reading him the paper, nor you, ma'am, bringing him his snuff. How he liked that snuff! Poor James!"

"O, yes, you'll miss him in a day or two more than you do now."

Silence invaded the room until memory reawakened it, Eliza speaking slowly—

"It was that chalice he broke . . . . Of course, it was all right. I mean it contained nothing. But still . . . They say it was the boy's fault. But poor James was so nervous, God be merciful to him."

"Yes, Miss Flynn, I heard that . . . about the chalice . . . He . . . his mind was a bit affected by that."

"He began to mope by himself, talking to no one, and wandering about. Often he couldn't be found. One night he was wanted, and they looked high up and low down and couldn't find him. Then the clerk suggested the chapel. So they opened the chapel (it was late at night), and brought a light to look for him . . . And there, sure enough, he was, sitting in his confession-box in the dark, wide awake, and laughing like softly to himself. Then they knew something was wrong."

"God rest his soul!"

Index

Most of the entries in the index refer to the page and line of *Dubliners* or *A Portrait of the Artist as a Young Man* under which the note appears, i.e., Abbey Theatre, *Por* C86:24; the entries in italics refer to pages in this book, i.e., Abbey Theatre, *p. 10*.

Designer:	Eric Jungerman
Compositor:	G & S Typesetters
Printer:	Vail-Ballou Press
Binder:	Vail-Ballou Press
Text:	Linotron 202 Plantin
Display:	VIP Plantin